*Everyman, I will go with thee,
and be thy guide*

THE EVERYMAN
LIBRARY

*The Everyman Library was founded by J. M. Dent
in 1906. He chose the name Everyman because he wanted
to make available the best books ever written in every
field to the greatest number of people at the cheapest possible
price. He began with Boswell's 'Life of Johnson';
his one-thousandth title was Aristotle's 'Metaphysics',
by which time sales exceeded forty million.*

*Today Everyman paperbacks remain true to
J. M. Dent's aims and high standards, with a wide range
of titles at affordable prices in editions which address
the needs of today's readers. Each new text is reset to give
a clear, elegant page and to incorporate the latest thinking
and scholarship. Each book carries the pilgrim logo,
the character in 'Everyman', a medieval morality play,
a proud link between Everyman
past and present.*

Arthur Morrison

A CHILD OF
THE JAGO

Edited by
PETER MILES
University of Wales, Lampeter

EVERYMAN
J. M. DENT · LONDON
CHARLES E. TUTTLE
VERMONT

J. M. Dent
Orion Publishing Group
Orion House, 5 Upper St Martin's Lane,
London WC2H 9EA
and
Charles E. Tuttle Co., Inc.
28 South Main Street,
Rutland, Vermont 05701, USA

Typeset in Sabon by CentraCet Ltd, Cambridge
Printed in Great Britain by
The Guernsey Press Co. Ltd, Guernsey, C. I.

British Library Cataloguing-in-Publication Data
is available upon request.

ISBN 0 460 87772 0

CONTENTS

To John, Viv, Nicholas and Jonathan

NOTE ON THE AUTHOR AND EDITOR

ARTHUR MORRISON (1863–1945) was born in Poplar. His father, an engine-fitter in the docks, died when Arthur was a child. Morrison rapidly bettered himself, rising through clerical work in the Architect's Department of the London School Board to a post at the People's Palace on the Mile End Road. Much favoured by the novelist and reformer Walter Besant, the People's Palace was an ambitious, purpose-built educational institution (a 'University for the People') offering courses and facilities designed to enhance the social, intellectual and cultural awareness of London's respectable working and lower middle class. Morrison organized events there and sub-edited the institution's *Journal*. As a teenager he had written light verse for cycling periodicals, and in his early twenties had serious journalism accepted by such newspapers as the *Globe*. In 1888 he published a series of sketches of London life in the *People* and in 1890 resigned from the People's Palace to become a full-time journalist and freelance contributor to the proliferating magazines of the period. He married in 1892. His first book dealt with spiritualism, but *Tales of Mean Streets* (1894), short stories that had mostly appeared in W. E. Henley's *National Observer*, gained him instant notoriety. For *A Child of the Jago* (1896), which turned from the commonplace streets of the East End to its worst slums, Morrison conducted on-the-spot research under the tutelage of the lionizing Reverend Arthur Osborne Jay, Vicar of Holy Trinity, Shoreditch. A later book, *To London Town* (1899), extended the concerns of *Mean Streets* and *A Child of the Jago*, while the much admired *The Hole in the Wall* (1902) put similar material to use in a thriller. *Cunning Murrell* (1900) was a Hardyesque tale of Essex rural life. Alongside such work, Morrison produced very successful detective fiction featuring his hero Martin Hewitt. Subsequently Morrison leant much more towards short stories and also one-act plays. Eventually his scholarly and commercial interest in Japanese Art took over.

His influential *Painters of Japan* appeared in 1911, while his dealing appears to have provided him with the means to retire from his journalistic and literary career. Relatively unknown to a new generation, Morrison died in Buckinghamshire in 1945.

PETER MILES lectures in English at the University of Wales, Lampeter. He is co-author (with Malcolm Smith) of *Cinema, Literature and Society: Elite and Mass Culture in Britain between the Wars* (1987) and author of *The Critics Debate: 'Wuthering Heights'* (1990). He has contributed to *The Art of Travel: Essays on Travel Writing* (1982) and *The Twentieth-Century British Working-Class Novel* (1984). With David Skilton he has co-edited Wilkie Collins's *The Woman in White* (1982) and Anthony Trollope's *Framley Parsonage* (1984). He has contributed to such journals as *Analytical and Enumerative Bibliography*, *ANQ*, *Book Collector*, *Library*, *Style* and *Studies in Bibliography*. He is the editor of the Everyman edition of Tobias Smollett's *The Expedition of Humphry Clinker* (1993).

CHRONOLOGY OF MORRISON'S LIFE

Year Age Life

1863   Arthur Morrison born in Poplar, London; his father George
                   an engine-fitter in the docks

CHRONOLOGY OF HIS TIMES

Year	Literary Context	Historical Events
1836	Charles Dickens, *Sketches by Boz*	
1837–9	Dickens, *Oliver Twist; or, The Parish Boy's Progress*	
1845	Benjamin Disraeli, *Sybil*	
1849	Henry Mayhew writing on the London poor for the *Morning Chronicle*	
1850	Thomas Carlyle, *Latter-Day Pamphlets*	
1854	Dickens, *Hard Times*	Crimean War begins
1855	Elizabeth Gaskell, *North and South*	
1856		Crimean War ends
1857	Gustav Flaubert, *Madame Bovary*	
1859	Charles Darwin, *On the Origin of Species* George Eliot, *Adam Bede*	
1861	Mayhew, *London Labour and the London Poor* (4 vols)	American Civil War begins
1862	Victor Hugo, *Les Misérables*	
1863	John Stuart Mill, *Utilitarianism*	
1865	Mendel, *Law of Heredity*	American Civil War ends
1866	Dostoevsky, *Crime and Punishment*	
1867		Second Reform Bill, enfranchising a million urban workers. Holy Trinity parish, Shoreditch, created
1868	Matthew Arnold, *Culture and Anarchy*	Disraeli becomes Prime Minister; succeeded by Gladstone

Year   Age   Life

1871   8   George Morrison dies from consumption, leaving his wife
              with Arthur and two other children

ᵀ875   12   Morrison's adolescence probably spent in the East End

1879   16   Morrison begins work as office boy in the Architect's
              Department of the London School Board at seven shillings a
              week. Later recalls, possibly at this period, frequenting
              secondhand bookshops in the Whitechapel Road
1880   17   Morrison's mother takes over haberdasher's shop in Grundy
              Street; Morrison's first publication – humorous verse in the
              magazine *Cycling*. Subsequently contributes to various
              cycling journals; engages in boxing and cycling. Later recalls,
              possibly at this period, holidays in Essex in company with
              John Louis Wimbush

Year	Literary Context	Historical Events
1869		Suez Canal opens
1870	Death of Dickens	Franco-Prussian War. Forster's Education Act
1871	Charles Darwin, *The Descent of Man* E. B. Tylor, *Primitive Culture*	Suppression of Paris Commune. Trade Unions legalized
1872	Charles Loring Brace, *The Dangerous Classes of New York* George Eliot, *Middlemarch*	
1873	Zola, *Le Ventre de Paris*	David Livingstone dies in Africa
1874		Disraeli's new ministry promotes slum clearance and public health. Factory Act: fifty-six and a half hour working week established. Modern bicycle invented
1875	Octavia Hill, *Homes of the London Poor*	Disraeli buys Suez Canal shares from Khedive of Egypt
1876		Queen Victoria assumes title of Empress of India. Bulgarian atrocities
1877	Zola, *L'Assommoir*	Outbreak of Russo-Turkish War
1878		Turkey defeated: Treaty of Berlin places Eastern Rumelia under Ottoman Empire
1879		Zulu Wars
1880	George Gissing, *Workers in the Dawn* George Wyld, *Theosophy and the Higher Life* Zola, *Nana*; *Le Roman Expérimental*	Gladstone's second Ministry

Year   Age   Life

1885   22   Morrison's first serious journalism, in the *Globe*

Year	Literary Context	Historical Events
1881		Land Act gives Irish tenant farmers greater rights. Death of Disraeli. (Social) Democratic Federation founded. Assassination of Czar Alexander II
1882	Annie Besant, *Reincarnation* Walter Besant, *All Sorts and Conditions of Men* Robert Louis Stevenson, *Treasure Island* R. A. Woods, 'The University Settlement Idea' in *Philanthropy and Social Progress*	British Protectorate of Egypt established. Society for Psychical Research founded
1883	Alfred Alsop, *Street Children Sought and Found, and Other Stories* Edward Carpenter, *Towards Socialism* Andrew Mearns, *The Bitter Cry of Outcast London* George Sims, *How the Poor Live*	Death of Karl Marx. Fabian Society founded
1884	Gissing, *The Unclassed* G. B. Shaw, *An Unsocial Socialist* Zola, *La Joie de Vivre*	Third Reform Act extends vote to many rural workers. Socialist League founded. Royal Commission on Housing; Edwin Chadwick, pioneer of housing and sanitation reform knighted
1885	Alsop, *Below the Surface: or, Down in the Slums, by A. Delver* Eleanor Grundy, *Life Below the Surface; Being the True Incidents of Child Life in the Slums of Manchester* Rider Haggard, *King Solomon's Mines* Zola, *Germinal*	Revolution in Eastern Rumelia; outbreak of Serbo-Bulgarian War. Death of General Gordon at Khartoum. Birth of D. H. Lawrence

Year	Age	Life
1886	23	Having risen to 'junior' and then 'third-class clerk', Morrison appointed secretary to the Beaumont Trustees, the body administering the People's Palace (Sept); in charge of social and educational facilities
1888	25	Obtains reader's ticket to British Museum. Contributes 13 sketches entitled 'Cockney Corners' to the *People* on such districts as Poplar, Soho, Clerkenwell, Bow Street, Whitechapel, Jacob's Island, Greenwich Park and Epping Forest; describes markets, trades, the condition of the unemployed and the ill
1889	26	Becomes sub-editor of *Palace Journal*; reprints such pieces as 'Whitechapel' (Apr), 'On Blackwall Pier' (May) and 'Christmas Eve in the Streets' (Dec); sub-editorials commenting on books, pictures, critical taste and urging membership of the Literary Society. Writes of the sufferings of the poor; Dock Strike inspires story 'Without Visible Means'

Year	Literary Context	Historical Events
1886	Frances Hodgson Burnett, *Little Lord Fauntleroy* Gissing, *Demos: A Story of English Socialism* Thomas Hardy, *The Mayor of Casterbridge* Henry James, *The Princess Casamassima* William Morris, *A Dream of John Ball* R. L. Stevenson, *Dr Jekyll and Mr Hyde* Zola, *La Terre*	Pall Mall and Trafalgar Square riots. Gladstone's third Ministry. Colonial and Indian Exhibition
1887	Arthur Conan Doyle, *A Study in Scarlet* Gissing, *Thyrza* Margaret Harkness, *A City Girl: A Realistic Story* Mark Rutherford, *The Revolution in Tanner's Lane*	Arthur Osborne Jay takes up parish duties in Shoreditch and the Old Nichol. Queen Victoria opens the People's Palace. 'Bloody Sunday' rioting in Trafalgar Square broken up by the Lifeguards. Queen Victoria's Golden Jubilee
1888	Harkness, *Out of Work* Emma Leslie, *How the Strike Began: A Story for Girls*	Jack the Ripper murders in Whitechapel continue into 1889. London Matchgirls' Strike
1889	Charles Booth, *East London*, one-volume version of *Life and Labour of the People in London* Gissing, *The Nether World* Harkness, *Captain Lobe*, reissued in 1891 as *In Darkest London* George Sims, *Horrible London* Fabian Essays	Gas Workers' Strike wins eight-hour working day. Great Dock Strike. Imprisonment of Vizetelly, Zola's English publisher. Second International founded

Year   Age   Life

1890   27   Resigns (from 30 Sept) from People's Palace. Joins editorial
             staff of the evening *Globe*; takes lodgings in the Strand.
             Subsequently freelances, publishing another short story in the
             People. His friend Harold Parlett goes to Japan and later
             helps Morrison acquire paintings

1891   28   First book, *The Shadows Around Us*: narratives of the
             supernatural originally published in the *People*. Contributes
             'A Street' to *Macmillan's* (Oct)

1892   29   Collaborates with illustrator J. A. Shepherd on 'My
             Neighbours' Dogs' and other animal sketches for the *Strand*.
             Marries Elizabeth Thatcher at Forest Gate (Aug). They live
             at Chingford and then Salcombe House, Loughton, Essex.
             Success of 'The Legend of Lapwater Hall' (ghost story) in
             Macmillan's

Year	Literary Context	Historical Events
1890	William Booth, *In Darkest England and the Way Out* Harkness, *A Manchester Shirtmaker* Rudyard Kipling, 'The Record of Badalia Herodsfoot' in *Harper's Weekly* Morris, *News from Nowhere* W. M. Stanley, *In Darkest Africa* Jacob Riis, *How the Other Half Lives: Studies Among the Tenements of New York* Sidney Webb, *Socialism in England*	London's first underground railway line
1891	Booth, *Life and Labour of the People in London* (2 vols) Gissing, *New Grub Street* Hardy, *Tess of the d'Urbervilles* Rev. A. O. M. Jay, *Life in Darkest London: A Hint to General Booth* Leslie, *The Seed She Sowed: A Tale of the Great Dock Strike* William Tirebuck, *Dorrie* Beatrice Webb, *The Co-operative Movement in Great Britain* Oscar Wilde, *The Picture of Dorian Grey*	
1892	Booth, *Life and Labour of the People in London* (9 vols, to 1897) Doyle, *The Adventures of Sherlock Holmes* Kipling, *Barrack Room Ballads* Riis, *The Children of the Poor* Israel Zangwill, *Children of the Ghetto*	Gladstone's fourth Ministry (to 1894). Keir Hardie wins parliamentary seat

Year   Age   Life

1893   30   W. E. Henley, editor of the *National Observer* and
            continuing friend provides an outlet for more stories of
            working-class life (Dec 1892–4); joins Kipling, Barrie,
            Hardy, Wells and Yeats as one of Henley's 'Regatta' of
            writers. Guy Morrison born

1894   31   First Martin Hewitt detective story, 'The Lenten Croft
            Robberies' appears in the *Strand* (Mar). Two working-class
            stories published in *Pall Mall Budget* (Aug–Sept). With some
            revision, and addition of 'The Red Cow Group', *Tales of
            Mean Streets* collects these and most of the sketches from the
            National Observer; published 15 Nov and dedicated to
            Henley. Removed from Clerkenwell Library by local
            authorities; W. H. Smith temporarily refuse to supply it to
            circulating libraries. Also publishes *Martin Hewitt,
            Investigator* and *Zig-Zags at the Zoo*

1895   32   *Bookman* publishes interview (Jan). Writes to *Spectator*
            (Mar) about reviewers' over-reaction to 'Lizerunt'. Rev. Jay
            writes letter of appreciation; invites Morrison to visit the Old
            Nichol. Morrison's interest in Japanese art grows. Publishes
            Chronicles of Martin Hewitt

Year	Literary Context	Historical Events
1893	Robert Blatchford, *Merrie England* Charles Allen Clarke, *The Knobstick* Stephen Crane, *Maggie: A Girl of the Streets* Benjamin Orange Flower, *Civilization's Inferno: Studies in the Social Cellar* Jay, *The Social Problem and its Possible Solution* Zangwill, *Tragedies of the Ghetto*	Gissing accuses Jay of plagiarizing *The Nether World* in *The Social Problem*. Independent Labour Party formed
1894	Clementina Black, *An Agitator* Blatchford, *A Son of the Forge* George Du Maurier, *Trilby* George Moore, *Esther Waters*	Jay invites Gissing to visit him in Shoreditch. Gladstone resigns as Prime Minister over Irish Home Rule. Nicholas II becomes Czar. Anarchist attack at Greenwich
1895	Crane, *The Red Badge of Courage* Hardy, *Jude the Obscure* H. W. Nevinson, *Neighbours of Ours: Slum Stories of London* Edwin Pugh, *A Street in Suburbia* H. G. Wells, *The Time Machine*	Gissing visits Jay and sees 'his way to a big book'. LCC Boundary Street Scheme demolishes Old Nichol. Jay invites Gissing to opening of new church. London School of Economics founded. Death of Engels. Trial of Oscar Wilde

Year   Age   Life

1896   33   Begins writing up *A Child of the Jago* (Apr); published by
            Methuen (Nov) after part-serialization (chs 1–13) in Henley's
            New Review; published in USA by H. S. Stone. Also
            publishes *Adventures of Martin Hewitt*. Jacob Riis, great
            American social commentator, reviews *Tales of Mean Streets*
            in *Book Buyer*. 'How Realistic Fiction is Written' appears
            anonymously in *St. James's Gazette* (Dec), claiming
            plagiarism of Jay's *Life in Darkest London*; Jay defends
            Morrison in *Gazette*; 'C.R.' similarly defends Morrison in
            the *Academy*. *Daily News* publishes interview (Dec)

1897   34   Harold Boulton reviews *Jago* in *British Review* (Jan). Second
            edition of *Jago*. H. D. Traill's 'The New Realism'
            (*Fortnightly Review*) attacks 'extraordinary unreality' of
            Jago; Jay responds in *Fortnightly* (Feb) but Traill extends
            attack in *The New Fiction and Other Essays*. Morrison
            completes 'What is a Realist' for *New Review* (Feb–Mar),
            subsequently adapted as preface to third edition of *Jago*.
            Publishes *The Dorrington Deed-Box* (detective stories).
            Tauchnitz issues *Jago*

Year	Literary Context	Historical Events
1896	J. Ackworth, *Clog Shop Chronicles* J. M. Barrie, *Sentimental Tommy* W. Besant, 'A Riverside Parish' in *The Poor in Great Cities* Marie Corelli, *The Mighty Atom* First English ed.(with bowdlerized title) of Crane's *Maggie: A Child of the Streets* S. R. Crockett, *Cleg Kelly: Arab of the City* Jay, *A Story of Shoreditch: Being a Sequel to 'Life in Darkest London'* Pugh, *The Man of Straw* Wells, *The Island of Dr Moreau* Death of William Morris	Jay interviewed for *London* under headline 'To Check the Survival of the Fittest'
1897	Joseph Conrad, *The Nigger of the Narcissus* Somerset Maugham, *Liza of Lambeth* Robert Sherard, *The White Slaves of England* Bram Stoker, *Dracula* Ethel L. Voynich, *The Gadfly*	Queen Victoria's Diamond Jubilee. Revolt on Indian North-West Frontier
1898	Pugh, *Tony Drum: A Cockney Boy*	Death of Gladstone

Year	Age	Life
1899	36	Publishes *To London Town* as completion of trilogy begun with *Mean Streets* and *Jago*
1900	37	Publishes *Cunning Murrell*
1901	38	'A Workman's Budget' (Apr) in *Cornhill* and 'Hooliganism' in *Pall Mall*
1902	39	Publishes *The Hole in the Wall*; also series of articles on Japanese art in *Monthly Review*. Fourth edition of *Jago*
1903	40	Publishes *The Red Triangle* (short stories)
1904	41	Publishes *The Green Eye of Goona: Stories of a Case of Tokay* (as *The Green Diamond* in USA); also successful one-act play version of 'That Brute Simmons' from *Mean Streets*, in collaboration with Herbert C. Sargent

Year	Literary Context	Historical Events
1899	W. Besant, *East London* Blatchford, *Dismal England* G. T. Kimmin, *Polly of Parker's Rents* William Pett Ridge, *A Son of the State* Clarence Rook, *The Hooligan Nights* and *Billy the Snide* Richard Whiteing, *No.5 John Street* William Wyckoff, *The Workers – The West* Conrad, *Heart of Darkness* (serial)	Boer War begins
1900	Blatchford, 'On Realism,' in his *My Favourite Books* Conrad, *Lord Jim*	Labour Representation Committee founded. Boxer Rebellion in China
1901	Kipling, *Kim* Frank Norris, *The Octopus* B. S. Rowntree, *Poverty: A Study of Town Life* Wells, *The First Men in the Moon*	Theodore Roosevelt becomes President of USA. Queen Victoria dies; accession of Edward VII
1902	Arnold Bennett, *Anna of the Five Towns* Booth, *Life and Labour of the People in London* (17 vols) C. F. G. Masterman, *From the Abyss*	Boer War ends. Jack London visits East End. Death of Zola
1903	W. Besant, *As We Are and As We Might Be* Samuel Butler, *The Way of All Flesh* Jack London, *The People of the Abyss* W.B.N., *Penal Servitude* Pett Ridge, *Up Side Streets* Olivia Rossetti, *A Girl Among the Anarchists*	Lenin becomes leader of the Russian Bolsheviks. Wright Brothers make first powered air-flight
1904	Conrad, *Nostromo: A Tale of the Seaboard*	Russo-Japanese War begins

Year	Age	Life
1905	42	Publishes *Divers Vanities* (short stories)
1906	43	Sells collection of Japanese woodcuts to British Museum
1907	44	Morrison's one-act play *A Stroke of Business* is well received. *The Dumb-Cake* published, another one-act play, adapted in collaboration with Richard Pryce from *Divers Vanities*
1909	46	Publishes *Green Ginger* (short stories)
1910	47	Parlett made Consul at Dairen
1911	48	Publishes the authoritative *Painters of Japan*, 2 vols, largely illustrated with paintings in his own collection. *Jago* reaches sixth edition
1913	50	Retires from journalism; moves to High Beech, Essex; continues interests in art collecting and dealing

Year	Literary Context	Historical Events
1905	Wells, *Kipps*	First Russian Revolution. Russia defeated by Japan
1906	Bramwell Booth, ed., *Essays and Sketches: The Salvation Army* John Galsworthy, *The Man of Property* Andersen Nexö, *Pelle the Conqueror* Upton Sinclair, *The Jungle* Robert Tressell writing *The Ragged Trousered Philanthropists*	Liberal Election victory; Labour electoral successes
1907	Conrad, *The Secret Agent* Maxim Gorky, *Mother* London, *The Iron Heel*	
1908	Blatchford, *Britain for the British* Bennett, *The Old Wives' Tale* Frank Harris, *The Bomb* Wells, *The War in the Air*	
1909	E. M. Forster, *Howards End* Masterman, *The Condition of England*	Old Age Pension introduced
1910	Sidney Webb, *English Poor Law Policy* Wells, *The History of Mr Polly*	Death of Edward VII; accession of George V Tonypandy riots
1911	Bennett, *Clayhanger* Conrad, *Under Western Eyes* Strindberg, *Miss Julie* in English translation. Sidney Webb, *The Prevention of Destitution*	*Daily Herald* founded. Liberal Government brings in national unemployment and medical insurance. Population of England and Wales reaches 36 million (double that in 1851)
1912	Doyle, *The Lost World*	First Balkan War. Loss of *Titanic*
1913	D. H. Lawrence, *Sons and Lovers*	Second Balkan War. Panama Canal opened

Year	Age	Life
1914	51	Guy serves in army. Morrison's collection of Japanese art bought by Sir Watkin Gwynne Evans (for £4,000) and presented to British Museum; publication of *Guide to an Exhibition of Japanese and Chinese Paintings Principally from the Arthur Morrison Collection* and *Exhibition of Japanese Screens Decorated by Old Masters, Held at the Galleries of the Royal Society of British Artists, January 26th to February 26th, 1914*
1915	52	Morrison acting as Special Constable in Essex; credited with telephoning news of the first Zeppelin raid on London
1921	58	Guy dies from malaria at his parents' home in Cavendish Square, London
1924	61	Morrison elected member of Royal Society of Literature

Year	Literary Context	Historical Events
1914	Robert Tressell, *The Ragged Trousered Philanthropists* James Joyce, *Dubliners*	Outbreak of First World War
1915	Lawrence, *The Rainbow*	Gallipoli
1916	Henri Barbusse, *Le Feu*	Battles of Verdun and Somme. Ireland: Easter Rising
1917		Battle of Passchendaele. Russian Revolution. USA enters war
1918		First World War ends in Armistice. Women over thirty and men over twenty-one obtain vote
1919	J. M. Keynes, *The Economic Consequences of the Peace*	Treaty of Versailles. Socialist uprising in Berlin suppressed
1920	Lawrence, *Women in Love* Wilfred Owen, *Poems*	League of Nations meets
1921		In London, Marie Stopes founds first birth-control clinic. Irish Free State founded
1922	T. S. Eliot, *The Waste Land* Joyce, *Ulysses*	Italy· Mussolini comes to power
1924	Forster, *A Passage to India*	Ramsay MacDonald becomes first Labour Prime Minister. Russia: Stalin achieves complete power
1925	Eisenstein, *The Battleship Potemkin* Sean O'Casey, *Juno and the Paycock* Virginia Woolf, *Mrs Dalloway*	Stanley Baldwin heads Conservative government
1926	Mrs Cecil Chesterton, *In Darkest London* Franz Kafka, *The Castle*	General Strike
1927	F. C. Boden, *Pit-Head Poems* Woolf, *To the Lighthouse*	Lindbergh flies New York–Paris

Year	Age	Life
1929	66	Publication of retrospective volume by Morrison in *Short Stories of Today and Yesterday* series
1930	67	Moves to final home, 'High Barn', Chalfont St Peter, Buckinghamshire
1933	70	Publishes *Fiddle o' Dreams and More* (short stories)
1935	72	Elected to Council of Royal Society of Literature
1936	73	Presents manuscript of *Jago* to Bethnal Green Library

Year	Literary Context	Historical Events
1928	Lawrence, *Lady Chatterley's Lover*	Vote given to women aged twenty-one
1929	Boden, *Out of the Coalfields* Robert Graves, *Goodbye to All That* Ernest Hemingway, *A Farewell to Arms*	Wall Street Crash
1931	Lionel Britton, *Hunger and Love* James Hanley, *Boy* Woolf prefaces *Life As We Have Known It*, by Co-operative Working Women.	
1932	Boden, *Miner* Aldous Huxley, *Brave New World*	Franklin D. Roosevelt becomes President of USA
1933	Walter Greenwood, *Love on the Dole* George Orwell, *Down and Out in Paris and London*	Hitler becomes Chancellor of Germany. First concentration camps. Roosevelt launches New Deal
1934	Lewis Grassic Gibbon, *Grey Granite* Graham Greene *It's a Battlefield* J. B. Priestley, *English Journey*	
1935	Walter Brierley, *Means Test Man* A. J. Cronin, *The Stars Look Down* Beatrice and Sidney Webb, *Soviet Communism: A New Civilization*	Italy invades Abyssinia
1936	P. G. Wodehouse, 'Archibald and the Masses' in *Young Men in Spats*	Spanish Civil War begins. Battle of Cable Street in East End. George V dies; Edward VIII succeeds and abdicates; accession of George VI

Year *Age* *Life*

1944 81   V. S. Pritchett's essay in *New Statesman and Nation* signals renewal of interest in Morrison

1945 82   Arthur Morrison dies (Dec). His will presents 140 Japanese paintings and woodcuts and collection of tea ceremony porcelain to British Museum. He directs his library to be sold and his notebooks and papers to be burned

1946   Penguin Books publish an edition of *Jago*

1956   Mrs Morrison dies. She bequeaths a collection of Chinese lacquer to British Museum

Year	Literary Context	Historical Events
1937	Ralph Fox, *The Novel and the People* Lewis Jones, *Cwmardy* Orwell, *The Road to Wigan Pier* Wal Hannington, *The Problem of the Distressed Areas*	
1938		Hitler takes Austria; Munich agreement gives Hitler Czechoslovakia
1939	Bert Coombes, *These Poor Hands* Greenwood, *How the Other Man Lives* Frank Griffin, *October Day* Jones, *We Live* John Steinbeck, *The Grapes of Wrath*	Germany invades Poland; outbreak of Second World War
1940	Orwell, 'My Country Right or Left'	Germany invades Denmark and Norway; Battle of Britain; Blitz begins, particularly affecting East End
1941	Orwell, 'The Lion and the Unicorn' Priestley, *Out of the People*	Germany invades Belgium, Holland, Russia, France; Japan attacks Pearl Harbor; USA enters war
1942	Evelyn Waugh, *Put Out More Flags*	Beveridge Report, laying foundations of Welfare State
1943		Warsaw Ghetto killings; Allies invade Italy
1944		D-Day landings; V1 and V2 rocket raids on London
1945	Orwell, *Animal Farm* Waugh, *Brideshead Revisited*	Defeat of Germany; Atomic bombs on Hiroshima and Nagasaki; Japan surrenders. Landslide Labour victory; Clement Attlee becomes Prime Minister
1946		Nationalization policies implemented
1948		National Health Service founded

INTRODUCTION

At the turn of the century Jane Findlater recalled that during the 1890s 'we all read the books of Arthur Morrison and shuddered over them'. Thereafter, something happened. An extraordinary change occurred in memory and perception of the incendiary Arthur Morrison whose *Tales of Mean Streets* (1894) and *A Child of the Jago* (1896) had once set the Thames on fire and the literary establishments of two continents singing praises or spitting feathers. Morrison's writing once prompted comparisons with Balzac, Zola, Daudet and Kipling, with Hogarth and Whistler; *A Child of the Jago* was seen by contemporaries as transmitting to posterity a '*locus classicus*' of the Victorian age. Habitually invoked as a figurehead of 'Realism', Morrison's name had regularly been twinned with that of the author of *The Red Badge of Courage*. That conjunction, moreover, even when fashioned by his fiercest detractors, had consistently worked to underline Morrison's status as the greater artist, the 'heavyweight' in H. G. Wells' words and, in H. D. Traill's, the 'trained craftsman' by whose side Stephen Crane was but a 'crude amateur'. Yet in 1967 Morrison's literary standing was such that the title of an article by P. J. Keating, simply asking 'Who Knows Arthur Morrison?', sounded distressingly like an appeal to find a missing person. Keating highlighted what had become not only a matter of readers' limited acquaintance with Morrison's books but of scholars' limited knowledge of the man. It now emerged that even such information as Morrison's place of birth (Kent? Poplar?) and his social class (working? middle?) had been only uncertainly or erroneously recorded. Keating correctly inferred that this situation was partly owing to false trails laid by Morrison himself, but the fact remained that by 1967 such judgements of the relative achievement of Morrison and Crane as Wells and Traill had offered or conceded seemed only rash and untenable. Thirty years on, Morrison's self-assisted submergence into the cellar of literary history, like his partial rescue, appears explicable in terms of altering valuations of his writing as shaped by trajectories of change in British culture and society over the last one hundred years. The heart of the matter is that Morrison's writings have spoken most intensely to readers at moments when the value of community and popular concern at unsatisfactory social conditions have been in the ascendant.

Born in 1863, Morrison had his greatest impact in the 1890s. Traces of him survive from the First World War when he was reported, as a special constable in Essex, to have been the first to telephone London with news of an airship attack. (One Zeppelin bombed Stoke Newington station and inflicted casualties with bombs and grenades as it tracked across Dalston, Hoxton, Shoreditch and Whitechapel; one was photographed over Morrison's childhood home of Poplar.) However, the fact that Morrison was also still living when the Luftwaffe was blitzing the East End docks and that he died as late as 1945 – after long silence and half a century after *A Child of the Jago* – can seem curiously out of synchronization with his literary biography. If the dimming of a bestseller's star is not a sufficient explanation, Jocelyn Bell captured something of the nature of the fading of man and writing from the consciousness of the culture in observing that Morrison 'was one of those contemporary bestsellers who could be found on every Edwardian bookshelf, but who vanished in the Great War and were unknown to the new and changed generation which followed'.

After the First World War, in the era of an élite literary Modernism by definition antipathetic to realism, there was little by which Morrison could have been known. His writing career had been intimately bound up with the magazine culture of the 1890s; once that connection ended, a dynamic in both the creation and reception of his work was lost. Most of his books went out of print; scholarship took little heed of them. Besides, fiction by and about the working class shifted its focus from the East End slums to the Distressed Areas of the Depression. After the Russian Revolution the politics of writing by and about the working class took new directions; such 1930s novelists as Lewis Grassic Gibbon, Lewis Jones and even Walter Greenwood imaged the working class from viewpoints and on premises very different to Arthur Morrison's. *A Child of the Jago* had its allegiances to the genre of documentary-style 'descent into the abyss' not just through the nature of the first-hand research that Morrison conducted for the novel, but through the dramatic role of its fictional Father Sturt and the historical role of that character's model, Father Arthur Osborne Jay, the enterprising Vicar of Holy Trinity, Shoreditch. The genre did still flourish: Jack London's *People of the Abyss* (1903), Ada Chesterton's *In Darkest London* (1926), her egregiously titled *I Lived in a Slum* (1936) and George Orwell's *The Road to Wigan Pier* (1937) carried further the spirit of Jay's and Morrison's descents into the Shoreditch slums. Yet the second, discursively political, part of *Wigan Pier* signals what changed. *A Child of the Jago* and Frank Griffin's *October Day* are both East End novels, but by the time of Griffin's in 1939 the issue in the East End's streets had moved beyond the mobilization of liberal compassion for slum-dwellers (or fears concerning them) to the outright confrontations of fascism and socialism. The politics of interwar representation of the working class hardly fostered rediscovery of a novelist Jane Findlater had assigned to a 'School of Pity'. If it was later than one thought, it was certainly too late for pity.

Morrison's cooperation in the submergence of his writings involved his vanishing into semi-retirement in the home counties. The very little that is known of him after the First World War suggests a modestly successful survivor from the world of the Edwardian men-of-letters turned skilful collector and dealer in Oriental art. While that interest has been misunderstood (the American novelist and socialist Jack London fumed about those who organized exhibitions of Japanese art for the people), there exists little evidence to counter an impression of Morrison as a man who no longer felt the need to write when he could well afford not to, as someone who in later years had found his own fairly comfortable 'way out'. In 1914 the British Museum celebrated with a catalogue its acquisition of Morrison's recently sold collection of Japanese and Chinese prints and paintings; in 1924 he was elected to the Royal Society of Literature and in 1935 to its Council. In 1933 one more new collection of short stories had drifted onto the scene, but more indicative was a little anthology of 1929, a reprise of his tales from the 1890s onwards. An unaccented selection published in a series that processed Bennett, Chesterton, Gissing and W. W. Jacobs to the same formula, it comprised a few stories from *Tales of Mean Streets* (the once notorious 'Lizerunt' not among them) outweighed by similar numbers taken from each of his subsequent, increasingly light, humorous and inconsequential collections. A brief preface to *Short Stories of Today and Yesterday* written by another hand made no mention of any shudders Morrison had once induced but quaintly recalled him as earstwhile explorer of the patois and strategies of London's criminals; Morrison's own minimalist 'Author's Note' spoke of stories published from 'twenty to thirty-four years ago' for which, however, he had no intention of claiming 'the interest of antiquity'. In contrast to the tone of the angry prophet's denunciation used as the epigraph to *A Child of the Jago*, this was a voice echoing round the very flower-garden of art that Morrison had so despised in his preface to the novel, the voice of a man as happy as anyone to cultivate oblivion towards his identity in an antique yesterday.

In fact, something had survived – and survives still. A typical language ('Social Problem discourse') evolved in the late nineteenth century to capture the lived experience of slums, overcrowding, violence and the downward spiral of poverty in large cities. In particular, it generated many metaphors that enabled the middle class to gain some inkling of a previously inconceivable other world of the urban poor and working class. The underclass became 'the Submerged' of the 'Abyss' or 'the Subterranean' of a 'Nether World', their lives given some perceptible shape, even if suffering ideological distortion in the process. Morrison's own contribution to such ways of seeing was a view from street level. Whether he coined the term or just impelled it with a new force, it was he who inscribed into the phrase 'mean streets' a distinct vision of the city that has ever since been reworked and reapplied. Morrison in fact used the term not to denote the alleyways of an Old Nichol (the original of his 'Jago'), but rather the featureless street 'hundreds of miles long' constituting London's ever-building East End – those 'newish' houses, as Somerset Maugham termed them in *Liza of Lambeth*, rising to fill the fields between what previously had been only hamlets. The writer and reformer Walter Besant, champion of the People's Palace and author of the novel *All Sorts and Conditions of Men*, stressed that this mushrooming city-in-itself stretching out towards Essex had a population the size of Philadelphia or Berlin, but only a fraction of those cities' amenities. Where, asked Besant, were the bookshops, libraries, churches, cathedrals, educational institutions, concert-halls, even the hotels – where was the civic administration and where the police? The East End had its public houses, corner shops, boxing saloons, occasional music-halls and theatres (such as the 'Britannia' at Hoxton), but principally, in Morrison's eyes (and at times he seems to have suppressed his awareness of the more cheerful and vigorous street-life that he presented in his article 'Christmas Eve in the Streets'), there tailed off into the distance a monotony of similar houses and lives, 'respectable' as their inhabitants might be. (Besant declared that the very 'omphalos of dreariness' was situated somewhere in the Mile End Road.) These were Morrison's 'mean streets' as he first defined them. In the aftermath of Jack the Ripper, however, the extraordinary impact of one short story skewed the reception of Morrison's first collection of working-class tales and the meaning of its title phrase. This was the account in 'Lizerunt' of the making of a Commercial Road street-prostitute from pickle-factory girl, dramatizing the workings of environment, heredity, early marriage, male violence and poverty in the commodification of women on London's 'windy street' – historyless women as they were so often observed from tram or omnibus by Morrison's middle-class readers, now given history through his tragic narrative. Repeatedly Morrison emphasized that the dealings of 'Lizerunt' with 'the great pollution' (as one reviewer termed it) was representative of neither the collection nor the East End as a whole. Yet for readers it was the particular meanness of Lizerunt's street that invested the phrase: when A Child of the Jago appeared, the association was compounded. 'Mean streets' became shorthand for the blind detachment of the processes of Darwinian nature from the suffering individual, now transposed into an urban setting: the phrase connoted a claustrophobic world red in knife and fist, characterizable only in terms of the otherness of Hell, a denatured world of bricks, dirt and dust-filtered light where the fittest might survive but where the most degenerate also lived on to threaten the fittest with contamination. With the exception of 'a few dusty fowls' and those imagined by Tommy Rann as targets for shooting, the only birds in Morrison's Jago are caged; the only animals are rats or else beasts of burden typified by Jerry Gullen's Canary who when not in harness is condemned – symbolically like any other Jago

– to chewing to splinters the palings of its wasteland compound even as the blood drips from its mouth. It is in these mean streets that a human child grows up remembering her jailed father as 'a man who lived in a cage'. In 1898, in an issue of *Home Magazine*, Dr Barnardo took up the phrase in presenting his own 'Tale of a Mean Street'; a century on from Morrison's volume of short stories, in December 1995, the *Independent* newspaper reported riot damage in Brixton by captioning its lead photograph of an elderly woman making her way past burnt-out buildings 'Mean Streets'.

American usage of 'mean', implying hardness and hostility in addition to narrowness and cultural impoverishment, consolidated the phrase and its vision. It percolated from Social Problem discourse into the repertoire of the Blues. The Raymond Chandler who in 1944 wrote 'Down these mean streets a man must go who is not himself mean, who is neither tarnished nor afraid', was formerly a Dulwich College schoolboy in turn-of-the-century Britain who quite possibly encountered *Tales of Mean Streets* by way of an interest in Morrison's fictional detective Martin Hewitt. Beyond Chandler and the mediation of his writing by *film noir*, moreover, lies Martin Scorsese's study *Mean Streets* (1974) depicting, in the director's words, 'second-generation Italians caught in the cloistered world of New York's lower east side'. It is through this ever-diffusing mythology of urban experience that Morrison and *A Child of the Jago* have been present. Scorsese described his own *Mean Streets* as 'no slice of life film'; rather, he declared, it was 'opera-like'; 'casual, intense and violent and it's both ultra-realistic and ultra-naturalistic, servile in many places and yet very stylised. There is no basic plot really; the people of the movie are the story.' This thread in the perception of urban life on both sides of the Atlantic makes it less than fortuitous that Scorsese's epitome of his film can serve as a characterization of *A Child of the Jago*; it too has its operatic dimensions; the cloistered world that it depicts is rendered in terms ultra-realistic and ultra-naturalistic, while it too has been seen as a stylised 'fairyland of horror' and a 'Voyage to the Houyhnhnms' – as essentially a symbolic as much as a realistic text.

In 1944 V. S. Pritchett rediscovered Morrison for a Britain in which the East End was being iconized in flame-lit silhouettes of common men standing heroically together. No longer perceived as a centre of infection and the alien, the East End was coming to symbolize national resistance and community. (When Buckingham Palace was bombed, the Queen Mother reportedly remarked that now at least she would be able to look the people of the East End in the face.) Life in wartime, though not without abrasions, broached class-distinctions – in the armed services, home guard, war-work and through rationing and the evacuation of London children to the countryside. Wartime propaganda stressed mutual dependence, while writers such as J. B. Priestley anticipated a peace in which political bills for the cross-class effort would have to be met. Pritchett's response to Morrison's writing was thus informed by new experiences of social tolerance and by pride in adaptation to a restricted life maintained under desperate circumstances: 'In Mr Morrison's book,' he wrote, 'slum life is the accepted life, a dirty but not a turgid stream. In their position, you say – as one ought to say of all human beings – these people have lived, they've kept their heads above water for a spell. Man is the animal who adapts himself.' In 1946 Penguin Books published *A Child of the Jago* in paperback; in 1947 Morrison's 1902 novel *The Hole in the Wall* reappeared with a preface by Pritchett and in the glow of his valuation of it as a 'minor masterpiece'. The ideology of 'The People's War', which had functioned to bring the classes of Britain together in the fight against Nazism (and with the promise of a fairer society thereafter), the establishment of the Welfare State and the drive for reconstruction through slum clearance and housing policy encouraged a return to *A Child of the Jago*, its social experiences and the focus its preface provided on the value of communal responsibility: 'If the community have left horrible places and horrible lives ... then the fault is the community's ... For the existence of this place, and for the evils it engendered, the community was, and is responsible; so that every member of the community was, and is, responsible to his degree.' Yet Morrison's recovery was by no means fully consolidated. Two decades on, another burst of activity pushed Morrison to the foreground: Keating's edition of *A Child of the Jago* appeared in the late 1960s; the 1970s brought a television adaptation and Folio Society edition of *The Hole in the Wall*; the early 1980s brought Michael Krzak's edition of *Tales of Mean Streets*. If British culture has since then been in danger of again marginalizing Morrison, the reasons may well lie in a subsequent swing towards a public ethos of individual responsibility and self-reliance where 'society', let alone communal responsibility, has been held not to exist at all. In the 1980s, images from television's 'EastEnders' – its 'Queen Vic' pub, street market, and elderly residents reminiscing about the Blitz – iconized communal values, though effectively as a nostalgic rearguard action. Beyond such images the physical redevelopment of Docklands overlaid the material elements of the national myth of community with a topography and commercially oriented architecture symbolizing new public values and rewriting the East End as Canary Wharf rather than as Albert Square.

It needs to be said, however, that the terms of Morrison's immediately postwar rediscovery were unbalanced, for *A Child of the Jago* was more than nominally a product of Victorian values. If it contributed to an atmosphere in which early twentieth-century Liberal legislation created Old Age pensions and national medical and unemployment insurance schemes, there are aspects of the book that in fact sit most uncomfortably with the values of the wartime Beveridge Report and its outline of a peacetime Welfare State, in the shade of which V. S. Pritchett composed his eulogy of Morrison's social writings. Elsewhere Morrison's hostility towards anarchism and his satire of socialism, as in 'The Rodd Street Revolution' (*Green Ginger*), requires little comment:

> 'The selfishness prevalent at the present time is due to the rotten state of s'ciety an' the oppression of the privileged classes. When we 'ave the social revolution, an' free an' absolute liberty o' the individual, then selfishness'll be swep' out o' the world' (said Sotcher).
>
> 'Yes,' answered Teddy blankly. 'but what – what am I a-goin' to do till it is?'
>
> 'Wave aloft the banner o' free an' unrestricted brotherhood and liberty in the face o' the bloated circles o' class an' capitalistic privilege,' replied Sotcher, with the fluency of a fresh-oiled machine.
>
> 'What?'
>
> 'I said we'd raise our free 'ands an' voices in the sacred cause o' universal anarchy an' proudly march in the van of progress to the

glorious consummation o' the social upheaval,' Sotcher continued, knowing that one sentence meant as much as the other, and airing them, therefore, in turn.

'Yes – jesso,' replied Teddy Mills, turning his uneasy glance toward the little front door; 'but what about the washin'?' (pp. 160–161)

For his own part Morrison valued 'firmness' over 'false sentiment' in dealing with the underclass, a stance which in fact conceals an iron fist. His ideal of communal responsibility for the Jagos ran not just to welfarism but, as the conversation between Sturt and the Surgeon indicates, to measures in emigration, penal settlements, eugenic apartheid and other constraints on their reproduction (Chap. 28). Differing emphatically from H. G. Wells, the problems that Morrison saw in the slums were due not just to environment, but also to heredity. Any lasting solution, in consequence, needed to be not just social but eugenic. 'Let the weed,' he chillingly maintained, in expounding the social politics of *A Child of the Jago*, 'die out'; only then can we 'raise the raisable'. Later, he softened his terms, talking instead – and more like the Salvation Army's General Booth in his study *In Darkest England and the Way Out* – of transportation to a 'colony' where the inhabitants might have 'bicycles and any luxuries you like'. However, his endorsement of the principle of 'segregation' whereby slum-dwellers 'would cease to be a danger to the community by propagating their kind' never altered. In the light of this alliance of fierce idealism with such expediency, the death of Dicky Perrott becomes double-edged, still moving to pity and underwriting liberal intervention, but in its disturbing status as dramatized euthanasia, also raising ghosts of more than one twentieth-century horror fuelled by misguided idealism. 'That is why I killed Dicky Perrott,' mused Morrison in December 1896, 'he could not escape from his environment, and had he lived, would have become perforce, as bad as his surroundings.'

Arthur Morrison, it has been clarified by P. J. Keating and Michael Krzak, was a working-class boy from Poplar who, there is every reason to suppose, grew up in the East End as son of an engine-fitter in the docks. His family may have had connections with rural Essex, a county to which he showed devotion as a cyclist, holiday-maker and then resident, as also in the homages paid in his short stories and in his Hardyesque novel of 1900, *Cunning Murrell*. (Hardy's influence is a tangible one, for example through echoes of *Tess of the d'Urbervilles*.) In print, however, Morrison was not frank about his background. He never once defended his version of the East End on the authority of his being himself an East Ender. (It was in 1897 that he told the compilers of *Who's Who* that he had been born in Kent and had been sent to private schools.) Instead, he defended the accuracy of his writing by asserting other means as his route to first-hand knowledge of East London; in the preface to *A Child of the Jago* he wrote of having lived there 'for certain years' and of an intimacy with its people founded not on a role as social explorer, but as 'familiar and equal friend'. Resorting to the corroboration of other observers rather than stating all his credentials, he persistently concealed his roots. Misconceptions did follow. Reviewers read him as a fellow middle-class onlooker and felt the freer to challenge him. One even gently explained what often went wrong when a gentleman of culture and education (presumably such as Morrison and himself) tried to make sense of the working class. Morrison's evasions and deceptions on this score, Keating suggested, revealed snobbery. Taken with Morrison's ironic style, with the terms of his retirement and under direction from the uncompromising charge made by Alan Sillitoe, author of *Saturday Night and Sunday Morning*, that Morrison 'wrote from too far above his characters', the indictment understandably lies on the books. Yet, in the face of the British class system, one might also acknowledge that there are kinds of equivocal pragmatism that lie somewhere between heroic self-immolation as working-class hero and the bruising tactics of John Braine's novel-hero Joe Lampton on the way to his 'room at the top'; this was something that Benny Green, himself an East Ender, recognized in introducing the work of another slum-writer of the 1890s – Clarence Rook and his *Hooligan Nights*: 'most of the residents of Morrison's mean streets,' Green observed, 'housed in pigsties at the very apogée of Empire, aspired to graduate from the bugs to the grouse, figuratively speaking'. Besides, there may have been psychological reasons for Morrison's pragmatic deceptions. In particular, the effect of his father's death when Arthur was only eight should not be underestimated. The situations of all his principal heroes – Dicky Perrott, Johnny May in *To London Town* (1899) and Stephen Kemp in *The Hole in the Wall* – echo that death and project the scale of the horror, isolation and fear so induced in casting those boys' bereavements as occurring through the excesses of murder, or imprisonment and execution (what Keating calls 'the wholesale slaughter of parents or parent figures'). The recurring patterns of these texts also project a composite mother figure, either absent or poorly equipped to cope with difficult times and the practical consequences of widowhood. And there is also a composite adolescent boy suffering unfairly premature anxieties over money and over the survival of his family. The early 'Lizerunt' and *A Child of the Jago* figured the bleakest versions of that anxiety – ejection onto the windy street, the desperate life of the street arab and the consequence, unstated or stated, of death. In 1899, by which time Morrison's writing must have made him moderately secure in financial terms, *To London Town* continued to reveal the same deep-rooted anxiety but also showed it being steadily overcome by a Johnny May who commits himself to work and the dignity of its skills, to taking charge courageously of family affairs, and who ultimately returns to the site of his grandfather's murder to confront the fact of it and what he now recognizes as the mundaneness of the event. In *The Hole in the Wall* the typical situation and fears are as ingrained as ever and crucially shape the consciousness of Stephen Kemp, but they are now romantically displaced into a milieu and a plot which, while retaining its grasp on the world of Jacob's Island, also savours to a degree of *Treasure Island*. Through these works, in short, there is a progressive accommodation and finally romanticization of deep childhood insecurity, and this unifying thread offers a psychological perspective on Morrison's rather awkward retrospective trilogization of *To London Town* with *Mean Streets* and *A Child of the Jago*. What, however, is most evident is that the graph of that accommodation of insecurity runs in parallel to the rise and rise of Arthur Morrison.

Morrison began work as a clerk in the Architect's Department of the London School Board. Probably while he was there, aged seventeen or eighteen, his first publications appeared in the cycling periodicals of the day. He moved on to the People's Palace in the Mile End Road, organizing social, cultural and educational events and sub-editing *The Palace Journal*. By then he had already begun to break into serious journalism. The practical experience of his work on the *Journal* in turn gave him the confidence in the late 1880s to move into full-time work in newspapers. By the time he was thirty Morrison was married, a father, and had a house in Essex. He was finding success through his writing in newspapers, magazines and then books, developing his skills, making new contacts, though doubtless when returning to those 'familiar and equal friends' in the East End the fragility of his success was still apparent, or to him at least. Certainly the Royal Society of Literature was yet a long way off for this exceptionally hard-working denizen of Gissing's New Grub Street. Indeed, a further flaw in the rediscovery of Morrison has been a deficient appreciation of the range of his activity in writing, of which *Mean Streets* and *A Child of the Jago* formed only a part. Morrison could indeed write stories of working-class life, but he could also put together a newspaper, knock out a pot-boiler on the spirit world and weave around such commitments the composition of a number of volumes of Martin Hewitt detective stories that rivalled the adventures of Sherlock Holmes in their popularity. Indeed, it is in the latter stories that one finds the most telling image of Morrison in the 1890s mirrored in his own Dr Watson, a hard-working journalist by the name of Brett who makes copy out of Martin Hewitt's investigations. In 'The Ivy Cottage Mystery' Brett reports:

I had been working double tides for a month: at night on my morning paper, as usual; and in the morning on an evening paper as *locum tenens* for another man who was taking a holiday. This was an exhausting plan of work, although it only actually involved some six hours' attendance a day, or less, at the two offices. I turned up at the headquarters of my own paper at ten in the evening, and by the time I had seen the editor, selected a subject, written my leader, corrected the slips, chatted, smoked, and so on, and cleared off, it was very usually one o'clock. This meant bed at two, or even three, after supper at the club.

This was all very well at ordinary periods, when any time in the morning would do for rising, but when I had to be up again soon after seven, and round at the evening paper office by eight, I naturally felt a little worn and disgusted with things by midday, after a sharp couple of hours' leaderette scribbling and paragraphing, with attendant sundries. (*Chronicles of Martin Hewitt*, pp.3–4)

This is an instance of the mirror's edge catching the reflection of the professional artist: Arthur Morrison, on a working day. In *New Grub Street*, his study of the world of late nineteenth-century journalism and publishing, the novelist George Gissing presented the writer's options as a choice between the path of the archetypal trimmer Jasper Milvain, ever alert to the chance of making a quick guinea, or the selfless artistry of an impoverished Harold Biffen devoting his life-blood (eventually literally) to his Balzacian epic *Mr Bailey, Grocer*. Morrison perhaps took his hint from the H. G. Wells who declared that he had rather be thought of as a journalist than an artist, but there was in any case a relatively small gap to traverse between the reporting of Morrison's bread-and-butter journalism and the realistic art of *A Child of the Jago*: in a less guarded moment he recalled, 'I naturally went to my experiences when I became a journalist. Still, I felt that I could not say in newspaper articles all I had to say; I felt it must be said in fiction.' So while Gissing brooded on the irreconcilable conflicts facing the writer, Morrison squared the circle and played Milvain early and late, and Biffen in between. That there was embourgeoisement goes without saying: Morrison clearly found no self-definition in the loneliness of the long-distance runner; he refused to lose the race for the sake of class solidarity. That his evasions were the self-protective measures of a hard-working man seeking to escape the very causes of his personal insecurity seems likely (and also a likely explanation of his sense of the necessity of *fiction* to do justice to his otherwise unrevealable experiences); that these factors combined with his acquisition of a journalist's sense of social responsibility that negotiated the interests of one class with another's rather than just espousing his roots seems also the case. Cut it how one may, this may still only add up to 'snobbery' on the road to a Buckinghamshire flower-garden; yet the application of that simplifying word to a complex and driven human experience is seldom wholly satisfying.

In its day, *A Child of the Jago* was a synonym for realism, for the impartially photographic or, as the French novelist Stendhal had expressed it, for a mirror walking down a road. The road in this case was the Old Nichol and the quality of the text's reflection, it was understood, could be tested by sampling the author's 'accuracy'. The text was assumed to deliver a proxy seeing that would allow readers to respond to social problems that the novel did not so much represent as disclose: the journalist and critic H. D. Traill, for example, faulted the novel for not giving him the feeling that he had 'just paid a visit to the actual district under the protection of the police'. Though by no means accepting all Traill's assumptions about the mode of his writing, Morrison and his allies were in fact quick to defend the accuracy of *A Child of the Jago*. The originals of Father Sturt, Dicky and Josh Perrott, Aaron Weech and Sally Green were all triumphantly brought forward as irrefutable testimony to the novel's 'truth'; the literary press was sprinkled with witnesses to life and events in the Old Nichol who confirmed or threw doubt on Morrison's portrait of the area. At the same time the realism of *A Child of the Jago* attracted hostility for its assumed insistence on the aesthetic necessity of both the investigative observation that underlay its composition and the kind of setting and spectrum of human behaviour with which it dealt. As the camera was seen to threaten painting, so the extremes of literary realism were seen to threaten literary art. For these reasons Morrison's 'notebook' and his journalistic 'methods' became totems in debate, while his violation of artistic 'reticence' by descriptions of squalor and violence also figured large. As realism shaded into naturalism, objections were also posed to the determining roles of heredity and environment on such as Dicky Perrott: 'What of the force of human nature?' asked some, and 'What of the human spirit?' More damagingly, and in some ways paradoxically, others saw Morrison's realism as utterly undermined by echoes between his text and Jay's earlier writing about his Shoreditch parish (*see* 'Notes'). Here, contributors to the argument about the 'truth' of Morrison's realism found a labyrinth of issues to discuss in which the same piece of evidence might from one perspective provide corroboration of the author's 'accuracy', yet from another apparently demonstrate bare-faced 'plagiarism' of Father Jay's writings. It was certainly ironic that George Gissing should have accused Jay of plagiarizing Gissing's novel *The Nether World*, that others should then have accused Morrison of plagiarizing one of Jay's books, and that Gissing should then have read *A Child of the Jago* and have judged it 'poor stuff'. (Sour grapes, perhaps: Jay only courted Morrison to write up the Old Nichol after wooing Gissing and possibly the *Daily Telegraph*'s socially concerned journalist James Greenwood with the same object in mind; Gissing, indeed, had been planning a 'big book' on the subject.)

It is important to recover just how significant debates over 'realism' were in the nineteenth century, particularly in their implications for estimates of the seriousness of novels as literary art. From the very beginnings of the novel as a form, realism had been recognized as its defining characteristic; through the eighteenth and nineteenth centuries the rise in influence and authority of natural philosophy and the social sciences effectively worked to confirm and amplify the claim of realism to be the inevitable mode of representation and analysis of a responsible literature. In the 1860s the French critic Taine observed that 'It doesn't matter whether the facts are physical or moral, they will still have causes; there are causes for ambition, courage, and truthfulness as there are for digestion, muscular movement, and animal warmth'; on such a basis was founded the claim of the realistic novel to approach the condition of a new moral science, particularly where the notation of causes or 'conditions' tended towards the construction of deterministic matrices of human behaviour. Balzac set himself the task of assembling through his novels a zoology of humankind. Zola compared the construction of a novel to the setting up of a scientific experiment: if the mechanics were correctly operated, conditions understood and observations correctly taken, then the result would be not so much an entertainment as scientific knowledge of the sector of human life selected for investigation. The tendency of realism to leap boundaries of social and sexual reticence could consequently seem an imperative. It is to this tendency that the *Blackwood's* reviewer of *A Child of the Jago* alluded when referring to literature 'highly spiced with vice and the peculiar kind of garbage upon which the French novel-reader has chosen to feed'. In fact, following the reception of 'Lizerunt', Morrison did not dwell on sexual relationship in *A Child of the Jago*; Dicky passes through puberty with hardly a thought on such matters – and when it does come, dismisses it ('the Jago girls affected him with an odd feeling of repulsion'). Infant mortality and couples living in sin are certainly fore-grounded matters, though not so emphatically pursued as the issue of premature marriage and childbirth; the Jago does have its prostitutes, but there is little focus on them beyond their role as accomplices in the more sensationalized practice of 'cosh-carrying'. In consequence the *Blackwood's* reviewer could grudgingly applaud the 'historian of the Jago' for showing 'all the uncleanness of the streets excepting that' ('that' being 'the odious question of sex' and, very particularly, prostitution). The less reticent socialist writer Robert Blatchford, founder of the *Clarion*, recognized that such an omission, like the sanitization of swearing in the book, in fact left the realism of *A Child of the Jago*, in absolute terms, highly questionable.

Although Morrison vigorously defended the truth of *A Child of the Jago* he himself resisted the artistic label of 'realist' and in part, there is room to conclude, because he knew better than the labellers. The reflections on Japanese art that preface *A Child of the Jago* reveal him distrustful of any monolithic concept of realism, acutely aware of realisms and concerned to see them as matters of cultural history, cultural politics and cultural relativity. In short, Morrison knew that one man's realism, as an artistic mode, was another man's stylization. Over the years his preface to *A Child of the Jago* (especially in its version as the essay 'What is a Realist?') has been criticized for failing to develop a strong, coherent theory of realism. Yet the terms of his resistance to providing one are interesting because they suggest just how far he was from being a naive realist and how uneasy he may have been about the danger of locking himself into a commitment to any such mode. In his essay 'Whitechapel' he referred affectionately to *A Journal of the Plague Year* and referred to its author as that 'realistic old deceiver De Foe'. Undoubtedly he used the term to highlight the element of hoax in Defoe's book (which represented itself as an eye-witness account of the Great Plague of 1665); yet to see Morrison playing with a concept of 'realistic deception' is to see him moving beyond a commitment to mere 'realism'. This perspective gains in force with a recognition of Morrison's awareness of language as a shifting, vulnerable, provisional medium. His short stories show a sustained interest in alternative languages, in accent and dialect, in such special codes as secret writing, thieves' slang, nicknames and pseudonyms and, as in 'The Case of the Missing Hand', the use of little known languages such as Romany as subversive mediums of communication. Such interest culminates in his short story 'The Lost Foreigner'. Here he explored the practical problems of representation and communication experienced by an individual possessing little command of the English language and plunged through nervous shock into utter loss of the abilities to write (*agraphia*) and to speak coherently (*dysphasia*). The philosophical issues with which the story deals point towards an appreciation of the precariousness of language as a medium of representation and communication. Indeed, Morrison's detective Martin Hewitt only solves the case by interpreting the lost foreigner's graphic doodlings as visual signs and symbols in an unconscious narrative recording the existence of an anarchist plot of which the terrified man has been an incidental casualty. Language has to be bypassed in order to reach the truth; the reader is left with a story that seems anything but the product of a writer wedded to a simple conviction of language as a wholly dependable means of representing the world. At the same time one suspects that Morrison the journalist was practical enough not to register a philosophical flaw as a political objection: if the language of realism was the current discourse of power – and Morrison the journalist knew that to be the case – why allow philosophical reservation to deflect one from engaging with that power in the interests of change, through such a work as *A Child of the Jago*? If Morrison could not wholeheartedly subscribe to his public categorization as 'realist', the role of 'realistic deceiver' yet remained open. In this context it becomes less surprising that in 'Whitechapel' Morrison should also allude to Beaumont and Fletcher's self-conscious play *The Knight of the Burning Pestle*, and that at one point in 'Christmas Eve in the Streets' he declares: 'We *will* have our Christmas Eve frosted; there shall be snow on the roofs, but a dry, swept, pavement; enough snow in the corners to make an occasional snowball of, but no more because more in London gets dirty and sludgy. Our Christmas Eve is an ideal one, and we will not have bad weather on Christmas Eve when we can get good.' The Jago was real enough for those who knew the Old Nichol to recognize it; but as the product of the pen of a realistic deceiver who could change the weather on Christmas Eve, the Jago was also decidedly of Morrison's making.

Morrison's focus on Dicky Perrott as child allowed him to demonstrate his hypotheses concerning heredity and environment through the most evident 'control experiment'. Placing Dicky centre stage, while echoing *Oliver Twist*, also reflected the pragmatic priorities and strategies of social commentators and reformers in relation to urban situations that were seen as spiralling out of control. In 1878, referring to New York in *The Night Sides of City Life*, the Reverend Charles de Witt Talmadge stressed, 'You see I speak more in regard to the youth and the children of the country, because old villains are seldom reformed, and therefore I talk more about the little ones'; Jacob Riis, in *How the Other Half Lives* (1890), observed, 'Nothing is now better understood than that the rescue of the children is the key to the problem of city poverty as presented for our solution to-day; that character may be formed where to reform it would be a hopeless task.' In *The Children of the Poor* (1892) Riis specifically commented that 'No investment gives a better return to-day on the capital put out than work among the children of the poor.' Walter Besant reiterated the view in words and actions while in 'Whitechapel' Morrison himself remarked: 'Children must not be left in these unscoured corners. Their fathers and mothers are hopeless, and must not be allowed to rear a numerous and equally hopeless race.' If this widespread concern for children was practical and humanitarian, the 'child' that appeared so frequently in Social Problem discourse in the deterministic formulation 'Child / Children / Daughter of the X' (where 'X' = Jago, Gutter, Ghetto, Streets or some related term) gained its rhetorical force through its barely concealed opposition to the concept of humankind as Child of God: in this implicit opposition there was thus placed at issue the definition of humankind as spiritual or – as the animal and body imagery of *A Child of the Jago* goes to suggest – as merely material being. In *Culture and Anarchy* Matthew Arnold commented scathingly on the 'immense pretension' of society terming itself 'children of God': 'and the work which we collective children of God do, our grand centre of life, our *city* which we have builded for us to dwell in, is London!' On first publication in England of Stephen Crane's *Maggie*, the novel's sub-title was altered from '*A Girl of the Streets*' to '*A Child of the Streets*': it is a minor change to modern eyes, but to a late Victorian sensibility the first phrase risked indecency while the second obliquely appealed to a sense of the sacred. In consequence, *A Child of the Jago* is partly about spiritual and material paternity, about a battle between various parents for Dicky Perrott – a battle, it has already been suggested, in which Morrison had a considerable personal interest. Dicky is the child of the Perrotts, but also the child of the Jago and heir to a 'black inheritance'. While he remains pathetically loyal to his biological parents, he is morally confused, neglected and emotionally blocked by them at every turn: his tears and secrets are confided to a battered donkey; odd shillings in his hand raise the possibility (sadly disappointed) of 'buying sympathy of his father and mother'. In this situation Dicky is fought over by surrogate fathers in the form of 'Father' Sturt and the fence Aaron Weech, as Oliver Twist had earlier been fought over by Mr Brownlow and Fagin. Each possesses, or poses as having, an authoritative 'omniscience' that commands Dicky's attention. Sturt attempts to salvage Josh as Dicky's true father by teasing him away from crime, encouraging him into church and towards work; at the same time Sturt draws out of Dicky the kind of love, respect, trust – and briefly the aspiration – that might normally be expected of the relationship of child and parent. Meanwhile Weech, as the living instrument of the Jago, self-interestedly but by no means ineffectively parodies the moral guidance of a parent, keeping Dicky's rate of thieving up to scratch while maintaining that he gives Dicky 'good advice like a father' (not to mention 'an' a bloater an' all'). More than this, Weech actively undermines his parental rivals by engineering Dicky's dismissal from the job that Father Sturt arranges and by betraying Josh to the police, thus clearing the way for his continued influence over the boy. Father Sturt's faith is justified by the evidence of Dicky's love for Looey, his bursts of generosity, his response to what music and art comes his way, his interest in reading, his intuition of, and desire for, a decent way of living beyond what the Jago offers. What in other circumstances might have existed between biological father and son is shadowed in Dicky's excitement at the fight with Billy Leary ('"Go it, father! Fa-ther! Fa-ther!" Dicky screamed from the window') and even in Josh's motivations in murdering Weech ('My boy was goin' straight, an' earnin' wages; someone got 'im chucked'). Going into his last fight Dicky paradoxically yells 'Come on Father Sturt's boys'; before he dies the slum's battle-cry 'Hold tight, Jago' rings out – the same cry from which his father gains strength as he goes to the gallows. But in the drama of paternity, such ironies and pathos only reinforce the tragic victory of the Jago and Weech, the fence finally revealed, beneath Josh's bludgeoning, as a mere 'bubbling Thing'. That Hannah Perrott's last child is named 'Little Josh' constitutes a bitter confirmation of the cycle of paternity and inheritance. In the hideous extremes that the Jago presents, a child of God is lost as another rough beast slouches towards Bethlehem.

It was Father Jay's perception that the poverty of London was the poverty of the world, 'for thither in helpless shoals flock the unskilled and unfortunate from all the quarters of the globe'. Morrison, one must conclude, saw this too and felt it as part of the threat that the Jago offered. Through his West End and East End there ghost connotations of the Empire and Orient, of Christendom and its boundaries, of the known and the Other. In 1899 Walter Besant wrote that 'It is the street which provides the casual hand; it is also the street which produces the drunkard, the loafer, the man who cannot work, the man who will not work, the street rough, the street sneak, and the street thief.' Some of these phrases are lifted from Joseph Conrad's *The Nigger of the Narcissus* (1897) where they apply to Donkin, the slum-dweller turned sailor whose shiftlessness threatens the whole system of society as Conrad models it in the microcosm of the ship and its crew. Donkin's more ominous and insidious partner in threat is the 'nigger' himself, James Wait, the racially different outsider, the symbolic alien whose subtle influence brings about even the threat of mutiny. Conrad's conjunction of Donkin and Wait is significant. The East End lent itself to being constructed as the ultimate Other, a heart of darkness, a place of dirt and disease, a breeding ground of the alien whether defined as Irish and Catholic, Eastern European and Jewish, criminal, anarchist or socialist, ungodly or morally and physically degenerate. What could by some be construed as worse than its diversity was its amazing capacity for unity – the East End spirit of sticking together. The Bloody Sunday riots of 1887 stemmed from a march about both unemployment and the Irish Question; a good proportion of matchgirls in the 1888 strike, as also dock-workers in the Great Strike of 1889, had Irish roots; the growth of trades unionism forged new constituencies of interest between such immigrant communities as Irish dockers and Yiddish-speaking Jewish tailors from Russia and Poland. In many respects *A Child of the Jago* corroborated such perceptions and fears. Elsewhere, as in 'The Missing Hand', Morrison frankly located threat as coming from the margins: it is not just a gipsy but a 'foreign gipsy' from the Wallachian area of Roumania who is at the root of that story's mystery. It might just as well have been Transylvania. In *A Child of the Jago*, no matter how much Morrison was the insider and sympathetic first-hand observer of the East End, he was also, as the writer escaping the insecurity of his roots through writing, the subject of an ideology that feared and suspected what he described. For readers one hundred years later, still faced with urban complexities and on the verge of confronting a new phase in the building of Fortress Europe, it is this fascinating – and at times appalling – mix of sympathy and fear, of identification and distance, of holy indignation and unholy distaste, of imperatives towards liberal action and illiberal repression, that makes *A Child of the Jago* such a challenging text to measure ourselves against.

PETER MILES

NOTE ON THE TEXT

This edition of *A Child of the Jago* follows the first edition of the novel (London: Methuen, 1896). The text of Morrison's 'Preface' follows its first printing in the third edition (1897). Obvious mistakes have been corrected. Chapters have been so designated and their numbers modernized from Roman to Arabic. Some practices in punctuation (such as the use of a comma in association with a dash) have been modernized. Emendation has otherwise been light and principally directed towards maintaining the consistency of the first edition's own compositorial and editorial practices. The original dedication has been retained.

Particular divergences from P. J. Keating's edition include: the retention of some instances of capitalization involved in creating ironic effects; retention of a few instances of italicization of words and parts of words where this has been deemed to create emphasis or to echo the rhythm of characters' speech patterns; retention of the 'Sketch Plan' of the Jago and its lettering as printed in the first edition.

The first edition ran to 345 pages (making use of white space with the freedom of its period). It contained two pages of extracts from reviews advertising Morrison's *Tales of Mean Streets* (*see* 'Morrison and his Critics'); it also contained Methuen's thirty-nine-page catalogue of books for October 1896.

A CHILD OF THE JAGO

TO

ARTHUR OSBORNE JAY

VICAR OF HOLY TRINITY, SHOREDITCH

PREFACE TO THE THIRD EDITION

I am glad to take this, the first available opportunity, to acknowledge the kindness with which *A Child of the Jago* has been received: both by the reading public, from which I have received many gratifying assurances that what I have tried to say has not altogether failed of its effect: and by the reviewers, the most of whom have written in very indulgent terms.

I think indeed, that I am the more gratified by the fact that this reception has not been unanimous: because an outcry and an opposition, even from an unimportant minority, are proofs that I have succeeded in saying, however imperfectly, something that was worth being said. Under the conditions of life as we know it there is no truth worth telling that will not interfere with some hearer's comfort. Various objections have been made to *A Child of the Jago*, and many of them had already been made to *Tales of Mean Streets*. And it has been the way of the objectors as well as the way of many among the kindest of my critics, to call me a 'realist'. The word has been used sometimes, it would seem, in praise; sometimes in mere indifference as one uses a phrase of convenient description; sometimes by way of an irremediable reproach. It is natural, then, not merely that I should wish to examine certain among the objections made to my work, but that I should feel some interest in the definition and description of a realist. A matter never made clear to me.

Now it is a fact that I have never called myself a 'realist', and I have never put forth any work as 'realism'. I decline the labels of the schoolmen and the sophisters: being a simple writer of tales, who takes whatever means lie to his hand to present life as he sees it; who insists on no process; and who refuses to be bound by any formula or prescription prepared by the catalogu-ers and the pigeon-holers of literature.

So it happens that when those who use the word 'realist' use it with no unanimity of intent and with a loose, inapprehensive application, it is not easy for me, who repudiate it altogether, to make a guess at its meaning. Nevertheless, it seems to me that the man who is called a 'realist' is one who, seeing things with his own eyes, discards the conventions of the schools, and presents his matter in individual terms of art. For a while the schoolmen abuse him as a realist; and in twenty years' time, if his work have life in it, he becomes a classic. Constable* was called a realist; so was Corot.* Who calls these painters realists now? The history of Japanese art affords a continuous illustration. From the day when Iwasa Matahei* impudently arose and dared to take his subjects from the daily life of the people, to the day when Hiroshigé,* casting away the last rag of propriety, adventurously drew a cast shadow, in flat defiance of all the canons of Tosa and Kano* – in all this time, and through all the crowded history of the School of Ukioyé,* no artist bringing something of his own to his art but was damned for a realist. Even the classic Harunobu* did not escape. Look now at the work of these men, and the label seems grotesque enough. So it goes through the making of all art. A man with the courage of his own vision interprets what he sees in fresh terms, and gives to things a new reality and an immediate presence. The schoolmen peer with dulled eyes from amid the heap of precedents and prescriptions about them, and, distracted by seeing a thing sanctioned neither by precedent nor by prescription, dub the man realist, and rail against him for that his work fits none of their pigeon-holes. And from without the schools many cry out and complain: for truth is strong meat, and the weakling stomach turns against it, except in minim doses smothered in treacle. Thus we hear the feeble plea that the function of imagination is the distortion of fact: the piteous demand that the artist should be shut up in a flower-garden,* and forbidden to peep through the hedge into the world. And they who know nothing of beauty, who are innately incapable of comprehending it, mistake it for mere prettiness, and call aloud for comfits; and among them that cannot understand, such definitions of the aims of art are bandied, as mean, if they mean anything, that art finds its most perfect expression in pink lollipops and gilt boxes. But in the end the truth prevails, if it be well set forth; and the schoolmen, groaning in their infinite labour, wearily write another prescription, admit another precedent, and make another pigeon-hole.

I have been asked, in print,* if I think that there is no phase of life which the artist may not touch. Most certainly I think this. More, I know it. It is the artist's privilege to seek his material where he pleases, and it is no man's privilege to say him nay. If the community have left horrible places and horrible lives before his eyes, then the fault is the community's; and to picture these places and these lives becomes not merely his privilege, but his duty. It was my fate to encounter a place in Shoreditch, where children were born and reared in circumstances which gave them no reasonable chance of living decent lives: where they were born fore-damned to a criminal or semi-criminal career. It was my experience to learn the ways of this place, to know its inhabitants, to talk with them, eat, drink, and work with them. For the existence of this place, and for the evils it engendered, the community was, and is, responsible; so that every member of the community was, and is, responsible in his degree. If I had been a rich man I might have attempted to discharge my peculiar responsibility in one way; if I had been a statesman I might have tried another. Being neither of these things, but a mere writer of fiction, I sought to do my duty by writing a tale wherein I hoped to bring the conditions of this place within the apprehension of others. There are those who say that I should have turned away my eyes and passed by on the other side: on the very respectable precedent of the priest and the Levite* in the parable.

Now, when the tale was written and published it was found, as I have said, to cause some discomfort to some persons. It is needless to say more of the schoolmen. Needless, too, to say much of the merely genteel: who were shocked to read of low creatures, as Kiddo Cook and Pigeony Poll, and to find my pages nowhere illuminated by a marquis. Of such are they who delight to read of two men in velvet and feathers perforating each other's stomachs with swords; while Josh Perrott and Billy Leary, punching each other's heads, present a scene too sickening and brutal to consider without disgust. And it was in defiance of the maunderings of such as these that Charles Lamb wrote much of his essay *On the Genius and Character of Hogarth*.* But chiefly this book of mine disturbed those who had done nothing, and preferred to do nothing, by way of discharging their responsibility toward the Jago and the people in it. The consciousness of duty neglected is discomforting, and personal comfort is the god of their kind. They firmly believe it to be the sole function of art to minister to their personal comfort – as upholstery does. They find it comfortable to shirk consideration of the fate of the Jago children, to shut their eyes to it, to say that all is well and the whole world virtuous and happy. And this mental attitude they nickname optimism, and vaunt it – exult in it as a quality. So that they cry out at the suggestion that it is no more than a selfish vice; and finding truth where they had looked for the materials of another debauch of self-delusion, they moan aloud: they protest, and they demand as their sacred right that the bitter cup be taken from before them. They have moaned and protested at *A Child of the Jago*, and, craven and bewildered, any protest seemed good enough to them. And herein they have not wanted for allies among them that sit in committee-rooms, and tinker. For your professed philanthropist, following his own spirit,* and seeing nothing, honestly resents the demonstration that his tinkering profits little. There is a story current in the East End of London, of a distracted lady who, being assailed with a request for the loan of a saucepan, defended herself in these words: – 'Tell yer mother I can't lend 'er the saucepan, consek-ince o' 'avin' lent it to Mrs Brown, besides which I'm a-usin' of it meself, an' moreover it's gone to be mended, an' what's more I ain't got one.' In a like spirit of lavish objection* it has been proclaimed in a breath that I transgress: – because (1) I should not have written of the Jago in all the nakedness of truth; (2) my description is not in the least like; (3) moreover, it is exaggerated; (4) though it may be true, it is quite unnecessary, because the Jago was already quite familiar, and everybody knew all about it; (5) the Jago houses have been pulled down; and (6) there never was any such place as the Jago at all.

To objections thus handsomely variegated it is not easy to reply with the tripping brevity wherewith they may be stated; and truly it is little reply that they call for, except, perhaps, in so far as they may be taken to impugn the sincerity of my work and the accuracy of my picture. A few of the objectors have caught up enough of their wits to strive after a war in my own country. They take hold of my technical method, and accuse me of lack of 'sympathy';* they claim that if I write of the Jago I should do so 'even weeping'. Now, my technical method is my own, and is deliberately designed to achieve a certain result, as is the method of every man – painter, poet, sculptor, or novelist

– who is not the slave and the plaything of his material. My tale
is the tale of my characters, and I have learned better than to
thrust myself and my emotions between them and my reader.
The cant of the charge stares all too plainly from the face of it.
It is not that these good people wish me to write 'even weeping':
for how do they know whether I weep or not? No: their wish is,
not that I shall weep, but that I shall weep obscenely in the
public gaze. In other words, that I shall do their weeping for
them, as a sort of emotional bedesman: that I shall make public
parade of sympathy in their behalf, so that they may keep their
own sympathy for themselves, and win comfort from the belief
that they are eased of their just responsibility by vicarious
snivelling.

But the protest that my picture of the Jago is untrue, is
another thing. For the most part it has found very vague
expression, but there are instances of rash excursion into
definiteness. Certain passages have been denoted as exaggera-
tions – as impossibilities. Now, I must confess that, foreseeing
such adventurous indiscretions, I had, for my own diversion, set
A Child of the Jago with traps. For certain years I have lived in
the East End of London, and have been, not an occasional
visitor, but a familiar and equal friend in the house of the East-
Ender in all his degrees; for, though the steps between be
smaller, there are more social degrees in the East End than ever
in the West. In this experience I have seen and I have heard
things that persons sitting in committee-rooms would call dia-
bolical fable; nevertheless, I have seen them, and heard them.
But it was none of my design to write of extreme instances:
typical facts were all I wanted; these, I knew, would be met – or
shirked – with incredulity; so that, whenever I saw reason to
anticipate a charge of exaggeration – as for instance, in the
matter of faction fighting – I made my typical incident the cold
transcript of a simple fact, an ordinary, easy-going fact, a fact
notorious in the neighbourhood, and capable of any amount of
reasonable proof. If I touched my fact at all, it was to subdue it;
that and no more. The traps worked well. Not one definite
charge of exaggeration has been flung but it has been aimed at
one of the normal facts I had provided as a target: not one.
Sometimes the effect has had a humour of its own; as when a
critic in a literary journal, beginning by selecting two of my
norms as instances of 'palpable exaggeration',* went on to

assure me that there was no need to describe such life as the life in the Jago, because it was already perfectly familiar to everybody.

Luckily I need not vindicate my accuracy. That has been done for me publicly by independent and altogether indisputable authority. In particular, the devoted vicar of the parish, which I have called the Jago, has testified* quite unreservedly to the truth of my presentation. Others also, with special knowledge,* have done the same; and though I refer to them, and am grateful for their support, it is with no prejudice to the validity of my own authority. For not only have I lived in the East End of London (which one may do, and yet never see it) but observation is my trade.

I have remarked in more than one place the expression of a foolish fancy that because the houses of the Old Jago have been pulled down, the Jago difficulty has been cleared out of the way. That is far from being the case. The Jago, as mere bricks and mortar, is gone.* But the Jago in flesh and blood still lives, and is crowding into neighbourhoods already densely over-populated.

In conclusion: the plan and the intention of my story made it requisite that, in telling it, I should largely adhere to fact; and I did so. If I write other tales different in scope and design, I shall adhere to fact or neglect it as may seem good to me: regardless of anybody's classification as a realist, or as anything else. For though I have made a suggestion, right or wrong, as to what a realist may be, whether I am one or not is no concern of mine; but the concern (if it be anybody's) of the tabulators and the watersifters.

A.M.

February 1897.

... Woe unto the foolish prophets,* that follow their own spirit, and have seen nothing! ...

Because, even because they have seduced my people, saying, Peace; and there was no peace; and one built up a wall, and lo, others daubed it with untempered mortar:

Say unto them which daub it with untempered mortar, that it shall fall: there shall be an overflowing shower; and ye, O great hailstones, shall fall; and a stormy wind shall rend it.

Lo, when the wall is fallen, shall it not be said unto you, Where is the daubing wherewith ye have daubed it? –

EZEKIEL xiii. 3 ... 10–12.

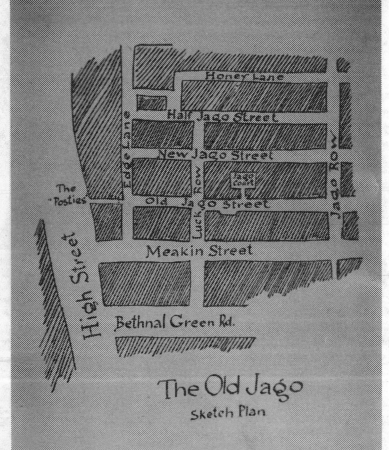

Honey Lane

Half Jago Street

New Jago Street

Jago Court

Old Jago Street

Meakin Street

Bethnal Green Rd.

Edge Lane

Luck Row

Jago Row

The "Posties"

High Street

The Old Jago
Sketch Plan

A CHILD OF THE JAGO

CHAPTER I

It was past the mid of a summer night in the Old Jago. The narrow street was all the blacker for the lurid sky; for there was a fire in a farther part of Shoreditch, and the welkin was an infernal coppery glare. Below, the hot, heavy air lay, a rank oppression, on the contorted forms of those who made for sleep on the pavement: and in it, and through it all, there rose from the foul earth and the grimed walls a close, mingled stink – the odour of the Jago.

From where, off Shoreditch High Street, a narrow passage, set across with posts,* gave menacing entrance on one end of Old Jago Street, to where the other end lost itself in the black beyond Jago Row; from where Jago Row began south at Meakin Street, to where it ended north at Honey Lane – there the Jago, for one hundred years the blackest pit in London,* lay and festered; and half way along Old Jago Street a narrow archway gave upon Jago Court, the blackest hole in all that pit.

A square of two hundred and fifty yards or less – that was all there was of the Jago. But in that square the human population swarmed in thousands. Old Jago Street, New Jago Street, Half Jago Street lay parallel, east and west: Jago Row at one end and Edge Lane at the other lay parallel also, stretching north and south: foul ways all. What was too vile for Kate Street, Seven Dials, and Ratcliff Highway in its worst day,* what was too useless, incapable and corrupt – all that teemed in the Old Jago.

Old Jago Street lay black and close under the quivering red sky; and slinking forms, as of great rats, followed one another quickly between the posts in the gut by the High Street, and scattered over the Jago. For the crowd about the fire was now small, the police was there in force, and every safe pocket had been tried. Soon the incursion ceased, and the sky, flickering and brightening no longer, settled to a sullen flush. On the pavement some writhed wearily, longing for sleep; others, despairing of it, sat and lolled, and a few talked. They were not there for lack of shelter, but because in this weather repose was less unlikely in the street than within doors: and the lodgings of the few who nevertheless abode at home were marked here and there by the lights visible from the windows. For in this place none ever slept without a light, because of three sorts of vermin that light in some sort keeps at bay: vermin which added to existence here a terror not to be guessed by the unafflicted: who object to being told of it. For on them that lay writhen and gasping on the pavement; on them that sat among them; on them that rolled and blasphemed in the lighted rooms; on every moving creature in this, the Old Jago, day and night, sleeping and walking,* the third plague of Egypt,* and more, lay unceasing.

The stifling air took a further oppression from the red sky. By the dark entrance to Jago Court a man rose, flinging out an oath, and sat with his head bowed in his hands.

'Ah—h—h—h,' he said. 'I wish I was dead: an' kep' a cawfy shop.'* He looked aside from his hands at his neighbours; but Kiddo Cook's* ideal of heaven was no new thing, and the sole answer was a snort from a dozing man a yard away.

Kiddo Cook felt in his pocket and produced a pipe and a screw of paper.* 'This is a bleed'n' unsocial sort o' evenin' party, this is,' he said. 'An' 'ere's the on'y real toff in the mob with 'ardly 'arf a pipeful left, an' no lights. D' y' 'ear, me lord' – leaning toward the dozing neighbour – 'got a match?'

'Go t' 'ell!'

'O wot 'orrid langwidge! It's shocking, blimy.* Arter that y' ought to find me a match. Come on.'

'Go t' 'ell!'

A lank, elderly man, who sat with his back to the wall, pushed up a battered tall hat from his eyes, and, producing a box of matches, exclaimed 'Hell? And how far's that? You're in it!'* He flung abroad a bony hand, and glanced upward. Over his forehead a greasy black curl dangled and shook as he shuddered back against the wall. 'My God, there can be no hell after this!'

'Ah,' Kiddo Cook remarked, as he lit his pipe in the hollow of his hands, 'that's a comfort, Mr Beveridge, any'ow.' He returned the matches, and the old man, tilting his hat forward, was silent.

A woman, gripping a shawl about her shoulders, came furtively along from the posts, with a man walking in her tracks – a little unsteadily. He was not of the Jago, but a decent young workman, by his dress. The sight took Kiddo Cook's idle eye, and when the couple had passed, he said meditatively: 'There's Billy Leary in luck ag'in: 'is missis do pick 'em up, s'elp me. I'd carry the cosh meself if I'd got a woman like 'er.'

Cosh-carrying was near to being the major industry of the Jago. The cosh was a foot length of iron rod, with a knob at one end, and a hook (or a ring) at the other. The craftsman carrying it in his coat sleeve, waited about dark staircase corners till his wife (married or not)* brought in a well drunken stranger: when, with a sudden blow behind the head, the stranger was happily coshed, and whatever was found on him as he lay insensible was the profit on the transaction. In the hands of capable practitioners this industry yielded a comfortable subsistence for no great exertion. Most, of course, depended on the woman: whose duty it was to keep the other artist* going in subjects. There were legends of surprising ingatherings achieved by wives of especial diligence: one of a woman who had brought to the cosh some six-and-twenty on a night of public rejoicing. This was, however, a story years old, and may have been no more than an exemplary fiction designed, like a Sunday School book, to convey a counsel of perfection to the dutiful matrons* of the Old Jago.

The man and woman vanished in a doorway near the Jago Row end, where, for some reason, dossers were fewer than about the portal* of Jago Court. There conversation flagged, and a broken snore was heard. It was a quiet night, as quietness was counted in the Jago; for it was too hot for most to fight in that stifling air – too hot to do more than turn on the stones and swear. Still the last hoarse yelps of a combat of women came intermittently from Half Jago Street in the further confines.

In a little while something large and dark was pushed forth from the door-opening near Jago Row which Billy Leary's spouse had entered. The thing rolled over, and lay tumbled on the pavement, for a time unnoted. It might have been yet another would-be sleeper, but for its stillness. Just such a thing it seemed, belike, to two that lifted their heads and peered from a few yards off, till they rose on hands and knees and crept to where it lay: Jago rats both. A man it was; with a thick smear across his face, and about his head the source of the dark trickle that sought the gutter deviously over the broken flags. The drab stuff of his pockets peeped out here and there in a crumpled bunch, and his waistcoat gaped where the watch-guard had been. Clearly, here was an uncommonly remunerative cosh – a cosh so good that the boots had been neglected, and remained on the man's feet. These the kneeling two unlaced deftly, and, rising, prize in hand, vanished in the deeper shadow of Jago Row.

A small boy, whom they met full tilt at the corner, staggered out to the gutter and flung a veteran curse after them. He was a slight child, by whose size you might have judged his age at five. But his face was of serious and troubled age. One who knew the children of the Jago, and could tell, might have held him eight, or from that to nine.

He replaced his hands in his trousers pockets, and trudged up the street. As he brushed by the coshed man he glanced again toward Jago Row, and, jerking his thumb that way, 'Done 'im for 'is boots,' he piped. But nobody marked him till he reached Jago Court, when old Beveridge, pushing back his hat once more, called sweetly and silkily, 'Dicky Perrott!' and beckoned with his finger.

The boy approached, and as he did so the man's skeleton hand suddenly shot out and gripped him by the collar. 'It – never – does – to – see – too – much!' Beveridge said, in a series of shouts, close to the boy's ear. 'Now go home,' he added, in a more ordinary tone, with a push to make his meaning plain: and straightway relapsed against the wall.

The boy scowled and backed off the pavement. His ragged jacket was coarsely made from one much larger, and he hitched the collar over his shoulder as he shrank toward a doorway some few yards on. Front doors were used merely as firewood* in the Old Jago, and most had been burnt there many years ago. If perchance one could have been found still on its hinges, it stood ever open and probably would not shut. Thus at night the Jago doorways were a row of black holes, foul and forbidding.

Dicky Perrott entered his hole with caution, for anywhere, in the passage and on the stairs, somebody might be lying drunk, against whom it would be unsafe to stumble. He found nobody, however, and climbed and reckoned his way up the first stair-flight with the necessary regard for the treads that one might step through and the rails that had gone from the side. Then he pushed open the door of the first-floor back* and was at home.

A little heap of guttering grease, not long ago a candle end, stood and spread on the mantelpiece, and gave irregular light from its drooping wick. A thin-railed iron bedstead, bent and staggering, stood against a wall, and on its murky coverings a half-dressed woman sat and neglected a baby that lay by her, grieving and wheezing. The woman had a long dolorous face, empty of expression and weak of mouth.*

'Where 'a' you bin, Dicky?' she asked, rather complaining than asking. 'It's sich low hours for a boy.'

Dicky glanced about the room. 'Got anythink to eat?' he asked.

'I dunno,' she answered listlessly. 'P'raps there's a bit o' bread in the cupboard. I don't want nothin', it's so 'ot. An' father ain't bin 'ome since tea-time.'

The boy rummaged and found a crust. Gnawing at this, he crossed to where the baby lay. ''Ullo, Looey,' he said, bending and patting the muddy cheek. ''Ullo!'

The baby turned feebly on its back, and set up a thin wail. Its eyes were large and bright, its tiny face was piteously flea-bitten and strangely old. 'Wy, she's 'ungry, mother,' said Dicky Perrott, and took the little thing up.

He sat on a small box, and rocked the baby on his knees, feeding it with morsels of chewed bread. The mother, dolefully inert, looked on and said: 'She's that backward I'm quite wore out; more 'n ten months old, an' don't even crawl yut. It's a never-endin' trouble, is children.'

She sighed, and presently stretched herself on the bed. The boy rose, and carrying his little sister with care, for she was dozing, essayed to look through the grimy window. The dull flush still spread overhead, but Jago Court lay darkling below, with scarce a sign of the ruinous back yards that edged it on this and the opposite sides, and nothing but blackness between.

The boy returned to his box, and sat. Then he said: 'I don't s'pose father's 'avin' a sleep outside, eh?'

The woman sat up with some show of energy. 'Wot?' she said sharply. 'Sleep out in the street like them low Ranns an' Learys? I should 'ope not. It's bad enough livin' 'ere at all, an' me being used to different things once, an' all. You ain't seen 'im outside, 'ave ye?'

'No, I ain't seen 'im: I jist looked in the court.' Then, after a pause: 'I 'ope 'e's done a click,'* the boy said.

His mother winced. 'I dunno wot you mean, Dicky,' she said, but falteringly. 'You – you're gittin' that low an' an'—'

'Wy, copped somethink, o' course. Nicked somethink. You know.'

'If you say sich things as that I'll tell 'im wot you say, an' 'e'll pay you. We ain't that sort o' people, Dicky, you ought to know. I was alwis kep' respectable an' straight all my life, I'm sure, an'—'

'I know. You said so before, to father – I 'eard: w'en 'e brought 'ome that there yuller prop – the necktie pin. Wy, where did 'e git that? 'E ain't 'ad a job for munse and munse: where's the yannups come from wot's bin for to pay the rent, an' git the toke, an' milk for Looey? Think I dunno? I ain't a kid. I know.'

'Dicky, Dicky! you mustn't say sich things!' was all the mother could find to say, with tears in her slack eyes. 'It's wicked an' – an' low. An' you must alwis be respectable an' straight, Dicky, an' you'll – you'll git on then.'

'Straight people's fools, I reckon. Kiddo Cook says that, an' 'e's as wide as Broad Street. W'en I grow up I'm goin' to git toffs' clo'es an' be in the 'igh mob. They does big clicks.'

'They git put in a dark prison for years an' years, Dicky – an' – an' if you're sich a wicked low boy, father'll give you the strap – 'ard,' the mother returned, with what earnestness she might. 'Gimme the baby, an' you go to bed, go on; 'fore father comes.'

Dicky handed over the baby, whose wizen face was now relaxed in sleep, and slowly disencumbered himself of the ungainly jacket, staring at the wall in a brown study. 'It's the mugs wot git took,' he said, absently. 'An' quoddin' ain't so bad.' Then, after a pause, he turned and added suddenly: 'S'pose father'll be smugged some day, eh, mother?'

His mother made no reply, but bent languidly over the baby, with an indefinite pretence of settling it in a place on the bed. Soon Dicky himself, in the short and ragged shirt he had worn under the jacket, burrowed head first among the dingy coverings at the foot, and protruding his head at the further side, took his accustomed place crosswise at the extreme end.

The filthy ceiling lit and darkened by fits as the candle-wick fell and guttered to its end. He heard his mother rise and find another fragment of candle to light by its expiring flame, but he lay still wakeful. After a time he asked: 'Mother, why don't you come to bed?'

'Waitin' for father. Go to sleep.'

He was silent for a little. But brain and eyes were wide awake, and soon he spoke again. 'Them noo 'uns in the front room,' he said. 'Ain't the man give 'is wife a 'idin' yut?'

'No.'

'Nor yut the boy – 'umpty-backed 'un?'

'No.'

'Seems they're mighty pertickler. Fancy theirselves too good for their neighbours; I 'eard Pigeony Poll say that; on'y Poll said – '

'You mustn't never listen to Pigeony Poll, Dicky. Ain't you 'eard me say so? Go to sleep. 'Ere comes father.' There was, indeed, a step on the stairs, but it passed the landing, and went on to the top floor. Dicky lay awake, but silent, gazing upward and back through the dirty window just over his head. It was very hot, and he fidgeted uncomfortably, fearing to turn or toss lest the baby should wake and cry. There came a change in the hue of the sky, and he watched the patch within his view, until the red seemed to gather in spots, and fade a spot at a time. Then at last there was a tread on the stairs, that stayed at the door; and father had come home. Dicky lay still, and listened.

'Lor, Josh, where ye bin?' Dicky heard his mother say. 'I'm almost wore out a-waitin'.'

'Awright, awright' – this in a hoarse grunt, little above a whisper. 'Got any water up 'ere? Wash this 'ere stick.'

There was a pause, wherein Dicky knew his mother looked about her in vacant doubt as to whether or not water was in the room. Then a quick, undertoned scream, and the stick rattled heavily on the floor. 'It's sticky!' his mother said. 'O my Gawd, Josh, look at that – an' bits o' 'air, too!' The great shadow of an open hand shot up across the ceiling and fell again. 'O Josh! O my Gawd! You ain't, 'ave ye? Not – not – not that?'

'Not wot? Gawblimy, not what? Shutcher mouth. If a man fights, you're got to fight back, ain' cher? Any one 'ud think it was a murder, to look at ye. I ain't sich a damn fool as that. 'Ere – pull up that board.'

Dicky knew the loose floor-board that was lifted with a slight groaning jar. It was to the right of the hearth, and he had shammed sleep when it had been lifted once before. His mother whimpered and cried quietly. 'You'll git in trouble, Josh,' she said. 'I wish you'd git a reg'lar job, Josh, like what you used – I do – I do.'

The board was shut down again. Dicky Perrott through one opened eye saw the sky a pale grey above, and hoped the click had been a good one: hoped also that it might bring bullock's liver for dinner.

Out in the Jago the pale dawn brought a cooler air and the chance of sleep. From the paving of Old Jago Street sad grey faces, open-mouthed, looked upward as from the Valley of Dry Bones.* Down by Jago Row the coshed subject, with the blood dry on his face, felt the colder air, and moved a leg.

CHAPTER 2

Three-quarters of a mile east of the Jago's outermost limit was the East End Elevation Mission and Pansophical Institute:* such was the amazing success whereof, that a new wing had been built, and was now to be declared open by a Bishop of great eminence and industry.

The triumphs of the East End Elevation Mission and Pansophical Institute were known and appreciated far from East London, by people who knew less of that part than of Asia Minor.* Indeed, they were chiefly appreciated by these. There were kept, perpetually on tap for the aspiring East Ender, the Higher Life, the Greater Thought, and the Wider Humanity: with other radiant abstractions, mostly in the comparative degree,* specifics all for the manufacture of the Superior Person. There were many Lectures given on still more subjects. Pictures* were borrowed and shown, with revelations to the Uninformed of the morals ingeniously concealed by the painters. The Uninformed were also encouraged to debate and to produce papers on literary and political matters, while still unencumbered with the smallest knowledge thereof: for the Enlargement of the Understanding and the Embellishment of the Intellect. And there were classes, and clubs, and newspapers, and games of draughts, and musical evenings,* and a brass band, whereby the life of the Hopeless Poor might be coloured, and the Misery of the Submerged* alleviated. The wretches who crowded to these benefits were tradesmen's sons, small shopkeepers and their families, and neat clerks, with here and there a smart young artisan of one of the especially respectable trades. They freely patronised the clubs, the musical evenings, the brass band, and the bagatelle board;* and those who took themselves seriously debated and Mutually-Improved* with pomp. Others, subject to savage fits of wanting-to-know, made short rushes at random evening classes, with intervals of disgusted apathy. Altogether, a number of decently-dressed and mannerly young men passed many evenings at the Pansophical Institute in harmless pleasures, and often with an agreeable illusion of intellectual advance.

Other young men, more fortunately circumstanced, with the educational varnish fresh and raw upon them, came from afar, equipped with a foreign mode of thought and a proper ignorance of the world and the proportions of things, as Missionaries.* Not without some anxiety to their parents, they plunged into the perilous deeps of the East End, to struggle – for a fortnight – with its suffering and its brutishness. So they went among the tradesmen's sons and the shopmen, who endured them as they endured the nominal subscription; and they came away with a certain relief, and with some misgiving as to what impression they had made, and what they had done to make it. But it was with knowledge and authority that they went back among those who had doubted their personal safety in the dark region.* The East End, they reported, was nothing like what it was said to be. You could see much worse places up West.* The people were quite a decent sort, in their way: shocking Bounders, of course; but quite clean and quiet, and very comfortably dressed, with ties and collars and watches.

But the Missionaries were few, and the subscribers to the Elevation Mission were many. Most had been convinced, by what they had been told, by what they had read in charity appeals, and perhaps by what they had seen in police-court and inquest reports,* that the whole East End was a wilderness of slums: slums packed with starving human organisms without minds and without morals, preying on each other alive. These subscribers visited the Institute by twos and threes, on occasions of particular festivity among the neat clerks, and were astonished at the wonderful effects of Pansophic Elevation on the degraded classes, their aspect and their habits. Perhaps it was a concert where nobody was drunk: perhaps a little dance where nobody howled a chorus, nor wore his hat, nor punched his partner in the eye. It was a great marvel, whereunto the observers testified: so that more subscriptions came, and the new wing was built.

The afternoon was bright, and all was promising. A small crowd of idlers hung about the main door of the Institute, and stared at a string of flags. Away to the left stood the new wing, a face of fair, clean brick; the ornamentation, of approved earnestness, in terra-cotta squares at regular intervals. Within sat many friends and relations of the shopmen and superior mechanics, and waited for the Bishop; the Eminences of the Elevation Mission sitting apart on the platform. Without, among the idlers, waited Dicky Perrott. His notions of what were going on were indistinct, but he had a belief, imbibed through rumour and tradition, that all celebrations at such large buildings were accompanied by the consumption, in the innermost recesses, of cake and tea. Even to be near cake was something. In Shoreditch High Street was a shop where cake stood in the window in great slabs, one slab over another, to an incalculable value. At this window – against it, as near as possible, his face flattened white – Dicky would stand till the shopkeeper drove him off: till he had but to shut his eyes to see once more, in the shifting black, the rich yellow sections with their myriad raisins. Once a careless errand-boy, who had bought a slice, took so clumsy a bite as he emerged that near a third of the whole piece broke and fell; and this Dicky had snatched from the paving and bolted with, ere the owner quite saw his loss. This was a superior sort of cake, at a penny. But once he had managed to buy himself a slice of an inferior sort for a halfpenny, in Meakin Street.

Dicky Perrott, these blessed memories in his brain, stood unobtrusively near the door, with the big jacket buttoned over as decently as might be, full of a desperate design: which was to get inside by whatsoever manner of trick or opportunity he might, and so, if it were humanly possible, to the cake.

The tickets were being taken at the door by an ardent young Elevator – one of the missionaries. Him, and all such washed and well-dressed people, Dicky had learnt to hold in serene contempt when the business in hand was dodging. There was no hurry: the Elevator might waste his vigilance on the ticket-holders for some time yet. And Dicky knew better than to betray the smallest sign of a desire for entrance while his enemy's attention was awake.

Carriages drew up, and yielded more Eminences: toward the end the Bishop himself, whom Dicky observed but as a pleasant-looking old gentleman in uncommon clothes; and on whom he bestowed no more thought than a passing wonder at what might be the accident to his hat which had necessitated its repair with string.*

But at the spikes of the Bishop's carriage* came another; and out of that there got three ladies, friends of the ticket-receiver,

on whom they closed, greeting and shaking hands; and in a flash
Dicky Perrott was beyond the lobby and moving obscurely along
the walls of the inner hall, behind pillars and in shadow, seeking
cake.

The Choral Society sang their lustiest, and there were
speeches. Eminences expressed their surprise and delight at
finding the people of the East End, gathered in the Institute
building, so respectable and clean, thanks to persistent, indefa-
tigable, unselfish Elevation.

The good Bishop, amid clapping of hands and fluttering of
handkerchiefs, piped cherubically of everything. He rejoiced to
see that day, whereon the helping hand of the West was so
unmistakably made apparent in the East. He rejoiced also to
find himself in the midst of so admirably typical an assemblage
– so representative, if he might say so, of that great East End of
London, thirsting and crying out for – for Elevation: for that –
ah – Elevation which the more fortunately circumstanced deni-
zens of – of other places, had so munificently – laid on. The
people of the East End had been sadly misrepresented – in
popular periodicals and in – in other ways.* The East End, he
was convinced, was not so black as it was painted.* (Applause.)
He had but to look about him. *Etcetera, etcetera.* He questioned
whether so well-conducted, morally-given, and respectable a
gathering could be brought together in any West End parish
with which he was acquainted. It was his most pleasant duty on
this occasion – and so on and so forth.

Dicky Perrott had found the cake. It was in a much smaller
room at the back of the hall, wherein it was expected that the
Bishop and certain Eminences of the platform would refresh
themselves with tea after the ceremony. There were heavy,
drooping curtains at the door of this room, and deep from the
largest folds the ratling from the Jago watched. The table was
guarded by a sour-faced man – just such a man as drove him
from the window of the cake shop in Shoreditch High Street.
Nobody else was there yet, and plainly the sour-faced man must
be absent or busy ere the cake could be got at.

There was a burst of applause in the hall: the new wing had
been declared open. Then there was more singing, and after that
much shuffling and tramping, for everybody was free to survey
the new rooms on the way out; and the Importances from the
platform came to find the tea.

Filling the room and standing about in little groups; chatting, munching, and sipping, while the sour-faced man distractedly floundered amid crockery: not a soul of them all perceived an inconsiderable small boy, ducking and dodging vaguely among legs and round skirts, making, from time to time, a silent snatch at a plate on the table: and presently he vanished altogether. Then the amiable Bishop, beaming over the tea-cup six inches from his chin, at two courtiers of the clergy, bethought him of a dinner engagement, and passed his hand downward over the rotundity of his waistcoat.

'Dear, dear,' said the Bishop, glancing down suddenly, 'why – what's become of my watch?'*

There hung three inches of black ribbon, with a cut end. The Bishop looked blankly at the Elevators about him.

Three streets off, Dicky Perrott, with his shut fist deep in his breeches pocket, and a gold watch in the fist, ran full drive for the Old Jago.

CHAPTER 3

There was nobody in chase; but Dicky Perrott, excited by his novel exploit, ran hard: forgetting the lesson first learnt by every child of the Jago, to avoid, as far as may be, suspicious flight in open streets. He burst into the Old Jago from the Jago Row corner, by Meakin Street; and still he ran. A small boy a trifle bigger than himself made a sharp punch at him as he passed, but he took no heed. The hulking group at the corner of Old Jago Street, ever observant of weaklings with plunder, saw him, and one tried to catch his arm, but he had the wit to dodge. Past the Jago Court passage he scudded, in at the familiar doorway, and up the stairs. A pale hunchbacked child, clean and wistful, descended, and him Dicky flung aside and half downstairs with 'Git out, 'ump!'

Josh Perrott sat on the bed, eating fried fish from an oily paper; for it was tea-time. He was a man of thirty-two, of middle height and stoutly built, with a hard, leathery face as of one much older. The hair about his mouth seemed always three days old – never much less nor much more. He was a plasterer – had, at least, so described himself at police-courts. But it was long since he had plastered, though he still walked abroad splashed and speckled, as though from an eruption of inherent plaster. In moments of pride he declared himself the only member of his family who had ever learned a trade, and worked at it. It was a long relinquished habit, but while it lasted he had married a decent boiler-maker's daughter,* who had known nothing of the Jago till these latter days. One other boast Josh Perrott had: that nothing but shot or pointed steel could hurt him.* And this, too, was near being a true boast; as he had proved in more than one fight in the local arena – which was Jago Court. Now he sat peaceably on the edge of the bed, and plucked with his fingers at the oily fish, while his wife grubbed hopelessly about the cupboard shelves for the screw of paper which was the sugar-basin.

Dicky entered at a burst. 'Mother – father – look! I done a click! I got a clock – a red 'un!'

Josh Perrott stopped, jaw and hand, with a pinch of fish poised in air. The woman turned, and her chin fell. 'O, Dicky, Dicky,' she cried, in real distress, 'you're a awful low, wicked boy. My Gawd, Josh, 'e – 'e'll grow up bad: I said so.'

Josh Perrott bolted the pinch of fish, and sucked his fingers as he sprang to the door. After a quick glance down the stairs he shut it, and turned to Dicky. 'Where d'je get that, ye young devel?' he asked, and snatched the watch.

'Claimed it auf a ol' bloke w'en 'e was drinkin' 'is tea,' Dicky replied, with sparkling eyes. 'Let's 'ave a look at it, father.'

'Did 'e run after ye?'

'No – didn't know nuffin' about it. I cut 'is bit o' ribbin with my knife.' Dicky held up a treasured relic of blade and handle, found in a gutter. 'Ain' cher goin' to let's 'ave a look at it?'

Josh Perrott looked doubtfully toward his wife: the children were chiefly her concern. Of her sentiments there could be no mistake. He slipped the watch into his own pocket, and caught Dicky by the collar.

'I'll give you somethink, you dam young thief,' he exclaimed, slipping off his belt. 'You'd like to have us all in stir for a year or two, I s'pose; goin' thievin' watches like a growed-up man.' And he plied the belt savagely, while Dicky, amazed, breathless and choking, spun about him with piteous squeals, and the baby woke and puled in feeble sympathy.

There was a rip, and the collar began to leave the old jacket. Feeling this, Josh Perrott released it, and with a quick drive of the fist in the neck sent Dicky staggering across the room. Dicky caught at the bed frame, and limped out to the landing, sobbing grievously in the bend of his sleeve.

It was more than his mother had intended, but she knew better than to attempt interference. Now that he was gone, she said, with some hesitation: ''Adn't you better take it out at once, Josh?'

'Yus, I'm goin',' Josh replied, turning the watch in his hand. 'It's a good 'un – a topper.'

'You – you won't let Weech 'ave it, will ye, Josh? 'E – 'e never gives much.'

'No bloomin' fear. I'm goin' up 'Oxton with this 'ere.'

*   *   *

Dicky sobbed his way down the stairs and through the passage to the back. In the yard he looked for Tommy Rann, to sympathise. But Tommy was not, and Dicky paused in his grief to reflect that perhaps, indeed, in the light of calm reason, he would rather cast the story of the watch in a more heroic mould, for Tommy's benefit, than was compatible with tears and a belted back. So he turned and squeezed through a hole in the broken fence, sobbing again, in search of the friend that shared his inmost sorrows.

The belting was bad – very bad. There was broken skin on his shins where the strap had curled round, and there was a little sticky blood under the shirt half way up his back: to say nothing of bruises. But it was the hopeless injustice of things that shook him to the soul. Wholly unaided, he had done, with neatness and credit, a click that anybody in the Jago would have been proud of. Overjoyed, he had hastened to receive the commendations of his father and mother, and to place the prize in their hands, freely and generously, though perhaps with some hope of hot supper by way of celebration. And his reward was this. Why? He could understand nothing: could but feel the wrong that broke his heart. And so, sobbing, he crawled through two fences to weep on the shaggy neck of Jerry Gullen's canary.

Jerry Gullen's canary was no bird, but a donkey: employed by Jerry Gullen in his occasional intervals of sobriety to drag a cranky shallow, sometimes stored with glass bottles, rags, and hearthstone:* sometimes with firewood manufactured from a convenient hoarding, or from the joinery of an empty house: sometimes with empty sacks covering miscellaneous property suddenly acquired and not for general inspection. His vacations, many and long, Jerry Gullen's canary spent, forgotten and unfed, in Jerry Gullen's backyard: gnawing desperately at fences, and harrowing the neighbourhood with his bray. Thus the nickname, facetiously applied by Kiddo Cook in celebration of his piteous song, grew into use; and 'Canary' would call the creature's attention as readily as a mouthful of imprecations.

Jerry Gullen's canary was gnawing, gnawing, with a sound as of a crooked centre-bit.* Everywhere about the foul yard, ten or twelve feet square, wood was rounded and splintered and bitten white, and as the donkey turned his heavy head, a drip of blood from his gums made a disc on the stones. A twitch of the ears welcomed Dicky, grief-stricken as he was; for it was commonly thus that he bethought him of solace in Jerry Gullen's backyard. And so Dicky, his arms about the mangy neck, told the tale of his wrongs till consolation came in composition of the heroic narrative designed for Tommy Rann.

'O, Canary, it is a blasted shame!'

CHAPTER 4

When Dicky Perrott came running into Jago Row with the
Bishop's watch in his pocket, another boy punched a fist at him,
and at the time Dicky was at a loss to guess the cause – unless it
were a simple caprice – but stayed neither to inquire nor to
retaliate. The fact was that the Ranns and the Learys were
coming out, fighting was in the air, and the small boy, meeting
another a trifle smaller, punched on general principles. The
Ranns and the Learys, ever at war or in guarded armistice, were
the great rival families – the Montagues and the Capulets* – of
the Old Jago. The Learys indeed, scarce pretended to rivalry –
rather to factious opposition. For the Ranns gloried in the style
and title of the 'Royal Family', and dominated the Jago; but
there were mighty fighters, men and women, among the Learys,
and when a combat arose it was a hard one and an animated.
The two families ramified throughout the Jago; and under the
Rann standard, whether by kin or by custom, were the Gullens,
the Fishers, the Spicers, and the Walshes; while in the Leary
train came Dawsons, Greens, and Harnwells. So that near all the
Jago was wont to be on one side or the other, and any of
the Jago which was not, was apt to be the worse for it; for
the Ranns drubbed all them that were not of their faction in the
most thorough and most workmanlike manner, and the Learys
held by the same practice; so that neutrality meant double
drubbing. But when the Ranns and Learys combined, and the
Old Jago issued forth in its entire might against Dove Lane, then
the battle was one to go miles to see.

This, however, was but a Rann and Leary fight; and it was
but in its early stages when Dicky Perrott, emerging from Jerry
Gullen's backyard, made for Shoreditch High Street by way of
the 'Posties' – the passage with posts at the end of Old Jago
Street. His purpose was to snatch a handful of hay from some
passing waggon, or of mixed fodder from some unguarded
nosebag, wherewith to reward the sympathy of Jerry Gullen's

canary. But by the 'Posties', at the Edge Lane corner, Tommy Rann, capless, and with a purple bump on his forehead, came flying into his arms, breathless, exultant, a babbling braggart. He had fought Johnny Leary and Joe Dawson, he said, one after the other, and pretty nigh broke Johnny Leary's blasted neck; and Joe Dawson's big brother was after him now with a bleed'n' shovel. So the two children ran on together, and sought the seclusion of their own back yard; where the story of Johnny Rann's prowess, with scowls and the pounding of imaginary foes, and the story of the Bishop's watch, with suppressions and improvements, mingled and contended in the thickening dusk. And Jerry Gullen's canary went forgotten and unrequited.

That night fighting was sporadic and desultory in the Jago. Bob the Bender* was reported to have a smashed nose, and Sam Cash had his head bandaged at the hospital. At the Bag of Nails in Edge Lane, Snob Spicer* was knocked out of knowl-edge* with a quart pot,* and Cocko* Harnwell's missis had a piece bitten off of one ear. As the night wore on, taunts and defiances were bandied from window to door, and from door to window, between those who intended to begin fighting tomorrow; and shouts from divers corners gave notice of isolated scuffles. Once a succession of piercing screams seemed to betoken that Sally Green had begun. There was a note in the screams of Sally Green's opposites which the Jago had learned to recognise. Sally Green, though of the weaker faction, was the female champion of the Old Jago: an eminence won and kept by fighting tactics peculiar to herself. For it was her way, reserving teeth and nails, to wrestle closely with her antagonist, throw her by a dexterous twist on her face, and fall on her, instantly seizing the victim's nape in her teeth, gnawing and worrying. The sufferer's screams were audible afar, and beyond their invariable eccentricity of quality – a quality vaguely suggestive of dire surprise – they had mechanical persistence, a pump-like regularity that distinguished them, in the accustomed ear, from other screams.

Josh Perrott had not been home all the evening: probably the Bishop's watch was in course of transmutation into beer. Dicky, stiff and domestically inclined, nursed Looey and listened to the noises without till he fell asleep, in hopeful anticipation of the morrow. For Tommy Rann had promised him half of a broken iron railing wherewith to fight the Learys.

CHAPTER 5

Sleep in the Jago was at best a thing of intermission, for reasons – reasons of multitude – already denoted; nevertheless Dicky slept well enough to be unconscious of his father's homecoming. In the morning, however, there lay Josh Perrott, snoring thunderously on the floor, piebald with road-dust. This was not a morning whereon father would want breakfast – that was plain: he would wake thirsty and savage. So Dicky made sure of a crust from the cupboard, and betook himself in search of Tommy Rann. As to washing, he was never especially fond of it, and in any case there were fifty excellent excuses for neglect. The only water was that from the little tap in the back yard. The little tap was usually out of order, or had been stolen bodily by a tenant; and if it were not, there was no basin there, nor any soap, nor towel; and anything savouring of moderate cleanliness was resented in the Jago* as an assumption of superiority.*

Fighting began early, fast and furious. The Ranns got together soon, and hunted the Learys up and down, and attacked them in their houses: the Learys' chances only coming when straggling Ranns were cut off from the main body. The weapons in use, as was customary, rose in effectiveness by a swiftly ascending scale. The Learys, assailed with sticks, replied with sticks torn from old packing-cases, with protruding nails. The two sides bethought them of coshes simultaneously, and such as had no coshes – very few – had pokers and iron railings. Ginger Stagg,* at bay in his passage, laid open Pud Palmer's* cheek with a chisel; and, knives thus happily legitimised with the least possible preliminary form, everybody was free to lay hold of whatever came handy.

In Old Jago Street, half way between Jago Court and Edge Lane, stood the Feathers, the grimiest and vilest of the four public-houses in the Jago. Into the Feathers some dozen Learys were driven, and for a while they held the inner bar and the taproom against the Ranns, who swarmed after them, chairs, bottles, and pewter pots flying thick, while Mother Gapp, the landlady, hung hysterical on the beer-pulls in the bar, supplicating and blubbering aloud. Then a partition came down with a crash, bringing shelves and many glasses with it, and the Ranns rushed over the ruin, beating the Learys down, jumping on them, heaving them through the back windows. Having thus cleared the house of the intruding enemy, the Ranns demanded recompense of liquor, and took it, dragging handles off beer-engines, seizing bottles, breaking into the cellar, and driving in bungs.* Nobody better than Mother Gapp could quell an ordinary bar riot – even to knocking a man down with a pot; but she knew better than to attempt interference now. Nothing could have made her swoon, but she sat limp and helpless, weeping and blaspheming.

The Ranns cleared off, every man with a bottle or so, and scattered, and this for a while was their undoing. For the Learys rallied and hunted the Ranns in their turn: a crowd of eighty or a hundred sweeping the Jago from Honey Lane to Meakin Street. Then they swung back through Edge Lane to Old Jago Street, and made for Jerry Gullen's – a house full of Ranns. Jerry Gullen, Bill Rann, and the rest took refuge in the upper floors and barricaded the stairs. Below, the Learys broke windows and ravaged the rooms, smashing whatsoever of furniture was to be found. Above, Pip Walsh, who affected horticulture on his window-sill, hurled down flower-pots. On the stairs, Billy Leary, scaling the barricade, was flung from top to bottom, and had to be carried home. And then Pip Walsh's missis scattered the besiegers on the pavement below with a kettleful of boiling water.

There was a sudden sortie of Ranns from Jago Court, but it profited nothing; for the party was small, and, its advent being unexpected, there was a lack of prompt co-operation from the house. The Learys held the field.

Down the middle of Old Jago Street came Sally Green: red faced, stripped to the waist, dancing, hoarse and triumphant. Nail-scores wide as the finger striped her back, her face, and her throat, and she had a black eye; but in one great hand she dangled a long bunch of clotted hair,* as she whooped defiance to the Jago. It was a trophy newly rent from the scalp of Norah Walsh, champion of the Rann womankind, who had crawled away to hide her blighted head, and be restored with gin. None

answered Sally's challenge, and, staying but to fling a brickbat
at Pip Walsh's window, she carried her dance and her trophy
into Edge Lane.

The scrimmage on Jerry Gullen's stairs was thundering anew,
and parties of Learys were making for other houses in the street,
when there came a volley of yells from Jago Row, heralding a
scudding mob of Ranns. The defeated sortie-party from Jago
Court, driven back, had gained New Jago Street by way of the
house-passages behind the Court, and set to gathering the
scattered faction. Now the Ranns came, drunk, semi-drunk, and
otherwise, and the Learys, leaving Jerry Gullen's, rushed to meet
them. There was a great shock, hats flew, sticks and heads made
a wooden rattle, and instantly the two mobs were broken into
an uproarious confusion of tangled groups, howling and grap-
pling. Here a man crawled into a passage to nurse a broken
head; there a knot gathered to kick a sprawling foe. So the fight
thinned out and spread, resolving into many independent com-
bats, with concerted rushes of less and less frequency, till once
again all through the Jago each fought for his own hand. Kiddo
Cook, always humorous, ran hilariously through the streets,
brandishing a long roll of twisted paper, wherewith he smacked
the heads of Learys all and sundry, who realised too late that
the paper was twisted round a lodging-house poker.*

Now, of the few neutral Jagos: most lay low. Josh Perrott,
however, hard as nails and respected for it, feared neither Rann
nor Leary, and leaving a little money with his missis, carried his
morning mouth in search of beer. Pigeony Poll,* harlot and
outcast, despised for that she neither fought nor kept a cosh-
carrier, like a respectable married woman, slunk and trembled
in corners and yards, and wept at the sight of bleeding heads.
As for old Beveridge, the affair so grossly excited him that he
neglected business (he cadged and wrote begging screeves)* and
stayed in the Jago, where he strode wildly about the streets, lank
and rusty, stabbing the air with a carving knife, and incoherently
defying 'all the lot' to come near him. Nobody did.

Dicky Perrott and Tommy Rann found a snug fastness in Jago
Row. For there was a fence with a loose board, which, pushed
aside, revealed a hole where through a very small boy might
squeeze; and within were stored many barrows and shallows,
mostly broken, and of these one, tilted forward and bottom up,
made a hut or den, screened about with fence and barrows.

Here they hid while the Learys swept the Jago, and hence they issued from time to time to pound such youngsters of the other side as might come in sight. The bits of iron railing made imposing weapons, but were a trifle too big and heavy for rapid use in their puny hands. Still, Dicky managed to double up little Billy Leary with a timely lunge in the stomach, and Tommy Rann made Bobby Harnwell's nose bleed very satisfactorily. On the other hand, the bump on Tommy Rann's forehead was widened by the visitation of a stick, and Dicky Perrott sustained a very hopeful punch in the eye, which he cherished enthusiastically with a view to an honourable blackness. In the snuggery intervals they explained their prowess one to another, and Dicky alluded to his intention, when he was a man, to buy a very long sword wherewith to cut off the Learys' heads: Tommy Rann inclining, however, to a gun, with which one might also shoot birds.

The battle flagged a little toward midday, but waxed lively again as the afternoon began. It was then that Dicky Perrott, venturing some way from the retreat, found himself in a scrimmage, and a man snatched away his piece of iron and floored a Leary with it. Gratifying as was the distinction of aiding in the exploit, Dicky mourned the loss of the weapon almost unto tears, and Tommy Rann would not go turn-about with the other, but kept it wholly for himself; so Dicky was fain to hunt sorrowfully for a mere stick. Even a disengaged stick was not easy to find just then. So Dicky, emerging from the Jago, tried Meakin Street, where there were shops, but unsuccessfully, and so came round by Luck Row, a narrow way from Meakin Street by Walker's cook shop, up through the Jago.

Dicky's mother, left with the baby, fastened the door as well as she might, and trembled. Indeed she had reason. The time of Josh Perrott's return was a matter of doubt, but when he did come he would want something to eat; it was for that he had left the money. But Dicky was out, and there was nothing in the cupboard. From the window she saw divers fights in Jago Court; and a man lay for near two hours on the stones with a cut on his temple. As for herself, she was no favourite in the neighbourhood at any time. For one thing, her husband did not carry the cosh. Then she was an alien who had never entirely fallen into Jago ways; she had soon grown sluttish and dirty, but she was never drunk, she never quarrelled, she did not gossip freely. Also her husband beat her but rarely, and then not with a chair nor a poker. Justly irritated by such superiorities as these, the women of the Jago were ill-disposed to brook another: which was, that Hannah Perrott had been married in church. For these reasons she was timid at the most peaceful of times, but now, with Ranns and Learys on the war-path, and herself obnoxious to both, she trembled. She wished Dicky would come and do her errand. But there was no sign of him, and midday wore into afternoon. It was late for Josh as it was, and he would be sure to come home irritable: it was his way when a bad head from overnight struggled with morning beer. If he found nothing to eat there would be trouble.

At length she resolved to go herself. There was a lull in the outer din, and what there was seemed to come from the farther parts of Honey Lane and Jago Row. She would slip across by Luck Row to Meakin Street and be back in five minutes. She took up little Looey and went.

And as Dicky, stickless, turned into Luck Row, there arose a loud shriek and then another, and then in a changed voice a succession of long screams with a regular breath-pause. Sally Green again! He ran, turned into Old Jago Street, and saw.

Sprawled on her face in the foul road lay a writhing woman and screamed; while squeezed under her arm was a baby with mud in its eyes and a cut cheek, crying weakly; and spread over all, clutching her prey by hair and wrist, Sally Green hung on the nape like a terrier, jaws clenched, head shaking.

Thus Dicky saw it in a flash, and in an instant he had flung himself on Sally Green, kicking, striking, biting and crying, for he had seen his mother and Looey. The kicks wasted themselves among the woman's petticoats, and the blows were feeble; but the sharp teeth were meeting in the shoulder-flesh, when help came.

Norah Walsh, vanquished champion, now somewhat recovered, looked from a window, saw her enemy vulnerable, and ran out armed with a bottle. She stopped at the kerb to knock the bottom off the bottle, and then, with an exultant shout, seized Sally Green by the hair and stabbed her about the face with the jagged points. Blinded with blood, Sally released her hold on Mrs Perrott and rolled on her back, struggling fiercely; but to no end, for Norah Walsh, kneeling on her breast, stabbed and stabbed again, till pieces of the bottle broke away. Sally's yells and plunges ceased, and a man pulled Norah off. On him she turned, and he was fain to run, while certain Learys found a truck* which might carry Sally to the hospital.

Hannah Perrott was gone indoors, hysterical and helpless. She had scarce crossed the street on her errand when she had met Sally Green in quest of female Ranns. Mrs Perrott was not a Rann, but she was not a Leary, so it came to the same thing. Moreover, there was her general obnoxiousness. She had tried to run, but that was useless; and now, sobbing and bleeding, she was merely conscious of being gently led, almost carried, indoors and upstairs. She was laid back on the bed, and somebody loosened her hair and wiped her face and neck, giving her hoarse, comforting words. Then she saw the face – scared though coarse and pitted, and red about the eyes – that bent over her. It was Pigeony Poll's.

Dicky had followed her in, no longer the hero of the Jago Row retreat, but with his face tearful and distorted, carrying the baby in his arms, and wiping the mud from her eyes. Now he sat on the little box and continued his ministrations, with fear in his looks as he glanced at his mother on the bed.

Without, the fight rallied once more. The Learys ran to avenge Sally Green, and the Ranns met them with a will. Down by the Bag of Nails a party of Ranns was driven between the posts and through the gut into Shoreditch High Street, where a stand was made until Fag Dawson* dropped, with a shoemaker's knife sticking under his arm-pit. Then the Ranns left, with most of the Learys after them, and Fag Dawson was carried to a chemist's by the police, never to floor a Rann again. For he was chived in the left lung.

Thus the fight ended. For a faction fight in the Jago, with a few broken heads and ribs and an odd knife wound here and there – even with a death in the hospital from kicks or what not – was all very well; but when it came to homicide in the open High Street, the police drew the line, and entered the Jago in force. Ordinarily, a peep now and again from a couple of policemen between the 'Posties' was all the supervision the Jago had, although three policemen had been seen to walk the length of Old Jago Street together, and there were raids in force for special captures. There was a raid in force now, and the turmoil ceased. Nothing would have pleased both Ranns and Learys better than to knock over two or three policemen, for kicking-practice; but there were too many for the sport, and for hours they patrolled the Jago's closest passages. Of course nobody knew who chived Fag Dawson. No inquiring policeman ever found anybody in the Old Jago who knew anything, even to the harm of his bitterest foe. It was the sole commandment that ran there: – 'Thou shalt not nark.'

That night it was known that there would be a fight between Josh Perrott and Billy Leary, once the latter grew well. For Josh Perrott came home, saw his wife, and turned Rann on the spot. But for the police in the Jago that night, there would have been many a sore head, if no worse, among the Learys, by visitation of Josh Perrott. Sally Green's husband had fled years ago, and Billy Leary, her brother, was the obvious mark for Josh's vengeance. He was near as eminent a fighter among the men as his sister among the women, and a charming scrap was antici-pated. It would come off, of course, in Jago Court one Sunday morning, as all fights of distinction did; and perhaps somebody in the High Mob would put up stakes.

CHAPTER 6

In the morning the police still held the Jago. Their presence embarrassed many, but none more than Dicky Perrott, who would always take a turning, or walk the other way, at sight of a policeman. Dicky got out of Old Jago Street early, and betook him to Meakin Street, where there were chandlers' shops with sugar in their windows, and cook-shops with pudding. He designed working through by these to Shoreditch High Street, there to crown his solace by contemplation of the cake-shop. But, as he neared Weech's coffee-shop, scarce half through Meakin Street, there stood Weech himself at the door, grinning and nodding affably, and beckoning him. He was a pleasant man, this Mr Aaron Weech,* who sang hymns aloud in the back parlour, and hummed the tunes in the shop: a prosperous, white-aproned, whiskered, half-bald, smirking tradesman, who bent and spoke amiably to boys, looking sharply in their eyes, but talked to a man mostly with his gaze on the man's waistcoat.

Indeed, there seemed to be something about Mr Aaron Weech especially attractive to youth. Nearly all his customers were boys and girls, though not boys and girls who looked likely to pay a great deal in the way of refreshment, much as they took. But he was ever indulgent, and at all times accessible to his young clients. Even on Sunday (though, of course, his shutters were kept rigidly up on the Day of Rest) a particular tap would bring him hot-foot to the door: not to sell coffee, for Mr Weech was no Sabbath-breaker.*

Now he stood at his door, and invited Dicky with nods and becks. Dicky, all wondering, and alert to dodge in case the thing were a mere device to bring him within striking distance, went.

'W'y Dicky Perrott,' quoth Mr Weech in a tone of genial surprise, 'I b'lieve you could drink a cup o' cawfy!'

Dicky, wondering how Mr Weech had learnt his name, believed he could.

'An' eat a slice o' cake too, I'll be bound,' Mr Weech added.

Dicky's glance leapt. Yes, he could eat a slice of cake too.

'Ah, I knew it,' said Mr Weech, triumphantly; 'I can always tell.' He rubbed Dicky's cap about his head, and drew him into the shop, at this hour bare of customers. At the innermost compartment they stopped, and Mr Weech, with a gentle pressure on the shoulders, seated Dicky at the table.

He brought the coffee, and not a single slice of cake, but two. True, it was not cake of Elevation Mission quality, nor was it so good as that shown at the shop in High Street: it was of a browner, dumpier, harder nature, and the currants were gritty and few. But cake it was, and to consider it critically were unworthy. Dicky bolted it with less comfort than he might, for Mr Weech watched him keenly across the table. And, indeed, from some queer cause, he felt an odd impulse to cry. It was the first time that he had ever been given anything, kindly and ungrudgingly.*

He swallowed the last crumb, washed it down with the dregs of his cup, and looked sheepishly across at Mr Weech.

'Goes down awright, don't it?' that benefactor remarked. 'Ah, I like to see you enjoyin' of yerself. I'm very fond o' you young 'uns: 'specially clever 'uns like you.'

Dicky had never been called clever before, so far as he could recollect, and he wondered at it now. Mr Weech, leaning back, contemplated him smilingly for some seconds, and then proceeded. 'Yus,' he said, 'you're the sort o' boy as can 'ave cawfy and cake w'enever you want it, you are.'

Dicky wondered more, and his face said as much. 'You know,' Mr Weech pursued, winking amain, grinning and nodding. 'That was a fine watch you found the other day. Y'ought to 'a' brought it to me.'

Dicky was alarmed. How did Mr Weech learn about the watch? Perhaps he was a friend of the funny old man who lost it. Dicky half rose, but his affable patron leaned across and pushed him back on the seat. 'You needn't be frightened,' he said. 'I ain't goin' to say nothink to nobody. But I know all about it, mind, an' I could if I liked. You found the watch, an' it was a red 'un, on a bit o' ribbin. Well, then you went and took it 'ome, like a little fool. Wot does yer father do? W'y 'e ups an' lathers you with 'is belt, an' 'e keeps the watch 'isself. That's all you git for yer pains. See — I know all about it.' And Mr Weech gazed on Dicky Perrott with a fixed grin.

'Oo toldjer?' Dicky managed to ask at last.

'Ah!' – this with a great emphasis and a tapping of the forefinger beside the nose* – 'I don't want much tellin': it ain't much as goes on 'ereabout I don't know of. Never mind 'ow. P'raps I got a little bird as w'ispers – p'raps I do it some other way. Any'ow I know. It ain't no good any boy tryin' to do somethink unbeknownst to me, mindjer.'

Mr Weech's head lay aside, his grin widened, his glance was sidelong, his forefinger pointed from his temple over Dicky's head, and altogether he looked so very knowing that Dicky shuffled in his seat. By what mysterious means was this new-found friend so well informed? The doubt troubled him, for Dicky knew nothing of Mr Aaron Weech's conversation, an hour before, with Tommy Rann.

'But it's awright, bless yer,' Mr Weech went on presently. 'Nobody's none the wuss for me knowin' about 'em . . . Well, we was a-talkin' about the watch, wasn't we? All you got after sich a lot o' trouble was a woppin' with a belt. That was too bad.' Mr Weech's voice was piteous and sympathetic. 'After you a-findin' sich a nice watch – a red 'un an' all! – you gits nothink for yerself but a beltin'. Never mind, you'll do better next time – I'll take care o' that. I don't like to see a clever boy put upon. You go an' find another, or somethink else – anythink good – an' then you bring it 'ere.'

Mr Weech's friendly sympathy extinguished Dicky's doubt. 'I didn't find it,' he said, shy but proud. 'It was a click – I sneaked it.'

'Eh?' ejaculated Mr Weech, a sudden picture of blank incomprehension. 'Eh? What? Click? Wot's a click? Sneaked? Wot's that? I dunno nothink about no talk o' that sort, an' I don't want to. It's my belief it means somethink wrong – but I dunno, an' I don't want to. 'Ear that? Eh? Don't let me 'ave no more o' that, or you'd better not come near me agin. If you *find* somethink, awright: you come to me an' I'll give ye somethink for it, if it's any good. It ain't no business of anybody's *where* you find it, o' course, an' I don't want to know. But clicks and sneaks – them's Greek to me, an' I don't want to learn 'em. Unnerstand that? Nice talk to respectable people, with yer clicks an' sneaks!'

Dicky blushed a little, and felt very guilty without in the least understanding the offence. But Mr Weech's virtuous indignation subsided as quickly as it had arisen, and he went on as amiably as ever.

'When you *find* anythink,' he said, 'jist like you found that watch, don't tell nobody, an' don't let nobody see it. Bring it 'ere quiet, when there ain't any p'liceman in the street, an' come right through to the back o' the shop, an' say, "I come to clean the knives."* Unnerstand? "I come to clean the knives." There ain't no knives to clean – it's on'y a way o' tellin' me you got somethink without other people knowin'. An' then I'll give you somethink for it – money p'raps, or p'raps cake or wot not. Don't forgit. "I come to clean the knives." See?'

Yes, Dicky understood perfectly; and Dicky saw a new world of dazzling delights. Cake – limitless cake, coffee, and the like whenever he might feel moved thereunto; but more than all, money – actual money. Good broad pennies,* perhaps whole shillings – perhaps even more still: money to buy bullock's liver for dinner, or tripe, or what you fancied: saveloys, baked potatoes from the can on cold nights, a little cart to wheel Looey in, a boat from a toy-shop with sails!

'There's no end o' things to be found all over the place, an' a sharp boy like you can find 'em every day. If you don't find 'em, someone else will; there's plenty on 'em about on the look-out, an' you got jist as much right as them. On'y mind!' – Mr Weech was suddenly stern and serious, and his forefinger was raised impressively – 'you know you can't do anythink without I know, an' if you say a word – if you say a word,' his fist came on the table with a bang, 'somethink'll happen to you. Somethink bad.'

Mr Weech rose, and was pleasant again, though business-like. 'Now, you just go an' find somethink,' he said. 'Look sharp about it, an' don't go an' git in trouble. The cawfy's a penny, an' the cake's a penny – ought prop'ly to be twopence, but say a penny this time. That's twopence you owe me, an' you better bring somethink an' pay it off quick. So go along.'

This was an unforeseen tag to the entertainment. For the first time in his life Dicky was in debt. It was a little disappointing to find the coffee and cake no gift after all: though, indeed, it now seemed foolish to have supposed they were; for in Dicky Perrott's world people did not give things away – that were the act of a fool. Thus Dicky, with his hands in his broken pockets, and thought in his small face, whereon still stood the muddy streaks of yesterday's tears, trudged out of Mr Aaron Weech's shop-door, and along Meakin Street.

Now he was beginning the world seriously, and must face the fact. Truly the world had been serious enough for him hitherto, but that he knew not. Now he was of an age when most boys were thieving for themselves, and he owed money like a man. True it was, as Mr Weech had said, that everybody – the whole Jago – was on the look-out for himself. Plainly he must take his share, lest it fall to others. As to the old gentleman's watch, he had but been beforehand. Through foolish ingenuousness he had lost it, and his father had got it, who could so much more easily steal one for himself; for he was a strong man, and had but to knock over another man at any night-time. Nobody should hear of future clicks but Mr Weech. Each for himself? Come, he must open his eyes.

CHAPTER 7

There was no chance all along Meakin Street. The chandlers and the keepers of cook-shops knew their neighbourhood too well to leave articles unguarded. Soon Dicky reached Shoreditch High Street. There things were a little more favourable. There were shops, as he well remembered, where goods were sometimes exhibited at the doors and outside the windows; but today there seemed to be no chance of the sort. As for the people, he was too short to try pockets, and indeed the High Street rarely gave passage to a more unpromising lot. Moreover, from robbery from the person he knew he must abstain, except for such uncommon opportunities as that of the Bishop's watch, for some years yet.

He hung about the doors and windows of shop after shop, hoping for a temporary absence of the shop-keeper, which might leave something snatchable. But he hoped in vain. From most shops he was driven away, for the Shoreditch trader is not slow to judge the purpose of a loitering boy. So he passed nearly two hours: when at last he saw his chance. It came in an advantageous part of High Street, not far from the 'Posties', though on the opposite side of the way. A nurse-girl had left a perambulator at a shop door, while she bought inside, and on the perambulator lay loose a little skin rug, from under which a little fat leg stuck and waved aloft. Dicky set his back to the shop, and sidled to within reach of the perambulator. But it chanced that at this moment the nurse-girl stepped to the door, and she made a snatch at his arm as he lifted the rug. This he dropped at once, and was swinging leisurely away (for he despised the chase of any nurse-girl) when a man took him suddenly by the shoulder. Quick as a weasel, Dicky ducked under the man's arm, pulled his shoulder clear, dropped forward and rested an instant on the tips of his fingers to avoid the catch of the other hand, and shot out into the road. The man tried to follow, but Dicky ran under the belly of a standing horse, under the head of another that trotted, across the fore-platform of a tramcar – behind the driver's back – and so over to the 'Posties'.

He slouched into the Jago, disappointed. As he crossed Edge Lane, he was surprised to perceive a stranger – a toff, indeed – who walked slowly along, looking up right and left at the grimy habitations about him. He wore a tall hat, and his clothes were black, and of a pattern that Dicky remembered to have seen at the Elevation Mission. They were, in fact, the clothes of a clergyman. For himself, he was tall and soundly built, with a certain square muscularity of face, and of age about thirty-five. He had ventured into the Jago because the police were in possession, Dicky thought; and wondered in what plight he would leave, had he come at another time. But losing view of the stranger, and making his way along Old Jago Street, Dicky perceived that indeed the police were gone, and that the Jago was free.

He climbed the broken stairs and pushed into the first-floor back, hopeful, though more doubtful, of dinner. There was none. His mother, tied about the neck with rags, lay across the bed nursing the damage of yesterday, and commiserating herself. A yard from her lay Looey, sick and ailing in a new way, but disregarded. Dicky moved to lift her, but at that she cried the more, and he was fain to let her lie. She rolled her head from side to side, and raised her thin little hand vaguely toward it, with feverishly working fingers. Dicky felt her head and she screamed again. There was a lump at the side, a hard, sharp lump; got from the stones of the roadway yesterday. And there was a curious quality, a rather fearful quality, in the little wails: uneasily suggestive of the screams of Sally Green's victims.

Father was out, prowling. There was nothing eatable in the cupboard, and there seemed nothing at home worth staying for. He took another look at Looey, but refrained from touching her, and went out.

The opposite door on the landing was wide open, and he could hear nobody in the room. He had never seen this door open before, and now he ventured on a peep: for the tenants of the front room were strangers, late arrivals, and interlopers. Their name was Roper. Roper was a pale cabinet-maker, fallen on evil times and out of work. He had a pale wife, disliked because of her neatly-kept clothes, her exceeding use of soap and water, her aloofness from gossip. She had a deadly pale baby; also there was a pale hunchbacked boy of near Dicky's age. Collectively the Ropers were disliked as strangers: because they furnished their own room, and in an obnoxiously complete style; because Roper did not drink, nor brawl, nor beat his wife, nor do anything all day but look for work; because all these things were a matter of scandalous arrogance, impudently subversive of Jago custom and precedent. Mrs Perrott was bad enough, but such people as these! . . .

Dicky had never before seen quite such a room as this. Everything was so clean: the floor, the windows, the bed-clothes. Also there was a strip of old carpet on the floor. There were two perfectly sound chairs; and two pink glass vases on the mantel-piece; and a clock. Nobody was in the room, and Dicky took a step farther. The clock attracted him again. It was a small, cheap, nickel-plated, cylindrical thing, of American make,* and it reminded him at once of the Bishop's watch. It was not gold, certainly, but it was a good deal bigger, and it could go – it was going. Dicky stepped back and glanced at the landing. Then he darted into the room, whipped the clock under the breast of the big jacket, and went for the stairs.

Half way down he met the pale hunchback ascending. Left at home alone, he had been standing in the front doorway. He saw Dicky's haste, saw also the suspicious bulge under his jacket, and straightway seized Dicky's arm. 'Where 'a' you bin?' he asked sharply. 'Bin in our room? What you got there?'

'Nothin' o' yours, 'ump. Git out o' that!' Dicky pushed him aside. 'If you don't le' go I'll corpse* ye!'

But one arm and hand was occupied with the bulge, and the other was for the moment unequal to the work of driving off the assailant. The two children wrangled and struggled down-stairs, through the doorway and into the street: the hunchback weak, but infuriate, buffeting, biting and whimpering; Dicky infuriate too, but alert for a chance to break away and run. So they scrambled together across the street, Dicky dragging away from the house at every step; and just at the corner of Luck Row, getting his fore-arm across the other's face, he back-heeled him, and the little hunchback fell heavily, and lay breathless and sobbing, while Dicky scampered through Luck Row and round the corner into Meakin Street.

Mr Weech was busier now, for there were customers. But Dicky and his bulge he saw ere they were well over the threshold.

'Ah yus, Dicky,' he said, coming to meet him. 'I was expectin' you. Come in –

> *In the swe-e-et by an' by,*
> *We shall meet on that beautiful shaw-er!**

Come in 'ere.' And still humming his hymn, he led Dicky into the shop parlour.

Here Dicky produced the clock, which Mr Weech surveyed with no great approval. 'You'll 'ave to try an' do better than this, you know,' he said. 'But any'ow 'ere it is, sich as it is. It about clears auf wot you owe, I reckon. Want some dinner?'

This was a fact, and Dicky admitted it.

'Awright –

> *In the swe-e-e-t by an' by –*

come out an' set down. I'll bring you somethink 'ot.'

This proved to be a very salt bloater, a cup of the usual muddy coffee, tasting of burnt toast, and a bit of bread: afterwards supplemented by a slice of cake. This to Dicky was a banquet. Moreover, there was the adult dignity of taking your dinner in a coffee-shop, which Dicky supported indomitably now that he began to feel at ease in Mr Weech's: leaning back in his seat, swinging his feet, and looking about at the walls with the grocers' almanacks* hanging thereto, and the Sunday School Anniversary bills* of past date, gathered from afar to signalise the elevated morals of the establishment.

'Done?' queried Mr Weech in his ear. 'Awright, don't 'ang about 'ere then. Bloater's a penny, bread a 'a'peny, cawfy a penny, cake a penny. You'll owe thrippence a'peny now.'

CHAPTER 8

When Dicky Perrott and the small hunchback were hauling and struggling across the street, Old Fisher came down from the top-floor back, wherein he dwelt with his son Bob, Bob's wife and two sisters, and five children: an apartment in no way so clean as the united efforts of ten people might be expected to have made it. Old Fisher, on whose grimy face the wrinkles were deposits of mud, stopped at the open door on the first floor, and, as Dicky had done, he took a peep. Perplexed at the monstrous absence of dirt, and encouraged by the stillness, Old Fisher also ventured within. Nobody was in charge, and Old Fisher, mentally pricing the pink glass vases at threepence, made for a small chest in the corner of the room, and lifted the lid. Within lay many of Roper's tools, from among which he had that morning taken such as he might want on an emergent call to work, to carry as he tramped Curtain Road. Clearly these were the most valuable things in the place;* and, slipping a few small articles into his pockets, Old Fisher took a good double handful of the larger, and tramped upstairs with them. Presently he returned with Bob's missis, and together they started with more. As they emerged, however, there on the landing stood the little hunchback, sobbing and smearing his face with his sleeve. At sight of this new pillage he burst into sharp wails, standing impotent on the landing, his streaming eyes following the man and woman ascending before him. Old Fisher, behind, stumped the stairs with a clumsy affectation of absent-mindedness; the woman, in front, looked down, merely indifferent. Scarce were they vanished above, however, when the little hunchback heard his father and mother on the lower stairs.

CHAPTER 9

Dicky came moodily back from his dinner at Mr Weech's, plunged in mystified computation: starting with a debt of twopence, he had paid Mr Weech an excellent clock – a luxurious article in Dicky's eyes – had eaten a bloater, and had emerged from the transaction owing threepence halfpenny. Of what such a clock cost he had no notion, though he felt it must be some inconceivable sum. As Mr Weech put it, the adjustment of accounts would seem to be quite correct; but the broad fact that all had ended in increasing his debt by three halfpence, remained and perplexed him. He remembered having seen such clocks in a shop in Norton Folgate. To ask the price, in person, were but to be chased out of the shop; but they were probably ticketed, and perhaps he might ask some bystander to read the ticket. This brought the reflection that, after all, reading was a useful accomplishment on occasion: though a matter of too much time and trouble to be worth while. Dicky had never been to school; for the Elementary Education Act ran in the Jago no more than any other Act of Parliament. There was a Board School,* truly, away out of the Jago bounds, by the corner of Honey Lane, where children might go free, and where some few Jago children did go now and again, when boots where to be given away, or when tickets were to be had,* for tea, or soup, or the like. But most parents were of Josh Perrott's opinion: that school-going was a practice best never begun; for then the child was never heard of, and there was no chance of inquiries or such trouble. Not that any such inquiries were common in the Jago, or led to anything.

Meantime Dicky, minded to know if his adventure had made any stir in the house, carried his way deviously toward home. Working through the parts beyond Jago Row, he fetched round into Honey Lane, so coming at New Jago Street from the farther side. Choosing one of the houses whose backs gave on Jago Court, he slipped through the passage, and so, by the back yard, crawled through the broken fence into the court. Left and right were the fronts of houses, four a side. Before him, to the right of the narrow archway leading to Old Jago Street, was the window of his own home. He gained the back yard quietly, and at the kitchen door met Tommy Rann.

'Come on,' called Tommy. ''Ere's a barney! They're a-pitchin' into them noo 'uns – Roperses. Roperses sez Fisherses is sneaked their things. They *are* a-gittin' of it!'

From the stairs, indeed, came shouts and curses, bumps and sobs and cries. The first landing and half the stairs were full of people, men and women, Ranns and Learys together. When Ranns joined Learys it was an ill time for them they marched against; and never were they so ready and so anxious to combine as after a fight between themselves, were but some common object of attack available. Here it was. Here were these pestilent outsiders, the Ropers, assailing the reputation of the neighbourhood by complaining of being robbed. As though their mere presence in the Jago, with their furniture and their superiority, were not obnoxious enough: they must turn about and call their neighbours thieves! They had been tolerated too long already. They should now be given something for themselves, and have some of their exasperating respectability knocked off; and if, in the confusion, their portable articles of furniture and bedclothing found their way into more deserving hands – why, serve them right.

The requisite volleys of preliminary abuse having been discharged, more active operations began under cover of fresh volleys. Dicky, with Tommy Rann behind him, struggled up the stairs among legs and skirts, and saw that the Ropers, the man flushed, but the woman paler than ever, were striving to shut their door. Within, the hunchback and the baby cried, and without, those on the landing, skidding the door with their feet, pushed inward, and now began to strike and maul. Somebody seized the man's wrist, and Norah Walsh got the woman by the hair and dragged her head down. In a peep through the scuffle Dicky saw her face, ashen and sweat-beaded, in the jamb of the door, and saw Norah Walsh's red fist beat into it twice. Then somebody came striding up the stairs, and Dicky was pushed farther back. Over the shoulders of those about him, Dicky saw a tall hat, and then the head beneath it. It was the stranger he had seen in Edge Lane – the parson: active and resolute.* Norah

Walsh he took by the shoulder, and flung back among the others, and as he turned on him, the man who held Roper's wrist released it and backed off.

'What is this?' demanded the new-comer, stern and hard of face. 'What is all this?' He bent his frown on one and another about him, and, as he did it, some shrank uneasily, and on the faces of others fell the blank lack of expression that was wont to meet police inquiries in the Jago. Dicky looked to see this man beaten down, kicked and stripped. But a well-dressed stranger was so new a thing in the Jago, this one had dropped among them so suddenly, and he had withal so bold a confidence, that the Jagos stood irresolute. A toff was not a person to be attacked without due consideration. After such a person there were apt to be inquiries, with money to back them, and vengeance sharp and certain: the thing, indeed, was commonly thought too risky. And this man, so unflinchingly confident, must needs have reason for it. He might have the police at instant call* – they might be back in the Jago at the moment. And he flung them back, commanded them, cowed them with his hard, intelligent eyes, like a tamer among beasts.

'Understand this, now,' he went on, with a sharp tap of his stick on the floor. 'This is a sort of thing I will *not* tolerate in my parish – in this parish: nor in any other place where I may meet it. Go away, and try to be ashamed of yourselves – go. Go, all of you, I say, to your own homes: I shall come there and talk to you again soon. Go along, Sam Cash – you've a broken head already, I see. Take it away: I shall come and see you too.'

Those on the stairs had melted away like punished school-children. Most of the others, after a moment of averted face and muttered justification one to another, were dragging their feet, each with a hang-dog pretence of sauntering airily off from some sight no longer interesting. Sam Cash, who had already seen the stranger in the street, and was thus perhaps a trifle less startled than the others at his advent, stood, however, with some assumption of virtuous impudence, till amazed by sudden address in his own name:* whereat, clean discomfited, he ignominiously turned tail and sneaked downstairs in meaner case than the rest. How should this strange parson know him, and know his name? Plainly he must be connected with the police. He had brought out the name as pat as you please. So argued Sam Cash with his fellows in the outer street: never recalling that Jerry Gullen had called aloud to him by name, when first he observed the parson in the street; had called to him, indeed, to haste to the bashing of the Ropers; and thus had first given the stranger notice of the proceeding. But it was the way of the Jago that its mean cunning saw a mystery and a terror where simple intelligence saw there was none.

As the crowd began to break up, Dicky pushed his own door a little open behind him, and there stood on his own ground, as the others cleared off; and the hunchback ventured a peep from behind his swooning mother. 'There y'are, that's 'im!' he shouted, pointing at Dicky. "'E begun it! 'E took the clock!' Dicky instantly dropped behind his door, and shut it fast.

The invaders had all gone – the Fishers had made upstairs in the beginning – before the parson turned and entered the Ropers' room. In five minutes he emerged and strode upstairs: whence he returned, after a still shorter interval, herding before him Old Fisher and Bob Fisher's missis, sulky and reluctant, carrying tools.

And thus it was that the Reverend Henry Sturt first addressed his parishioners. The parish, besides the Jago, comprised Meakin Street and some small way beyond, and it was to this less savage district that his predecessor had confined his attention: preaching every Sunday in a stable, in an alley behind a disused shop, and distributing loaves and sixpences* to the old women who attended regularly on that account. For to go into the Jago were for him mere wasted effort. And so, indeed, the matter had been since the parish came into being.*

CHAPTER 10

When Dicky retreated from the landing and shut the door behind him, he slipped the bolt, a strong one, put there by Josh Perrott himself, possibly as an accessory to escape by the window in some possible desperate pass. For a little he listened, but no sound hinted of attack from without, and he turned to his mother.

Josh Perrott had been out since early morning, and Dicky, too, had done no more than look in for a moment in search of dinner. Hannah Perrott, grown tired of self-commiseration, felt herself neglected and aggrieved – slighted in her state of invalid privilege. So she transferred some of her pity from her sore neck to her desolate condition as misprized wife and mother, and the better to feel it, proceeded to martyrise herself, with melancholy pleasure, by a nerveless show of 'setting to rights' in the room – a domestic novelty, perfunctory as it was. Looey, still restless and weeping, she left on the bed, for, being neglected herself, it was not her mood to tend the baby; she would aggravate the relish of her sorrows in her own way. Besides, Looey had been given something to eat a long time ago, and had not eaten it yet: with her there was nothing else to do. So that now, as she dragged a rag along the grease-strewn mantelpiece, Mrs Perrott greeted Dicky: – 'There y'are, Dicky, comin' 'inderin' 'ere just when I'm a-puttin' things to rights.' And she sighed with the weight of another grievance.

Looey lay on her back, faintly and vainly struggling to turn her fearful little face from the light. Clutched in her little fist was the unclean stump of bread she had held for hours. Dicky plucked a soft piece and essayed to feed her with it, but the dry little mouth rejected the morsel, and the head turned feverishly from side to side to the sound of that novel cry. She was hot wherever Dicky touched her, and presently he said: – 'Mother, I b'lieve Looey's queer. I think she wants some med'cine.'

His mother shook her head peevishly. 'O, you an' Looey's a

noosance,' she said. 'A lot you care about *me* bein' queer, you an' yer father too, leavin' me all alone like this, an' me feelin' ready to drop, an' got the room to do an' all. I wish you'd go away an' stop 'inderin' of me like this.'

Dicky took but another look at Looey, and then slouched out. The landing was clear, and the Ropers' door was shut. He wondered what had become of the stranger with the tall hat – whether he was in the Ropers' room or not. The thought hurried him, for he feared to have that stranger asking him questions about the clock. He got out into the street, thoughtful. He had some compunctions in the matter of that clock, now. Not that he could in any reasonable way blame himself. There the clock had stood at his mercy, and by all Jago custom and ethic it was his if only he could get clear away with it. This he had done, and he had no more concern in the business, strictly speaking. Nevertheless, since he had seen the woman's face in the jamb of the door, he felt a sort of pity for her – that she should have lost her clock. No doubt she had enjoyed its possession, as, indeed, he would have enjoyed it himself, had he not had to take it instantly to Mr Weech. And his fancy wandered off in medita- tion of what he would do with a clock of his own. To begin with, of course, he would open it, and discover the secret of its works and its ticking: perhaps thereby discovering how to make a clock himself. Also he would frequently wind it up, and he would show the inside to Looey, in confidence. It would stand on the mantelpiece, and raise the social position of the family. People would come respectfully to ask the time, and he would tell them, with an air. Yes, certainly a clock must stand eminent among the things he would buy, when he had plenty of money. He must look out for more clicks: the one way to riches.

As to the Ropers, again. Bad it must be, indeed, to be deprived suddenly of a clock, after long experience of the joys it brought; and Norah Walsh had punched the woman in the face, and clawed her hair, and the woman could not fight. Dicky was sorry for her, and straightway resolved to give her another clock, or, if not a clock, something that would please her as much. He had acquired a clock in the morning; why not another in the afternoon? Failing a clock, he would try for something else, and the Ropers should have it. The resolve gave Dicky a virtuous exaltation of spirit, the reward of the philanthropist.

Again he began the prowl after likely plunder that was to be his daily industry. Meakin Street he did not try. The chandlers' and the cook-shops held nothing that might be counted a consolatory equivalent for a clock. Through the 'Posties' he reached Shoreditch High Street at once, and started.

This time his movements aroused less suspicion. In the morning he had no particular prize in view, and loitered at every shop, waiting his chance at anything portable. Now, with a more definite object, he made his promenade easily, but without stopping or lounging by shop-fronts. The thing, whatsoever it might be, must be small, handsome, and of an interesting character – at least as interesting as the clock was. It must be small, not merely for facility of concealment and removal – though these were main considerations – but because stealthy presentation were then the easier. It would have pleased Dicky to hand over his gift openly, and to bask in the thanks and the consideration it would procure. But he had been accused of stealing the clock, and an open gift would savour of admission and peace-offering, whereas in that matter stark denial was his plain course.

A roll of print stuff would not do; apples would not do; and fish was wide of his purpose. Up one side and down the other side of High Street he walked, his eyes instant for suggestion and opportunity. But all in vain. Nobody exposed clocks out of doors, and of those within not one but an attempt on it were simple madness. And of the things less desperate of access nothing was proper to the occasion: all were too large, too cheap, or too uninteresting. Oddly, Dicky feared failure more than had he been hunting for himself,

He tried farther south, in Norton Folgate. There was a shop of cheap second-hand miscellanies: saddles, razors, straps,* dumb-bells, pistols, boxing gloves, trunks, bags, and billiard-balls. Many of the things hung about the door-posts in bunches, and within all was black, as in a cave. At one door-post was a pistol. Nothing could be more interesting than a pistol – indeed it was altogether a better possession than a clock; and it was a small, handy sort of thing. Probably the Ropers would be delighted with a pistol. He stood and regarded it with much interest. There were difficulties. In the first place it was beyond his reach; and in the second, it hung by the trigger-guard on a stout cord. Just then, glancing within the shop, he perceived a pair of fiery eyes regarding him, panther-like, from the inner gloom; and he hastily resumed his walk, as the Jew shopkeeper reached the door, and watched him safely away.

Now he came to Bishopsgate Street, and here at last he chose the gift. It was at a toy-shop: a fine, flaming toy-shop, with carts, dolls, and hoops dangling above, and wooden horses standing below, guarding two baskets by the door. One contained a mixed assortment of tops, whips, boats, and woolly dogs; the other was lavishly filled with shining, round metal boxes, nobly decorated with coloured pictures,* each box with a little cranked handle. As he looked, a tune, delightfully tinkled on some instrument, was heard from within the shop. Dicky peeped. There was a lady, with a little girl at her side who was looking eagerly at just such a shining, round box in the saleswoman's hands, and it was from that box, as the saleswoman turned the handle, that the tune came. Dicky was enchanted. This – this was the thing, beyond debate: a pretty little box that would play music whenever you turned a handle. This was a thing worth any fifty clocks. Indeed it was almost as good as a regular barrel-organ, the first thing he would buy if he were rich.

There was a shop-boy in charge of the goods outside the window, and his eyes were on Dicky. So Dicky whistled absently, and strolled carelessly along. He swung behind a large waggon, crossed the road, and sought a convenient doorstep; for his mind was made up, and his business was now to sit down before the toy-shop, and wait his opportunity.

A shop had been boarded up after a fire, and from its doorstep one could command a perfect view of the toy-shop across the broad thoroughfare with its crowded traffic – could sit, moreover, safe from interference. Here he took his seat, secure from the notice of the guardian shop-boy, whose attention was given to passengers on his own side. The little girl, gripping the new toy in her hand, came out at her mother's side and trotted off. For a moment Dicky reflected that the box could be easily snatched. But after all the little girl had but one: whereas the shopwoman had many, and at best could play on no more than one at a time.

He resumed his watch of the shop-boy, confident that sooner or later a chance would come. A woman stopped to ask the price of something, and Dicky had half crossed the road ere the boy had begun to answer. But the answer was short, and the boy's attention was released too soon.

At last the shopwoman called the boy within, and Dicky darted across – not directly, but so as to arrive invisibly at the side next the basket of music boxes. A quick glance behind him, a snatch at the box with the reddest picture, and a dash into the traffic did it.

The dash would not have been called for but for the sudden re-appearance of the shop-boy ere the box had vanished amid the intricacies of Dicky's jacket. Dicky was fast, but the boy was little slower, and was, moreover, bigger, and stronger on his legs; and Dicky reached the other pavement and turned the next corner into Widegate Street, the pursuer scarce ten yards behind.

It was now that he first experienced 'hot beef' – which is the Jago idiom denoting the plight of one harried by the cry 'Stop thief'. Down Widegate Street, across Sandys Row and into Raven Row he ran his best, clutching the hem of his jacket and the music box that lay within. Crossing Sandys Row a loafing lad shouldered against the shop-boy, and Dicky was grateful, for he made it a gain of several yards.

But others had joined in the hunt, and Dicky for the first time began to fear. This was a bad day – twice already he had been chased; and now – it was bad. He thought little more, for a stunning fear fell upon him: the fear of the hunted, that calculates nothing, and is measured by no apprehension of consequences. He remembered that he must avoid Spitalfields Market, full of men who would stop him; and he knew that in many places where a man would be befriended many would make a virtue of stopping a boy. To the right along Bell Lane he made an agonised burst of speed, and for a while he saw not nor remembered anything; heard no more than dreadful shouts drawing nearer his shoulders, felt only the fear. But he could not last. Quick enough when fresh, he was tiny and ill fed, and now he felt his legs trembling and his wind going. Something seemed to beat on the back of his head, till he wondered madly if it were the shop-boy with a stick. He turned corners, and chose his way by mere instinct, ashen-faced, staring, open-mouthed. How soon would he give in, and drop? A street more – half a street – ten yards? Rolling and tripping, he turned one last corner and almost fell against a vast, fat, unkempt woman whose clothes slid from her shoulders.

"Ere y' are, boy,' said the woman, and flung him by the shoulder through the doorway before which she stood.

He was saved at his extremity, for he could never have reached the street's end. The woman who had done it (probably she had boys of her own on the crook) filled the entrance with her frowsy bulk, and the chase straggled past. Dicky caught the stair-post for a moment's support, and then staggered out at the back of the house. He gasped, he panted, things danced blue before him, but still he clutched his jacket hem and the music box lying within. The back door gave on a cobble-paved court, with other doors, two coster's barrows, and a few dusty fowls. Dicky sat on a step where a door was shut, and rested his head against the frame.

The beating in his head grew slower and lighter, and presently he could breathe with no fear of choking. He rose and moved off, still panting, and feeble in the legs. The court ended in an arched passage, through which he gained the street beyond. Here he had but to turn to the left, and he was in Brick Lane, and thence all was clear to the Old Jago. Regaining his breath and his confidence as he went, he bethought him of the Jago Row retreat, where he might examine his prize at leisure, embowered amid trucks and barrows. Thither he pushed his way, and soon, in the shade of the upturned barrow, he brought out the music box. Bright and shiny, it had taken no damage in the flight, though on his hands he found scratches, and on his shins bruises, got he knew not how. On the top of the box was the picture of a rosy little boy in crimson presenting a scarlet nosegay to a rosy little girl in pink, while a red brick mansion filled the distance and solidified the composition. The brilliant hoop that made the sides (silver, Dicky was convinced) was stamped in patterns, and the little brass handle was an irresistible temptation. Dicky climbed a truck, and looked about him, peeping from beside the loose fence-plank. Then, seeing nobody very near, he muffled the box as well as he could in his jacket, and turned the handle.

This was indeed worth all the trouble. *Gently Does the Trick* * was the tune, and Dicky, with his head aside and his ear on the bunch of jacket that covered the box, listened: his lips parted, his eyes seeking illimitable space. He played the tune through, and played it again, and then growing reckless, played it with the box unmuffled, till he was startled by a bang on the fence from without. It was but a passing boy with a stick, but Dicky was sufficiently disturbed to abandon his quarters and take his music elsewhere.

What he longed to do was to take it home and play it to Looey, but that was out of the question: he remembered the watch. But there was Jerry Gullen's canary, and him Dicky sought and found. Canary blinked solemnly when the resplendent box was flashed in his eyes, and set his ears back and forward as, muffled again in Dicky's jacket, it tinkled out its tune.

Tommy Rann should not see it, lest he prevail over its beneficent dedication to the Ropers. Truly, as it was, Dicky's resolution was hard to abide by. The thing acquired at such a cost of patience, address, hard flight, and deadly fear was surely his by right – as surely, quite, as the clock had been. And such a thing he might never touch again. But he put by the temptation manfully, and came out by Jerry Gullen's front door. He would look no more on the music box, beautiful as it was: he would convey it to the Ropers before temptation came again.

It was not easy to devise likely means. Their door was shut fast, of course. For a little while he favoured the plan of setting the box against the threshold, knocking, and running off. But an opportunity might arise of doing the thing in a way to give him some glimpse of the Ropers' delight, an indulgence he felt entitled to. So he waited a little, listened a little, and at last came out into the street, and loafed.

It was near six o'clock, and a smell of bloater hung about Jerry Gullen's door and window; under the raised sash Jerry Gullen, close-cropped and foxy of face, smoked his pipe, sprawled his elbows, and contemplated the world. Dicky, with the music box stowed out of sight, looked as blank of design and as destitute of possession as he could manage; for there were loafers near Mother Gapp's, loafers at the Luck Row corner – at every corner – and loafers by the 'Posties', all laggard of limb and alert of eye. He had just seen a child, going with an empty beer can, thrown down, robbed of his coppers and a poor old top, and kicked away in helpless tears; and the incident was commonplace enough, or many would have lacked pocket-money. Whosoever was too young, too old, or too weak to fight for it must keep what he had well hidden, in the Jago.

Down the street came Billy Leary, big, flushed and limping,

and hanging to a smaller man by a fistful of his coat on the shoulder. Dicky knew the small man for a good toy-getter – (which = watch stealer) – and judged he had had a good click, the proceeds whereof Billy Leary was battening upon in beershops. For Billy Leary rarely condescended to anything less honourable than bashing, and had not yet fallen so low as to go about stealing for himself. His missis brought many to the cosh, and his chief necessity – another drink – he merely demanded of the nearest person with the money to buy it, on pain of bashing. Or he walked into the nearest public-house, selected the fullest pot, and spat in it: a ceremony that deprived the purchaser of further interest in the beer, and left it at his own disposal. There were others, both Ranns and Learys, who pursued a similar way of life; but Billy Leary was biggest among them – big men not being common in the Jago – and rarely came to a difficulty: as, however, he did once come, having invaded the pot of a stranger, who turned out to be a Mile End pugilist exploring Shoreditch. It was not well for any Jago who had made a click to have Billy Leary know of it; for then the clicker was apt to be sought out, clung to, and sucked dry; possibly bashed as well, when nothing more was left, if Billy Leary were still but sober enough for the work.

Dicky gazed after the man with interest. It was he whom his father was to fight in a week or so – perhaps in a few days: on the first Sunday, indeed, that Leary should be deemed fit enough. How much of the limp was due to yesterday's disaster and how much to today's beer, Dicky could not judge. But there seemed little reason to look for a long delay before the fight.

As Dicky turned away a man pushed a large truck round the corner from Edge Lane, and on the footpath beside it walked the parson, calm as ever, with black clothes and tall hat, whole and unsoiled. He had made himself known in the Jago in the course of that afternoon. He had traversed it from end to end, street by street and alley by alley. His self-possession, his readiness, his unbending firmness, abashed and perplexed the Jagos, and his appearance just as the police had left could but convince them that he must have some mysterious and potent connection with the force. He had attempted very little in the way of domiciliary visiting, being content for the time to see his parish, and speak here a word and there another with his parishioners. An encounter with Kiddo Cook did as much as anything toward securing him a proper deference. In his second walk through Old Jago Street, as he neared the Feathers, he was aware of a bunch of grinning faces pressed against the bar window, and as he came abreast, forth stepped Kiddo Cook from the door, impudently affable, smirking and ducking with mock obsequiousness, and offering a quart pot.*

'An' 'ow jer find jerself, sir?' he asked, with pantomime cordiality. 'Hof'ly shockin' these 'ere lower classes, ain't they? Er – yus; disgustin', weally. Er – might I – er – prepose – er – a little refreshment? Ellow me.'

The parson, grimly impassive, heard him through, took the pot, and instantly jerking it upward, shot the beer, a single splash, into Kiddo's face. 'There are things I must teach you, I see, my man,' he said, without moving a muscle, except to return the pot.

Kiddo Cook, coughing, drenched and confounded, took the pot instinctively and backed to Mother Gapp's door, while the bunch of faces at the bar window tossed and rolled in a joyous ecstasy: the ghost whereof presently struggled painfully among Kiddo's own dripping features, as he realised the completeness of his defeat, and the expedience of a patient grin. The parson went calmly on.

Before this, indeed when he left the Ropers' room, and just after Dicky had started out, he had looked in at the Perrotts' quarters to speak about the clock. But plainly no clock was there, and Mrs Perrott's flaccid indignation at the suggestion, and her unmistakable ignorance of the affair, decided him to carry the matter no further, at any rate for the present. Moreover, the little hunchback's tale was inconclusive. He had seen no clock in Dicky's possession – had but met him on the stairs with a bulging jacket. The thing might be suspicious, but the new parson knew better than to peril his influence by charging where he could not convict. So he duly commiserated Hannah Perrott's troubles, suggested that the baby seemed unwell and had better be taken to a doctor, and went his way about the Jago.

Now he stopped the truck by Dicky's front door and mounted to the Ropers' room. For he had seen that the Jago was no place for them now, and had himself found them a suitable room away by Dove Lane. And so, emboldened by his company, the Ropers came forth, and with the help of the man who had brought the truck, carried down the pieces of their bedstead, a bundle of bedding, the two chairs, the pink vases, and the strip of old carpet, and piled them on the truck with the few more things that were theirs.

Dicky, with his hand on the music box in the lining of his jacket, sauntered up by the tail of the truck, and, waiting his chance, plunged his gift under the bundle of bedding, and left it there. But the little hunchback's sharp eyes were jealously on him, and 'Look there!' he squealed, ''e put 'is 'and in the truck an' took somethink!'

'Ye lie!' answered Dicky, indignant and hurt, but cautiously backing off; 'I ain't got nothink.' He spread his hands and opened his jacket in proof. 'Think I got yer bloomin' bedstead?'

He had nothing, it was plain. In fact, at the tail of the truck there was nothing he could easily have moved at all, certainly nothing he could have concealed. So the rest of the little removal was hurried, for heads were now at windows, the loafers began to draw about the truck, and trouble might break out at any moment: indeed, the Ropers could never have ventured from their room but for the general uneasy awe of the parson. For nothing was so dangerous in the Jago as to impugn its honesty. To rob another was reasonable and legitimate, and to avoid being robbed, so far as might be, was natural and proper. But to accuse anybody of a theft was unsportsmanlike, a foul outrage, a shameful abuse, a thing unpardonable. You might rob a man, bash a man, even kill a man; but to 'take away his character'* – even when he had none – was to draw down the execrations of the whole Jago; while to assail the pure fame of the place – to 'give the street a bad name' – this was to bring the Jago howling and bashing about your ears.

The truck moved off at last, amid murmurings, mutterings, and grunts from the onlookers. The man of the truck pulled, Roper shoved behind, and his wife, with her threadbare decency and her meagre, bruised face, carried the baby, while the hunchbacked boy went by her side. All this under convoy of the Reverend Henry Sturt.

A little distance gave more confidence to a few, and, when the group had reached within a score of yards of Edge Lane, there came a hoot or two, a 'Yah!' and other less spellable sounds, expressive of contempt and defiance. Roper glanced back nervously, but the rest held on their way regardless. Then came a brickbat, which missed the woman by very little and struck the truck wheel. At this the parson stopped and turned on his heel, and Cocko Harnwell, the flinger, drove his hands into his breeches pockets and affected an interest in Mother Gapp's window; till, perceiving the parson's eyes directed sternly upon him, and the parson's stick rising to point at him, he ingloriously turned tail and scuttled into Jago Court.

And so the Ropers left the Jago. Dove Lane was but a stone's-throw ahead when some of the load shifted, and the truck was stopped to set the matter right. The chest was pushed back, and the bedding was lifted to put against it, and so the musical box came to light. Roper picked it up and held it before the vicar's eyes. 'Look at that, sir,' he said. 'You'll witness I know nothing of it, won't you? It ain't mine, an' I never saw it before. It's bin put in for spite to put a theft on us. When they come for it you'll bear me out, sir, won't you? That was the Perrott boy as was put up to do that, I'll be bound. When he was behind the truck.'

But nobody came for Dicky's gift, and in the Jago twilight Dicky vainly struggled to whistle the half-remembered tune, and to persuade himself that he was not sorry that the box was gone.

Josh Perrott reached home late for tea but in good humour. He had spent most of the day at the Bag of Nails, dancing attendance on the High Mobsmen. Those of the High Mob* were the flourishing practitioners* in burglary, the mag,* the mace,* and the broads,* with an outer fringe of such dippers – such pickpockets – as could dress well, welshers,* and snidesmen.* These, the grandees of rascality, lived in places far from the Jago, and some drove in gigs and pony traps. But they found the Bag of Nails a convenient and secluded exchange and house of call,* and there they met, made appointments, designed villainies, and tossed for sovereigns: deeply reverenced by the admiring Jagos, among whom no ambition flourished but this – to become also of these resplendent ones. It was of these that old Beveridge had spoken one day to Dicky, in language the child but half understood. The old man sat on a curb in view of the Bag of Nails, and smoked a blackened bit of clay pipe. He hauled Dicky to his side, and, pointing with his pipe, said: – 'See that man with the furs?'

'What?' Dicky replied. Mean 'im in the ice-cream coat,* smokin' a cigar? Yus.'

'And the other with the brimmy* tall hat, and the red face, and the umbrella?'

'Yus.'

'What are they?'

''Igh mob. 'Ooks. Toffs.'

'Right. Now, Dicky Perrott, you Jago whelp, look at them – look hard. Some day, if you're clever – cleverer than anyone in the Jago now – if you're only scoundrel enough, and brazen enough, and lucky enough – one of a thousand – maybe you'll be like them: bursting with high living, drunk when you like, red and pimply. There it is – that's your aim in life – there's your pattern. Learn to read and write, learn all you can, learn cunning, spare nobody and stop at nothing, and perhaps – ' he waved his hand toward the Bag of Nails. 'It's the best the world has for you, for the Jago's got you, and that's the only way out,* except gaol and the gallows. So do your devilmost, or God help you, Dicky Perrott – though he won't: for the Jago's got you!'

Old Beveridge had eccentric talk and manners, and the Jago regarded him as a trifle 'barmy', though anything but a fool. So that Dicky troubled little to sift the meaning of what he said.

Josh Perrott's mission among the High Mob had been to discover some Mobsman who might be disposed to back him in the fight with Billy Leary. For though a private feud was the first cause of the turn-up, still business must never be neglected, and a feud or anything else that could produce money must be made to produce it, and when a fight of exceptional merit is placed before spectators, it is but fair that they should pay for their diversion.

But few High Mobsmen were at the Bag of Nails that day. Sunday was the day of the chief gatherings of the High Mob: Sunday the market day, so to speak, of the Jago, when such rent as was due weekly was paid (most of the Jago rents were paid daily and nightly) and other accounts were settled or fought out. Moreover, the High Mob were perhaps a trifle shy of the Jago at the time of a faction fight; and one was but just over, and that cut short at a third of the usual span of days.* So that Josh waited long and touted vainly, till a patron arrived who knew him of old; who had employed him, indeed, as 'minder' – which means a protector or a bully, as you please to regard it – on a racecourse adventure involving bodily risk. On this occasion Josh had earned his wages with hard knocks given and taken, and his employer had conceived a high and thankful opinion of his capacity. Wherefore he listened now to the tale of the coming fight, and agreed to provide something in the way of stakes, and to put something on for Josh himself: looking for his own profit to the bets he might make at favourable odds with his friends. For Billy Leary was notorious as being near prime ruffian of the Jago, while Josh's reputation was neither so evil nor so wide. And so it was settled, and Josh came pleased to his tea; for assuredly Billy Leary would have no difficulty in finding another notable of the High Mob to cover the stakes.

Dicky was at home, sitting by Looey on the bed; and when he called his father it seemed pretty plain to Josh that the baby was out of sorts. 'She's rum about the eyes,' he said to his wife. 'Blimy if she don't look as though she was goin' to squint.'

Josh was never particularly solicitous as to the children, but he saw that they were fed and clothed – perhaps by mere force of the habit of his more reputable days of plastering. He had brought home tripe, rolled in paper, and stuffed into his coat pocket, to make a supper on the strength of the day's stroke of business. When this tripe was boiled, he and Dicky essayed to drive morsels into Looey's mouth, and to wash them down with beer; but to no end but choking rejection. Whereat Josh decided that she must go to the dispensary in the morning. And in the morning he took her, with Dicky at his heels; for not only did his wife still nurse her neck, but in truth she feared to venture abroad.

The dispensary was no charitable institution,* but a shop so labelled in Meakin Street, one of half a dozen such kept by a medical man who lived away from them, and bothered himself as little about them as was consistent with banking the takings and signing the death-certificates. A needy young student, whose sole qualification was cheapness, was set to do the business of each place, and the uniform price for advice and medicine was sixpence. But there was a deal of professional character in the blackened and gilt-lettered front windows, and the sixpences came by hundreds. For hospital letters* but rarely came Meakin Street way. Such as did were mostly in the hands of tradesmen, who subscribed* for the purpose of getting them, and gave them to their best customers, as was proper and business-like. And so the dispensary flourished, and the needy young student grew shifty and callous, and no doubt there were occasional faith-cures. Indeed, cures of simple science were not at all impossible. For there was always a good supply of two drugs in the place – Turkey rhubarb and sulphuric acid: both very useful, both very cheap, and both going very far in varied preparation, properly handled. An ounce or two of sulphuric acid, for instance, costing something fractional, dilutes with water into many gallons of physic. Excellent medicines they made too, and balanced each other very well by reason of their opposite effects.* But indeed they were not all, for sometimes there were two or three other drugs in hand,* interfering, perhaps troublesomely, with the simple division of therapeutics into the two provinces of rhubarb and sulphuric acid.

Business was brisk at the dispensary: several were waiting, and medicine and advice were going at the rate of two minutes for sixpence. Looey's case was not so clear as most of the others: she could not describe its symptoms succinctly, as 'a pain here', or 'a tight feeling there'. She did but lie heavily, staring blankly upward (she did not mind the light now), with the little cast in her eyes, and repeat her odd little wail; and Dicky and his father could tell very little. The young student had a passing thought that he might have known a trifle more of the matter if he had had time to turn up Ross on nerve and brain troubles* – were such a proceeding consistent with the dignity of the dispensary; but straightway assigning the case to the rhubarb province, made up a powder, ordered Josh to keep the baby quiet, and pitched his sixpence among the others, well within the two minutes.

And faith in the dispensary was strengthened, for indeed Looey seemed a little better after the powder; and she was fed with spoonfuls of a fluid bought at a chandler's shop, and called milk.*

CHAPTER 12

'Dicky Perrott, come 'ere,' said Mr Aaron Weech in a voice of sad rebuke, a few days later. 'Come 'ere, Dicky Perrott.'

He shook his head solemnly as he stooped. Dicky slouched up.

'What was that you found the other day an' didn't bring to me?'

'Nuffin'.' Dicky withdrew a step.

'It's no good you a-tellin' me that, Dicky Perrott, when I know better. You know very well you can't pervent me knowin'.' His little eyes searched Dicky's face, and Dicky sulkily shifted his own gaze. 'You're a wicked, ungrateful young 'ound, an' I've a good mind to tell a p'liceman to find out where you got that clock. Come 'ere now – don't you try runnin' away. Wot! after me a-takin' you in when you was 'ungry, an' givin' you cawfy an' cake, an' good advice like a father, an' a bloater an' all, an' you owin' me thrippence a'peny besides, then you goes an' – an' takes yer findin's somewhere else!'

'I never!' protested Dicky stoutly. But Mr Weech's cunning, equal to a shrewd guess that since his last visit Dicky had probably had another 'find', and quick to detect a lie, was slack to perceive a truth.

'Now don't you go an' add on a wicked lie to yer sinful ungratefulness, wotever you do,' he said, severely. 'That's wuss, an' I alwis know. Doncher know the little 'ymn?* –

> An' 'im as does one fault at fust
> An' lies to 'ide it, makes it two.

It's bad enough to be ungrateful to me as is bin so kind to you, an' it's wuss to break the fust commandment.* If the bloater don't inflooence you, the 'oly 'ymn ought. 'Ow would you like me to go an' ask yer father for that thrippence a'peny you owe me? That's wot I'll 'ave to do if you don't mind.'

Dicky would not have liked it at all, as his frightened face testified.

'Then find somethink an' pay it at once, an' then I won't. I won't be 'ard on you, if you'll be a good boy. But don't git playin' no more tricks – 'cos I'll know all about 'em. Now go an' find somethink quick.' And Dicky went.

CHAPTER 13

Ten days after his first tour of the Old Jago, the Reverend Henry Sturt first preached in the parish church made of a stable, in an alley behind Meakin Street, but few yards away, though beyond sight and sound of the Jago. There, that Sunday morning was a morning of importance, a time of excitement, for the fight between Billy Leary and Josh Perrott was to come off in Jago Court. The assurance that there was money in the thing was a sovereign liniment for Billy Leary's bruises – for they were but bruises – and he hastened to come by that money, lest it melt by caprice of the backers, or the backers themselves fall at unlucky odds with the police. He made little of Josh Perrott, his hardness and known fighting power notwithstanding. For was there not full a stone and a half between their weights? And had Billy not four or five inches the better in height and a commensurate advantage in reach? And Billy Leary's own hardness and fighting power were well proved enough.

It was past eleven o'clock. The weekly rents – for the week forthcoming – had been extracted, or partly extracted, or scuffled over. Old Poll Rann, who had made money in sixty-five years of stall-farming* and iniquity, had made the rounds of the six houses she rented, to turn out the tenants of the night who were disposed to linger. Many had already stripped themselves to their rags at pitch-and-toss* in Jago Court; and the game still went busily on in the crowded area and in overflow groups in Old Jago Street; and men found themselves deprived, not merely of the money for that day's food and that night's lodging, but even of the last few pence set by to back a horse for Tuesday's race. A little-regarded fight or two went on here and there as usual, and on kerbs and doorsteps sat women, hideous at all ages, filling the air with the rhetoric of the Jago.

Presently down from Edge Lane and the 'Posties' came the High Mobsmen, swaggering in check suits and billycocks, gold chains and lumpy rings: stared at, envied, and here and there pointed out by name or exploit. 'Him as done the sparks in from Regent Street for nine centuries o' quids';* 'Him as done five stretch* for a snide bank bill an' they never found the oof'; 'Him as maced the bookies in France an' shot the nark in the boat'; and so forth. And the High Mob being come, the fight was due.

Of course, a fight merely as a fight was no great matter of interest: the thing was too common. But there was money on this; and again, it was no common thing to find Billy Leary defied, still less to find him challenged. Moreover, the thing had a Rann and Leary complexion, and it arose out of the battle of less than a fortnight back. So that Josh Perrott did not lack for partisans, though not a Rann believed he could stand long before Billy Leary. Billy's cause, too, had lost some popularity because it had been reported that Sally Green, in hospital, had talked of 'summonsing' Norah Walsh in the matter of her mangled face: a scandalous device to overreach, a piece of foul practice repugnant to all proper feeling; more especially for such a distinguished Jago as Sally Green – so well able to take care of herself. But all this was nothing as affecting the odds. They ruled at three to one on Billy Leary, with few takers, and went to four to one before the fight began.

Josh Perrott had been strictly sober for a full week. And the family had lived better, for he had brought meat home each day. Now he sat indifferently at the window of his room, and looked out at the crowd in Jago Court till such time as he might be wanted. He had not been out of the room that morning: he was saving his energy for Billy Leary.

As for Dicky, he had scarce slept for excitement. For days he had enjoyed consideration among his fellows on account of this fight. Now he shook and quivered, and nothing relieved his agitation but violent exertion. So he rushed downstairs a hundred times to see if the High Mob were coming, and back to report that they were not. At last he saw their overbearing checks, and tore upstairs, face before knees, with "'Ere they are, father! 'Ere they are! They're comin' down the street, father!' and danced frenzied about the room and the landing.

Presently Jerry Gullen and Kiddo Cook came, as seconds, to take Josh out, and then Dicky quieted a little externally, though he was bursting at the chest and throat, and his chin jolted his teeth together uncontrollably. Josh dragged off his spotted coat and waistcoat and flung them on the bed, and then was helped out of his ill-mended blue shirt. He gave a hitch to his trousers-band, tightened his belt, and was ready.

'Ta-ta, ol' gal,' he said to his wife, with a grin; 'back agin soon.'

'With a bob or two for ye,' added Kiddo Cook, grinning likewise.

Hannah Perrott sat pale and wistful, with the baby on her knees. Through the morning she had sat so, wretched and helpless, sometimes putting her face in her hands, sometimes breaking out hopelessly: – 'Don't, Josh, don't – good Gawd, Josh, I wish you wouldn't!' or 'Josh, Josh, I wish I was dead!' Josh had fought before, it was true, and more than once, but then she had learned of the matter afterward. This preparation and long waiting were another thing. Once she had even exclaimed that she would go with him – though she meant nothing.

Now, as Josh went out at the door, she bent over Looey and hid her face again. 'Good luck, father,' called Dicky, 'go it!' Though the words would hardly pass his throat, and he struggled to believe that he had no fear for his father.

No sooner was the door shut than he rushed to the window, though Josh could not appear in Jago Court for three or four minutes yet. The sash-line was broken, and the window had been propped open with a stick. In his excitement Dicky dislodged the stick, and the sash* came down on his head, but he scarce felt the blow, and readjusted the stick with trembling hands, regardless of the bruise rising under his hair.

'Aincher goin' to look, mother?' he asked. 'Wontcher 'old up Looey?'

But his mother would not look. As for Looey, she looked at nothing. She had been taken to the dispensary once again, and now lay drowsy and dull, with little more movement than a general shudder and a twitching of the face at long intervals. The little face itself was thinner and older than ever: horribly flea-bitten still, but bloodlessly pale. Mrs Perrott had begun to think Looey was ailing for something; thought it might be measles or whooping-cough* coming, and complained that children were a continual worry.

Dicky hung head and shoulders out of the window, clinging to the broken sill and scraping feverishly at the wall with his toes. Jago Court was fuller than ever. The tossing went on, though now with more haste, that most might be made of the remaining time. A scuffle still persisted in one corner. Some stood to gaze at the High Mob, who, to the number of eight or ten, stood in an exalted group over against the back fences of New Jago Street; but the thickest knot was about Cocko Harnwell's doorstep, whereon sat Billy Leary, his head just visible through the press about him, waiting to keep his appointment.

Then a close group appeared at the archway, and pushed into the crowd, which made way at its touch, the disturbed tossers pocketing their coppers, but the others busily persisting, with no more than a glance aside between the spins. Josh Perrott's cropped head and bare shoulders marked the centre of the group, and as it came, another group moved out from Cocko Harnwell's doorstep, with Billy Leary's tall bulk shining pink and hairy in its midst.

''E's in the court, mother,' called Dicky, scraping faster with his toes.

The High Mobsmen moved up toward the middle of the court, and some from the two groups spread and pushed back the crowd. Still half a dozen couples, remote by the walls, tossed and tossed faster than ever, moving this way and that as the crowd pressed.

Now there was an irregular space of bare cobble stones and house refuse, five or six yards across, in the middle of Jago Court, and all round it the shouting crowd was packed tight, those at the back standing on sills and hanging to fences. Every window was a clump of heads, and women yelled savagely or cheerily down and across. The two groups were merged in the press at each side of the space, Billy Leary and Josh Perrott in front of each, with his seconds.

'Naa then, any more 'fore they begin?' bawled a High Mobsman, turning about among his fellows. 'Three to one on the big 'un – three to one! 'Ere, I'll give fours – four to one on Leary! Fourer one! Fourer one!'

But they shook their heads; they would wait a little. Leary and Perrott stepped out. The last of the tossers stuffed away his coppers, and sought for a hold on the fence.

'They're a-sparrin', mother!' cried Dicky, pale and staring, elbows and legs a-work, till he was like to pitch out of window.

From his mother there but jerked a whimpering sob, which he did not hear.

The sparring was not long. There was little of subtlety in the milling of the Jago: mostly no more than a rough application of the main hits and guards,* with much rushing and ruffianing. What there was of condition in the two men was Josh's: smaller and shorter, he had a certain hard brownness of hide that Leary, in his heavy opulence of flesh, lacked; and there was a horny quality in his face and hands that reminded the company of his boast of invulnerability to anything milder than steel. Also his breadth of chest was great. Nevertheless all odds seemed against him, by reason of Billy Leary's size, reach, and fighting record.

The men rushed together, and Josh was forced back by weight. Leary's great fists, left and right, shot into his face with smacking reports, but left no mark on the leathery skin, and Josh, fighting for the body, drove his knuckles into the other's ribs with a force that jerked a thick grunt from Billy's lips at each blow.

There was a roar of shouts. 'Go it, father! Fa—ther! Fa—ther!' Dicky screamed from the window, till his voice broke in his throat and he coughed himself livid. The men were at holds, and swaying this way and that over the uneven stones. Blood ran copiously from Billy Leary's nose over his mouth and chin, and, as they turned, Dicky saw his father spit away a tooth over Leary's shoulder. They clipped and hauled to and fro, each striving to break the other's foothold. Then Perrott stumbled at a hole, lost his feet, and went down, with Leary on top.

Cheers and yells rent the air, as each man was taken to his own side by his seconds. Dicky let go the sill and turned to his mother, wild of eye, breathless with broken chatter.

'Father 'it 'im on the nose, mother, like that – 'is ribs is goin' black where father pasted 'em – 'e was out o' breath fust – there's blood all over 'is face, mother – father would 'a' chucked 'im over if 'e 'adn't tumbled in a 'ole – father 'it 'im twice on the jore – 'e – O!'

Dicky was back again on the sill, kicking and shouting, for time was called, and the two men rushed again into a tangled knot. But the close strife was short. Josh had but closed to spoil his man's wind, and, leaving his head to take care of itself, stayed till he had driven left and right on the mark, and then got back. Leary came after him, gasping and blowing already, and

Josh feinted a lead and avoided, bringing Leary round on his heel and off again in chase. Once more Josh met him, drove at his ribs, and got away out of reach. Leary's wind was going fast, and his partisans howled savagely at Josh – perceiving his tactics – taunting him with running away, daring him to stand and fight. 'I'll take that four to one,' called a High Mobsman to him who had offered the odds in the beginning. 'I'll stand a quid on Perrott!'

'Not with me you won't,' the other answered. 'Evens, if you like.'

'Right. Done at evens, a quid.'

Perrott, stung at length by the shouts from Leary's corner, turned on Billy and met him at full dash. He was himself puffing by this time, though much less than his adversary, and, at the cost of a heavy blow (which he took on his forehead), he visited Billy's ribs once more.

Both men were grunting and gasping now, and the sound of blows was as of the confused beating of carpets. Dicky, who had been afflicted to heart-burst by his father's dodging and running, which he mistook for simple flight, now broke into excited speech once more: –

'Father's 'it 'im on the jore ag'in' – 'is eye's a-bungin' up – *Go it, father, bash 'i-i-i-m!* Father's landin' 'im – 'e—'

Hannah Perrott crept to the window and looked. She saw the foul Jago mob, swaying and bellowing about the shifting edge of an open patch, in the midst whereof her husband and Billy Leary, bruised, bloody and gasping, fought and battered infuriately; and she crept back to the bed and bent her face on Looey's unclean little frock: till a fit of tense shuddering took the child, and the mother looked up again.

Without, the round ended. For a full minute the men took and gave knock for knock, and then Leary, wincing from another body-blow, swung his right desperately on Perrott's ear, and knocked him over.

Exulting shouts rose from the Leary faction, and the blow struck Dicky's heart still. But Josh was up almost before Kiddo Cook reached him, and Dicky saw a wide grin on his face as he came to his corner. The leathery toughness of the man, and the advantage it gave him, now grew apparent. He had endured to the full as much and as hard punching as had his foe – even more, and harder; once he had fallen on the broken cobble-stones with all Leary's weight on him; and once he had been knocked down on them. But, except for the sweat that ran over his face and down his back, and for a missing front tooth and the lip it had cut, he showed little sign of the struggle; while Leary's left eye was a mere slit in a black wen, his nose was a beaten mass, which had ensanguined him (and indeed Josh) from crown to waist, and his chest and flanks were a mottle of bruises.

'Father's awright, mother – I see 'im laughin'! And 'e's smashed Leary's nose all over 'is face!'

Up again they sprang for the next round, Perrott active and daring, Leary cautious and a trifle stiff. Josh rushed in and struck at the tender ribs once more, took two blows callously on his head, and sent his left at the nose, with a smack as of a flail on water. With that Leary rushed like a bull, and Josh was driven and battered back, for the moment without response. But he ducked, and slipped away, and came again, fresh and vicious. And now it was seen that Perrott's toughness of hand was lasting. Leary's knuckles were raw, cut, and flayed, and took little good by the shock when they met the other's stubborn muzzle; while Josh still flung in his corneous fists, hard and lasting as a bag of bullets.

But suddenly, stooping to reach the mark once more, Josh's foot turned on a projecting stone, and he floundered forward into Billy's arms. Like a flash his neck was clipped in the big man's left arm: Josh Perrott was in chancery. Quick and hard Leary pounded the imprisoned head, while Jerry Gullen and Kiddo Cook danced distracted and dismayed, and the crowd whooped and yelled.

Dicky hung delirious over the sill, and shrieked he knew not what. He saw his father fighting hard at the back and ribs with both hands, and Leary hammering his face in a way to make pulp of an ordinary mazzard. Then suddenly Josh Perrott's right hand shot up from behind, over Leary's shoulder, and gripped him at the chin. Slowly, with tightened muscles, he forced his man back over his bent knee, Leary clinging and swaying, but impotent to struggle. Then, with an extra wrench from Josh, up came Leary's feet from the ground, higher, higher, till suddenly Josh flung him heavily over, heels up, and dropped on him with all his weight.

The Ranns roared again. Josh was up in a moment, sitting on Kiddo Cook's knee, and taking a drink from a bottle. Billy Leary lay like a man fallen from a house-top. His seconds turned him on his back, and dragged him to his corner. There he lay limp and senseless, and there was a cut at the back of his head.

The High Mobsman who held the watch waited for half a minute and then called 'Time!' Josh Perrott stood up, but Billy Leary was knocked out of knowledge, and heard not. He was beaten.

Josh Perrott was involved in a howling, dancing crowd, and was pushed, grinning, this way and that, slapped on the back, and offered drinks. In the outskirts the tossers, inveterate, pulled out their pence and resumed their game.

Dicky spun about, laughing, flushed, and elated, and as soon as the door was distinct to his dazzled sight, he ran off downstairs. His mother, relieved and even pleased, speculated as to what money the thing might bring. She put the baby on the bed, and looked from the window.

Josh, in the crowd, shouted and beckoned her, pointing and tapping his bare shoulder. He wanted his clothes. She gathered together the shirt, the coat, and the waistcoat, and hurried downstairs. Looey could come to no harm lying on the bed for a few minutes. And, indeed, Hannah Perrott felt that she would be a person of distinction in the crowd, and was not sorry to have an excuse for going out.

'Three cheers for the missis!' sang out Kiddo Cook as she came through the press. 'I said 'e'd 'ave a bob or two for you, didn't I?' Josh Perrott, indeed, was rich – a capitalist of five pounds. For a sovereign a side had been put up, and his backer had put on a sovereign for him at three to one. So that now it became him to stand beer to many sympathisers. Also, he felt that the missis should have some part in the celebration, for was it not her injury that he had avenged on Sally Green's brother? So Hannah Perrott, pleased though timorous, was hauled away with the rest to Mother Gapp's.

Here she sat by Josh's side for an hour. Once or twice she thought of Looey, but with native inertness she let the thought slip. Perhaps Dicky would be back, and at any rate it was hard if she must not take half an hour's relaxation once in a way. At last came Dicky, urgent perplexity in his face, looking in at the door. Josh, minded to be generous all round, felt for a penny.

'Mother,' said Dicky, plucking at her arm, 'Pigeony Poll's at 'ome, nussin' Looey; she told me to tell you to come at once.'

Pigeony Poll? What right had she in the room? The ghost of Hannah Perrott's respectability rose in resentment. She supposed she must go. She arose, mystified, and went, with Dicky at her skirts.

Pigeony Poll sat by the window with the baby in her arms, and pale misgiving in her dull face. 'I – I come in, Mrs Perrott, mum,' she said, with a hush in her thick voice, 'I come in 'cos I see you goin' out, an' I thought the baby'd be alone. She – she's 'ad a sort o' fit – all stiff an' blue in the face and grindin' 'er little mouth. She's left auf now – but I – I dunno what to make of 'er. She's so – so – '

Hannah Perrott stared blankly, and lifted the child, whose arm dropped and hung. The wizen age had gone from Looey's face, and the lids were down on the strained eyes; her pale lips lay eased of the old pinching – even parted in a smile. For she looked in the face of the Angel that plays with the dead children.

Hannah Perrott's chin fell. 'Lor',' she said bemusedly, and sat on the bed.

An odd croaking noise broke in jerks from Pigeony Poll as she crept from the room, with her face bowed in the bend of her arm, like a weeping schoolboy. Dicky stared, confounded. . . . Josh came and gazed stupidly, with his mouth open, walking tip-toe. But at a word from Kiddo Cook, who came in his tracks, he snatched the little body and clattered off to the dispensary, to knock up the young student.

The rumour went in the Jago that Josh Perrott was in double luck. For here was insurance money without a doubt. But in truth that was a thing the Perrotts had neglected.

Hannah Perrott felt a listless relief; Josh felt nothing in particular, except that there was no other thing to be done, and that Mother Gapp's would be a cheerful place to finish the day in, and keep up the missis's pecker.

So that eight o'clock that evening at Perrotts' witnessed a darkening room wherein an inconsiderable little corpse lay on a bed; while a small ragamuffin spread upon it with outstretched arms, exhausted with sobbing, a soak of muddy tears: – 'O Looey, Looey! Can't you 'ear? Won't you never come to me no more?'

And the Reverend Henry Sturt, walking from church through

Luck Row toward his lodgings in Kingsland Road, heard shouts and riot behind the grimy panes of Mother Gapp's, and in the midst the roar of many voices joined in the Jago chant: –

> *Six bloomin' long months in a prison,*
> * Six more bloomin' months I must stay,*
> *For meetin' a bloke in our alley,*
> * An' takin' 'is uxter away!*

> * Toora-li—toora-li—looral,*
> * Toora-li—toora-li—lay,*
> * A-coshin' a bloke in our alley,*
> * An' takin' 'is uxter away!*

CHAPTER 14

On an autumn day four years after his first coming to the Jago, the Reverend Henry Sturt left a solicitor's office in Cheapside, and walked eastward, with something more of hope and triumph in him than he had felt since the Jago fell to his charge. For the ground was bought whereon should be built a church and buildings accessory, and he felt, not that he was like to see any great result from his struggle, but that perhaps he might pursue it better armed and with less of grim despair than had been his portion hitherto.

It had taken him four years to gather the money for the site, and some of it he was paying from his own pocket. He was unmarried, and had therefore no reason to save. Still, he must be careful, for the sake of the parish: the church must be built, and some of the money would probably be wanted for that. Moreover, there were other calls. The benefice brought a trifle less than £200 a year, and out of that, so far as it would go, he paid (with some small outside help) £130 for rent of the temporary church and the adjacent rooms; the organist's salary; the rates and the gas-bills; the cost of cleaning, care, and repair; the sums needed for such relief as was impossible to be withheld; and a thousand small things beside. While the Jagos speculated wildly among themselves as to the vast sums he must make by his job. For what toff would come and live in the Jago except for a consideration of solid gain? What other possible motive could there be, indeed?

Still, he had an influence among them such as they had never known before. For one thing, they feared in him what they took for a sort of supernatural insight. The mean cunning of the Jago, subtle as it was, and baffling to most strangers, foundered miserably before his relentless intelligence; and crafty rogues – 'wide as Broad Street',* as their proverb went – at first sulked, faltered and prevaricated transparently, but soon gave up all hope or effort to deceive him. Thus he was respected. Once he had made it plain that he was no common milch-cow in the matter of gratuities: to be bamboozled for shillings, cajoled for coals, and bullied for blankets: then there became apparent in him qualities of charity and loving-kindness, well-judged and governed, that awoke in places a regard that was in a way akin to affection. And the familiar habit of the Jago slowly grew to call him Father Sturt.

Father Sturt was not to be overreached: that was the axiom gloomily accepted by all in the Jago who lived by what they accounted their wits. You could not juggle shillings and clothing (convertible into shillings) out of Father Sturt by the easy fee-faw-fum of repentance and salvation that served with so many. There were many of the Jagos (mightily despised by some of the sturdier ruffians) who sallied forth from time to time into neighbouring regions in pursuit of the profitable sentimentalist: discovering him – black-coated, earnest, green – sometimes a preacher, sometimes a layman, sometimes one having authority on the committee of a charitable institution; dabbling in the East End on his own account, or administering relief for a mission, or disbursing a Mansion House Fund.* He was of two chief kinds: the Merely-Soft* – the 'man of wool' as the Jago word went – for whom any tale was good enough, delivered with the proper wistful misery: and the Gullible-Cocksure, confident in a blind experience, who was quite as easy to tap, when approached with a becoming circumspection. A rough and ready method, which served well in most cases with both sorts, was a profession of sudden religious awakening. For this, one offered an aspect either of serene happiness or of maniacal exaltation, according to the customer's taste. A better way, but one demanding greater subtlety, was the assumption of the part of Earnest Inquirer, hesitating on the brink of Salvation. For the attitude was capable of indefinite prolongation, and was ever productive of the boots, the coats, and the half-crowns used to coax weak brethren into the fold. But with Father Sturt, such trouble was worse than useless; it was, indeed, but to invite a humiliating snub. Thus, when Fluffy Pike* first came to Father Sturt with the intelligence that he had at last found Grace, then Father Sturt asked if he had found it in a certain hamper – a hamper hooked that morning from a railway van – and if it were of a quality likely to inspire an act of restoration to the goods office. Nothing was to be done with a man of this disgustingly practical turn of mind, and the Jagos soon ceased from trying.

Father Sturt had made more of the stable than the make-shift church he had found. He had organised a club in a stable adjoining, and he lived in the rooms over the shut-up shop. In the club he gathered the men of the Jago indiscriminately, with the sole condition of good behaviour on the premises. And there they smoked, jumped, swung on horizontal bars, boxed,* played at cards and bagatelle, free from interference save when interference became necessary. For the women there were sewing-meetings and singing. And all governed with an invisible discipline, which, being brought to action, was found to be of iron.

Now there was ground on which might be built a worthier church; and Father Sturt had in mind a church which should have by its side a cleanly lodging-house, a night-shelter, a club, baths and washhouses. And at a stroke he would establish this habitation and wipe out the blackest spot in the Jago. For the new site comprised the whole of Jago Court and the houses that masked it in Old Jago Street.

This was a dream of the future – perhaps of the immediate future, if a certain new millionaire* could only be interested in the undertaking – but of the future certainly. The money for the site alone had been hard enough to gather. In the first place the East London Elevation Mission and Pansophical Institute was asking very diligently for funds – and was getting them. It was to that, indeed, that people turned by habit when minded to invest in the amelioration of the East End. Then about this time there had arisen a sudden quacksalver, a Panjandrum of philanthropy, a mummer of the market-place, who undertook, for a fixed sum, to abolish poverty and sin together;* and many, pleased with the new gaudery,* poured out before him the money that had gone to maintain hospitals and to feed proved charities. So that gifts were scarce and hard to come by – indeed, were apt to be thought unnecessary, for was not misery to be destroyed out of hand? Moreover, Father Sturt wanted not for enemies among the Sentimental-Cocksure. He was callous and cynical in face of the succulent penitence of Fluffy Pike and his kind. He preferred the frank rogue before the calculating snivelmonger. He had a club at which boxing was allowed, and dominoes – flat ungodliness.* He shook hands familiarly every day with the lowest characters: his tastes were vulgar and brutal.

And the company at his club was really dreadful. These things the Cocksure said, with shaking of heads; and these they took care should be known among such as might give Father Sturt money. Father Sturt! – the name itself was sheer papistry.* And many comforted themselves by writing him anonymous letters, displaying hell before his eyes, and dealing him vivid damnation.

So Father Sturt tramped back to the Jago, and to the strain and struggle that ceased not for one moment of his life, though it left never a mark of success behind it. For the Jago was much as ever. Were the lump once leavened by the advent of any denizen a little less base than the rest, were a native once ridiculed and persuaded into a spell of work and clean living, then must Father Sturt hasten to drive him from the Jago ere its influence suck him under for ever; leaving for his own community none but the entirely vicious. And among these he spent his life: preaching little, in the common sense, for that were but idle vanity in this place; but working, alleviating, growing into the Jago life, flinging scorn and ridicule on evil things, grateful for tiny negative successes – for keeping a few from ill-behaviour but for an hour; conscious that wherever he was not, iniquity flourished unreproved; and oppressed by the remembrance that albeit the Jago death-rate ruled full four times that of all London* beyond, still the Jago rats bred and bred their kind unhindered, multiplying apace and infecting the world.

In Luck Row he came on Josh Perrott, making for home with something under the skirt of his coat.

'How d'ye do, Josh?' said Father Sturt, clapping a hand on Josh's shoulder, and offering it as Josh turned about.

Josh, with a shifting of the object under his coat, hastened to tap his cap-peak with his forefinger before shaking hands. He grinned broadly, and looked this way and that, with mingled gratification and embarrassment, as was the Jago way in such circumstances. Because one could never tell whether Father Sturt would exchange a mere friendly sentence or two, or, with concealed knowledge, put some disastrous question about a watch, or a purse, or a breastpin, or what not.

'Very well, thanks, Father,' answered Josh, and grinned amiably at the wall beyond the vicar's elbow.

'And what have you been doing just lately?'

'Oo – odd jobs, Father.' Always the same answer, all over the Jago.

'Not quite such odd jobs as usual, I hope, Josh, eh?' Father Sturt smiled, and twitched Josh playfully by the button-hole as one might treat a child. 'I once heard of a very odd job in the Kingsland Road that got a fine young man six months' holiday. Eh, Josh?'

Josh Perrott wriggled and grinned sheepishly; tried to frown, failed, and grinned again. He had only been out a few weeks from that six moon.* Presently he said: – 'Awright, Father; you do rub it into a bloke, no mistake.'

The grin persisted as he looked first at the wall, then at the pavement, then down the street, but never in the parson's face.

'Ah, there's a deal of good in a blister* sometimes, isn't there, Josh? What's that I see – a clock? Not another odd job, eh?'

It was indeed a small nickel-plated American clock which Josh had under his coat, and which he now partly uncovered with positive protests. 'No, s'elp me, Father, it's all straight – all fair trade, Father – jist a swop for somethink else, on me solemn davy. That's wot it is, Father – straight.'

'Well, I'm glad you thought to get it, Josh,' Father Sturt pursued, still twitching the button-hole. 'You never have been a punctual church-goer, you know, Josh, and I'm glad you've made arrangements to improve. You'll have no excuse now, you know, and I shall expect you on Sunday morning – promptly. Don't forget: I shall be looking for you.' And Father Sturt shook hands again, and passed on, leaving Josh Perrott still grinning dubiously, and striving to assimilate the invitation to church.

The clock was indeed an exchange, though not altogether an innocent one: the facts being these. Early that morning Josh had found himself scrambling hastily along a turning out of Brick Lane, accompanied by a parcel of nine or ten pounds of tobacco, and extremely conscious of the hasty scrambling of several other people round the corner. Some of these people turned that corner before Josh reached the next, so that his course was observed, and it became politic to get rid of his parcel before a possible heading-off in Meakin Street. There was one place where this might be done, and that was at Weech's. A muddy yard, one of a tangle of such places behind Meakin Street, abutted on Weech's back fence; and it was no uncommon thing for a Jago on the crook, hard pressed, to pitch his plunder over the fence, double out into the crowd, and call on Mr Aaron Weech for the purchase-money as soon as opportunity served.

The manœuvre was a simple one, facilitated by the plan of the courts; but it was only adopted in extreme cases, because Mr Aaron Weech was at best but a mean paymaster, and with so much of the upper hand in the bargain as these circumstances conferred, was apt to be meaner than ever. But this case seemed to call for the stratagem, and Josh made for the muddy yard, dropped the parcel over the fence, with a loud whistle, and backed off by the side passage in the regular way.

When he called on Mr Aaron Weech a few hours later, that talented tradesman, with liberal gestures, told out shillings singly in his hand, pausing after each as though that were the last. But Josh held his hand persistently open, till Mr Weech, having released the fifth shilling, stopped altogether, scandalised at such rapacity. But still Josh was not satisfied, and as he was not quite so easy a customer to manage as the boys who commonly fenced at the shop, Mr Weech compromised, in the end, by throwing in a cheap clock. It had been in hand for a long time; and Josh was fain to take it, since he could get no more. And thus it was that Dicky, coming in at about five o'clock, was astonished to see on the mantelpiece, amid the greasy ruins of many candle ends, the clock that had belonged to the Ropers four years before.

CHAPTER 15

As for Dicky, he went to school. That is to say, he turned up now and again, at irregular intervals, at the Board School just over the Jago border in Honey Lane. When anything was given away, he attended as a matter of course; but he went now and again without such inducement – perhaps because he fancied an afternoon's change, perhaps because the weather was cold and the school was warm. He was classed as a half-timer, an arrangement which variegated the register, but otherwise did not matter. Other boys, half-timers or not, attended as little as he. It was long since the managers had realised the futility of attempting compulsion in the Jago.*

Dicky was no fool, and he had picked up some sort of reading and writing as he went along. Moreover, he had grown an expert thief, and had taken six strokes of a birch-rod by order of a magistrate. As yet he rarely attempted a pocket, being, for most opportunities, too small; but he was comforted by the reflection that probably he would never get really tall, and thus grow out of pocket-picking when he was fully experienced, as was the fate of some. For no tall man can be a successful pickpocket, because he must bend to his work, and so advertise it to every beholder.

Meantime Dicky practised that petty larceny which is possible in every street in London; and at odd times he would play the scout among the practitioners of the 'fat's a-running'* industry. If one crossed Meakin Street by way of Luck Row and kept his way among the courts ahead, he presently reached the main Bethnal Green Road, at the end whereof stood the great goods depot of a railway company.* Here carts and vans went to and fro all day, laden with goods from the depot, and certain gangs among the Jagos preyed on these continually. A quick-witted scout stood on the look-out for such vehicles as went with unguarded tailboards. At the approach of one such he sent the shout '*Fat's a-runnin'!*' up Luck Row, and, quick at the signal, a gang scuttled down, by the court or passage which his waved hand might hint at, seized whatever could be snatched from the cart, and melted away into the courts, sometimes leaving a few hands behind to hinder and misdirect pursuit. Taking one capture with another, the thing paid very well; and besides, there were many vans laden with parcels of tobacco, not from the railway depot but from the tobacco factories hard by,* a click from which was apt to prove especially lucrative. Dicky was a notable success as scout. The department was a fairly safe one, but it was not always easy to extract from the gang the few coppers that were regarded as sufficient share for service done. Moreover, Mr Weech was not pleased; for by now Dicky was near to being his most remunerative client, and the cart robberies counted nothing, for the fat's a-running boys fenced their swag with a publican at Hoxton. And though Dicky had grown out of his childish belief that Mr Weech could hear a mile away and see through a wall, he had a cautious dread of the weapon he supposed to lie ever to his patron's hand – betrayal to the police. In other respects things were easier. His father took no heed of what he did, and even his mother had so far accepted destiny as to ask if he had a copper or two, when there was a scarcity. Indeed Hannah Perrott filled her place in the Jago better than of old. She would gossip, she drew no very rigid line as to her acquaintance, and Dicky had seen her drunk. Still, for Old Jago Street she was a quiet woman, and she never brawled nor fought. Of fighting, indeed, Josh could do enough for the whole family, once again four in number. For the place of Looey, forgotten, was supplied by Em, aged two.

When Dicky came home and recognised the clock on the mantelpiece, being the more certain because his mother told him it had come from Weech's, the thing irritated him strangely. Through all those four years since he had carried that clock to Mr Weech, he had never got rid of the wretched hunchback. He, too, went to the Board School in Honey Lane (it lay between Dove Lane and the Jago), but he went regularly, worked hard, and was a favourite with teachers. So far, Dicky was unconcerned. But scarce an ill chance came to him but, sooner or later, he found the hunchback at the back of it. If ever a teacher mysteriously found out that it was Dicky who had drawn his portrait, all nose and teeth, on the blackboard, the tale had come from Bobby Roper. Whenever Dicky, chancing upon school by ill luck on an afternoon when sums were to be done, essayed to copy answers from his neighbour's slate, up shot the hunchback's hand in an instant, the tale was told, and handers were Dicky's portion. Once, dinnerless and hungry, he had stolen a sandwich from a teacher's desk; and, though he had thought himself alone and unseen, the hunchback knew it, and pointed him out, white malice in his thin face and eager hate in his thrust finger. For a fortnight Dicky dared not pass a little fruit shop in Meakin Street, because of an attempt on an orange, betrayed by his misshapen schoolfellow, which brought him a hard chase from the fruiterer and a bad bruise on the spine from a board flung after him. The hunchback's whole energies – even his whole time – seemed to be devoted to watching him. Dicky, on his part, received no injuries meekly. In the beginning he had tried threats and public jeers at his enemy's infirmity. Then, on some especially exasperating occasion, he pounded Bobby Roper savagely about the head and capsized him into a mud-heap. But bodily reprisal, though he erected it into a practice, proved no deterrent. For the little hunchback, though he might cry at the pummelling, retorted with worse revenge of his own sort. And once or twice bystanders, seeing a deformed child thus treated, interfered with clouts on Dicky's ears. The victim, moreover, designed another retaliation. He would go to some bigger boy with a tale that Dicky had spoken vauntingly of fighting him and beating him hollow, with one hand. This brought the big boy after Dicky at once, with a hiding: except on some rare occasion when the hunchback rated his instrument of vengeance too high, and Dicky was able to beat him in truth. But this was a very uncommon mistake. And after this Dicky did not wait for specific provocation: he 'clumped' Bobby Roper, or rolled him in the gutter, as a matter of principle, whenever he could get hold of him.

That afternoon Dicky had suffered again. Two days earlier, tea and cake had been provided by a benevolent manager for all who attended the school. Consequently the attendance was excellent, and included Dicky. But his attempt to secrete a pocketful of cake, to carry home for Em, was reported by Bobby Roper; and Dicky was hauled forth, deprived of his plunder, and expelled in disgrace. He waited outside and paid off the score fiercely, by the help of a very long and pliant cabbage stalk. But this afternoon Bill Bates, a boy a head taller than himself and two years older, had fallen on him suddenly in Lincoln Street, and, though Dicky fought desperately and kicked with much effect, had dealt him a thrashing that left him bruised, bleeding, dusty, and crying with rage and pain. This was the hunchback's doing, without a doubt. Dicky limped home, but was something comforted by an accident in Shoreditch High Street, whereby a coster's barrow-load of cough-drops was knocked over by a covered van, and the cough-drops were scattered in the mud. For while the carman* and the coster flew at each other's name and address, and defamed each other's eyes and mother,* Dicky gathered a handful of cough-drops, muddy, it is true, but easy to wipe. And so he made for home more cheerfully disposed: till the sight of the Ropers' old clock brought the hunchback to mind once more, and in bitter anger he resolved to search for him forthwith, and pass on the afternoon's hiding, with interest.

As he emerged into the street, a hand was reached to catch him, which he dodged by instinct. He rushed back upstairs, and emptied his pockets, stowing away in a safe corner the rest of the cough-drops, the broken ruin he called his knife, some buttons and pieces of string, a bit of chalk, three little pieces of slate pencil* and two marbles. Then he went down again into the street, confident in his destitution, and watched, forgetting the hunchback in the excitement of the spectacle.

The loafers from the corners had conceived a sudden notion of co-operation* and had joined forces to the array of twenty or thirty. Confident in their numbers, they swept the street, stopping every passenger – man, woman or child – and emptying all pockets. A straggler on the outskirts of the crowd, a hobbledehoy like most of the rest, had snatched at but had lost Dicky, and was now busy, with four or five others, rolling a woman, a struggling heap of old clothes and skinny limbs, in the road. It was Biddy Flynn, too old and worn for anything but honest work, who sold oranges and nuts from a basket, and who had been caught on her way out for her evening's trade in High Street. She was a fortunate capture, being a lone woman with all her possessions about her. Under her skirt, and tied round her waist with string, she kept her money-bag; and it was soon found and dragged away, yielding two and eightpence farthing and a lucky shoe-tip, worn round and bright. She had, moreover, an old brass brooch; but unfortunately her wedding ring, worn to pin-wire, could not be got past the knotted knuckle – though it would have been worth little in any case. So Biddy Flynn, exhausted with plunging and screaming, was left, and her empty basket was flung at her. She staggered away, wailing and rolling her head, with her hand to the wall; and the gang, sharing out, sucked oranges with relish, and turned to fresh exploits. Dicky watched from the Jago Court passage.

Business slackened for a little while, and the loafers were contemplating a raid in force on Mother Gapp's till, when a grown lad ran in pell-mell from Luck Row with a square parcel clipped under his arm – a parcel of aspect well known among the fat's a-running boys – a parcel that meant tobacco. He was collared at once.

'Stow it, Bill!' he cried breathlessly, recognising his captor. 'The bloke's a-comin'!'

But half-a-dozen hands were on his plunder, it was snatched away, and he was flung back on the flags. There was a clatter on the stones of Luck Row, and a light van came rattling into Old Jago Street, the horse galloping, the carman lashing and shouting: – 'Stop 'im! Stop thief!'

The sight was so novel that for a moment the gang merely stared and grinned. This man must be a greenhorn – new to the neighbourhood – to venture a load of goods up Luck Row. And it was tobacco, too. He was pale and flustered, and he called wildly, as he looked this way and that: – 'A man's stole somethin' auf my van. Where's 'e gawn?'

'No good, guv'nor,' cried one. 'The ball's stopped rollin'.* You're lawst 'im.'

'My Gawd!' said the man, in a sweat, 'I'm done. There's two quid's worth o' 'bacca – an' I on'y got the job o' Monday – bin out nine munse!'

'Was it a parcel like this 'ere?' asked another, chuckling, and lifting a second packet over the tailboard.

'Yus – put it down! Gawd – wotcher up to? 'Ere – 'elp! 'elp!'

The gang were over the van, guffawing and flinging out the load. The carman yelled aloud, and fought desperately with his whip – Bill Hanks is near blind of an eye now from one cut; but he was the worse for it. For he was knocked off the van in a heap, and, as he lay, they cleared his pockets, and pulled off his boots; those that had caught the sting of the whip kicking him about the head till it but shifted in the slime at the stroke, an inanimate lump.

There was talk of how to deal with the horse and van. To try to sell them was too large a job, and too risky. So, as it was growing dusk, the senseless carman was put on the floor of the van, the tailboard was raised, and one of the gang led the horse away, to lose the whole thing in the busy streets.

Here was a big haul, and many of the crowd busied themselves in getting it out of sight, and scouting out among the fences to arrange sales. Those who remained grew less active, and hung at the corner of Luck Row, little more than an ordinary corner-group of loafers.

Then Dicky remembered the hunchback, and slouched off to Dove Lane. But he could see nothing of Bobby Roper. The Jago and Dove Lane were districts ever at feud, active or smouldering, save for brief intervals of ostentatious reconciliation, serving to render the next attack on Dove Lane the more savage – for invariably the Jagos were aggressors and victors. Dicky was careful in his lurkings, therefore: lest he should be recognised and set upon by more Dove Lane boys than would be convenient. He knew where the Ropers lived, and he went and hung about the door. Once he fancied he could hear a disjointed tinkle, as of a music-box grown infirm, but he was not sure of it. And in the end he contented himself, for the present, with flinging a stone through the Ropers' window, and taking to his heels.

The Jago was black with night, the rats came and went, and the cosh-carriers lurked on landings. On a step, Pigeony Poll, drunk because of a little gin and no food, sang hideously and wept. The loafers had dispersed to spend their afternoon's makings. The group which Dicky had left by Luck Row corner, indeed, had been discouraged early in the evening in consequence of an attempt at 'turning over' old Beveridge, as he unsuspectingly stalked among them, in from his city round. For the old man whipped out his case-knife and drove it into the flesh of Nobber Sugg's* arm, at the shoulder – stabbed, too, at another, and ripped his coat. So Nobber Sugg, with blood streaming through his sleeve, went off with two more to tie up the arm; and old Beveridge, grinning and mumbling fiercely, strode about the street, knife in hand, for ten minutes, ere he grew calm enough to go his way. This Tommy Rann told Dicky, sitting in the back yard and smoking a pipe; a pipe charged with tobacco pillaged from a tin-full which his father had bought, at about fourpence a pound, from a loafer. And both boys crawled indoors deadly sick.

CHAPTER 16

Josh Perrott was at church on Sunday morning, as Father Sturt had bid him. Not because of the bidding, but because the vicar overtook him and Kiddo Cook in Meakin Street, and hauled them in, professing to be much gratified at their punctuality, and charging them never to fall away from the habit. The two Jagos, with dubious grins, submitted as they must, and were in a little while surprised to find others arriving, friends and acquaintances never suspected of church-going. The fact was, that Father Sturt, by dint of long effort, had so often brought so many to his stable-church, as he had now brought Josh and Kiddo, that the terrors and embarrassments of the place had worn off, and many, finding nothing more attractive elsewhere, would make occasional attendances of their own motion. Wet Sundays, particularly, inclined them to church: where there might be a fire, where at least there was a clean room, with pictures on the wall, where there were often flowers,* where there was always music, and where Father Sturt made an address of a quarter of an hour, which nobody ever suspected of being a sermon; an address which one might doze over or listen to, as one might be disposed; but which most listened to, more or less, partly because of an uneasy feeling that Father Sturt would know if they did not, and partly because it was very easy to understand, was not oppressively minatory, was spoken with an intimate knowledge of themselves, and was, indeed, something of a refreshing novelty, being the simple talk of a gentleman.

Josh Perrott and Kiddo Cook were not altogether sorry they had come. It was a rest. Stable though it had been, they had never sat in so pleasant a room before. There was nothing to do, no constant watch to be kept, no police to avoid, and their wits had a holiday. They forgot things. Their courage never rose so high as to build the thought; but in truth pipes would have made them happy.

The address being done, Father Sturt announced the purchase

of the site for the new church, and briefly described his scheme. He would give tenants good notice, he said, before the houses were destroyed. Meantime, they must pay rent; though most of the amounts would be reduced.*

And after the benediction, Father Sturt, from his window over the closed shop, saw Josh Perrott and Kiddo Cook guffawing and elbowing one another up Luck Row. Each was accusing the other of having tried to sing.

CHAPTER 17

There was much talk of Father Sturt's announcement. Many held it a shame that so much money, destined for the benefit of the Jago, should be spent in bricks and mortar, instead of being distributed among themselves. They fell to calculating the price of the land and houses, and to working it out laboriously in the denomination of pots and gallons. More: it was felt to be a grave social danger that Jago Court should be extinguished. What would become of the Jago without Jago Court? Where would Sunday morning be spent? Where would the fights come off, and where was so convenient a place for pitch and toss? But mainly they feared the police. Jago Court was an unfailing sanctuary, a city of refuge ever ready, ever secure.* There were times when two or three of the police, hot in the chase, would burst into the Jago at the heels of a flying marauder. Then the runaway would make straight for the archway, and, once he was in Jago Court, danger was over. For he had only to run into one of the ever-open doors at right or left, and out into back-yards and other houses; or, better, to scramble over the low fence opposite, through the back door before him, and so into New Jago Street. Beyond the archway the police could not venture, except in large companies. A young constable who tried it once, getting ahead of two companions in his ardour, was laid low as he emerged from the passage, by a fire-grate adroitly let drop* from an upper window.

The blotting out of such a godsend of a place as this would be a calamity. The Jago would never be the same again. As it was, the Old Jago was a very convenient, comfortable sort of place, they argued. They could not imagine themselves living anywhere else. But assuredly it would be the Jago no longer without Jago Court. And this thing was to be done, too, with money got together for their benefit! The sole explanation the Jago could supply was the one that at last, with arithmetical variations, prevailed. The landlords were to be paid a sum (varying in Jago estimation from a hundred pounds to a hundred thousand) for the houses and the ground, and of this they were secretly to return to Father Sturt a certain share (generally agreed on as half), as his private fee for bringing about so desirable a transaction. Looked at from all points, this appeared to be the most plausible explanation: for no other could reasonably account for Father Sturt's activity. No wonder he could afford to reduce some of the rents! Was he not already receiving princely wages* (variously supposed to be something from ten pounds to thirty pounds a week) from the Government, for preaching every Sunday?

Still the rents were to be reduced: that was the immediate consideration, and nothing but an immediate consideration carried weight in the Jago,* where a shilling today was to be preferred to a constant income beginning in a month's time. The first effect of the announcement was a rush of applications for rooms in the doomed houses, each applicant demanding to be accommodated by the eviction of somebody already established, but now disinterestedly discovered to be a bad tenant. They were all disappointed, but the residents had better luck than they had hoped. For the unexpected happened, and the money for a part of the new buildings was suddenly guaranteed. Wherefore Father Sturt, knowing that many would be hard put to it to find shelter when the houses came down, and guessing that rents would rise with the demand, determined to ask none for the little while the tenements endured. Scarce had he made his decision known ere he regretted it, popular as it was. For he reflected that the money saved would merely melt, and that at the inevitable turning out, not a soul would be the better off for the relief, but, indeed, might find it harder than ever to pay rent after the temporary easement. It would have been better rigidly to exact the rent, and return it in lump to each tenant as he left. The sum would have been an inducement to leave peaceably – a matter in which trouble was to be expected. But then, what did any windfall of shillings bring in the Jago? What but a drunk? This was one of Father Sturt's thousand perplexities, and he could but hope that, perhaps, he had done right after all.

The old buildings were sold, as they stood, to the house-wreckers, and on the house-wreckers devolved the work of getting the lodgers out. For weeks the day was deferred, but it drew very near at last, and a tall hoarding was put up. Next morning it had vanished; but there was a loud crackling where the Jagos boiled their pots; Dicky Perrott and Tommy Rann had a bonfire in Edge Lane; and Jerry Gullen's canary sweated abroad before a heavy load of cheap firewood.

Then Josh Perrott and Billy Leary, his old enemy, were appointed joint guardians of the new hoarding, each to get half-a-crown on every morning when the fence was found intact. And in the end there came eviction day, and once more the police held the Jago in force, escorting gangs of men with tumbrils.*

As for the Perrotts, they could easily find another room, at the high rent always charged for the privilege of residence in the Jago. To have remained in one room four or five years, and to have paid rent with indifferent good regularity was a feat sufficiently rare to be notorious, and to cause way to be made for them wherever a room was falling vacant, or could be emptied. They went no farther than across the way, to a room wherein a widow had died over her sack-making two days before, and had sat on the floor with her head between her knees for hours, while her children, not understanding, cried that they were hungry. These children were now gone to the workhouse: more fortunate than the many they left behind. And the room was a very fair one, ten feet square or so.

The rest of the tenants thought not at all of new quarters, and did nothing to find them, till they found themselves and their belongings roofless in Old Jago Street. Then with one accord they demanded lodgings of the vicar. Most of them had never inhabited any rooms so long as they had these which they must now leave – having been ejected again and again because of unpaid rent. Nevertheless, they clamoured for redress as they might have clamoured had they never changed dwellings in their lives.

Nobody resisted the police; for there were too many of them. Moreover, Father Sturt was there, and few had hardihood for any but their best behaviour in his presence. Still, there were disputes among the Jagos themselves, that sometimes came very near to fights. Ginger Stagg's missis professed to recognise a long-lost property in a tin kettle brought into the outer air among the belongings of Mrs Walsh. The miscellaneous rags and sticks that were Cocko Harnwell's household goods got mingled in the roadway with those appertaining to the Fishers;

and their assortment without a turn of family combat was a task which tried the vicar's influence to the utmost. Mrs Rafferty, too, was suspected of undue pride in a cranky deal washstand, and thereby of a disposition to sneer at the humbler turn-out of the Regans from the next floor: giving occasion for a shrill and animated row.

The weather was dry, fortunately, and the evicted squatted in the roadway, by their heaps, or on them, squabbling and lamenting. Ginger Stagg, having covered certain crockery with the old family mattress, forgetfully sat on it, and came upon Father Sturt with an indignant demand for compensation.

Father Sturt's efforts to stimulate a search for new lodgings met with small success at first. It was felt that, no doubt, there were lodgings to be had, but they would be open to the fatal objection of costing something; and the Jago temperament could neither endure nor understand payment for what had once been given for nothing. Father Sturt, the Jagos argued, had given them free quarters for so long. Then why should he stop now? If they cleared out in order to make room for his new church, in common fairness he should find them similar lodging on the same terms. So they sat and waited for him to do it.

At length the vicar set to work with them in good earnest, carried away with him a family or two at a time, and inducted them to rooms of his own finding. And hereat others, learning that in these cases rent in advance was exacted, bestirred themselves: reflecting that if rent must be paid they might as well choose their own rooms as take those that Father Sturt might find. Of course the thing was not done without payments from the vicar's pocket.* Some were wholly destitute; others could not muster enough to pay that advance of rent which alone could open a Jago tenancy. Distinguishing the genuine impecuniosity from the merely professed, with the insight that was now a sixth sense with him, Father Sturt helped sparingly and in secret; for a precedent of almsgiving was an evil thing in the Jago, confirming the shiftlessness which was already a piece of Jago nature, and setting up long affliction for the almsgiver. Enough of such precedents existed; and the inevitable additions thereto were a work of anxious responsibility and jealous care.

So the bivouac in Old Jago Street melted away. For one thing, there were those among the dispossessed who would not waste time in unproductive inactivity just then; for war had arisen with Dove Lane, and spoils were going. Dove Lane was no very reputable place, but it was not like the Jago. In the phrase of the district, the Dove Laners were pretty thick, but the Jagos were thick as glue. There were many market-porters among the Dove Laners, and at this, their prosperous season,* they and their friends resorted to a shop in Meakin Street, kept by an 'ikey' tailor, there to buy the original out-and-out downy benjamins,* or the celebrated bang-up kicksies, cut saucy, with artful buttons and a double fakement* down the sides. And hereabout they were apt to be set upon by Jagos; overthrown by superior numbers; bashed; and cleaned out. Or, if the purchases had been made, they were flimped of their kicksies, benjies or daisies,* as the case might be. So that a fight with Dove Lane might be an affair of some occasional profit; and it became no loyal Jago to idle in the stronghold.

Father Sturt's task was nearly over, when, returning to Old Jago Street, he saw Dicky Perrott sitting by a still-remaining heap – a heap small and poor even among those others. The Perrotts had been decorously settled in their new home since early morning; but here was Dicky, guarding a heap with a baby on it, and absorbed in the weaving of rush bags.

'That's right, Dicky my boy,' said Father Sturt in the approving voice that a Jago would do almost anything – except turn honest – to hear. And Dicky, startled, looked up, flushed and happy, over his shoulder.

'Rush bags, eh?' the vicar went on, stooping and handing Dicky another rush from the heap. 'And whose are they?'

The bags, the rushes, the heap, and the baby belonged to Mrs Bates, the widow, who was now in search of a new room. Dicky had often watched the weaving of fishmongers' frails,* and, since it was work in which he had had no opportunity of indulging, it naturally struck him as a fascinating pastime. So that he was delighted by the chance which he had taken, and Mrs Bates, for her part, was not sorry to find somebody to mind her property. Moreover, by hard work and the skill begot of much practice, she was able to earn a sum of some three farthings an hour at the rush bags: a profit which her cupidity made her reluctant to lose, for even half an hour. And thus to have Dicky carry on the business* – and in his enthusiasm he did it very well – was a further consideration.

Father Sturt chatted with Dicky till the boy could scarce plait for very pride. Would not Dicky like to work regularly every day, asked Father Sturt, and earn wages? Dicky could see no graceful answer but the affirmative; and in sober earnest he thought he would. Father Sturt took hold of Dicky's vanity. Was he not capable of something better than other Jago boys? Why should he not earn regular wages, and live comfortably, well fed and clothed, with no fear of the police, and no shame for what he did? *He* might do it, when others could not. They were not clever enough. They called themselves 'clever' and 'wide'; 'but,' said Father Sturt, 'is there one of them that can deceive me?' And Dicky knew there was not one. Most did no work, the vicar's argument went on, because they had neither the pluck to try nor the intelligence to accomplish. Else why did they live the wretched Jago life instead of take the pleasanter time of the decent labourer?

Dicky, already zealous at work as exampled in rush bag-making, listened with wistful pride. Yes, if he could, he would work and take his place over the envious heads of his Jago friends. But how? Nobody would employ a boy living in the Jago. That was notorious. The address was a topsy-turvy testimonial for miles round.

All the same when Mrs Bates at last took away her belongings, Dicky ran off in delighted amaze to tell his mother and Em that he was going to tea at Father Sturt's rooms.

And the wreckers tore down the foul old houses, laying bare the secret dens of a century of infamy; lifting out the wide sashes of the old 'weavers' windows'* – the one good feature in the structures; letting light and air at last into the subterraneous basements where men and women had swarmed, and bred, and died, like wolves in their lairs; and emerging from clouds of choking dust, each man a colony of vermin. But there were rooms which the wreckers – no jack-a-dandies neither – flatly refused to enter;* and nothing would make them but much coaxing, the promise of extra pay, and the certainty of much immediate beer.

CHAPTER 18

Mr Grinder* kept a shop in the Bethnal Green Road. It was announced in brilliant lettering as an 'oil, colour and Italian warehouse', and there, in addition to the oil and the colour, and whatever of Italian there might have been, he sold pots, pans, kettles, brooms, shovels, mops, lamps, nails, and treacle. It was a shop ever too tight for its stock, which burst forth at every available opening, and heaped so high on the paving that the window was half buried in a bank of shining tin. Father Sturt was one of the best customers: the oil, candles and utensils needed for church and club all coming from Mr Grinder's. Mr Grinder was losing his shop-boy, who had found a better situation; and Father Sturt determined that, could but the oilman be persuaded, Dicky Perrott should be the new boy. Mr Grinder was persuaded. Chiefly perhaps, because the vicar undertook to make good the loss, should the experiment end in theft; partly because it was policy to oblige a good customer; and partly, indeed, because Mr Grinder was willing to give such a boy a chance in life, for he was no bad fellow, as oil-and-colourmen go, and had been an errand boy himself.

So that there came a Monday morning when Dicky, his clothes as well mended as might be (for Hannah Perrott, no more than another Jago, could disobey Father Sturt), and a cut-down apron of his mother's tied before him, stood by Mr Grinder's bank of pots and kettles, in an eager agony to sell something, and near blind with the pride of the thing. He had been waiting at the shop-door long ere Mr Grinder was out of bed; and now, set to guard the outside stock – a duty not to be neglected in that neighbourhood – he brushed a tin pot here and there with his sleeve, and longed for some Jago friend to pass and view him in his new greatness. The goods he watched over were an unfailing source of interest; and he learned by much repetition the prices of all the saucepans, painted in blue distemper on the tin, and ranging from eightpence-halfpenny, on the big pots in the bottom row, to three-halfpence on the very little ones at the top. And there were long ranks of little paraffin lamps at a penny – the sort that had set fire to a garret in Half Jago Street a month since, and burnt old Mother Leary to a greasy cinder. With a smaller array of a superior quality at fourpence-halfpenny – just like the one that had burst at Jerry Gullen's, and burnt the bed. While over his head swung door-mats at one-and-eightpence, with penny mousetraps dangling from their corners.

When he grew more accustomed to his circumstances, he bethought him to collect a little dirt, and rub it down the front of his apron,* to give himself a well-worked and business-like appearance; and he greatly impeded women who looked at the saucepans and the mousetraps, ere they entered the shop, by his anxiety to cut them off from Mr Grinder and serve them himself. He remembered the boy at the toy-shop in Bishopsgate Street, years ago, who had chased him through Spitalfields; and he wished that some lurching youngster would snatch a mousetrap, that he might make a chase himself.

At Mr Grinder's every call Dicky was prompt and willing; for every new duty was a fresh delight, and the whole day a prolonged game of real shopkeeping. And at his tea – he was to have tea each day in addition to three and sixpence every Saturday – he took scarce five minutes. There was a trolley – just such a thing as porters used at railway stations, but smaller – which was his own particular implement, his own to pack parcels on for delivery to such few customers as did not carry away their own purchases: and to acquire the dexterous man-agement of this trolley was a pure joy. He bolted his tea to start the sooner on a trolley-journey to a public-house two hundred yards away.

His enthusiasm for work as an amusement cooled in a day or two, but all his pride in it remained. The fight with Dove Lane waxed amain, but Dicky would not be tempted into more than a distant interest in it. In his daydreams he saw himself a tradesman, with a shop of his own and the name 'R. Perrott', with a gold flourish, over the door. He would employ a boy himself then; and there would be a parlour, with stuff-bottomed chairs and a shade of flowers, and Em grown up and playing on the piano. Truly Father Sturt was right: the hooks were fools, and the straight game was the better.

Bobby Roper, the hunchback, went past the shop once, and saw him. Dicky, minding his new dignity, ignored his enemy, and for the first time for a year and more, allowed him to pass without either taunt or blow. The other, astonished at Dicky's new occupation, came back and back again, staring, from a safe distance, at Dicky and the shop. Dicky, on his part, took no more notice than to assume an ostentatious vigilance: so that the hunchback, baring his teeth in a snigger of malice, at last turned on his heel and rolled off.

Twice Kiddo Cook passed, but made no sign of recognition beyond a wink; and Dicky felt grateful for Kiddo's obvious fear of compromising him. Once old Beveridge came by, striding rapidly, his tatters flying, and the legend 'Hard Up' chalked on his hat, as was his manner in his town rambles. He stopped abruptly at sight of Dick, stooped, and said: – 'Dicky Perrott? Hum – hum – hey?' Then he hurried on, doubtless conceiving just such a fear as Kiddo Cook's. As for Tommy Rann, his affections were alienated by Dicky's outset refusal to secrete treacle in a tin mug for a midnight carouse; and he did not show himself. So matters went for near a week.

But Mr Weech missed Dicky sadly. It was rare for a day to pass without a visit from Dicky, and Dicky had a way of bringing good things. Mr Weech would not have sold Dicky's custom for ten shillings a week. So that when Mr Weech inquired, and found that Dicky was at work in an oil-shop, he was naturally annoyed. Moreover, if Dicky Perrott got into *that* way of life, he would have no fear for himself, and might get talking inconveniently among his new friends about the business affairs of Mr Aaron Weech. And at this reflection that philanthropist grew thoughtful.

CHAPTER 19

Dicky had gone on an errand, and Mr Grinder was at the shop door, when there appeared before him a whiskered and smirking figure, with a quick glance each way along the street, and a long and smiling one at the oil-man's necktie.

'Good mornin', Mr Grinder, good mornin' sir.' Mr Weech stroked his left palm with his right fist and nodded pleasantly. 'I'm in business meself, over in Meakin Street – name of Weech: p'r'aps you know the shop? I – I just 'opped over to ask' – Grinder led the way into the shop – 'to ask (so's to make things quite sure y'know, though no doubt it's all right) to ask if it's correct you're awfferin' brass roastin'-jacks at a shillin' each.'

'Brass roastin'-jacks at a shillin'?' exclaimed Grinder, shocked at the notion. 'Why, no!'

Mr Weech appeared mildly surprised. 'Nor yut seven-poun' jars o' jam an' pickles at sixpence?' he pursued, with his eye on those ranged behind the counter.

'No! '

'Nor doormats at fourpence?'

'Fourpence? Cert'nly not!'

Mr Weech's face fell into a blank perplexity. He pawed his ear with a doubtful air, murmuring absently: – 'Well I'm sure 'e *said* fourpence: an' sixpence for pickles, an' bring 'em round after the shop was shut. But there,' he added, more briskly, 'there's no 'arm done, an' no doubt it's a mistake.' He turned as though to leave, but Grinder restrained him.

'But look 'ere,' he said, 'I want to know about this. Wotjer mean? 'Oo was goin' to bring round pickles after the shop was shut? 'Oo said fourpence for doormats?'

'Oh, I expect it's jest a little mistake, that's all,' answered Weech, making another motion toward the door; 'an' I don't want to git nobody into trouble.'

'Trouble? Nice trouble I'd be in if I sold brass smoke-jacks* for a bob! There's somethink 'ere as I ought to know about. Tell me about it straight.'

Weech looked thoughtfully at the oil-man's top waistcoat button for a few seconds, and then said: – 'Yus, p'raps I better. I can feel for you, Mr Grinder, 'avin' a feelin' 'art, an' bein' in business meself. Where's your boy?'

'Gawn out.'

'Comin' back soon?'

'Not yut. Come in the back-parlour.'

There Mr Weech, with ingenuous reluctance, assured Mr Grinder that Dicky Perrott had importuned him to buy the goods in question at the prices he had mentioned, together with others – readily named now that the oil-man swallowed so freely – and that they were to be delivered and paid for at night when Dicky left work. But perhaps, Mr Weech concluded, parading an obstinate belief in human nature, perhaps the boy, being new to the business, had mistaken the prices, and was merely doing his best to push his master's trade.

'No fear o' that,' said Grinder, shaking his head gloomily. 'Not the least fear o' that. 'E knows the cheapest doormats I got's one an' six – I 'eard him tell customers so outside a dozen times; an' anyone can see the smoke-jacks is ticketed five an' nine' – as Mr Weech had seen, when he spoke of them. 'I thought that boy was too eager an' willin' to be quite genavin,' Dicky's master went on. ''E ain't 'ad me yut, that's one comfort: if anythin' 'ud bin gawn I'd 'a' missed it. But out 'e goes as soon as 'e comes back: you can take yer davy o' that!'

'Ah,' replied Mr Weech, 'it's fearful the wickedness there is about, ain't it? It's enough to break yer 'art. Sich a neighb'r'ood too! Wy, if it was known as I'd give you this 'ere little friendly information, bein' in business meself an' knowin' wot it is, my life wouldn't be safe a hower. It wouldn't, Mr Grinder.'

'Wouldn't it?' said Mr Grinder. 'You mean them in the Jago, I s'pose.'

'Yus. They're a awful lot, Mr Grinder – you've no idear. The father o' this 'ere boy as I've warned you aginst, 'e's in with a desprit gang, an' they'd murder me if they thought I'd come an' told you honest, w'en you might 'a' bin robbed, as is my nature to. They would indeed. So o' course you won't say wot I toldjer, nor 'oo give you this 'ere honourable friendly warnin' – not to nobody.'

'That's awright,' answered the simple Grinder, 'I won't let on. But out 'e goes, promp'. I'm obliged to ye, Mr Weech. Er – r wot'll ye take?'

Weech put away the suggestion with a virtuous palm: – 'Nothink at all, Mr Grinder, thanks all the same. I never touch nothink; an' I'm glad to – to do any moral job, so to speak, as comes in my way. "Scatter seeds o' kindness" you know, as the – the Psalm says,* Mr Grinder. Your boy ain't back, is 'e?'

And after peering cautiously, Mr Weech went his way.

CHAPTER 20

Dicky completed his round, and pushed his unladen trolley Grinder-ward with a fuller sense of responsibility than ever. For he carried money. A publican had paid him four and threepence, and he had taken two and tenpence elsewhere. He had left his proud signature, pencilled large and black, on two receipts, and he stopped in a dozen doorways to count the money over again, and make sure that all was right. Between the halts he added four and three to two and ten mentally, and proved his sum correct by subtracting each in turn from seven and a penny. And at last he stood his trolley on end by the bank of saucepans, and entered the shop.

'Walker's is paid, an' Wilkins is paid,' said Dicky, putting down the money. 'Two an' ten an' four an' three's seven an' a penny.'

Mr Grinder looked steadily and sourly at Dicky, and counted. He pitched the odd penny into the till and shook the rest of the coins in his closed hand, still staring moodily in the boy's face. 'It's three an' six a week you come 'ere at,' he said.

'Yus sir,' Dicky replied, since Grinder seemed to expect an answer. The supreme moment when he should take his first wages had been the week's beacon to him, reddening and brightening as Saturday night grew nearer.

'Three an' six a week an' yer tea.'

Dicky wondered.

'So as if I found out anythink about – say Brass Roastin'-jacks for instance – I could give ye yer three an' six an' start y' auf, unless I did somethin' wuss.'

Dicky was all incomprehension; but something made him feel a little sick.

'But s'posin' I *didn't* find out anythink about – say Seven-pun' Jars o' Pickles – an' s'pose I wasn't disposed to suspect anythink in regard to – say Doormats; then I could either give ye a week's notice or pay y' a week's money an' clear y' out on the spot, without no more trouble.'

Mr Grinder paused, and still looked at Dicky with calm dislike. Then he added, as though in answer to himself, 'Yus.' . . .

He dropped the money slowly from his right hand to his left. Dicky's mouth was dry, and the drawers and pickle-jars swam before him at each side of Grinder's head. What did it mean?

'Ere y' are,' cried Mr Grinder, with sudden energy, thrusting his hand across the counter. 'Two three-and-sixes is seven shillin's, an' you can git yer tea at 'ome with yer dirty little sister. Git out o' my shop!'

Dicky's hand closed mechanically on the money, and after a second's pause, he found broken speech. 'W—w—wot for, sir?' he asked, huskily. 'I ain't done nothink!'

'No, an' you sha'n't do nothink, that's more. Out ye go! If I see ye near the place agin I'll 'ave ye locked up!'

Dicky slunk to the door. He felt the sobs coming, but he turned at the threshold and said with tremulous lips: – 'Woncher gimme a chance, sir? S'elp me, I done me best. I—'

Mr Grinder made a short rush from the back of the shop, and Dicky gave up and fled.

It was all over. There could never be a shop with 'R. Perrott' painted over it, now; there would be no parlour with stuff-bottomed chairs and a piano for Em to play. He was cut off from the trolley for ever. Dicky was thirteen, and at that age the children of the Jago were past childish tears; but tears he could not smother, even till he might find a hiding-place: they burst out shamefully in the open street.

He took dark turnings, and hid his head in doorways. It was very bitter. At last, when the sobs grew fewer, he remembered the money gripped in his wet first. It was a consolation. Seven shillings was a vast sum in Dicky's eyes; until that day he had never handled so much in his life. It would have been handsome recompense, he thought, for any trouble in the world but this. He must take it home, of course; it might avail to buy sympathy of his father and mother. But then, to think he might have had as much every fortnight of his life, a good tea every day, and the proud responsibility, and the trolley! At this his lips came awry again, his eyes sought his sleeve, and he turned to another doorway.

His glance fell on the white apron, now smudged and greased in good earnest. It made him feel worse; so he untied it and stuffed it away under his jacket. He wondered vaguely what had occurred to irritate Mr Grinder, and why he talked of pickles and doormats; but the sorrow of it all afflicted him to the extinction of such minor speculation. And in this misery he dragged his reluctant feet toward the Old Jago.

CHAPTER 21

He handed his father the seven shillings, and received a furious belting for losing his situation. He cried quietly, but it was not because of the strap. All he feared now was to meet Father Sturt. He had rather fifty beltings than Father Sturt's reproaches; and, having disgraced himself with Mr Grinder in some mysterious way which it was beyond his capacity to understand, what but reproaches could he expect from the vicar? The whole world was against him. As for himself, he was hopeless: plainly he must have some incomprehensible defect of nature, since he offended, do as he might, and could neither understand nor redeem his fault. He wondered if it had been so with little Neddy Wright, who had found the world too ruthless for him at ten; and had tied a brick to his neck, as he had seen done with needless dogs, and let himself timidly down into the canal at Haggerstone Bridge.

So he shuffled through Jago Row, when a hand came on his shoulder and a hoarse voice said: – 'Wot's the matter, Dicky?'

He turned, and saw the mild, coarse face of Pigeony Poll, the jaw whereof was labouring on something tough and sticky. Poll pulled from her pocket a glutinous paper, clinging about a cohesive lump of broken toffee – the one luxury of her moneyed times. ''Ave a bit,' she said. 'Wot's the matter?'

But Dicky thrust the hand away and fled, for he feared another burst of tears. His eyes were bad enough as it was, and he longed to hide himself in some hole.

He turned into New Jago Street. Hither it was that Jerry Gullen had betaken himself with his family and the canary, after the great eviction. Dicky slackened his pace, loitered at Jerry's doorway, and presently found himself in the common passage. It was long since he had had a private interview with Jerry Gullen's canary: for, indeed, he was thirteen – he was no longer a child, in fact! – and it was not well that he should indulge in such foolish weakness. Nevertheless he went as far as the back door. There stood the old donkey, mangy and infirm as ever, but apparently no nearer the end. The wood of the fence was bitten in places, but it was not as yet gnawed to the general whiteness and roundness of that in Canary's old abode. Canary, indeed, was fortunate today, for at the sound of Dicky's step he lifted his nose from a small heap of straw, dust, and mouldy hay, swept into a corner. Dicky stepped into the yard, and put his hand on Canary's neck; presently he glanced guiltily at the windows above. Nobody was looking. And in five minutes Dicky, aged as he was, had told Canary his troubles, while new tears wetted the ragged crest* and dropped into the dusty straw.

Now his grief lost some of its edge. Ashamed as he was, he had a shapeless, unapprehended notion that Canary was the sole creature alive that could understand and feel with him. And Canary poked his nose under the old jacket and sniffed in sympathy, as the broken lining tickled him. Dicky's intellectuals began to arrange themselves. Plainly, Mr Weech's philosophy was right after all. He was of the Jago, and he must prey on the outer world, as all the Jago did; not stray foolishly off the regular track in chase of visions, and fall headlong. Father Sturt was a creature of another mould. Who was he, Dicky Perrott, that he should break away from the Jago habit, and strain after another nature? What could come of it but defeat and bitterness? As old Beveridge had said, the Jago had got him. Why should he fight against the inevitable, and bruise himself? The ways out of the Jago old Beveridge had told him, years ago. Gaol, the gallows and the High Mob. There was his chance, his aspiration, his goal: the High Mob. To dream of oil-shops or regular wages was foolishness. His bed was made in the Jago, and he must lie on it. His hope in life, if he might have a hope at all, was to be of the High Mob. Spare nobody, stop at nothing, do his devilmost: old Beveridge had said that years ago. The task was before him, and he must not balk at it. As for gaol and the gallows, well! There they were, and he could not help it; ill ways out of the Jago, both, but still – ways out.

He rubbed his face carefully with his sleeve, put away his foolish ambitions, and went forth with a brave heart: to accomplish his destiny for well or ill – a Jago rat. To do his devilmost. But to avoid Father Sturt.

Out he went into Shoreditch High Street, and there he prowled the evening away; there and in Norton Folgate. But he touched for* nothing – nothing at all. He feared lest his week's honesty had damaged his training. Even an apple on a stall he failed at, and had to run. And then he turned into Bethnal Green Road.

But here a thought checked him suddenly. What of Mr Grinder? He had threatened to have Dicky locked up if he came near the shop again. But a child of the Jago knew too much to be frightened by such a threat as that. He went on. He felt interested to see how his late employer was getting along without him, and who was minding the goods outside the shop. Probably there was nobody: and this gave Dicky an idea.

He had forgotten his smudgy apron, folded and tucked away in the lining of his jacket. Now he pulled it out, and fastened it before him once more. He knew Mr Grinder's habits in the shop, and if he could seize a fitting opportunity he might be able, attired in his apron, to pick up or reach down any article that struck his fancy, fearless of interference from passers-by; for he would seem to be still shop-boy.

With that he hastened, for it was near closing time at Grinder's. He took the opposite side of the road, the better to observe unseen in the darkness. But Mr Grinder had already begun to carry things in from the pavement. As Dicky looked he came out with a long pole wherewith he unhooked from above a clattering cluster of pails and watering-pots, and a bunch of doormats. The doormats he let fall on the flags, while he carried in the pots and pails. Dicky knew that these pots and pails were kept at night in a shed behind the house; so he scuttled across the road, opening the blade of his old knife as he ran. He cut the string that held the mats together, selected a thick one, rolled it under his arm, and edged off into the shadow. Then he ran quietly across to the nearest turning.

Presently Mr Grinder came out, hooked his finger in the string among the mats, and pulled up nothing. He stooped, and saw that the string was cut. He looked about him suspiciously, flung the mats over, and counted them. Then he stood erect; stared up the street, down the street, and across the road, with his mouth open; and made short rushes left and right into the gloom. Then he returned to the mats and scratched his head. Finally, he gave another glance about the street, picked up the mats in his arms and carried them in, counting them as he went. And, the mats bestowed, whenever he came forth for a fresh armful of saucepans, he stood and gazed doubtfully, now this way, now that, about the Bethnal Green Road.

Mr Aaron Weech was pushing his last shutter into its place when 'Clean the knives,' said Dicky Perrott, in perfunctory repetition of the old formula.

Mr Weech seemed taken aback. 'Wot, that?' he asked, doubtfully, pointing at the doormat. Then, after a sharp look about the almost deserted street, he ran to Jago Row corner, twenty yards away, and looked down there. Nobody was hiding, and he came back. He led the way into the shop, and closed the door. Then, looking keenly in Dicky's face, he suddenly asked – "Oo toldjer to bring that 'ere?'

'Told me?' Dicky answered sullenly. 'Nobody told me. Don'cher want it?'

''Ow much did 'e tell ye t' ask for it?'

'Tell me? 'Oo?'

'*You* know. 'Ow much didjer say 'e said?'

Dicky was mystified. 'Dunno wotcher mean,' he replied.

Mr Weech suddenly broke into a loud laugh, but kept his keen look on the boy's face nevertheless. 'Ah, it's a good joke, Dicky, ain't it?' he said, and laughed again. 'But you can't 'ave me, ye know! Mr Grinder's a old friend o' mine, an' I know 'is little larks. Wot did 'e tell ye to do if I wouldn't 'ave that doormat?'

'Tell me?' asked Dicky, plainly more mystified than ever. 'Wy 'e never told me nothink. 'E gimme the sack this afternoon, an' chucked me out.'

'Then wotcher got yer apron on now for?'

'Oh,' said Dicky, looking down at it, 'I jist put it on agin – o' purpose.' And he glanced at the mat.

Mr Weech understood, and grinned – a genuine grin this time. 'That's right Dicky,' he said, 'never let yer wits go a-ramblin'. A sharp boy like you's a lot too good for a shop-boy, slavin' away from mornin' till night, an' treated ungrateful. Wot did 'e sack ye for?'

'I dunno. Took a fit in 'is 'ead, I s'pose. Wotcher goin' to gimme for this mat? It's a two an' three mat.'

'Want somethink to eat, doncher?' suggested Mr Weech, glancing at a heap of stale cake.

'No I don't,' Dicky answered, with sulky resolution. 'I want money.'

'Awright,' said Mr Weech, resignedly. 'You ain't 'ad much to eat an' drink 'ere for a long time, though. But I'll do the 'an'some, seein' you're bin treated ungrateful by Grinder. 'Ere's twopence.'

But Dicky held to the mat. 'Twopence ain't enough,' he said. 'I want fourpence.' He meant to spare nobody – not even Mr Weech.

'Wot? Fourpence?' gasped Mr Weech indignantly. 'Wy, you're mad. Take it away.'

Dicky rolled the mat under his arm and turned to the door.

'Ere,' said Mr Weech, seeing him going, 'I'll make it thrippence, seein' you're bin treated so bad. Thrippence – *and* a slice o' cake,' he added, perceiving that Dicky did not hesitate.

'I don't want no cake,' Dicky answered doggedly. 'I want fourpence, an' I won't take no less.'

The good Weech was unwilling that Dicky should find another market after all, so he submitted to the extortion. 'Ah well,' he said, with a sigh, pulling out the extra coppers, 'jist for this once, then. You'll 'ave to make it up next time. Mindjer, it's on'y 'cos I'm sorry for ye bein' treated ungrateful. Don't *you* go an' treat *me* ungrateful, now.'

Dicky pocketed his pence and made for home, while Mr Weech, chuckling gently at his morning prophecy of a doormat for fourpence, carried the plunder to the room reserved for new and unused stock; promising himself, however, a peep at Grinder's shop in the morning, to make quite sure that Dicky had really left.

So ended Dicky's dealings with the house of Grinder. When Father Sturt next saw the oil-man, and inquired of Dicky's progress, he was met with solemn congratulations that no larcenies were to pay for. Mr Grinder's sagacity, it seemed, had enabled him to detect and crush at the outset Dicky's plans for selling stock wholesale on his own account. Out of consideration for the vicar's recommendation he had refrained from handing the boy over to the police, but had paid him a week in advance and dismissed him. Father Sturt insisted on repaying the money, and went his way with a heavy heart. For if this were what came of the promising among his flock, what of the others? For some while he saw nothing of Dicky; and the incident fell back among a crowd of others in his remembrance: for Dicky was but one among thousands, and the disappointment was but one of many hundreds.

Lying awake that night, but with closed eyes, Dicky heard his mother, talking with his father, suggest that perhaps an enemy had earwigged Grinder, and told him a tale that had brought about Dicky's dismissal: somebody, perhaps, who wanted the situation for somebody else. Josh Perrott did no more than grunt at the guess, but it gave a new light to Dicky. Clearly that would account for Grinder's change. But who could the mischief-maker be?

The little clock on the mantelpiece ticked away busily in the silence, and Dicky instantly thought of the hunchback. He it must have been, without a doubt. Who else? Was he not hanging about the shop, staring and sneering, but a day or two back? And was it not he who had pursued him with malice on every occasion, in school and out? Had not Bobby Roper this very trick of lying tales? Where was the gratuitous injury in all these four years that had not been Bobby Roper's work? Dicky trembled with rage as he lay, and he resolved on condign revenge. The war with Dove Lane was over for the time being, but that made it easier for him to catch his enemy.

CHAPTER 22

The feud between the Jago and Dove Lane was eternal, just as was that between the Ranns and the Learys; but, like the Rann and Leary feud, it had its paroxysms and its intervals. And, in both cases, the close of a paroxysm was signalised by a great show of amity between the factions. Bob Rann and Billy Leary would drink affably from the same pot, and Norah Walsh and Sally Green would call each other 'mum'; while Jagos and Dove-Laners would mingle in bars and lend pinches of tobacco, and call each other 'matey'. A paroxysm in the war had now passed, and reconciliation was due. The Dove-Laners had been heavily thrashed: their benjamins and kicksies had been impounded in Meakin Street, and they had ceased from buying. Dove Lane itself had been swept from end to end by the victorious Jago, and the populations of both were dotted thickly with bandaged heads. This satisfactory state of things achieved, there was little reason left for fighting. Moreover, if fighting persisted too long at a time, the police were apt to turn up in numbers, subjecting the neighbourhood to much inconvenient scrutiny, and very often coming across Jagos – or even Dove-Laners – 'wanted' on old accounts. So peace was declared; and, as a visible sign thereof, it was determined that the Dove-Laners should visit the Jago in a body, there to join in a sing-song at Mother Gapp's. Mother Gapp's was chosen, not only because it *was* Mother Gapp's – an important consideration – but also because of the large room behind the bar, called the 'club-room', which had long ago been made of two rooms and a big cupboard, by the cutting away of crazy partitions from the crazy walls.

Scarce was it dark when the Dove-Laners, in a succession of hilarious groups – but withal a trifle suspicious – began to push through Mother Gapp's doors. Their caps pulled down to their ears, their hands in their pockets, their shoulders humped, and their jackets buttoned tight, they lurched through the Jago, grinning with uneasy affability at the greetings that met them, being less practised than the Jagos in the assumption of elaborate cordiality.

In the club-room of the Feathers there were but three or four of the other party, though the bar was packed. The three or four, of whom Josh Perrott was one, were by way of a committee of stewards deputed to bid the Dove-Laners welcome, and to help them to seats. The Jagos were in some sort in the situation of hosts, and it had been decided after debate that it would ill become them to take their places till their guests were seated. The punctilio of the Jago on such occasions was a marvel ever.

So Josh Perrott stood at one side of the club-room door and Billy Leary at the other, shaking hands with all who entered, and strenuously maintaining cheerful grins. Now the Jago smile was a smile by itself, unlike the smiles in other places. It faded suddenly, and left the face – the Jago face – drawn and sad and startling by contrast, as of a man betrayed into mirth in the midst of great sorrow. So that a persistent grin was known for a work of conscious effort.

The Dove-Laners came in still larger numbers than had been expected, and before long it was perceived that there would be little space in the club-room, if any at all, for the Jagos. Already the visitors seemed to fill the place, but they still kept coming, and found places by squeezing. There was some doubt as to what had best be done. Meanwhile the sing-song began, for at least a score were anxious to 'oblige' at once, and every moment fresh volunteers arose. Many Dove-Laners stood up, and so made more room; but more came, and still more, till the club-room could hold not another, and the very walls were like to burst. Under the low ceiling hung a layer of smoke that obscured the face of the man standing on the table at the end to sing; and under the smoke was a close-packed array of heads, hats, and clay pipes, much diversified by white bandages and black eyes.

Such Dove-Laners as came in now were fain to find places in the bar, if they could; and a crowd of Jagos, men and women, hung about the doors of the Feathers. More fortunate than other boys, Dicky, who would go anywhere to hear what purported to be music, had succeeded in worming himself through the bar and almost to the door of the club-room; but he could get no farther, and now he stood compressed, bounded on the face by Cocko Harnwell's coat-tails, and on the back of the head by Fluffy Pike's moleskin waistcoat, with pearlies down the front and the artful dodge over the pockets.* Pud Palmer – one of the reception committee – was singing. He accompanied his chorus by a step dance, and all the company stamped in sympathy: –

'She's a fighter, she's a biter, she's a swearer, she's a tearer,
    The gonophs down aar alley they calls 'er Rorty Sal;
    But as I'm a pertikiler sort o' bloke. I calls 'er Rorty SAIRER,*
    I'm goin'–'

Crack! – CRASH!

Dicky clung to Cocko Harnwell's coat-tails lest he were trampled to death; and for a while he was flung about, crushed and bruised, among rushing men, like a swimmer among breakers, while the air was rent with howls and the smash of glass. For the club-room floor had given way.

It had been built but slightly in the beginning, as floor for two small rooms and a cupboard, with little weight to carry. Old and rotten now, and put to the strain of a multitude, stamping in unison, it had failed utterly, and had let down a struggling mob of men five feet on the barrels in the cellar, panic-stricken and jumbled with tables, pots, wooden forms, lighted pipes and splintered joinery.

From the midst of the stramash a Dove-Laner bawled aloud that it was a trap,* and instantly Jagos and Dove-Laners were at each others' throats, and it was like to go hard with the few Jagos among the ruins. Billy Leary laid about him desperately with a ragged piece of flooring, while Josh Perrott and Pud Palmer battered Dove-Laners with quart pots. Then it was shouted without that the Dove-Laners were exterminating the Jagos within, and a torrent of Jagos burst through the doors, poured through the bar, and over the club-room threshold into the confusion below.

Dicky, bruised, frightened and flung like a rag this way and that, at last made shift to grasp a post, and climb up on the bar counter. Mother Gapp, a dishevelled maniac, was dancing amid pots and broken glass, black in the face, screaming inaudibly. Dicky stumbled along the counter, climbed over the broken end of a partition, and fell into the arms of Kiddo Cook, coming in with the rush. 'Put the boy out!' yelled Kiddo, turning and heaving him over the heads behind him. Somebody caught Dicky by a leg and an arm, his head hit the door post, the world turned a double-somersault about him, and he came down with a crash.

He was on the flags of Old Jago Street, with all his breath driven out of him.

But he was quickly on his feet again. A crowd beat against the front of Mother Gapp's, and reinforcements came running from everywhere, with the familiar rallying-cry, 'Jago! Jago 'old tight!' Dove Lane had abused the Jago hospitality; woe to the Dove-Laners!

There were scuffles here and there, where Dove-Laners, who had never reached the club-room, or who had been crowded out of it, made for escape. Dicky was shaken and sore, but he pulled himself together resolutely. He had seen a few Dove Lane boys about before he had got into the Feathers, and plainly it was his duty to find them and bash them. Moreover, he wondered what had become of his father. He hastened through the dark passage of the house next to Mother Gapp's, into the back yard, and through the broken fence. There was a door in the club-room wall, and through this he thought to see what was going forward.

The cellar – at any rate, at the farther end – was a pit of writhing forms, and the din rose loud as ever. A short figure stood black against the light, and held by the doorpost, looking down at the riot. Dicky knew it. He sprang at Bobby Roper, pulled him by the arm, and struck at him furiously. The hunchback, whimpering, did his best to retaliate and to get away; but Dicky, raging at the remembrance of his fancied injury, struck savagely, and struck again, till Bobby Roper tripped backward over the projecting end of a broken floor-board, and pitched headlong into the cellar. He struck a barrel and rolled over, falling into the space between that and two other barrels. Dicky looked, but the hunchback did not move. Then some of the Dove-Laners flung pots at the lamps hanging against the club-room walls. Soon they were smashed and fell, and there was a darkness; and under cover thereof the aliens essayed flight.

Dicky was a little frightened at what he had done, but he felt that with Bobby Roper anything was justifiable. Some Dove-Laners escaped by the back door – the cellar was low, and there was not five feet between the barrels and the broken joists – and these Dicky avoided by getting back through the fence. In the end, most of the enemy struggled away by one means or another, and when lights were brought at last the Jagos were found pummelling each other savagely in the gloom.

Father Sturt, apprised of something uncommon by the exodus of members from the club, finally locked the doors and came to investigate. He arrived as the Jagos were extricating themselves from the cellar, and it was he who lifted the little hunchback from among the barrels and carried him into the open air; he also who carried him home. No bone was broken, and no joint was disturbed, but there was a serious shock, many contusions, and a cut on the scalp. So said the surgeon whom Father Sturt took with him to Dove Lane. And Bobby Roper lay a fortnight in bed.

More plaster than ever embellished the heads of Dove Lane and the Jago that night; but for the Jagos there was compensation. For down among the barrels lay many a packet of tobacco, many a pair of boots, and many a corner stuffed with mixed property of other sorts: which Mother Gapp had fenced for many a month back. So that it happened to more than one warrior to carry home again something with which he had run between the 'Posties' long before, and had sold to Mother Gapp for what she would give.

The ground floor of the Feathers stood a battered shell. The damage of four years ago was inconsiderable compared to this. With tears and blasphemy Mother Gapp invaded the hoard of her long iniquity to buy a new floor; but it was the larceny – the taking of the tobacco and the boots, and the many other things from among the barrels – that cut her to the soul. A crool – a crool thing was such robbery – sheer robbery, said Mother Gapp.

Josh Perrott got a bad sprain in the cellar and had to be helped home. More, he took with him not a single piece of plunder, such was his painful disablement.

CHAPTER 23

For more than a week Josh Perrott could not walk about. And it was a bad week. For some little while his luck had been but poor, and now he found himself laid up with a total reserve fund of fourteenpence. A coat was pawned with old Poll Rann (who kept a leaving shop* in a first floor back in Jago Row) for ninepence. Then Josh swore at Dicky for not being still at Grinder's, and told him to turn out and bring home some money. Dicky had risen almost too sore and stiff to stand, on the morning after the fight at the Feathers, and he was little better now. But he had to go, and he went, though he well knew that a click was out of the question, for his joints almost refused to bend. But he found that the fat's a-running boys were contemplating business, and he scouted for them with such success as to bring home sevenpence in the evening. Then Kiddo Cook, who had left Mother Gapp's with a double armful on the night of the sing-song, found himself rich enough, being a bachelor, to lend Josh eighteenpence. And a shawl of Hannah Perrott's was pawned. That, though, was redeemed the next day, together with the coat. For Dicky brought home a golden sovereign.

It had been an easy click – scarce a click at all, perhaps, strictly speaking. Dicky had tramped into the city, and had found a crowd outside St Paul's – a well-dressed crowd, not being moved on: for something was going forward in the cathedral. He recognised one of the High Mob, a pogue-hunter – that is a pickpocket who deals in purses. Dicky watched this man's movements, by way of education; for he was an eminent practitioner, and worked alone, with no assistant to cover him. Dicky saw him in the thick of the crowd, standing beside and behind one lady after another; but it was only when his elbow bent to slip something into his own pocket that Dicky knew he had 'touched'. Presently he moved to another part of the crowd, where mostly men were standing, and there he stealthily let drop a crumpled newspaper, and straightway left the crowd. He had 'worked' it as much as he judged safe. Dicky wriggled toward the crumpled paper, slipped it under his jacket, and cleared away also. He knew that there was something in the paper besides news: that, in fact, there were purses in it – purses emptied and shed as soon as might be, because nobody can swear to money, but strange purses lead to destruction. Dicky recked little of this danger, but made his best pace to a recess in a back street, there to examine his pogues; for though the uxter was gone from them, they might yet bring a few coppers from Mr Weech, if they were of good quality. They were a fairly sound lot. One had a large clasp that looked like silver, and another was quite new, and Dicky was observing with satisfaction the shop-shininess of the lining, when he perceived a cunning pocket at the back, lying flat against the main integument – and in it was a sovereign! He gulped at the sight. Clearly the pogue-hunter, emptying the pogues in his pocket by sense of touch, had missed the flat pocket. Dicky was not yet able to run with freedom, but he never ceased from trotting till he reached his own staircase in Old Jago Street. And so the eight or nine days passed, and Josh went out into the Jago with no more than a tenderness about his ankle.

Now, he much desired a good click; so he went across High Street Shoreditch, to Kingsland Railway Station and bought a ticket for Canonbury.

Luck was against him, it was plain. He tramped the northern suburbs from three o'clock till dark, but touched for nothing. He spent money, indeed, for he feared to overwork his ankle, and for that reason rested in divers public-houses. He peeped in at the gates of quiet gardens, in the hope of garden-hose left unwatched, or tennis-rackets lying in a handy summer-house. But he saw none. He pried about the doors of private stable-yards, in case of absent grooms and unprotected bunches of harness, but in vain. He inspected quiet areas and kitchen entrances in search of unguarded spoons – even descended into one area, where he had to make an awkward excuse about buying old bottles, in consequence of meeting the cook at the door. He tramped one quiet road after another on the look out for a dead 'un – a house furnished, but untenanted. But there was never a dead 'un, it seemed, in all the northern district. So he grew tired and short-tempered, and cursed himself for that he had not driven off with a baker's horse and cart that had tempted him early in the afternoon.

It grew twilight, and then dark. Josh sat in a public-house, and took a long rest and some bread and cheese. It would never do to go home without touching, and for some time he considered possibilities with regard to a handful of silver money, kept in a glass on a shelf behind the bar. But it was out of reach, and there were too many people in the place for any attempt by climbing on the counter. Josh grew savage and soured. Plastering itself was not such troublesome work; and at least the pay was certain. It was little short of ten o'clock when he left the public-house and turned back toward Canonbury. He would have *something* on the way, he resolved, and he would catch the first train home. He would have to knock somebody over in a dark street, that was all. It was nothing new, but he would rather have made his click another way this time, because his tender ankle might keep him slow, or even give way altogether; and to be caught in a robbery with violence might easily mean something more than mere imprisonment; it might mean a dose of the 'cat':* and the cat was a thing the thought or the mention whereof sent shudders through the Old Jago.

But no: nobody worth knocking down came his way. Truly luck was out tonight. There was a spot by the long garden wall of a corner house that would have suited admirably, and as Josh lingered there, and looked about him, his eye fell on a ladder, reared nearly upright against the back wall of that same corner house, and lashed at the roof. It passed by the side of the second floor window, whereof the top sash was a little open. That would do. It was not his usual line of work, but it looked very promising.

He stuck his stick under his waistcoat by way of the collar, and climbed the wall with gingerly care, giving his sound foot all the hard work. The ladder offered no difficulty, but the bottom sash of the window was stiff, and he cracked a pane of glass in pushing at the frame with his stick. The sash lifted, however, in the end, and he climbed into the dark room, being much impeded by the dressing-table. All was quiet in the house, and the ticking of a watch on the dressing-table was distinct in the ear. Josh felt for it and found it, with a chain hanging from the bow.*

The house was uncommonly quiet. Could it possibly be a

dead 'un after all? Josh felt that he ought to have inspected the front windows before climbing the wall, but the excitement of the long-delayed chance had ruined his discretion. At any rate he would reconnoitre. The door was ajar and the landing was dark.

Down in the drawing-room a gross, pimply man, in shirt-sleeves and socks, sat up on the sofa at the sound of an opened window higher in the house. He took a drink from the glass by his side, and listened. Then he rose and went softly upstairs.

Josh Perrott came out on the landing. It was a long landing, with a staircase at the end, illuminated from somewhere below: so that it was not a case of a dead 'un after all. He tiptoed along to take a look down the stairs, nevertheless. Then he was conscious of a loud breathing, as of an over-gorged cow, and up behind the stair-rails rose a fat head, followed by a fat trunk, between white shirt-sleeves.

Josh sank into the shadow. The man had no light, but discover him he must, sooner or later, for the landing was narrow. Better sooner, and suddenly. As the man's foot was on the topmost stair, Josh sprang at him with a straight left-hander that took him on the broad chin, and sent him downstairs in a heap, with a crash and a roar. Josh darted back to the room he had just left, scrambled through the window, and slid down the ladder, as he had slid down many another when he was a plasterer's boy. He checked himself short of the bottom, sprang at the wall-coping, flung himself over, and ran up the dark by-street, with the sound of muffled roars and screams faint in his ears.

He ran a street or two, taking every corner as he came to it, and then fell into a walk. In his flight he had not spared his ankle, and now it was painful. Moreover, he had left his stick behind him, in the bedroom. But he was in Highbury, and Canonbury Road Station was less than half a mile away. He grinned silently as he went, for there was something in the aspect of the overfed householder, and in the manner of his downfall, that gave the adventure a comic flavour. He took a peep at his spoil as he passed under a street lamp, for all watches and chains are the same in the dark, and the thing might be a mere Waterbury on a steel guard.* But no: both were gold, and heavy: a red clock and slang* if ever there was one. And so Josh Perrott hobbled and chuckled his way home.

CHAPTER 24

But indeed Josh Perrott's luck was worse than he thought. For the gross, pimply man was a High Mobsman – so very high a mobsman that it would have been slander and libel, and a very great expense, to write him down a mobsman at all. He paid a rent of a hundred and twenty pounds a year, and heavy rates, and put half-a-crown into the plate at a very respectable chapel every Sunday. He was, in fact, the King of High Mobsmen, spoken of among them as the Mogul.* He did no vulgar thievery: he never screwed a chat, nor claimed a peter,* nor worked the mace. He sat easily at home, and financed (sometimes planned) promising speculations: a large swindle requiring much ground-baiting and preliminary outlay; or a robbery of specie from a mail train: or a bank fraud needing organization and funds. When the results of such speculations consisted of money he took the lion's share. When they were expressed in terms of imprisonment they fell to active and intelligent subordinates. So that for years the Mogul had lived an affluent and a blameless life, far removed from the necessity of injudicious bodily exercise, and characterised by every indulgence consistent with a proper suburban respectability. He had patronised, snubbed, or encouraged High Mobsmen of more temerarious habit, had profited by their exploits, and had read of their convictions and sentences with placid interest in the morning papers. And after all this, to be robbed in his own house and knocked downstairs by a casual buster was an outrage that afflicted the Mogul with wrath infuriate. Because that was a sort of trouble that had never seemed a possibility, to a person of his eminence: and because the angriest victim of dishonesty is a thief.

However, the burglar had got clean away, that was plain; and he had taken the best watch and chain in the house, with the Mogul's initials on the back. So that respectable sufferer sent for the police, and gave his attention to the alleviation of bumps and the washing away of blood. In his bodily condition a light blow was enough to let a great deal of blood – no doubt with benefit;* and Josh Perrott's blows were not light in any case.

So it came to pass that not only were the police on the look-out for a man with a large gold watch with the Mogul's monogram on the back; but also the word was passed as by telegraph through underground channels, till every fence in London was warned that the watch was the Mogul's; and ere noon next day there was not one but would as life have put a scorpion in his pocket as that same toy and tackle that Josh Perrott was gloating over in his back room in Old Jago Street.

As for Josh, his ankle was bad in the morning, and swelled. He dabbed at it perseveringly with wet rags, and rubbed it vigorously, so that by one o'clock he was able to lace up his boot and go out. He was anxious to fence his plunder without delay, and he made his way to Hoxton. The watch seemed to be something especially good, and he determined to stand out for a price well above the usual figure. For the swag of common thieves commended no such prices as did that of the High Mob. All of it was bought and sold on the simple system first called into being seventy years back and more by the prince of fences, Ikey Solomons.* A breast-pin brought a fixed sum, good or bad, and a roll of cloth brought the fixed price of a roll of cloth, regardless of quality. Thus a silver watch fetched six shillings, never more and never less; a gold watch was worth twice as much; an uncommonly good one – a rich man's watch – would bring as much as eighteen shillings, if the thief were judge enough of its quality to venture the demand. And as it commonly took three men to secure a single watch in the open street – one to 'front',* one to snatch, and a third to take from the snatcher – the gains of the toy-getting trade were poor, except to the fence. This time Josh resolved to put pressure on the fence, and to do his best to get something as near a sovereign as might be. And as to the chain, so thick and heavy, he would fight his best for the privilege of sale by weight. Thus turning the thing in his mind, he entered the familiar doorway of the old clothes shop.

'Vot is id?' asked the fence, holding out his hand with the customary air of contempt for what was coming, by way of discounting it in advance. This particular fence, by-the-bye, never bought anything himself.* He inspected whatever was brought on behalf of an occult friend; and the transaction was completed by a shabby third party in an adjoining court. But he had an amazingly keen regard for his friend's interests.

Josh put the watch into the extended hand. The fence lifted it to his face, turned it over, and started. He looked hard at Josh, and then again at the watch, and handed it hastily back, holding it gingerly by the bow. 'Don' vant *dot*', he said; 'nod me – nod 'im, I mean. No, no.' He turned away, shaking his hand as though to throw off contamination. 'Take id avay.'

'Wot's the matter?' Josh demanded, astonished. 'Is it 'cos o' the letters on the back? You can easy send it to church, can't ye?'

A watch is 'sent to church' when it is put into another case. But the fence waved away the suggestion. 'Take id avay I tell you,' he said. 'I – 'e von't 'ave nodden to do vid id.'

'Wot's the matter with the chain, then?' asked Josh. But the fence walked away to the back of the shop, wagging his hands desperately, like a wet man seeking a towel, and repeating only: – 'Nodden to do vid id – take id avay – nodden to do vid id.'

Josh stuffed his prize back into his pocket, and regained the street. He was confounded. What was wrong with Cohen? Did he suspect a police trick to entrap him? Josh snorted with indignation at the thought. He was no nark! But perhaps the police were showing a pressing interest in Cohen's business concerns just now, and he had suspended fencing for a while. The guess was a lame one, but he could think of none better at the moment, as he pushed his way to the Jago. He would try Mother Gapp.

Mother Gapp would not even take the watch in her hands; her eyes were good enough at that distance. 'Lor', Josh Perrott,' she said, 'wot 'a' ye bin up to now? Want to git me lagged now, do ye? Ain't satisfied with breakin' up the 'ouse an' ruinin' a pore widder that way, ain't ye? You git out, go on. I 'ad 'nough o' you!'

It was very extraordinary. Was there a general reclamation of fences? But there were men at work at the Feathers, putting down boards and restoring partitions; and two of them had been 'gone over' ruinously on their way to work, and now they came and went with four policemen. Possibly Mother Gapp feared the observation of carpenters. Be it as it might, there was nothing for it now but Weech's.

Mr Weech was charmed. 'Dear me, it's a wonderful fine

watch, Mr Perrott – a wonderful fine watch. An' a beautiful chain.' But he was looking narrowly at the big monogram as he said it. 'It's reely a wonderful article. 'Ow they do git 'em up, to be sure! Cost a lot o' money too, I'll be bound. Might you be thinkin' o' sellin' it?'

'Yus o' course,' replied Josh. 'That's wot I brought it for.'

'Ah, it's a lovely watch, Mr Perrott – a lov-erly watch; an' the chain matches it. But you mustn't be too 'ard on me. Shall we say four pound for the little lot?'

It was more than double Josh's wildest hopes, but he wanted all he could get. 'Five,' he said doggedly.

Weech gazed at him with tender rebuke. 'Five pound's a awful lot o' money, Mr Perrott,' he said. 'You're too 'ard on me, reely. I 'ardly know 'ow I can scrape it up. But it's a beautiful little lot, an' I won't 'aggle. But I ain't got all that money in the 'ouse now. I never keep so much money in the 'ouse – sich a neighb'r'ood, Mr Perrott! Bring it round tomorrer mornin' at eleven.'

'Awright, I'll come. Five quid, mind.'

'Ah yus,' answered Mr Weech, with a reproving smile. 'It's reely more than I ought!'

Josh was jubilant, and forgot his sore ankle. He had never handled such a sum as five pounds since his fight with Billy Leary, years ago; when, indeed, he had stooped to folly in the shape of lavish treating, and so had not enjoyed the handling of the full amount.

Mr Weech, also, was pleased. For it was a great stroke of business to oblige so distinguished a person as the Mogul. There was no telling what advantages it might not lead to in the way of trade.

That night the Perrotts had a hot supper, brought from Walker's cookshop in paper. And at eleven the next morning Josh, twenty yards from Mr Weech's door, with the watch and chain in his pocket, was tapped on the arm by a constable in plain clothes, while another came up on the other side. 'Mornin', Perrott,' said the first constable, cheerily. 'We've got a little business with you at the station.'

'Me? Wot for?'

'Oh well, come along; p'raps it ain't anything – unless there's a gold watch an' chain on you, from Highbury. It's just a turnin' over.'

'Awright,' replied Josh, resignedly. 'It's a fair cop. I'll go quiet.'

'That's right, Perrott; it ain't no good playin' the fool, you know.' They were moving along; and as they came by Weech's shop, a whiskered face, with a patch of shining scalp over it, peeped from behind a curtain that hung at the rear of the bloaters and plumcake in the window. As he saw it, Josh ducked suddenly, wrenching his arm free, and dashed over the threshold. Mr Weech, whiskers and apron flying, galloped through the door at the back, and the constables sprang upon Josh instantly and dragged him into the street. 'Wotcher mean?' cried the one who knew him, indignantly, and with a significant glance at the other. 'Call that goin' quiet?'

Josh's face was white and staring with rage. 'Awright,' he grunted through his shut teeth, after a pause. 'I'll go quiet now. I ain't got nothin' agin *you*.'

CHAPTER 25

Dicky's morning theft that day had been but a small one – he had run off with a new two-foot rule that a cabinet-maker had carelessly left on an unfinished office table at his shop door in Curtain Road. It was not much, but it might fetch some sort of a dinner at Weech's, which would be better than going home, and, perhaps, finding nothing. So about noon, all ignorant of his father's misfortune, he came by way of Holywell Lane and Bethnal Green Road to Meakin Street.

Mr Weech looked at him rather oddly, Dicky fancied, when he came in, but he took the two-foot rule with alacrity, and brought Dicky a rasher of bacon, and a slice of cake afterward. This seemed very generous. More: Mr Weech's manner was uncommonly amiable, and when the meal was over, of his own motion, he handed over a supplementary penny. Dicky was surprised; but he had no objection, and he thought little more about it.

As soon as he appeared in Luck Row he was told that his father had been 'smugged'. Indeed the tidings had filled the Jago within ten minutes. Josh Perrott was walking quietly along Meakin Street – so went the news – when up comes Snuffy* and another split, and smugs him. Josh had a go for Weech's door, to cut his lucky out at the back, but was caught. That was a smart notion of Josh's, the Jago opinion ran, to get through Weech's and out into the courts behind. But it was no go.

Hannah Perrott sat in her room, inert and lamenting. Dicky could not rouse her, and at last he went off by himself to reconnoitre about Commercial Street Police Station, and pick up what information he might; while a gossip or two came and took Mrs Perrott for consolation to Mother Gapp's. Little Em, unwashed, tangled and weeping, could well take care of herself and the room, being more than two years old.

Josh Perrott would be brought up tomorrow, Dicky ascertained, at the North London Police Court. So the next morning

found Dicky trudging moodily along the two miles of flags to
Stoke Newington Road; while his mother and three sympathis-
ing friends, who foresaw an opportunity for numerous tiny
drops with interesting circumstances to flavour them, took a
penny cast* on the way in a tramcar.

Dicky, with some doubt as to the disposition of the door-
keeping policeman toward ragged boys, waited for the four
women, and contrived to pass in unobserved among them.
Several Jagos were in the court, interested not only in Josh's
adventure, but in one of Cocko Harnwell's, who had indulged,
the night before, in an animated little scramble with three
policemen in Dalston; and they waited with sympathetic interest
while the luck was settled of a long string of drunk-and-
disorderlies.

At last Josh was brought in, and lurched composedly into the
dock, in the manner of one who knew the routine. The police
gave evidence of arrest, in consequence of information received,
and of finding the watch and chain in Josh's trousers pocket.
The prosecutor,* with his head conspicuously bedight with
sticking-plaster, puffed and grunted up into the witness-box,
kissed the book, and was a 'retired commission agent'.* He
positively identified the watch and chain, and he not less
positively identified Josh Perrott, whom he had picked out from
a score of men in the police-yard. This would have been a feat
indeed for a man who had never seen Josh, and had only once
encountered his fist in the dark, had it not been for the dutiful
though private aid of Mr Weech: who, in giving his information
had described Josh and his one suit of clothes with great fidelity,
especially indicating a scar on the right cheek-bone which would
mark him among a thousand. The retired commission agent was
quite sure of the prisoner. He had met him on the stairs, where
there was plenty of light from a lamp, and the prisoner had
attacked him savagely, beating him about the head and flinging
him downstairs. The policeman called by the prosecutor's
servant deposed to finding the prosecutor bruised and bleeding.
There was a ladder against the back of the house; a bedroom
window had been opened; there were muddy marks on the sill;
and he had found the stick – produced – lying in the bedroom.

Josh leaned easily on the rail before him while evidence was
being given, and said 'No, yer worship', whenever he was asked
if he desired to question a witness. He knew better than to run

the risk of incriminating himself by challenging the prosecutor's well-coloured evidence; and, as it was a certain case of committal for trial, it would have been useless in any event. He made the same reply when he was asked if he had anything to say before being committed: and straightway was 'fullied'. He lurched serenely out of the dock, waving his cap at his friends in the court, and that was all. The Jagos waited till Cocko Harnwell got his three months and then retired to neighbouring public-houses; but Dicky remembered his little sister, and hurried home.

The month's session at the Old Bailey had just begun, so that Josh had no long stay at Holloway.* Among the Jagos it was held to be a most creditable circumstance that Josh was to take his trial with full honours at the Old Bailey, and not at mere County Sessions at Clerkenwell, like a simple lob-crawler* or peter-claimer. For Josh's was a case of burglary with serious violence, such as was fitting for the Old Bailey, and not even a High Mobsman could come to trial with greater glory. 'As like as not it's laggin' dues,* after 'is other convictions,' said Bill Rann. And Jerry Gullen thought so too.

Dicky went, with his mother and Em, to see Josh at Newgate. They stood with other visitors, very noisy, before a double iron railing* covered with wire-netting, at the farther side whereof stood Josh and other prisoners, while a screaming hubbub of question and answer filled the air. Josh had little to say. He lounged against the farther railing with his hands in his pockets, asked what Cocko Harnwell had got, and sent a message to Bill Rann. While his wife did little more than look dolefully through the wires, and pipe: – 'Oh, Josh, wotever shall I do?' at intervals, with no particular emotion; while Em pressed her smudgy little face against the wires, and stared mightily; and while Dicky felt that if he had been younger he would have cried. When time was up, Josh waved his hand and slouched off, and his family turned out with the rest: little Em carrying into later years a memory of father as a man who lived in a cage.

In such a case as this, the Jago would have been for ever disgraced if Josh Perrott's pals had neglected to get up a 'break' or subscription to pay for his defence. Things were never very flourishing in the Jago. But this was the sort of break a Jago could not shirk, lest it were remembered against him when his own turn came. So enough was collected to brief an exceedingly junior counsel, who did his useless best. But the facts were too strong even for the most experienced advocate; the evidence of the prosecutor was nowhere to be shaken, and the jury found a verdict of guilty without leaving the box – indeed, with scarce the formality of collecting their heads together over the rails. Then Josh's past was most unpleasantly raked up before him. He had been convicted of larceny, of assaulting the police, and of robbery with violence. There were two sentences of six months' imprisonment recorded against him, one of three months, and two of a month. Besides fines. The Recorder* considered it a very serious offence. Not deterred by the punishments he had already received the prisoner had proceeded to a worse crime – burglary; and with violence. It was plain that lenience was wasted in such a case, and simple imprisonment was not enough. There must be an exemplary sentence. The prisoner must be kept in penal servitude for five years.

Lagging dues it was, as Bill Rann had anticipated. That Josh Perrott agreed with him was suggested by the fact that from the very beginning he described himself as a painter; because a painter in prison is apt to be employed at times in painting – a lighter and a more desirable task than falls to the lot of his fellows in other trades.

In a room by the court Josh saw his wife, Dicky, and Bill Rann (Josh's brother-in-law for the occasion) before his ride to Holloway, his one stopping place on the way to Chelmsford Gaol. Little Em had been left sprawling in the Jago gutters. This time Hannah Perrott wept in good earnest, and Dicky, notwithstanding his thirteen years, blinked very hard at the wall before him. The arrangement of Josh's affairs was neither a long nor a difficult labour. 'S'pose you'll 'ave to do wot you can with rush bags, an' sacks, and match-boxes, an' wot not,' he said to his wife, and she assented. Josh nodded: – 'An' if you 'ave to go in the 'ouse' – he meant the workhouse – 'well, it can't be 'elped. You won't be no wuss auf 'n me.'

'Oh, *she'll* be awright,' said Bill Rann, jerking his thumb cheerfully toward the missis. 'Wot about you? Think they'll make it Parkhurst?'

Josh shook his head moodily. Parkhurst being the prison reserved for convicts of less robust habit, he had little hope of enjoying its easier conditions.* Presently he said: – 'I bin put away this time – fair put away.'

'Wot?' answered Bill, 'narkin' dues is it?'

Josh nodded.

''Oo done it then? 'Oo narked?'

Josh shook his head. 'Never mind,' he said, 'I don't want 'im druv out o' the Jago 'fore I come out. I'd be sorry to miss 'im. *I* know 'im – that's enough.'

And then time was up. Josh suffered the missis to kiss him, and shook hands with Bill Rann. 'Good luck to all you Jagos,' he said. Dicky shook hands too, and said 'Goodbye, father!' in a voice of such laboured cheerfulness that a grin burst for a moment amid Josh's moody features as he was marched away, and so departed for the place – in Jago idiom – where the dogs don't bite.

CHAPTER 26

It was Father Sturt's practice to visit every family in his parish in regular order. But small as the parish was – insignificant, indeed, in mere area – its population exceeded eight thousand: so that the round was one of many months, for visiting was but one among innumerable duties. But Josh Perrott's lagging secured his family a special call. Not that the circumstances were in any way novel or at all uncommon; nor even that the vicar had any hope of being able to help. He was but the one man who could swim in a howling sea of human wreckage.* In the Jago, wives like Hannah Perrott, temporarily widowed by the absence of husbands 'in the country',* were to be counted in scores, and most were in worse case than she, in the matter of dependent children. Father Sturt's house-list revealed the fact that in Old Jago Street alone, near seventy of the males were at that moment on ticket-of-leave.*

In the Perrott case, indeed, the sufferers were fortunate, as things went. Mrs Perrott had but herself and the child of two to keep, for Dicky could do something, whether good or bad, for himself. The vicar might try to get regular work for Dicky, but it would be a vain toil, for he must tell an employer what he knew of Dicky's past and of that other situation. He could but give the woman the best counsel at his command, and do what he might to quicken any latent spark of energy. So he did his best, and that was all. The struggle lay with Hannah Perrott.

She had been left before, and more than once; but then the periods had been shorter, and, as a matter of fact, things had fallen out so well that scarce more than a meal here and there had had to be missed, though, when they came, the meals were apt to be but of crusts. And now there was more trouble ahead; for though she began her lonely time with but one small child on hand, she knew that ere long there would be two.

Of course, she had worked before; not only when Josh had been 'in' but at other times, to add to the family resources. She was a clumsy needle woman: else she might hope to earn some ninepence or a shilling a day at making shirts,* by keeping well to the needle for sixteen hours out of the twenty-four; and from the whole sum there would be no deductions, except for needles and cotton, and what the frugal employer might choose to subtract for work to which he could devise an objection. But, as it was, she must do her best to get some sack-making. They paid one-and-sevenpence a hundred for sacks, and, with speed and long hours, she could make a hundred in four days. Rush bag-making would bring even more, which would be desirable, considering the three-and-sixpence a week for rent: which, with the payments for other rooms, made the rent of the crazy den in Old Jago Street about equal, space for space, to that of a house in Onslow Square. Then there was a more lucrative employment still, but one to be looked for at intervals only: one not to be counted on at all, in fact, for it was a prize, and many sought after it. This was the making of matchboxes. For making one hundred and forty-four outside cases with paper label and sandpaper, and the same number of trays to slide into them – a gross of complete boxes, or two hundred and eighty-eight pieces in all – one got twopence farthing; indeed, for a special size one even got a farthing a gross more; and all the wood and the labels and the sandpaper were provided free: so that the fortunate operative lost nothing out of the twopence farthing but the cost of the paste, and the string for tying up the boxes into regularly numbered batches, and the time employed in fetching the work and taking it back again. And if seven gross were to be got, and could be done in a day – and it was really not very difficult for the skilful hand who kept at work long enough – the day's income was one-and-threepence three-farthings, less expenses: still better, that, than the shirts. But the work was hard to get. As the public-spirited manufacturers complained: people would buy Swedish matches, whereas if people would Support Home Industries* and buy no matches but theirs, they would be able to order many a twopence-farthingsworth of boxes more.

There might be collateral sources of income, but these were doubtful and irregular. Probably Dicky would bring in a few coppers now and again. Then judicious attendance at churches, chapels and prayer-meetings beyond the Jago borders was rewarded by coal-tickets, boots, and the like. It was necessary to know just where and when to go and what to say, else the sole result might be loss of time. There was a church in Bethnal Green, for instance, which it would be foolish to enter before the end of the Litany, for then you were in good time to get your half-quarter hundredweight of coals;* but at other places they might object to so late an appearance. Above all, one must know the ropes. There were several women in the Jago who made almost a living in this way alone. They were experts; they knew every fund, every meeting-house, all the comings and goings of the gullible; insomuch that they would take black umbrage at any unexpected difficulty in getting what they demanded. 'Wy,' one would say, 'I 'ad to pitch sich a bleed'n' 'oly tale I earned it twice over.' But these were the proficient, and proficiency in the trade was an outcome of long experience working on a foundation of natural gifts; and Hannah Perrott could never hope to be among them.

Turning these things in her mind, she addressed herself to her struggle. She managed to get some sacks, but for a week or two she could make nothing like twenty-five a day, though Dicky helped. Her fingers got raw; but she managed to complete a hundred within the first week. They might have been better done, as the employer said when he saw them. But she got her full one-and-sevenpence. She pawned her boots for fourpence, and wore two old odd ones of Josh's; and she got twopence on a petticoat. Dicky also helped a little; and at the end of a fortnight there came a godsend in the shape of material for matchboxes. Mrs Perrott was slow with them at first; but Dicky was quick, and even little Em began to learn to spread paste.

CHAPTER 27

Dicky grew slighter and lanker, dark about the eyes, and weaker. He was growing longitudinally, and that made his lateral wasting the quicker and the more apparent. A furtive, frighted look hung ever in his face, a fugitive air about his whole person. His mother's long face was longer than ever, and blacker under the eyes than Dicky's own, and her weak open mouth hung at the corners as that of a woman faint with weeping. Little Em's knees and elbows were knobs in the midst of limbs of unnatural length. Rarely could a meal be seen ahead; and when it came, it made Dicky doubtful whether or not hunger were really caused by eating. But his chief distress was to see that little Em cried not like a child, but silently, as she strove to thread needles or to smear matchbox labels. And when good fortune brought matchboxes, there was an undue loss on the twopence farthing in the matter of paste. The stuff was a foul mess, sour and faint, and it was kept in a broken tea-cup, near which Dicky had detected his sister sucking her fingers; for in truth little Em stole the paste.

On and off, by one way and another, Mrs Perrott made enough to keep the rent paid with indifferent regularity, and sometimes there was a copper or so left over. She did fairly well, too, at the churches and prayer-meetings; people saw her condition, and now and again would give her something beyond the common dole; so that she learned the trick of looking more miserable than usual at such places.

The roof provided, Dicky felt that his was the task to find food. Alone, he might have rubbed along clear of starvation, but there were his mother and his sister. Lack of victuals shook his nerve and made him timid. Moreover, his terror grew greater than ever at the prospect of being caught in a theft. He lay awake at night and sweated to think of it. Who would bring in things from the outer world for mother and Em then? And the danger was worse than ever. He had felt the police-court birch,* and it was bad, very bad. But he would take it every day and take it almost without a tear, rather than the chance of a reformatory. Magistrates were unwilling to send boys to reformatories while both father and mother were at hand to control them, for that were relieving the parents of their natural responsibility; but in a case like Dicky's, a 'schooling'* was a very likely thing. So that Dicky, as he prowled, was torn between implacable need and the fear of being cut off from all chance of supplying it.

It was his rule never to come home without bringing something, were it no more than a mildewed crust. It was a resolve impossible to keep at times, but at those times it was two in the morning ere he would drag himself, pallid and faint, into the dark room where the others might be – probably were – lying awake and unfed. Rather than face such a home-coming he had sometimes ventured on a more difficult feat than stealing in the outer world: he had stolen in the Jago. Sam Cash, for instance, had lost a bloater.

Dicky never ate at Weech's now. Rarely, indeed, would he take payment in kind, unless it were for something of smaller value than the average of his poor pilferings; and then he carried the food home. But cheaper things could be bought elsewhere, so that more usually he insisted on money payments: to the grief of Mr Weech, who set forth the odiousness of ingratitude at length; though his homilies had no sort of effect on Dicky's morals.

Father Sturt saw that Hannah Perrott gained no ground in her struggle, and urged her to apply for outdoor parish relief, promising to second her request with the guardians.* But with an odd throwback to the respectability of her boiler-making ancestry, she disliked the notion of help from the parish, and preferred to remain as she was; for there at least her ingrained inertness seemed to side with some phantom of self-respect. To her present position she had subsided by almost imperceptible degrees, and she was scarce conscious of a change. But to parish relief there was a distinct and palpable step: a step that, on the whole, it seemed easier not to take. But it was with eagerness that she took a Maternity Society's letter, wherewith the vicar had provided himself on her behalf. For her time was drawing near.

CHAPTER 28

Josh Perrott well understood the advantage of good prison-behaviour, and after six months in his Chelmsford cell he had earned the right to a visit from friends. But none came. He had scarcely expected that anybody would, and asked for the order merely on the general principle that a man should take all he can get, useful or not. For there would have been a five-shilling fare to pay for each visitor from London, and Hannah Perrott could as easily have paid five pounds. And indeed she had other things to think of.

Kiddo Cook had been less observed of late in the Jago. In simple fact he was at work. He found that a steady week of porterage at Spitalfields Market would bring him sixteen shillings and perhaps a little more: and he had taken Father Sturt's encouragement to try another week, and a week after that. Father Sturt too, had cunningly stimulated Kiddo's ambitions: till he cherished aspirations to a fruit and vegetable stall, with a proper tarpaulin cover for bad weather; though he cherished them in secret, confident that they were of his own independent conception. Perhaps the Perrotts saw as much of Kiddo as did anybody at this time. For Kiddo, seeing how it went with them (though indeed it went as badly with others too) built up laboriously a solemn and most circumstantial Lie.* There was a friend of his, a perfect gentleman, who used a beer-shop by Spitalfields Market, and who had just started an extensive and complicated business in the general provision line. He sold all sorts of fruit and vegetables fresh, and all sorts of meat, carrots, cabbages, saveloys, fried fish and pease-pudding cooked. His motto was: – 'Everything *of* the best.' But he had the misfortune to be quite unable himself to judge whether his goods were really of the best or not, in consequence of an injury to his palate, arising from a blow on the mouth with a quart pot, inflicted in the heat of discussion by a wealthy acquaintance. So that he, being a perfect gentleman, had requested Kiddo Cook, out of the friendship he bore him, to drop in occasionally and test his samples. 'Take a good big whack, you know,' said he, 'and get the advice of a friend or two, if *you* ain't sure.' So Kiddo would take frequent and handsome whacks accordingly, to the perfect gentleman's delight; and, not quite knowing what to do with all the whacks, or being desirous of an independent opinion on them (there was some confusion between these two motives) he would bring Mrs Perrott samples, from time to time, and hope it wouldn't inconvenience her. It never did.

It was late in the dusk of a rainy day that Kiddo Cook stumped into Old Jago Street with an apple in his pocket for Em. It was not much, but money was a little short, and at any rate the child would be pleased. As he climbed the stairs he grew conscious of sounds of anguish, muffled by the Perrotts' door. There might have been sobs, and there seemed to be groans; certainly little Em was crying, though but faintly, and something – perhaps boot-heels – scraped on the boards. Kiddo hesitated a little, and then knocked softly. The knock was unnoticed, so in the end he pushed the door open.

The day had been a bad one with the Perrotts. Dicky had gone out early, and had not returned. His mother had tramped unfed to the sackmakers, but there was no work to be got. She tried the rush bag people, with a like result. Nor was any matchbox material being given out. An unregarded turnip,* had rolled from a shop into the gutter, and she had seized it stealthily. It was not in nature to take it home whole, and once a corner was cleared, she dragged herself Jago-ward, gnawing the root furtively as she went. And so she joined Em at home late in the afternoon.

Kiddo pushed the door open and went in. At his second step he stood staring, and his chin dropped. 'Good Gawd!' said Kiddo Cook.

He cleared the stairs in three jumps. He stood but an instant on the flags before the house, with a quick glance each way, and then dashed off through the mud.

Pigeony Poll was erratic in residence, but just now she had a room by the roof of a house in Jago Row, and up the stairs of this house Kiddo ran, calling her by name.

'Go over to Perrotts', quick!' he shouted from the landing below as Poll appeared at her door. 'Run, for Gawd's sake, or the woman'll croak! I'm auf to Father's.' And he rushed away to the vicar's lodgings.

Father Sturt emerged at a run, and made for a surgeon's in Shoreditch High Street. And when the surgeon reached Hannah Perrott he found her stretched on her ragged bed, tended, with anxious clumsiness, by Pigeony Poll; while little Em, tearful and abashed, sat in a corner and nibbled a bit of turnip.

Hannah Perrott had anticipated the operation of the Maternity Society letter, and another child of the Jago had come unconsenting into its black inheritance.

Father Sturt met the surgeon as he came away in the later evening, and asked if all were well. The surgeon shrugged his shoulders. 'People would call it so,' he said. 'The boy's alive, and so is the mother. But you and I may say the truth. You know the Jago far better than I. Is there a child in all this place that wouldn't be better dead – still better unborn? But does a day pass without bringing you just such a parishioner? Here lies the Jago, a nest of rats, breeding, breeding, as only rats can; and we say it is well. On high moral grounds we uphold the right of rats to multiply their thousands.* Sometimes we catch a rat. And we keep it a little while, nourish it carefully, and put it back into the nest to propagate its kind.'

Father Sturt walked a little way in silence. Then he said: – 'You are right, of course. But who'll listen, if you shout it from the housetops? I might try to proclaim it myself, if I had time and energy to waste. But I have none – I must work, and so must you. The burden grows day by day, as you say. The thing's hopeless, perhaps, but that is not for me to discuss. I have my duty.'

The surgeon was a young man, but Shoreditch had helped him over most of his enthusiasms. 'That's right,' he said, 'quite right. People are so very genteel, aren't they?' He laughed, as at a droll remembrance. 'But, hang it all, men like ourselves needn't talk as though the world was built of hardbake. It's a mighty relief to speak truth with a man who knows – a man not rotted through with sentiment. Think how few men we trust with the power to give a fellow creature a year in gaol, and how carefully we pick them! Even damnation is out of fashion, I believe, among theologians. But any noxious wretch may damn human souls to the Jago, one after another, year in year out, and we respect his right: his sacred right.'

At the 'Posties' the two men separated. The rain, which had abated for a space, came up on a driving wind, and whipped Dicky Perrott home to meet his new brother.

CHAPTER 29

Things grew a little easier with the Perrotts. Father Sturt saw
that there was food while the mother was renewing her strength,
and he had a bag of linen sent. More, he carried his point as to
parish relief by main force. It was two shillings and three
quartern loaves a week. Unfortunately the loaves were imprinted
with the parish mark, or they might have been sold at the
chandler's, in order that the whole measure of relief might be
passed on to the landlord (a very respectable man, with a
chandler's shop of his own) for rent. As it was, the bread
perforce was eaten, and the landlord had the two shillings, as
well as eighteenpence which had to be got in some other way.
Of course, Hannah Perrott might have 'taken in lodgers' in the
room, as others did, but she doubted her ability to bully the rent
out of them, or to turn them out if they did not pay. Whatever
was pawnable had gone already, of course, except the little nickel-
plated clock. That might have produced as much as sixpence,
but she had a whim to keep it. She regarded it as a memorial of
Josh, for it was his sole contribution to the family appointments.

Dicky, with a cast-off jacket from the vicar's store, took to
hanging about Liverpool Street Station in quest of bags to carry.
Sometimes he got bags, and coppers for carrying them: sometimes he got kicks from porters. An hour or two of disappointment in this pursuit would send him off on the prowl to 'find'
new stock for Mr Weech. He went farther afield now: to the
market-places in Mile End and Stepney, and to the riverside,
where there were many chances – guarded jealously, however,
by the pirate boys of the neighbourhood, who would tolerate no
interlopers at the wharves. In the very early morning, too, he
practised the sand-bag fake, in the Jago. For there were those
among the Jagos who kept (two even bred) linnets and such
birds, and prepared them for julking, or singing matches at the
Bag of Nails. It was the habit of the bird-fanciers to hang their
little wooden cages on nails out of windows, and there they hung

through the night: for it had been noted, as a surprising peculiarity in linnets, that a bird would droop and go off song after a dozen or so of nights in a Jago room, in company with eight, ten or a dozen human sleepers, notwithstanding the thoughtful shutting of windows. So that any early riser provided with a little bag packed with a handful or so of sand, could become an opulent bird-owner in half-an-hour. Let but the sand-bag be pitched with proper skill at the bottom of a cage, and that cage would leave the nail, and come tumbling and fluttering down into the ready hands of the early riser. The sand-bag brought down the cage and fell quietly on the flags, which was why it was preferred before a stone. The sand-bag faker was moved by no particular love of linnets. His spoil was got rid of as soon as the bird-shops opened in Club Row. And his craft was one of danger.

Thus the months went with Dicky, and the years. There were changes in the Jago. The baby was but three months old when Father Sturt's new church was opened, and the club set going in new buildings; and it was at that time that Josh Perrott was removed to Portland. Even the gradual removal of the Old Jago itself was begun. For the County Council* bought a row of houses at the end of Jago Row, by Honey Lane, with a design to build big barrack dwellings on the site. The scenes of the Jago Court eviction were repeated, with less governed antics. For the County Council knew not Jago ways; and when deputations came forth weeping, protesting the impossibility of finding new lodgings, and beseeching a respite, they were given six weeks more, and went back delighted into free quarters. At the end of the six weeks a larger deputation protested a little louder, wept a great deal more, and poached another month; for it would seem an unpopular thing to turn the people into the street. Thus in the end, when the unpopular thing had to be done, it was with sevenfold trouble, loud cursing of the County Council in the public street, and many fights. But this one spot of the Jago cleared, the County Council began to creep along Jago Row and into Half Jago Street; and after long delay the crude yellow brick of the barrack dwellings* rose above the oft-stolen hoardings, and grew, storey by storey. Dicky was fourteen, fifteen, sixteen. If Josh Perrott had only earned his marks,* he would soon be out now.

CHAPTER 30

Josh Perrott earned his marks, and in less than four years from his conviction he came away from Portland. It was a mere matter of hours ere his arrival in London, when Dicky, hands in pockets, strolled along Old Jago Street, and by the 'Posties' to High Street.

Dicky was almost at his seventeenth birthday. He had grown his utmost, and stood five feet two. He wore a cap with a cloth peak and ear-laps tied at the top with strings, slap-up kicksies, cut saucy, and a bob-tail coat of the out-and-out description: though all these glories were torn and shabby, and had been bought second-hand. He was safe from any risk of the reformatory now, being well over the age;* and he had had the luck never to have taken by the police since his father's lagging – though there were escapes too narrow to be thought about with comfort. It was a matter for wonderment, and he spoke of it with pride. Here he was, a man of long experience, and near seventeen years old, yet he had never been in prison. Few, very few of such an age could say that.

Sometimes he saw his old enemy, the hunchback, who worked at a shoemaker's, but he saw him with unconcern. He cared nothing for tale-bearing now. The memory of old injuries had dulled, and, after all, this was a merely inconsiderable hunchback, whom it were beneath his dignity to regard with anything but tolerant indifference. Bob Roper steered clear at such encounters, and showed his teeth like a cat, and looked back malevolently. It didn't matter.

Dicky was not married, either in the simple Jago fashion or in church. There was little difference, as a matter of fact, so far as facility went. There was a church in Bethnal Green where you might be married for sevenpence if you were fourteen years old, and no questions asked – or at any rate they were questions answers whereunto were easy to invent. You just came in, drunk if possible, with a batch of some scores, and rowdied about the church with your hat on, and the curate worked off the crowd at one go, calling the names one after another. You sang, or you shouted, or you drank out of a bottle, or you flung a prayer-book at a friend, as the fancy took you; and the whole thing was not a bad joke for the money, though after all sevenpence is half-a-gallon,* and not to be wasted. But Dicky had had enough to do to look after his mother and Em and little Josh – as Hannah Perrott had called the baby. Dicky, indeed, had a family already. More: the Jago girls affected him with an odd feeling of repulsion. Not of themselves, perhaps, though they were squalid drabs long ere they were ripe for the sevenpenny church: but by comparison with the clean, remote shop-girls who were visible through the broad windows in the outer streets.

Dicky intended the day to be a holiday. He was not going 'out', as the word went, for ill-luck had a way of coming on notable days like this, and he might easily chance to 'fall'* before his father got home. He was almost too big now for carrying bags at Liverpool Street, because small boys looked cheaper than large ones – not that there was anything especially large about Dicky, beyond his height of five feet two; and at the moment he could think of nothing else that might turn a copper. He stood irresolute on the High Street footway, and as he stood, Kiddo Cook hove in sight, dragging a barrow-load of carrots and cabbages. Kiddo had not yet compassed the stall with the rain-proof awning. But it was almost in sight, for the barrow could scarce hold all that he could sell; and there was a joke abroad that he was to be married in Father Sturt's church: some facetiously suggesting that Mother Gapp would prove a good investment commercially, while others maintained the greater eligibility of old Poll Rann.

"Tcheer, Dicky!" said Kiddo, pulling up and wiping his cap-lining with a red cotton handkerchief. 'Ol' man out today, ain't 'e?'

'Yus,' Dicky answered. ''Spect 'im up tonight.'*

Kiddo nodded, and wiped his face. "Spose the mob'll git up a break for 'im,' he said; 'but 'e'll 'ave a bit o' gilt from stir as well, won't 'e? So 'e'll be awright.' And Kiddo stuffed his handkerchief into his trousers pocket, pulled his cap tight, and bent to his barrow-handles.

Dicky turned idly to the left, and slouched to the corner of Meakin Street. There he loafed for a little while, and then went as aimlessly up the turning. Meakin Street was much as ever. There were still the chandlers' shops, where tea and sugar were sold by the farthingsworth, and the barber's where hair was fashionably cut for three halfpence: though Jago hair was commonly cut in another place* and received little more attention. There was still Walker's cook-shop, foggy with steam, its windows all a-trickle, and there was the Original Slap-up Tog Emporium, with its kicksies and its benjamins cut saucy as ever, and its double fakements still artful. At the 'dispensary' there was another young student, but his advice and medicine were sixpence, just as his remote predecessor's had been for little Looey, long forgotten. And farther down on the opposite side, Mr Aaron Weech's coffee-shop, with its Sunday-school festival bills, maintained its general Band-of-Hope air,* and displayed its shrivelled bloaters, its doubtful cake, and its pallid scones in an odour of respectability and stale pickles. Dicky glanced in as he came by the door, and met the anxious eye of Mr Weech, whom he had not seen for a fortnight. For Dicky was no boy now, but knew enough to sell at Cohen's or elsewhere whenever possible, and to care not a rap for Mr Weech.

As that tradesman saw Dicky, he burst into an eager smile, and came forward. 'Good mornin' – er – ' with a quick glance – 'Mr Perrott! Good mornin'! You're quite a stranger, reely!'

Mister Perrott! Mr Weech was very polite. Dicky stopped, and grunted a cautious salutation.

'Do come in, Mr Perrott. Wy, is the good noos right wot I 'ear, about yer father a-comin' 'ome from – from the country?'

Dicky confirmed the news.

'Well I *am* glad t' 'ear that now.' Mr Weech grinned exceedingly, though there was something lacking in his delight. 'But there, wot'll you 'ave, Mr Perrott? Say anythink in the 'ole shop and welcome! It's sich an 'appy occasion, Mr Perrott, I couldn't think o' chargin' you a 'a'peny. 'Ave a rasher, now, do. There's one on at this very moment. Sairer! ain't that rasher done yut?'

Dicky did not understand this liberality, but he had long since adopted the policy of taking all he could get. So he sat at a table, and Mr Weech sat opposite.

'Jist like ole times, ain't it?' said Mr Weech. 'An' that reminds me I owe you a shillin'. It's that pair o' noo boots you chucked over the back fence a fortnight ago. W'en I come to look et 'em, they was better'n wot I thought, an' so I says to meself, "This won't do," says I. "On'y ninepence for a pair o' boots like them ain't fair," I says, "an' I'd rayther be at a lawss on 'em than not be fair. Fair's fair, as the apostle David says in the Proverbs,* an' them boots is worth very near *one*-an'-nine. So I'll give Mr Perrott another shillin'," I says, "the very next time I see 'im." An' there it is.'

He put the shilling on the table, and Dicky pocketed it, nothing loth. The thing might be hard to understand, but that concerned him not. There was the shilling. Likewise, there was the bacon, and the coffee that went with it, and Dicky went at them with a will, recking nothing of why they were there, and nothing of any matter which might make the giver anxious in the prospect of an early meeting with Josh.

'Ah,' Mr Weech went on, 'it'll be quite a pleasure to see yer father agin, that it will. Wot a blessed release!* "Free from the lor O 'appy condition," as the 'ymn says. I 'ope 'e'll be well an' 'arty. An' if – *if* there should be anythink in the way of a friendly lead* or a subscription or wot not, I 'ope – remember this, Mr Perrott, won'tcher? – I 'ope you'll let me 'ave a chance to put down somethink good. Not as I can reely afford it, ye know, Mr Perrott – trade's very pore, an' it's sich a neighb'r'ood! – but I'll do it for yer father – yus, if it's me last copper. Ye won't forgit that, will ye? An' if 'e'd like any little relish* w'en 'e comes 'ome – sich as a 'addick or a bit o' 'am – wy, I'll wrop it up an' send it.'

This was all very handsome, and Dicky wished some notion of the sort had occurred to Mr Weech on a few of the dinnerless days of the past four years. But he went away wondering if it might not be well to regard Mr Weech with caution for a while. For there must be a reason for all this generosity.

CHAPTER 31

It was in Mother Gapp's that Josh Perrott and his family met. Hannah had started out with an idea of meeting him at Waterloo Station; but, finding herself an object of distinction and congratulation among the women she met, she had lingered by the way, accepting many little drops, to prove herself not unduly proud, and so had failed of her intent. Josh, on his part, had not been abstinent. He had successfully run the gauntlet of Prisoners' Aid Societies* and the like, professing to have 'a job waiting for him' in Shoreditch, and his way across London had been freely punctuated at public-houses; for his prison gratuity* was a very pleasant and useful little sum. And now, when at last they met, he was not especially gracious. He wanted to know, not only why he had found nobody at home, but also why Hannah had never been to see him at Portland. As to the second question, the obvious and sufficient answer was that the return fare to Portland would have been some twenty-five shillings: a sum that Hannah had never seen together since Josh left her. As to the first, she protested, with muddled vehemence, that she had gone to meet him, and had missed him by some mistake as to arrival platforms. So that at length, urged thereto by the rest of the hour's customers at the Feathers, Josh kissed her sulkily and ordered her a drink. Em was distrustful at first, but drank her allowance of gin* with much relish, tipping the glass again and again to catch the last drop; and little Josh, now for the first time introduced to Josh the elder, took a dislike to his father's not particularly sober glare and grin, and roared aloud upon his knee, assailing him, between the roars, with every curse familiar in the Jago, amid the genial merriment of the company. Dicky came in quietly, and stood at his father's elbow with the pride natural to a dutiful son on such an occasion. And at closing-time they all helped each other home.

In the morning Josh rose late. He looked all the better for his lagging, browner than ever in the face, smarter and stouter. In a corner he perceived a little heap of made match-boxes, and, hard by, the material for more. It was Em's work of yesterday morning. 'Support 'ome indu*s*teries,' said Josh, musingly. 'Yus. Twopence-farden a gross.' And he kicked the heap to splinters.

He strolled out into the street, to survey the Jago. In the bulk it was little changed, though the County Council had made a difference in the north-east corner, and was creeping farther and farther still. The dispossessed Jagos had gone to infect the neighbourhoods across the border, and to crowd the people a little closer. They did not return to live in the new barrack-buildings; which was a strange thing, for the County Council was charging very little more than double the rents which the landlords of the Old Jago had charged. And so another Jago, teeming and villainous as the one displaced, was slowly growing, in the form of a ring, round about the great yellow houses. But the new church and its attendant buildings most took Josh's notice. They were little more than begun when last he walked Old Jago Street in daylight, and now they stood, large and healthy amid the dens about them, a wonder and a pride. As he looked, Jerry Gullen and Bill Rann passed.

'Wayo, brother-in-law!' sang out Bill Rann, who remembered the Old Bailey fiction of four years back, and thought it a capital joke.

'Nice sort o' thing, ain't it?' said Jerry Gullen with indignant sarcasm, jerking his thumb toward the new church. 'The street's clean ruined. Wot's the good o' livin' 'ere now? Wy, a man mustn't even do a click, blimy!'

'An' doncher?' asked Josh with a grin. Hereat another grin broke wide on Jerry Gullen's face, and he went his way with a wink and a whistle.

'And so you're back again, Josh Perrott!' said old Beveridge, seedier than ever, with the 'Hard Up' fresh chalked on the changeless hat. 'Back again! Pity you couldn't stay there, isn't it? Pity we can't all stay there.'

Josh looked after the gaunt old figure with much doubt and a vague indignation: for such a view was foreign to his understanding. And as he looked Father Sturt came out of the church, and laid his hand on Josh's shoulder.

'What!' exclaimed the vicar, 'home again without coming to see me! But there, you must have been coming. I hope you haven't been knocking long? Come in now, at any rate. You're looking wonderfully well. What a capital thing a holiday is, isn't it – a good long one?' Taking Josh by the arm he hauled him, grinning, sheepish and almost blushing, toward the club door. And at that moment Sam Cash came hurrying round Luck Row corner, with his finger through a string, and on that string a bunch of grouse.

'Dear me,' said Father Sturt, turning back, but without releasing Josh's arm. 'Here's our dear friend, Sam Cash, taking home something for his lunch. Come, Sam, with such a fine lot of birds as that, I'm sure you'll be proud to tell us where they came from. Eh?'

For a moment Sam Cash was a trifle puzzled, even offended. Then there fell over his face the mask of utter inexpression which the vicar had learned to know. Said Sam Cash, stolidly: 'I bin 'avin' a little shootin' with a friend.'

'Dear, dear, what a charming friend! And where are his moors? Nowhere about the Bethnal Green Road, I suppose, by the goods depot? Come now, I'm sure Josh Perrott would like to know. You didn't get any shooting in your little holiday, did you, Josh?' Josh grinned, delighted, but Sam shuffled uneasily, with a hopeless sidelong glance as in search of a hole wherein to hide. 'Ah, you see,' Father Sturt said, 'he doesn't want his friend's hospitality to be abused. Let me see – two, four, six – why there must be nine or ten brace, and all at one shot, too! Sam always makes his bag at one shot, you know, Josh, whatever the game is. Yes, wonderful shooting. And did you shoot the label at the same time, Sam? Come, I *should* like to look at that label!'

But the wretched Sam was off at a bolt, faster than a police pursuit would have sent him, while Josh guffawed joyously. To be 'rotted' by Father Sturt was the true Jago terror, but to the Jagos looking on it was pure delight. Theft was a piece of the Jago nature; but at least Father Sturt could wither the pride of it by such ridicule as the Jago could understand.

'There – he's very bashful for a sportsman, isn't he, Josh?' the vicar proceeded. 'But you must come and see the club at once. You shall be a member.'

Josh spent near an hour in the new buildings. Father Sturt showed him the club, the night shelter, the church, and his own little rooms. He asked, too, much about Josh's intentions for the future. Of course, Josh was 'going to look for a job'. Father

Sturt knew he would say that. Every Jago had been going to look for a job ever since the vicar first came to the place. But he professed to take Josh's word seriously, and offered to try to get him taken on as a plasterer at some of the new County Council buildings. He flattered Josh by reminding him of his command of a regular trade. Josh was a man with opportunities, and he should be above the pitiable expedients of the poor untradesmanlike about him. Indeed, he should leave the Jago altogether, with his family, and start afresh in a new place, a reputable mechanic.

To these things Josh Perrott listened with fidgety deference, answering only 'Yus, Father', when it seemed to be necessary. In the end he promised to 'think it over', which meant nothing, as the parson well knew. And in the mood in which Josh came away he would gladly have risked another lagging to serve Father Sturt's convenience; but he would rather have suffered one than take Father Sturt's advice.

He made the day a holiday. He had been told that he was in for a little excitement, for it was held that fitting time had arrived for another scrap with Dove Lane; but the affair was not yet moving. Snob Spicer had broken a window with a Dove-Laner's head, it was true, but nothing had come of it, and etiquette demanded that the next card should be played by Dove Lane. For the present, the Jago was content to take thought for Josh's 'friendly lead'. Such a thing was everybody's right on return from a lagging, and this one was fixed for a night next week.

All that day Mr Weech looked out anxiously, but Josh Perrott never passed his way.

CHAPTER 32

Bill Rann called for Josh early the next morning, and they strolled down Old Jago Street in close communion.

'Are you on for a job?' asked Bill. ''Cos I got one cut an' dried – a topper, an' safe as 'ouses.'

'Wot sort o' job's this?'

'Wy a bust – unless we can screw it.'

This meant a breaking-in, with a possibility of a quieter entrance by means of keys. It was unpleasantly suggestive of Josh's last exploit, but he answered: 'Awright. Depends, o' course.'

'O, it's a good un.' Bill Rann grinned for no obvious reason, and slapped his leg to express rapturous amusement. 'It's a good un – you can take yer davy o' that. I bin a thinkin' about it for a fortnight, but it wants two. Damme, it's nobby!' And Bill Ram grinned again, and made two taps of a step-dance.* 'Wotjer think,' he pursued, suddenly serious, 'wotjer think o' screwin' a fence?'

It was a novel notion, but in Josh's mind, at first flush, it seemed unsportsmanlike. 'Wot fence?' asked Josh.

Bill Rann's grin burst wide again. He bent low, with outstretched chin, and stuck his elbows out as he answered: 'Wy, ole Weech!'

Josh bared his teeth – but with no smile – looking sharply in the other's upturned face. Bill Rann, bent nearly double, and with hands in pockets, flapped his arms in the manner of wings, chuckled aloud, and, jerking his feet back and forth, went elaborately through the first movement of the gallows-flap.* 'Eh? eh?' said he. ''Ow's that strike ye, ole cock?'

Josh answered not, but his parted lips stretched wide, and his tongue-tip passed quickly over them while he thought.

'It'll be a fair cop for 'im,' Bill pursued, eagerly. ''E's treated us all pretty mean, one time or other. Wy, I bet 'e *owes* us fifty quid atween us, wot with all the times 'e's squeeged us for a bit. It'll on'y be goin' to bring away our own stuff!'

'G-r-r-r!' Josh growled, glaring fiercely; 'it was 'im as put me away for my laggin'! Bleed'n' swine!'

Bill Rann stopped, surprised. 'Wot – 'im?' he exclaimed. 'Ole Weech narked ye? 'Owjer know that?'

Josh told the tale of his negotiations in the matter of the Mogul's watch, and described Weech's terror at sight of his dash at the shop-door. 'I'm on,' said Josh in conclusion. 'It's one way o' payin' 'im, an' it'll bring a bit in. On'y 'e better not show 'isself w'ile I'm abaat! 'E wouldn't git auf with a punch on the chin, like the bloke at 'Ighbury!' Josh Perrott ended with a tigerish snarl and a white spot at the curl of each of his nostrils.

'Blimy!' said Bill Rann; 'an' so it was 'im, was it? I often wondered 'oo you meant. Well, flimpin' 'im's the best way. Won't 'e sing a bleed'n' 'ymn w'en 'e finds 'is stuff weeded!' Bill flung back his head, and laughed again. 'But there – let's lay it out.' And the two men fell to the discussion of methods.

Weech's back fence was to be his undoing. It was the obvious plan. The front shutters were impracticable in such a place as Meakin Street; but the alleys in the rear were a perfect approach. Bill Rann had surveyed the spot attentively, and, after expert consideration, he had selected the wash-house window as the point of entrance. Old boxes and packing-wood littered the yard, and it would be easy to mount a selected box, shift the catch of the little window, and wriggle in, feet first, without noise. True, the door between the wash-house and the other rooms might be fastened, but it could be worked at under cover; and Bill Rann had a belief that there must be a good deal of 'stuff' in the wash-house itself. There would be nobody in the house but Weech, because the wretched old woman, who swept the floors and cooked bloaters, was sent away at night; so that every room must be unoccupied but one.

As for tools, Josh had none, but Bill Rann undertook to provide them; and in the matter of time it was considered that that same night would be as good as any. It would be better than most, in fact, for it was Wednesday, and Bill Rann had observed that Mr Weech went to the bank in High Street, Shoreditch, pretty regularly on Thursday mornings.

This day also Mr Weech kept a careful watch for Josh Perrott, but saw him not.

CHAPTER 33

Hannah Perrott did her best to keep Josh from going out that night. She did not explain her objections, because she did not know precisely what they were, though they were in some sort prompted by his manner; and it was solely because of her constitutional inability to urge them with any persistence that she escaped forcible retort. For Josh was in a savage and self-centred mood.

'Wy, wot's up?' asked Bill Rann, when they met, looking doubtfully in his pal's face. 'You ain't bin boozin', 'ave ye?'

Josh repelled the question with a snarl. 'No I ain't,' he said. 'Got the tools?' There was a thickness in his voice, with a wildness in his eye, that might well explain his partner's doubt.

'Yus. Come under the light. I couldn't git no twirls, an' we sha'n't want 'em. 'Ere's a screwdriver, an' two gimlets, an' a knife for the winderketch, an' a little james, an' a neddy – '

'A neddy!' Josh cut in, scornfully pointing his thumb at the instrument, which some call life-preserver. 'A neddy for Weech! G-r-r-r! I might take a neddy to a *man*!'

'That's awright,' Bill replied. 'But it 'ud frighten 'im pretty well, wouldn't it? Look 'ere. S'pose we can't find the oof. W'y shouldn't we wake up Mr Weech very quiet an' respeckful, an' ask 'im t' 'elp us? 'E's all alone, an' I'm sure 'e'll be glad to 'blige, w'en 'e sees this 'ere neddy, without waitin' for a tap. W'y, blimy, I b'lieve 'e'd be afraid to sing out any'ow, for fear o' bringin' in the coppers to find all the stuff 'e's bought on the crook! It's all done, once we're inside!'

It was near midnight, and Bill Rann had observed Weech putting up his shutters at eleven. So the two Jagos walked slowly along Meakin Street, on the side opposite Weech's, with sharp eyes for the windows.

All was quiet; there was no visible light – none from the skylight over the shop door, none from the window above, none from the garret window above that. They passed on, crossed the road, strolled back, and listened at the door; there was no sound from within. The clock in a distant steeple struck twelve, and was joined at the fourth stroke by the loud bell of St Leonard's, hard by;* and ere the last mild note had sounded from the farthest clock in the awakened chorus, Josh Perrott and Bill Rann had taken the next turning, and were pushing their way to the alleys behind Weech's.

Foul rat-runs these alleys, not to be traversed by a stranger. Josh and Bill plunged into one narrow archway after another, each of which might have been the private passage of a house, and came at last, stealthy and unseen, into the muddy yard.

Weech's back fence was before them, and black house-backs crowded them round. There were but one or two lights in the windows, and those windows were shut and curtained. The rear of Weech's house was black and silent as the front. They peered over the fence. The yard was pitch-dark, but faint angular tokens here and there told of heaped boxes and lumber. 'We won't tip 'im the whistle this time,' whispered Bill Rann, with a smothered chuckle. 'Over!'

He bent his knee, and Josh straddled from it over the rickety fence with quiet care, and lowered himself gingerly on the other side. 'Clear 'ere,' he whispered. 'Come on.' Since Bill's display of the tools Josh had scarce spoken a word. Bill wondered at his taciturnity, but respected it as a business-like quality in the circumstances.

It was but a matter of four or five yards to the wash-house window, but they bent and felt their way. Josh took up an old lemonade-case as he went, and planted it on the ground below the window, stretching his hand for the knife as he did so. And now he took command and foremost place.

It was an old shoemaker's knife, with too long a handle; for there was a skew-joint in the sash, and the knife would not bend. Presently Bill Rann, below, could see that Josh was cutting away the putty from the pane, and in five minutes the pane itself was put into his hand. He stooped, and laid it noiselessly on the soft ground.

Josh turned the catch and lifted the sash. There was some noise, but not much, as he pushed the frame up evenly, with a thumb at each side. They waited; but it was quite still, and Josh, sitting on the sill, manœuvred his legs, one at a time, through the narrow opening. Then, turning over, he let himself down, and beckoned Bill Rann to follow.

Bill Rann had a small tin box, with an inch of candle on the inside of one end, so that when the wick was lit the contrivance made a simple but an effective lantern, the light whereof shone in front alone, and could be extinguished at a puff. Now a match was struck, and a quick view taken of the wash-house.

There was not much about; only cracked and greasy plates, jars, tins, pots and pans, and in a corner a miscellaneous heap, plainly cheap pilferings, covered with a bit of old carpet. The air was offensive with the characteristic smell of Weech's – the smell of stale pickles.

'There ain't nothin' to waste time over 'ere,' said Josh, aloud. 'Come on!'

'Shut up, you damn fool!' exclaimed Bill Rann, in a whisper. 'D'jer want to wake 'im?'

'Umph! Why not?' was the reply, still aloud. Bill began to feel that his pal was really drunk. But, silent once more, Josh applied himself to the door of the inner room. It was crank and old, worn and battered at the edges. Josh forced the wedge end of the jemmy through the jamb, splintering the perished wood of the frame, and, with a push, forced the striking-box* of the lock off its screws. There was still a bolt at the top; that at the bottom had lost its catch – but this gave as little trouble as the lock. Bill Rann strained the door open from below, the jemmy entered readily, and in a few seconds the top bolt was in like case with the bottom.

They entered the room behind the shop, and it was innocent and disappointing. A loo table,* four horse-hair covered chairs, a mirror, three coloured wall-texts,* two china figures and a cheap walnut sideboard – that was all. The slow step of a policeman without stopped, with a push at the shop-door, to test its fastenings, and then went on; and stronger than ever was the smell of stale pickles.

To try the shop would be mere waste of time. Weech's pocket was the till, and there could be no other prize. A door at the side of the room, latched simply, gave on the stairs. 'Take auf yer boots,' Bill whispered, unlacing his own, and slinging them across his shoulder by the tied laces.

But Josh would not, and he said so, with an oath. Bill could not understand him. *Could* it be drink? Bill wished him a mile away. 'Awright,' he whispered, 'you set down 'ere w'ile I slip upstairs an' take a peep. I bet the stuff's in the garret. Best on'y one goes, quiet.'

Josh sat, and Bill, taking his lantern, crept up the stairs noiselessly, save for one creak. He gained the stair-head, listened a moment, tiptoed along the small landing, and was halfway up the steep and narrow garret-stairs, when he heard a sound, and stopped. Somebody was on the lower flight.

There was a heavy tread, with the kick of a boot against stair or skirting-board; and then came noisy steps along the landing. Josh was coming up in his boots! Bill Rann was at his wits' end. He backed down the garret-stairs, and met Josh at the foot. 'Are ye barmy?' he hissed fiercely, catching Josh by the collar and pulling him into the turn of the stairs. 'D'ye want another five stretch?'

A loud creak and a soft thump sounded from behind the door at the other end of the landing; and then a match was struck. 'Keep back on the stairs,' Bill whispered. ''E's 'eard you.' Josh sat on a stair, perfectly still, with his legs drawn up out of sight from the door. Bill blew out his light. He would not venture open intimidation of Weech now, with Josh half muzzy, lest some burst of lunacy brought in the police.

A soft treading of bare feet, the squeak of a door-handle, a light on the landing, and Aaron Weech stood at his open door in his shirt, candle in hand, his hair rumpled, his head aside, his mouth a little open, his unconscious gaze upward; listening intently. He took a slight step forward. And then Bill Rann's heart turned over and over.

For Josh Perrott sprang from the stair, and, his shoulders humped and his face thrust out, walked deliberately across the landing. Weech turned his head quickly; his chin fell on his chest as by jaw-break; there were but dots amid the white of his eyes; his head lay slowly back, as the candle tilted and shot its grease on the floor. The door swung wider as his shoulder struck it, and he screamed, like a rabbit that sees a stoat. Then, with a wrench, he turned, letting drop the candle, and ran shrieking to the window, flung it open, and yelled into the black street. ''Elp! 'Elp! P'lice! *Murder! Murder! Murder! Murder!*'

'Run, Josh – run, ye blasted fool!' roared Bill Rann, bounding across the landing, and snatching at his arm.

'Go on – go on! I'm comin'!' Josh answered without turning

his head. And Bill took the bottom flight at a jump. The candle flared as it lay on the floor, and spread a greasy pool about it.

'Murder! Murder! Mu—r—r—'

Josh had the man by the shoulder, swung him back from the window, gripped his throat, and dragged him across the carpet as he might drag a cat, while Weech's arms waved uselessly, and his feet feebly sought a hold on the floor.

'Now!' cried Josh Perrott, glaring on the writhen face below his own, and raising his case-knife in the manner of a cleaver, 'sing a hymn! Sing the hymn as'll do ye most good! You'll cheat me when ye can, an' when ye can't you'll put me five year in stir, eh? Sing a hymn, ye snivellin' nark!'

From the street there came the noise of many hurrying feet and of a scattered shouting. Josh Perrott made an offer at slashing the slaty face, checked his arm, and went on.

'You'll put down somethin' 'an'some at my break, will ye? An' you'll starve my wife an' kids all to bones an' teeth four year! Sing a hymn, ye cur!'

He made another feint at slashing. Men were beating thunderously at the shop door, and there were shrill whistles.

'Won't sing yer hymn? There ain't much time! My boy was goin' straight, an' earnin' wages: someone got 'im chucked. A man 'as time to think things out, in stir! Sing, ye son of a cow! Sing! Sing!'

Twice the knife hacked the livid face. But the third hack was below the chin; and the face fell back.

The bubbling Thing dropped in a heap, and put out the flaring candle. Without, the shouts gathered to a roar, and the door shook under heavy blows. 'Open – open the door!' cried a deep voice.

He looked from the open window. There was a scrambling crowd, and more people were running in. Windows gaped, and thrust out noisy heads. The flash of a bull's-eye* dazzled him, and he staggered back. 'Perrott! Perrott!' came a shout. He had but glanced out, but he was recognised.

He threw down his knife, and made for the landing, slipping on the wet floor and stumbling against the Heap. There were shouts from behind the house now; they were few, but they were close. He dashed up the narrow stairs, floundered through the back garret, over bags and boxes and heaps of mingled commodities, and threw up the sash. Men were stumbling invisibly in the dark yard below. He got upon the sill, swung round by the dormer-frame, and went, hands and knees, along the roof. Yells and loud whistles rose clamant in the air, and his own name was shouted to and fro. Then the blows on the shop-door ceased with a splintering crash, and there was a trampling of feet on floor-boards.

The roofs were irregular in shape and height, and his progress was slow. He aimed at reaching the roof of Father Sturt's old club building, still empty. He had had this in mind from the moment he climbed from the garret-window; for in the work of setting the drains in order an iron ventilating pipe had been carried up from the stable-yard to well above the roof. It was a stout pipe, close by the wall, to which it was clamped with iron attachments. Four years had passed since he had seen it, and he trusted to luck to find it still standing, for it seemed his only chance. Down below people scampered and shouted. Crowds had sprung out of the dark night as by magic; and the police – they must have been lying in wait in scores. It seemed a mere matter of seconds since he had scaled the back fence; and now people were tearing about the house behind him, and shouting out of windows to those below. He hoped that the iron pipe might not be gone.

Good – it was there. He peered from the parapet down into the stable-yard, and the place seemed empty. He gripped the pipe with hands and knees, and descended.

The alley had no back way: he must take his chance in Meakin Street. He peeped. At the street end there was a dark obstruction, set with spots of light: a row of police. That way was shut; he must try the Jago – Luck Row was almost opposite, and no Jago would betray him. The hunters were already on the roofs. Men shouted up to them from the street, and kept pace with them, coming nearer. He took a breath and dashed across, knocking a man over at the corner.

Up Luck Row, into Old Jago Street he ran, past his own home, and across to a black doorway, just as Father Sturt, roused by the persistent din, opened his window. The passage was empty, and for an instant he paused, breathless. But there were howls without, and the pelting of many feet. The man knocked over at the corner had given the alarm, and the hunt was up.

Into the back-yard and over the fence; through another

passage into New Jago Street; with a notion to gain the courts by Honey Lane and so away. But he was thinking of the Jago as it had been – he had forgotten the demolition. As he neared Jago Row the place of it lay suddenly before him – an open waste of eighty yards square, skirted by the straight streets and the yellow barracks, with the Board School standing dark among them. And along the straight streets more men were rushing, and more police. They were newcomers: why not venture over? He rubbed his cheek, for something like a film of gum clung to it. Then he remembered, and peered closely at his hands. Blood, sticking and drying and peeling; blood on hands and face, blood on clothes, without a doubt. To go abroad thus were to court arrest, were he known or not. It must be got off; but how? To go home was to give himself up. The police were there long since – they swarmed the Jago through. Some half-dismantled houses stood at hand, and he made for the nearest.

There were cellars under these houses, reached from the back-yards. Many a Jago had been born, had lived, and had died in such a place. A cellar would hide him for an hour, while he groped himself clean as he might. Broken brickwork littered the space that had been the back-yard. Feeling in the dark for the steps, which stood in a little pit, his foot turned on a stone, and he pitched headlong.

The cellar itself was littered with rubbish, and he lay among it a little while, breathless and bruised. When he tried to rise, he found his ankle useless. It was the old sprain, got at Mother Gapp's before his lagging, and ever ready to assert itself. He sat among the brickbats to pull off the boot – that was foul and sticky too – and he rubbed the ankle. He had been a fool to think of the cellar: why not any corner among the walls above? He had given way to the mere panic instinct to burrow, to hide himself in a hole, and he had chosen one wherefrom there was no second way of escape – none at all but by the steps he had fallen in at. Far better to have struck out boldly across the streets by Columbia Market to the canal: who could have seen the smears in the darkness? And in the canal he might have washed the lot away, secure from observation, under a bridge. The thing might be possible, even now, if he could stand the pain. But no, the foot was useless when he tried it. He was trapped like a rat. He rubbed and kneaded the ankle diligently, and managed to draw the boot on. But stand on both legs he could not. He might have crawled up the steps on hands and knees, but what was the use of that? So he sat, and waited.

Knots of men went hurrying by, and he caught snatches of their talk. There had been a murder – a man was murdered in his bed – it was a woman – a man had murdered his wife – there were two murders – three – the tale went every way, but it was always Murder, Murder, Murder. Everybody was saying Murder: till in the passing footsteps, in the vague shouts in the distance, and presently in the mere black about him he heard the word still – Murder, Murder, Murder. He fell to contrasting the whispered fancy with the real screams in that bedroom. He wondered what Bill Rann thought of it all, and what had become of the james and the gimlets. He pictured the crowd in Old Jago Street, pushing into his room, talking about him, telling the news. He wondered if Hannah had been asleep when they came, and what she said when they told her. And more people hurried past the ruined house, all talking Murder, Murder, still Murder.

The foot was horribly painful. Was it swelling? Yes, he thought it was; he rubbed it again. What would Dicky do? If only Dicky knew where he was! That might help. There was a new burst of shouts in the distance. What was that? Perhaps they had caught Bill Rann; but that was unlikely. They knew nothing of Bill – they had seen but one man. Perhaps they were carrying away the Heap on a shutter:* that would be no nice job, especially down the steep stairs. There had been very little in the wash-house, and nothing in the next room; the garrets were pretty full of odd things, but no doubt the money was in the bedroom. The smell of stale pickles was very strong.

So his thoughts chased one another – eager, trivial, crowded – till his head ached with their splitting haste. To take heed for the future, to plan escape, to design expedients – these were merely impossible, sitting there inactive in the dark. He thought of the pipe he had slid down, what it cost, why they put it there, who the man was that he ran against at Luck Row, whether or not he hurt him, what the police would do with the bloaters and cake and bacon at the shop, and – again – of the smell of stale pickles.

Father Sturt was up and dressed, standing guard on the landing outside the Perrotts' door. The stairs were full of Jagos – mostly women – constantly joined by new-comers, all anxious to batter the door and belabour the hidden family with noisy sympathy and sedulous inquiries: all, that is, except the oldest Mrs Walsh in the Jago, who, possessed by an unshakable conviction that Josh's wife must have 'druv 'im to it', had come in a shawl and a petticoat to give Hannah a piece of her mind. But all were driven back and sent grumbling away, by Father Sturt.

Every passage from the Jago was held by the police, and a search from house to house was begun. With clear consciences the Jagos all could deny any knowledge of Josh Perrott's whereabouts; but a clear conscience was little valued in those parts, and one after another affirmed point blank that the man seen at the window was not Perrott at all, but a stranger who lived a long way off. This, of course, less by way of favouring the fugitive than of baffling the police: the Jago's first duty. But the police knew the worth of such talk, and the search went on.

Thus it came to pass that in the grey of the morning a party in New Jago Street, after telling each other that the ruins must be carefully examined, climbed among the rubbish, and were startled by a voice from underground.

'Awright,' cried Josh Perrott in the cellar. 'I'm done; it's a cop. Come an' 'elp me out o' this 'ole.'

CHAPTER 34

The Lion and Unicorn* had been fresh gilt since he was there before, but the white-headed old gaoler in the dock was much the same. And the big sword – what did they have a big sword for, stuck up there, over the red cushions, and what was the use of a sword six foot long? But perhaps it wasn't six foot after all – it looked longer than it was; and no doubt it was only for show, and probably a dummy with no blade. There was a well-dressed black man sitting down below among the lawyers. What did he want? Why did they let him in? A nice thing – to be made a show of, for niggers! And Josh Perrott loosened his neckcloth with an indignant tug of the forefinger, and went off into another train of thought. He had a throbbing, wavering head-ache, the outcome of thinking so hard about so many things. They were small things, and had nothing to do with his own business; but there were so many of them, and they all had to be got through at such a pace, and one thing led to another.

Ever since they had taken him he had been oppressed by this plague of galloping thought, with few intervals of rest, when he could consider immediate concerns. But of these he made little trouble. The thing was done. Very well then, he would take his gruel* like a man. He had done many a worse thing, he said, that had been thought less of.

The evidence was a nuisance. What was the good of it all? Over and over and over again. At the inquest, at the police-court, and now here. Repeated, laboriously taken down, and repeated again. And now it was worse than ever, for the judge insisted on making a note of everything, and wrote it down slowly, a word at a time. The witnesses were like barrel-organs, producing the same old tune mechanically, without changing a note. There was the policeman who was in Meakin Street at twelve-thirty on the morning of the fourth of the month, when he heard cries of Murder, and proceeded to the coffee-shop. There was the other policeman who also 'proceeded' there, and recognised the prisoner, whom he knew, at the first-floor window. And there was the sergeant who had found him in the cellar, and the doctor who had made an examination, and the knife, and the boots, and all of it. It was Murder, Murder, Murder still. Why? Wasn't it plain enough? He felt some interest in what was coming – in the sentence, and the black cap, and so on – never having seen a murder trial before. But all this repetition oppressed him vaguely amid the innumerable things he had to think of, one thing leading to another.

Hannah and Dicky were there, sitting together behind the glass partition that rose at the side of the dock. Hannah's face was down in her hands, and Dicky's face was thin and white, and he sat with his neck stretched, his lips apart, his head aside to catch the smallest word. His eyes, too, were red with strained, unwinking attention. Josh felt vaguely that they might keep a bolder face, as he did himself. His sprained foot was still far from well, but he stood up, putting his weight on the other. He might have been allowed to sit if he had asked, but that would look like weakness.

There was another judge this time, an older one, with spectacles. He had come solemnly in, after lunch, with a bunch of flowers* in his hand, and Josh thought he made an odd figure in his long red gown. Why did he sit at the end of the bench, instead of in the middle, under the long sword? Perhaps the old gentleman, who sat there for a little while and then went away, was the Lord Mayor. That would account for it. There was another room behind the bedroom at Weech's, which he had never thought about. Perhaps the money was there, after all. Could they have missed any hiding-place in the shop parlour? No: there was the round table, with the four chairs about it, and the little sideboard; besides the texts on the wall, and two china figures on the mantelpiece – that was all. There was a copper in the wash-house, but there was nothing in it. The garret was a very good place to keep things in; but there was a strong smell of stale pickles. He could smell it now – he had smelt it ever since.

The judge stopped a witness to speak of a draught from a window. Josh Perrott watched the shutting of the window – they did it with a cord. He had not noticed a draught himself. But pigeons were flying outside the panes and resting on the chimney-stacks. Pud Palmer tried to keep pigeons in Jago Row, but one morning the trap* was found empty. A poulterer gave fourpence each for them. They were ticketed at eighteenpence a pair in the shop, and that was fivepence profit apiece for the poulterer. Tenpence a pair profit on eleven pairs was nearly ten shillings – ten shillings all but tenpence. They wouldn't have given any more in Club Row.* A man had a four-legged linnet in Club Row, but there was a show in Bethnal Green Road with a two-headed sheep.* It was outside there that Ginger Stagg was pinched for lob-crawling. And so on, and so on, till his head buzzed again.

His counsel was saying something. How long had he been talking? What was the good of it? He had told him that he had no defence. The lawyer was enlarging on the dead man's iniquities, talking of provocation, and the heat of passion, and the like. He was aiming desperately at a recommendation to mercy. That was mere foolery.

But presently the judge began to sum up. They were coming to something at last. But it was merely the thrice-told evidence once more. The judge blinked at his notes, and went at it again; the policeman with his whistle, and the other with his lantern, and the doctor, and the sergeant, and the rest. It was shorter this time, though. Josh Perrott turned and looked at the clock behind him, with the faces over it, peering from the gallery. But when he turned to face the judge again he had forgotten the time, and crowded trivialities were racing through the narrow gates of his brain once more.

There was a cry for silence, and then a fresh voice spoke. 'Gentlemen of the jury, have you agreed upon your verdict?'

'We have.' The foreman was an agitated, colourless man, and he spoke in a low tone.

'Do you find the prisoner at the bar guilty, or not guilty?'

'Guilty.'

Yes, that was right; this was the real business. His head was clear and ready now.

'And is that the verdict of you all?'

'Yes.'

Was that Hannah sobbing?

A pale parson in his black gown came walking along by the bench, and stood like a tall ghost at the judge's side, his eyes raised and his hands clasped. The judge took a black thing from the seat beside him, and arranged it on his head. It was a sort of soft mortarboard* Josh noted curiously, with a large silk tassel hanging over one side, giving the judge, with his wig and his spectacles and his red gown, a horribly jaunty look. No brain could be clearer than Josh Perrott's now.

'Prisoner at the bar, have you anything to say why sentence of death should not be passed on you according to law?'

'No sir – I done it. On'y 'e was a worse man than me!'

The Clerk of Arraigns* sank into his place, and the judge spoke.

'Joshua Perrott, you have been convicted, on evidence that can leave no doubt whatever of your guilt in the mind of any rational person, of the horrible crime of wilful murder. The circumstances of your awful offence there is no need to recapitulate, but they were of the most brutal and shocking character. You deliberately, and with preparation, broke into the house of the man whose death you have shortly to answer for in a higher court than this: whether you broke in with a design of robbery as well as of revenge by murder I know not, nor is it my duty to consider: but you there, with every circumstance of callous ferocity, sent the wretched man to that last account which you must shortly render for yourself. Of the ill-spent life of that miserable man, your victim, it is not for me to speak, nor for you to think. And I do most earnestly beseech you to use the short time yet remaining to you on this earth in true repentance, and in making your peace with Almighty God. It is my duty to pronounce sentence of that punishment which not I, but the law of this country, imposes for the crime which you have committed. The sentence of the Court is: that you be taken to the place whence you came, and thence to a place of execution: and that you be there Hanged by the Neck till you be Dead: and may the Lord have Mercy on your Soul!'

'Amen!' It was from the tall black figure.

Well, well, that was over. The gaoler touched his arm. Right. But first he took a quick glance through the glass partition. Hannah was falling over, or something – a mere rusty swaying bundle – and Dicky was holding her up with both arms. Dicky's face was damp and grey, and twitching lines were in his cheeks. Josh took a step toward the partition, but they hurried him away.

CHAPTER 35

All this hard thinking would be over in half an hour or so. What was to come now didn't matter; no more than a mere punch in the eye. The worst was over on Saturday, and he had got through that all right. Hannah was very bad, and so was Dicky. Em cried in a bewildered sort of way, because the others did. Little Josh, conceiving that his father was somehow causing all the tears, kicked and swore at him. He tried to get Hannah to smile at this, but it was no go; and they had to carry her out at last. Dicky was well-plucked though, bad as he was. He felt him shake and choke when he kissed him, but he walked out straight and steady, with the two children. Well, it was over . . .

He hoped they would get up a break in the Jago for Hannah and the youngsters. His own break had never come off – they owed him one. The last break he was at was at Mother Gapp's, before the Dove-Laners fell through the floor. It must have cost Mother Gapp a deal of money to put in the new floor; but then she must have made a lot in her time, what with one thing and another. There was the fencing, and the houses she had bought in Honey Lane, and the two fourpenny doss-houses* in Hoxton that they said were hers, and – well, nobody could say what else. Some said she came of the gipsies that used to live at the Mount years ago.* The Mount was a pretty thick place now, but not so thick as the Jago: the Jagos were thick as glue and wide as Broad Street. Bob the Bender fell in Broad Street, toy-getting, and got a stretch and a half . . .

Yes, yes, of course, they always tolled a bell. But it was rather confusing, with things to think about.

Ah, they had come at last. Come, there was nothing more to think about now; nothing but to take it game. Hold tight – Jago hold tight . . . 'No thank you, sir – nothing to say, special. On'y much obliged to ye, thank ye kindly, for the grub an' – an' bein' kind an' wot not. Thanks all of ye, come to that. Specially you, sir.' It was the tall black figure again . . .

What, this was the chap, was it? Seedy-looking. Sort of undertaker's man to look at. All right – straps. Not cords to tie, then. Waist; wrists; elbows; more straps dangling below – do them presently. This was how they did it, then . . . This way?

'I am the resurrection and the life, saith the Lord: he that believeth in Me, though he were dead, yet shall he live: and whosoever liveth and believeth in Me shall never die.'

A very big gate, this, all iron, painted white. Round to the right. Not very far, they told him. It was dark in the passage, but the door led into the yard, where it was light and open, and sparrows were twittering. Another door: in a shed.

This was the place. All white, everywhere – frame too; not black after all. Up the steps . . . Hold tight: not much longer. Stand there? Very well.

'Man that is born of woman hath but a short time to live, and is full of misery. He cometh up, and is cut down, like a flower: he fleeth as it were a shadow, and never continueth in one stay.

'In the midst of life . . .'*

CHAPTER 36

It was but a little crowd that stood at the Old Bailey corner while the bell tolled, to watch for the black flag. This was not a popular murder. Josh Perrott was not a man who had been bred to better things; he did not snivel and rant in the dock; and he had not butchered his wife nor his child, nor anybody with a claim on his gratitude or affection; so that nobody sympathised with him, nor got up a petition for pardon, nor wrote tearful letters to the newspapers. And the crowd that watched for the black flag was a small one, and half of it came from the Jago.

While it was watching, and while the bell was tolling, a knot of people stood at the Perrotts' front-doorway, in Old Jago Street. Father Sturt went across as soon as the sleepers of the night had been seen away from the shelter, and spoke to Kiddo Cook, who stood at the stair-foot to drive off intruders.

'They say she's been settin' up all night, Father,' Kiddo reported, in a hushed voice. 'An' Poll's jest looked in at the winder from Walsh's, and says she can see 'em all kneelin' round a chair with that little clock o' theirs on it. It's – it's more'n 'alf an hour yut.'

'I shall come here myself presently, and relieve you. Can you wait? You mustn't neglect trade, you know.'

'I'll wait all day, Father, if ye like. Nobody sha'n't disturb 'em.'

When Father Sturt returned from his errand, 'Have you heard anything?' he asked.

'No, Father,' answered Kiddo Cook. 'They ain't moved.'

There were two faint notes from a distant steeple, and then the bell of St Leonard's beat out the inexorable hour.

Kiddo Cook prospered. The stall was a present fact, and the awning was not far off; indeed, he was vigilantly in search of a second-hand one, not too much worn. But with all his affluence he was not often drunk. Nothing could be better than his pitch – right out in the High Street, in the busiest part, and hard by the London and County branch bank. They called it Kiddo's Bank in the Jago, and made jokes about alleged deposits of his. If you bought a penn'orth of greens from Kiddo, said facetious Jagos, he didn't condescend to take the money himself; he gave you a slip of paper, and you paid at the bank. And Kiddo had indulged in a stroke of magnificence that no other Jago would have thought of. He had taken *two* rooms, in the new County Council dwellings. The secret was that Father Sturt had agreed to marry Kiddo Cook and Pigeony Poll. There would be plenty for both to do, what with the stall and the regular round with the barrow.

The wedding-day came when Hannah Perrott had been one week a widow. For a few days Father Sturt had left her alone, and had guarded her privacy. Then, seeing that she gave no sign, he went with what quiet comfort he might, and bespoke her attention to her concerns. He invented some charing work in his rooms for her. She did it very badly, and if he left her long alone, she would be found on the floor, with her face in a chair-seat, crying weakly. But the work was something for her to do and to think about, and by dint of bustling it and magnifying its importance, Father Sturt brought her to some degree of mind-fulness and calm.

Dicky walked that morning in a sort of numb, embittered fury. What should he do now? His devilmost. Spare nobody and stop at nothing. Old Beveridge was right that morning years ago. The Jago had got him, and it held him fast. Now he went doubly sealed of the outcasts:* a Jago with a hanged father. Father Sturt talked of work, but who would give *him* work?

And why do it, in any case? What came of it before? No, he was a Jago and the world's enemy; Father Sturt was the only good man in it; as for the rest, he would spoil them when he could. There was something for tomorrow night, if only he could get calmed down enough by then. A builder's yard in Kingsland with an office in a loft, and money in a common desk. Tommy Rann had found it, and they must do it together; if only he could get this odd numbness off him, and have his head clear. So much crying, perhaps, and so much trying not to, till his head was like to burst. Deep-eyed and pale, he dragged round into Edge Lane, and so into New Jago Street.

Jerry Gullen's canary was harnessed to the barrow, and Jerry himself was piling the barrow with rags and bottles. Dicky stood and looked; he thought he would rub Canary's head, but then he changed his mind, and did not move. Jerry Gullen glanced at him furtively once or twice, and then said: 'Good ole moke for wear, ain't 'e?'

'Yus,' Dicky answered moodily, his talk half random. ''E'll peg out soon now.'

''Im? Not 'im. Wy, I bet 'e'll live longer'n you will. 'E ain't goin' to die.'

'I think 'e'd like to,' said Dicky, and slouched on.

Yes, Canary would be better off, dead. So would others. It would be a comfortable thing for himself if he could die quietly then and there. But it would never do for mother and the children to be left helpless. How good for them all to go off easily together,* and wake in some pleasant place, say a place like Father Sturt's sitting-room, and perhaps find – but there, what foolishness!

What was this unendurable stupor that clung about him like a net? He knew everything clearly enough, but it was all in an atmosphere of dull heedlessness. There would be some relief in doing something violent – in smashing something to little pieces with a hammer.

He came to the ruined houses. There was a tumult of yells, and a crowd of thirty or forty lads went streaming across the open waste, waving sticks.

'Come on! Come on, Jago! 'Ere they are!'

A fight! Ah, what more welcome! And Dove Lane, too – Dove Lane, that had taken to bawling the taunt, 'Jago cut-throats', since . . .

He was in the thick of the raid. 'Come on, Jago! Jago! 'Ere they are!' Past the Board School and through Honey Lane they went, and into Dove Lane territory. A small crowd of Dove-Laners broke and fled. Straight ahead the Jagos went, till they were suddenly taken in flank at a turning by a full Dove Lane mob. The Jagos were broken by the rush, but they fought stoutly, and the street was filled with a surge of combat.

'Jago! Jago hold tight!'

Thin, wasted and shaken, Dicky fought like a tiger. He had no stick till he floored a Dove-Laner and took his from him, but then he bludgeoned apace, callous to every blow, till he fought through the thick, and burst out at the edge of the fray. He pulled his cap tight, and swung back, almost knocking over, but disregarding, a leather-aproned,* furtive hunchback, who turned and came at his heels.

'Jago! Jago hold tight!' yelled Dicky Perrott. 'Come on, Father Sturt's boys!'

He was down. Just a punch under the arm from behind. As he rolled, face under, he caught a single glimpse of the hunchback, running. But what was this – all this?

A shout went up. 'Stabbed! Chived! They chived Dicky Perrott!'

The fight melted. Somebody turned Dicky on his back, and he moaned, and lay gasping. He lifted his dabbled hands, and looked at them, wondering. They tried to lift him, but the blood poured so fast that they put him down. Somebody had gone for a surgeon.

'Take me 'ome,' said Dicky, faintly, with an odd gurgle in his voice. 'Not 'awspital.'

The surgeon came running, with policemen at his heels. He ripped away the clothes from about the wound, and shook his head. It was the lung. Water was brought, and cloths, and an old door. They put Dicky on the door, and carried him toward the surgery; and two lads who stayed by him were sent to bring his friends.

The bride and bridegroom, meeting the news on the way home, set off at a run, and Father Sturt followed.

'Good Gawd, Dicky,' cried Poll, tearing her way to the shutter as it stopped at the surgery door, 'wot's this?'

Dicky's eye fell on the flowered bonnet that graced the wedding, and his lip lifted with the shade of a smile. 'Luck, Pidge!'

He was laid out in the surgery. A crowd stood about the door, while Father Sturt went in. The vicar lifted his eyebrows questioningly, and the surgeon shook his head. It was a matter of minutes.

Father Sturt bent over and took Dicky's hand. 'My poor Dicky,' he said, 'who did this?'

'Dunno, Fa'er.'

The lie – the staunch Jago lie. Thou shalt not nark.

'Fetch mother an' the kids. Fa'er!'

'Yes, my boy?'

'Tell Mist' Beveridge there's 'nother way out – better.'

THE END

NOTES

p.3 **Preface to the third edition:** variant, shorter version of Morrison's essay 'What is a Realist?' – an essay engaging in more detail with H. D. Traill's objections to *A Child of the Jago* in the *Fortnightly Review* (*see* 'Morrison and his Critics').

p.4 **Constable:** John Constable (1776–1837), English landscape painter, particularly famous for his natural lighting effects, water reflections and cloud studies.

p.4 **Corot:** Jean Baptiste Camille Corot (1796–1875), French figure and landscape painter who worked in romantic and realist styles.

p.4 **Iwasa Matahei:** (or Matabei) (1578–1650) first Japanese artist publicly to identify himself with *genre* compositions depicting the lives of ordinary people. Previously such figures had played mainly subsidiary roles in paintings of noble or saintly characters. *See* Ukioyé below; also Morrison's *The Painters of Japan*.

p.4 **Hiroshigé:** (1797–1858) with Hokusai, master of colour-printed woodcuts of contemporary life and scenery of Japan. Exclusion of the natural cast shadow had been regarded as one of the defining characteristics of Japanese art; Hiroshigé's work was consequently better received in the West than in Japan.

p.4 **Tosa and Kano:** opposing traditions in Japanese art, each, from the earliest times, enjoying periods of particular dominance. Tosa, Buddhist in inspiration and typified by the art of Takayoshi, produced a native art of ceremony, grace and formal convention. Kano, which supplanted Tosa in the fifteenth century, was Zen in inspiration, Chinese-influenced and prioritized the subjective response of artist and viewer.

p.4 **School of Ukioyé:** (or, variously, Ukiyo-ye, Ukiyo-e) *See* Matahei and Hiroshigé above. Japanese school of *genre* painting and print-making which was developed in the seventeenth and eighteenth centuries by such artists as Moronobu, Haronobu, Okumura Masanobu, Kiyonaga and Utamora.

p.4 Harunobu: Suzuki Haronobu (1718–70), Japanese artist who advanced woodblock printing from the conventional two-colour technique to polychrome; he specialized in idyllic images of youth.

p.4 the artist should be shut up in a flower-garden: Morrison alludes, as in the reflection that follows concerning those who regard art as 'upholstery', to the *Bookman*'s review of *Jago*, which prioritized literature as 'a portion of the relaxation of life'. The *Critic*'s review, taking a similar stance even more emphatically, did not appear until April 1897 (*see* 'Morrison and his Critics').

p.4 I have been asked, in print: Chiming of the word 'phase' suggests Morrison is alluding to the *Blackwood's* review: 'Mr Morrison will say that he does not wish to please, but only to exhibit another phase of life' (*see* 'Morrison and his Critics').

p.5 the priest and the Levite: parable of the Good Samaritan, answering the question 'And who is my neighbour?': Luke, 10.29–37.

p.5 Hogarth: Charles Lamb (1775–1834), 'On the Genius and Character of Hogarth, with Some Remarks on a Passage in the Writings of the Late Mr. Barry', an essay first published in Leigh Hunt's *Reflector* (1811) and subsequently included by Lamb in his *Works* (1818). The essay praised the engraver, satirist and comic history painter William Hogarth (1697–1764), particularly for the quality of 'the real' in his depiction of the principal character in *The Rake's Progress*. Lamb defended Hogarth against the strictures of Sir Joshua Reynolds and those who deprecated 'the low' in Hogarth's compositions, particularly the Irishman James Barry R.A. (1741–1806), Professor of Painting at the Royal Academy, who had written adversely of Hogarth in the *Friend*. Lamb observed: 'Those persons seem to me to confound the painting of subjects in common or vulgar life with the being a vulgar artist. The quantity of thought which Hogarth crowds into every picture, would alone *unvulgarize* every subject which he might choose.' Doubtless the essay's attack on the 'rage for classification' also appealed to Morrison: 'We are for ever deceiving ourselves with names and theories'. This reference to Lamb's essay appears only in the preface and not in 'What is a Realist?'.

p.6 following his own spirit: *see* note on epigraph below.

p.6 a like spirit of lavish objection: the objections listed relate specifically to Traill's attack.

p.6 lack of 'sympathy': the *Bookman* found in *Jago* 'a horrible defiance of any sensitive feelings we may have'; Traill wrote of realists who 'sternly shut their eyes to the real pathos of the scenes and lives which they describe'. The *Critic* was shortly to suggest that some 'softening' might have 'created or evoked the sympathy which he longs for the reader to feel'; in December the *Academy* again charged him with 'lack of sympathy', without which 'there can be no really great imaginative writing'. Morrison had also already bridled at this charge in his *Daily News* interview (*see* 'Critical Responses').

p.7 'palpable exaggeration': review of *Jago* in the *Athenaeum*, 12 Dec. 1896 (*see* 'Morrison and his Critics').

p.8 the devoted vicar ... has testified: Rev. A. Osborne Jay, Vicar of Holy Trinity, Shoreditch, the novel's dedicatee and model for Father Sturt. 'What is a Realist?' mentions Jay corroborating Morrison's account 'four or five times at least in public print'. Jay wrote letters to the *St James's Gazette* and the *Fortnightly Review* and gave an interview to *London*; Morrison may also have in mind one or more of Jay's books: *Life in Darkest London: With a Hint to General Booth* (London: Webster and Cable, 1891); *The Social Problem and Its Possible Solution* (London: Simpkin and Marshall, 1893); *A Story of Shoreditch: A Sequel to Life in Darkest London* (London: Simpkin and Marshall, 1896).

p.8 Others ... with special knowledge: these included Harold Boulton, 'C.R', and the *East London Church Chronicle* (effectively, the Bishop of Stepney). *See* 'Critical Responses'.

p.8 The Jago ... is gone: *see* London County Council below.

p.9 Woe unto the foolish prophets: attack on false prophets prophesying 'concerning Jerusalem, and which see visions of peace for her, and there is no peace' (Ezekiel, 13.16). The idea of the destruction of Jerusalem had been applied to London since the Renaissance. This example, however, chimes particularly strongly with other *fin-de-siècle* projections of urban catastrophe: see, for example, Peter Miles, 'Richard Jefferies' Apocalypse Snow: Corn, Gold and the Politics of Urban Survival', *Imprimatur*, 2, iv (1996). In his preface Morrison identified such prophets with 'your professed philanthropist, following his own spirit and seeing nothing'. The epigraph also reinforces Morrison's assertion that 'observation is my trade' and alludes, in its figure of the ill-built building, to the condition of the Jago itself.

p.10 The Old Jago: Sketch Plan: excluding the historical (Shoreditch) High Street and Bethnal Green Road, T. Harper Smith (pp.42–3) translates this sketch-plan into the historical street system:

Old Jago Street:	Old Nichol Street
New Jago Street:	New Nichol Street
Half Jago Street:	Half Nichol Street
Jago Row:	Nichol Row
Edge Lane:	Boundary Street
Honey Lane:	Mead Street
Meakin Street:	Church Street

Smith does not translate 'Luck Row'. Morrison identified Jago Court as 'Orange Court' in his *Daily News* interview (*see* 'Morrison and his Critics' and Jay, p.61). One reviewer suggested that 'Jago' was a play on the name 'Jay' (i.e. 'Jay-go' as opposed to a 'No-go' area: *Athenaeum*, 3607, 12 Dec. 1896, pp. 832–3). Smith notes that Charles Booth's *Life and Labour of the People in London* contains 'a description of part of the Jago, really the "Nichol", house by house, under the name of Summer Gardens' (p.40).

p.11 set across with posts: designed to exclude horses and carts from subsequently narrowing passageways.

p.11 for one hundred years the blackest pit in London: the enormous growth of the East End occurred during the nineteenth century: 'The whole of that great city of a million souls, now called East London, consisted, until the end of the last century, of Whitechapel and Bethnal Green, still preserving something of the old rusticity; of Mile End, Stepney and Bow, and West Ham, hamlets set among fields, and market-gardens, and of that long fringe of riverside-streets and houses': 'A Riverside Parish' (1892); reprinted in *As We Are and As We May Be* (London: Chatto and Windus, 1903), p.108. In the wake of development, the 'Old' Jago, first occupied by Huguenot silk-weavers or their successors, was left to decay through what Morrison termed 'a century of infamy'.

p.11 What was too vile for Kate Street, Seven Dials, and Ratcliff Highway in its worst day: 'The Kate Street mob dropped on him in Brick Lane and bashed him full sore': Morrison, 'A Conversion', in *Tales of Mean Streets*, p.260.

Dickens wrote of the 'Dials' with its 'seven dark passages' in *Sketches by Boz* (Chap. 5): 'Where is there such another maze of streets, courts, lanes and alleys? Where such a pure mixture of Englishmen and Irishmen, as in this complicated part of London? ... The unexperienced wayfarer ... traverses streets of dirty straggling houses, with now and then an unexpected court composed of buildings as ill-proportioned and deformed as the half-naked children that wallow in the kennels.' In Morrison's 'The Case of the Lost Foreigner', Seven Dials is the locale of a Frenchman with anarchist connections (*Chronicles of Martin Hewitt*, pp.281–322).

The folk song 'As I was a-walking along Ratcliff Highway' captures this principal dockland road's associations with sailors, prostitutes and the press gang. Dickens called it 'that reservoir of dirt, drunkenness and drabs: thieves, oysters, baked potatoes and pickled salmon'. Besant characterized its history as 'street fighting and brawling all day long; the perpetual adoration of rum; quarrels over stolen goods; quarrels over drunken drabs ... a never-ending, still-beginning debauch' ('A Riverside Parish', p.117). Morrison set *The Hole in the Wall* here (vividly describing the Blue Gate slum): 'I think there could never have been another street in this country at once so foul and so picturesque as Ratcliff Highway at the time I speak of' (p.83). The area was subsequently cleaned up and the Highway's name changed to St George's Street; of St James, Ratcliff, Besant observed: 'Till lately there were forty-six [public houses], but ten have been suppressed' ('A Riverside Parish', p.125).

p.12   three sorts of vermin ... third plague of Egypt: fleas, flies and lice. Looey is 'horribly flea-bitten'; in Egypt, flies and lice followed the plague of frogs (Exodus, 9); Jay observed that 'only those who reside [here] can know the abject terror of the awful curse "lice in all their quarters", or the extreme reasonableness of the ordinary summer ejaculation, "They do bite this weather!"' (p.69).

p.12   sleeping and walking: Keating prints the more idiomatic 'sleeping and waking'; the first edition reading, however, has the merit of extending the theme of motion through 'writhen', 'rolled' and 'moving'.

p.12   I wish I was dead: an' kep' a cawfy shop: Jay: "I wish I were dead," is a common aspiration, "and kept a coffee-house" – a vision surely of peace which should touch the hearts of all the well-fed, who can get all they want as soon as they ask for it' (p.118). In 1951 Francis Le May, an inhabitant of Huguenot descent, recalled Bethnal Green in the 1880s and 1890s and explained the role of coffee shops and cook shops (such as Weech's) in the community: 'Gas cookers were unknown, so most of the food was bought already cooked. Every eating house supplied hot meals, vegetables, puddings etc. ... There were Cook Shops, Pie Shops and Coffee Shops everywhere, and people you passed carrying basins with a saucer for cover, or a beer can with soup, or a covered plate could be counted by the score': 'Memories of Bethnal Green', *East London Record*, 4 (1981), pp. 30–5, pp. 31–2.

p.12 Kiddo Cook: Jago nicknames connote wiliness, bravado or expertise. 'Kid' was a slang term of admiration for an expert young thief or pugilist. 'Kiddy' meant to fool ('kid'); as a noun it was what Morrison called 'a friendly synonym' for a professional thief assuming a 'flashness' of dress and manner (*OED*). 'Kiddy', meaning a 'bloke', survives in London and the south east, as also does 'kiddo' as a term of address importing 'friend'.

p.12 screw of paper: nineteenth-century equivalent of a paper bag. George Sturt teased his readers 'Do you know how to twist up paper into a small bag?': *A Small Boy in the Sixties* (1927; reprinted London: Caliban, 1982), p.135. At the Perrotts' a 'screw of paper' substitutes for a 'sugar basin'; Kiddo's keeping tobacco in this way (as Butson does in *To London Town*), indicates that he can not afford a tobacco-pouch.

p.12 O wot 'orrid langwidge! It's shocking, blimy: in *To London Town* Essex country-dwellers recoil from the language of visiting London 'beanfeasters' (Chap. 1). Besant, in 'From Thirteen to Seventeen' (1886; reprinted in *As We Are and As We May Be*), declared that he had never heard 'language more vile and depraved' than from fifteen-year-old working girls at Hampstead Heath fair; 'at mere profanity, of course, these girls would be easily defeated by men, but not in absolute vileness' (p.34). Kiddo theatrically mimics the offended sensibility of superior classes or of the posturing working class whose dropped 'aitches' and unconscious profanity ('[Cor] blimey' = 'God blind me') inadvertently announce the affectation.

p.12 Hell? And how far's that? You're in it!: infernal imagery pervades constructions of the East End, constituting a whole discourse as much as a discrete chain of literary transmission. Mephostophilis' 'Why, this is Hell, nor am I out of it' (Christopher Marlowe, *Dr Faustus*, iii, 78) offers a precedent, but so does Jay: '"There can be no hell hereafter," is a common expression of the people, "we live in it already"' (p.108); this phrasing is echoed in Morrison's *Daily News* interview. However, the sentiment equally chimes with Gissing's *The Nether World* (which Gissing had accused Jay of plagiarizing) where Mad Jack reports his dream of the underclass living in 'a state of punishment' inflicted for their misusing wealth in a former life: 'This life you are now leading is that of the damned; this place to which you are confined is Hell! . . . This is Hell – Hell – Hell!' (Chap. 37).

p.13 wife (married or not): middle-class horror of the underclass partly focused on perceived sexual immorality. Domestic Christian Missions encouraged marriage of those joined, as Morrison put it, 'in the simple Jago fashion' – or as Jay phrased it, 'only married, not churched' (p.110). Hence the later references to a Bethnal Green church 'where you might be married for sevenpence if you were fourteen years old and no questions asked'. Morrison's *Daily News* interviewer was himself a former East End curate and interpolated: 'my mind went back to a Christmas morning in an East End church, where I, as curate, stood marrying blaspheming youths and girls to one another . . . ghastly mockery'. In *Mean Streets* it is a rector who encourages 'early matrimony' by giving 'free weddings' who marries Lizerunt and Billy Chope. Harold Boulton commented that 'the institution of the family as sanctioned by the narrow formulae of Church and State had been stamped out' in the Old Nichol. Besant saw early marriage as a symptom of cultural poverty, indeed 'the greatest curse of East London' ('A Riverside Parish', p.129). Kijinski notes that Victorian ethnographic methodology in evaluating cultures gave special weight to the status of marriage.

p.13 industry . . . craftsman . . . profit . . . transaction . . . capable practitioners . . . duty . . . artist: long-lived extended metaphor presenting the criminal urban poor in relation to work and business, notably enshrined in Hogarth's 'Industry and Idleness' (where the industrious apprentice becomes Lord Mayor and the idle apprentice, turning to crime, is hanged); also in Dickens's *Oliver Twist* where Fagin refers to his boys' activities as examples of industry and craftsmanship. Terms such as 'trade', 'tradesman' and 'training' are used ironically throughout *Jago*, while an ironic version of the idle and industrious apprentices ghosts through the presentation of Dicky Perrott and Bobby Roper at the Board School.

p.13 exemplary fiction . . . Sunday School book . . . dutiful matrons: Joseph Alleine and John Wesley ran Sunday Schools earlier, but these institutions are particularly associated with Robert Raikes' organizing activity in the 1780s. They were subsequently promoted by Sunday School Unions and participated in the project of educating the poor working class into 'respectability'. St Mary's, Whitechapel, for example, was running a Sunday School in 1890 under its rector Arthur J. Robinson. Prize-books 'of the goody kind' for good attendance or scripture reading were produced for distribution by such specialist publishers as SPCK and Partridge (Besant, *East London* (London: Chatto, 1899; new ed., 1902), p.13). Their idealized stories inculcated such virtues as temperance, chastity, stoicism and filial duty. *The Ragged Trousered Philanthropists* was to mock their role as quietist political propaganda: see P. Miles, 'The Painter's Bible and the British Workman: Robert Tressell's Literary Activism', in J. Hawthorn, ed., *The British Working-Class Novel in the Twentieth Century* (London: Arnold, 1984), pp.1–17.

p.13 portal: elaborate, quasi-medieval gateway; Orange Court was noted for its narrow, tunnel-like entrance.

p.14 Front doors were used merely as firewood: Jago houses are in multiple occupation (Smith mentions that 53 Old Nichol Street 'with ten rooms had ninety persons'); the dismantling of front doors destroys their function as symbols of artisan respectability or of middle-class domesticity and privacy. In 'That Brute Simmons', in *Mean Streets*, the punctilious Mrs Simmons regards even an open front door as 'low', *see* E. Ross, 'Not the Sort that Would Sit on the Doorstep – Respectability in Pre-World-War-I London Neighbourhoods', *International Labour and Working-Class History*, no. 27 (1985), 39–59.

p.15 first-floor back: 'back' rooms, having less light and looking out on walls, waste areas or middens, commanded lower rents. (The Ropers, who with their 'threadbare decency' are seen as 'pertickler' and 'too good for their neighbours', occupy a 'front room'.) Visitors used coded knocks at the front door (when present) for particular tenants (*see* 'That Brute Simmons').

p.15 weak of mouth: physiognomy as a key to character flourished through the nineteenth century both in popular culture and in the novel. As a pseudo-science it cooperated in defining and locating 'degeneration'; while Hannah is 'weak of mouth', Father Sturt is 'tall and soundly built, with a certain square muscularity of face'. See Graeme Tytler, *Physiognomy in the European Novel: Faces and Fortunes* (1982) and Daniel Pick, *Faces of Degeneration: A European Disorder*.

p.16 done a click: pulled a job; committed a theft; Jay draws attention to the expression (p.98).

p.18 Valley of Dry Bones: the dead awaiting resurrection as a metaphor for the underclass awaiting 'a better way' (with an ironic quibble on the coshed man regaining consciousness). Ezekiel, 37. 1–2: 'The hand of the Lord was upon me, and carried me out in the Spirit of the Lord, and set me down in the midst of the valley which was full of bones, and caused me to pass by them round about: and, behold, there were very many in the open valley; and, lo, they were very dry.'

p.19 East End Elevation Mission and Pansophical Institute: the careful locating of the Institute suggests the satire is directed at Toynbee Hall, associated with St Jude's Church, Whitechapel, rather than Morrison's former place of employment, the People's Palace, located in Stepney, further east along the Mile End Road. However, Morrison satirizes the premises and principles of philanthropic activity rather than any particular institution.

The ostentatious title combines the spirit of Victorian civic and educational development ('Institute') with democratic humanist ('Pansophical') and evangelical religious impulses ('Mission'). In Matthew Arnold's terms, the Institute offers 'sweetness and light', cultural development and moral improvement. 'Elevation' was part of philanthropic and eugenic discourses; it carried a residual religious meaning ('the lifting up of the soul [in adoration]; a devout exaltation of feeling' [*OED*]) but also denoted a 'raising' of the lower classes physically, socially, morally and culturally. Besant saw the People's Palace as working for the 'purification and elevation of life'. Morrison saw such elevation as principally self-aggrandisement by the philanthropist: in *To London Town* 'superior vistors' to a Working Man's Institute come away 'oozing with inexpensive patronage' (p.222) and other visitors 'went home virtuously conscious of having done their duty towards the Submerged' (p.238). The term 'elevator' (as in 'ardent young Elevator') may be mildly ironic in that it principally meant a Salvation Army factory – such as Hanbury Street Elevator – resocializing the underclass into responsible work: *see* Besant, 'The Farm and the City', in Bramwell Booth, ed., *Essays and Sketches: The Salvation Army* (London: Salvation Army, 1906), p.60.

Besant defined the interests of the People's Palace as 'knowledge in all its branches'; 'its educational capacities are almost boundless ... there will be founded here a University for the People of a kind hitherto unknown and undreamed of' ('The People's Palace' (1887), reprinted in *As We Are and As We May Be*, pp.50–51). The concept (though not in this social context) of an Institute of Pansophy was variously associated with the Czech educational reformer Jan Komensky and William Hartlib, English analyst of the structure of knowledge. The *OED* notes two principal meanings of 'Pansophy': 'universal encyclopaedic knowledge; a scheme or encyclopaedic work embracing the whole body of human knowledge' and 'the claim or pretension' to such.

p.19 **people who knew less of that part than of Asia Minor:** widespread ignorance of conditions in the East End is a common theme in writing about it. 'Asia Minor' here implies the Ottoman Empire and the Balkan politics which so exercised Gladstone and affected debate about the aims of British Liberalism. As a result of the Russo-Turkish War (1877–8), Eastern Rumelia was placed under Ottoman control, but in 1885 a revolution led to the province joining Bulgaria. This in turn led to war between Serbia and Bulgaria and complex repercussions involving the Ottoman Empire, Russia, Austria, Greece and Roumania. The connotations of 'West' and 'East' thus oscillate between denoting parts of London and connoting a larger ideological geography opposing the West as Christendom to a threatening 'other' along Europe's Eastern and Southern borders characterized as Muslim, Serb or Semitic, often as pederastic, homosexual or otherwise deviant or degenerative: *see* Edward Said, *Orientalism* (1978). The Transylvania of Bram Stoker's *Dracula* (1897) is patent evidence of such anxiety but London with its 'street arabs' and increased racial diversity also provided a model of this opposition at home: *see* Ledger; also Morrison, 'Whitechapel', *Palace Journal* (24 April 1889), 1022–3. Besant, in his chapter 'The Aliens' in *East London*, celebrated Anglo-Saxony's cultural absorption of Romans, Vikings, Normans, Flemings and others but wrote with more discernible unease of the one hundred thousand Jewish immigrants arriving in the late nineteenth century.

p.19 **Higher Life, the Greater Thought, and the Wider Humanity: with other radiant abstractions, mostly in the comparative degree:** satire on the discourse of idealists and transcendentalists. The term 'Higher Life', denoting a state of personal spiritual sanctification, was common in evangelical and educational debate, as also in nonconformist theological stances. The Theosophy movement (founded in 1875 by Madame Blavatsky), influenced by Indian thought, used the term to signify higher mystical planes of existence (e.g. George Wyld's

Theosophy and the Higher Life: or, Spiritual Dynamics and the Divine and Miraculous Man; Annie Besant's *The Laws of the Higher Life*). Morrison had an arm's length interest in such matters. His first published book, *The Shadows Around Us*, dealt with spiritualism; some of his short stories touch on the paranormal and the occult.

p.19 Lectures ... Pictures: Besant judged Toynbee Hall's lecturers 'the most distinguished men in their own lines to be found; there is no talking "down" to the Whitechapel audience'. Easter art exhibitions were organized by the Rev. Samuel Barnett, Vicar of St Jude. Besant elaborated: 'In the evening ladies go round with small parties and give little talks upon the pictures, explaining what the artist meant and how his design has been carried out. Such a party I once watched before Burne-Jones's picture of "The Briar Rose". The people gazed; they saw the brilliant colouring, the briar-rose everywhere, the sleeping knights, the courtyard – all. Then the guide began, and their faces lit up with pleasure and understanding, and all went home that evening richer for the contemplation and the comprehension of one great work of art.' (*East London*, 311; 296–7).

p.19 Uninformed ... Hopeless Poor ... Misery of the Submerged: Social Problem discourse generated such terms as The Submerged, The Subterranean (prefiguring H. G. Wells' 'Morlocks'), The Unemployed, The Dispossessed, The Nether Worlders, The Great Unwashed, The Degraded Classes, The Vicious Classes. Besant characterized the Submerged as those who had fallen to the gutter from any height, whether starting as professional man, tradesman or workman; at the same time he observed: 'The word "submerged" likes me not. I have endeavoured to find or to invent another and a better word. So far without success.' (*East London*, p.229). *See*: R. H. Stoll, 'The Unthinkable Poor in Edwardian Writing', *Mosaic – A Journal for the Interdisciplinary Study of Literature*, 15, iv (1982), 23–45. 'The Uninformed' may be Morrison's invention or satire on conflation of the condition of the outcast poor with the very different issue of educational provision for the artisan and lower middle class. In *To London Town* Morrison wrote mockingly of those who spoke of 'the Degraded Classes, who were to be Raised from the Depths' by cultural education (p.222) or even of 'the Upraising of the Hopeless Residuum' (p.235).

p.19 debate and to produce papers on literary and political matters ... classes, and clubs ... and musical evenings: Morrison may here have in mind the People's Palace and his own former role in organizing such activities: *see* Michael Krzak's introduction (1983) to *Mean Streets*. Besant recorded: 'What Barnett and Toynbee Hall have done for the intellectual side, the People's Palace has done for the musical side. Its cheap concerts have led the people, naturally inclined to music, insensibly into ways of good taste ... They now have their own orchestra, vocal and instrumental ... Here is the finest gymnasium in London, and here are many clubs – for foot-ball, cricket, and games of all kinds' (*East London*, pp.312–13). Besant's greatest disappointment was that a literary prize he instituted produced responses of very low quality.

p.19 tradesmen's sons, small shopkeepers: Besant was clear about the constituency of the People's Palace. In 'The Amusements of the People' (1884), reprinted in *As We Are and As We May Be*, he commented: 'It can do nothing, absolutely nothing, to relieve the great starvation and misery which lies all about London, but more especially at the East-end ... We are concerned only with the well fed, those who are in steady work, the respectable artisans and *petits commis*, the artists in the hundred little industries which are carried on in the East-end; those, in fact, who have already acquired some power of enjoyment because they are separated by a sensible distance from their hand-to-mouth brothers and sisters' (pp.288–9).

p.19 bagatelle board: popular from the Regency period onwards, this forerunner of pinball machines was often found in pubs (as in the Sol's Arms in *Bleak House*); it is also played in Father Sturt's club (as it was in Jay's, though not for money). It did not figure as one of the rational recreations demanding 'skill, patience, discipline, drill, and obedience to law' that Besant encouraged ('The People's Palace', p.57); Morrison may be implying philanthropists' failure to inculcate desired recreational values.

p.19 Mutually-Improved: debating societies were sometimes termed 'Mutual Improvement Societies'; Morrison had already mocked them in *Mean Streets* (*see* 'A Street').

p.20 Other young men ... Missionaries: the Society for the Propagation of the Gospel in Foreign Parts was established in 1701. Theological debate further enhancing the duty of mission, the missionary became an icon of Victorian culture. The domestic dimension of mission grew in parallel; the need was demonstrated in an 1886 census in the East End which found that some 92 per cent of the population attended no religious service. University Settlements enabled those in training for the Church to gain experience of mission in deprived areas.

p.20 perilous deeps ... dark region: in Social Problem discourse deprived areas were typically constructed as deep (descent; the pit; the abyss; drowning at sea) and dark (night; the nether world; the African interior).

p.20 much worse places up West: Besant emphasized that the East End was not a city of slums, and singled out Devil's Acre, West London, as a far worse slum than any in the East End (*East London*, p.38). George Sturt wrote of the annual arrival in Farnham of hoppers 'from the slums of Reading or of West London' (p.76).

p.20 police-court and inquest reports: 'Police intelligence' was published in the daily newspapers (cf. Emma Sansom's trial in *To London Town*); Jack London compiled an entire chapter of *The People of the Abyss* (Chap. 16) with quotations from such reports. Besant suggested that publications like the *Police News Budget* represented the typical reading of the East Ender.

p.21 accident to his hat ... string: a bishop's hat resembled a low top hat with strings running from its sides to the brim.

p.21 spikes of the Bishop's carriage: designed to prevent people jumping on the back. George Sturt recalled a bishop 'who could not drive to church without two flunkeys clinging to the back of his carriage' (p.168).

p.22 popular periodicals and in – in other ways: the Bishop's hesitation suggests Morrison may be mischievously alluding to his own *Mean Streets*.

p.22 not so black as it was painted: the *Spectator*'s reviewer toyed with such a charge against *Mean Streets*: 'as if he were deluding consciously the public into taking too black a view of the East-End'. Charles Booth's Poverty Survey Maps of London used a seven-shade colour-coding system running between black ('lowest class') and yellow ('wealthy'). For Booth's map covering the Old Nichol *see* Terry McCarthy, ed., *The Great Dock Strike 1889* (London: TGWU and Weidenfeld and Nicolson, 1988), pp.96–7.

p.23 what's become of my watch?: elaboration of Jay's account of his new church's foundation ceremony: 'Outside for many hundred yards a dense crowd gathered; and within a Bishop, a Bishop-elect, and an Archdeacon graced the proceedings with their presence. Some of these eminent persons were on their way to attend a garden party at Lambeth, and I personally conducted them afterwards through the crowd, feeling sure that otherwise they would attend that gathering minus their watches' (p.65).

p.24 decent boiler-maker's daughter: boiler-makers counted themselves among the aristocracy of skilled labour, far higher socially than a plasterer (such as Josh claims to be). Morrison, as in the preface and his sketch 'On Blackwall Pier', was acutely aware of lower-class social distinctions: 'Here, perhaps, would muse the democratic observer, are no social distinctions – here all men are equal. Arcadian republic of Blackwall! Happy province of peaceful anarchy! But the democratic observer would be making a mistake': *Palace Journal*, 8 May 1889, p.1046. Boiler-making relates to Morrison's father's occupation as engine-fitter and to Tommy May's apprenticeship in engineering in *To London Town*.

p.24 nothing but shot or pointed steel could hurt him: an attribute claimed by the original of Josh Perrott as reported by Morrison in his *Daily News* interview (*see* 'Morrison and his Critics').

p.26 hearthstone: used for abrasive cleaning of hearths and doorsteps; typically supplied by rag-and-bone men in exchange for metal, glass, bones (for glue) and rags (for shoddy or paper). Jerry may thus be an occasional rag-and-bone man. In *Sketches by Boz* (Chap. 5) Dickens described the 'firewood and hearthstone line' as one requiring 'a floating capital of eighteenpence or thereabouts'.

p.26 centre-bit: carpenter's tool, favoured by burglars, used for making cylindrical holes: in *Oliver Twist* Bill Sykes requires only 'a centre-bit and a boy' to perform a burglary (Chap. 19); Tennyson referred to 'the villainous centre-bits' that 'Grind on the wakeful ear in the hush of the moonless nights' (*Maud*, I,xi).

p.28 Montagues and the Capulets: feuding families in Shakespeare's *Romeo and Juliet*.

p.29 Bob the Bender: 'Bender' was slang for a hard drinker; cf. 'go on a bender'. 'Jack the Bender' was a nickname in use in Jay's parish (p.37).

p.29 Snob Spicer: 'Snob' was slang for a shoemaker. Spicer is of the Rann persuasion; Fag Dawson (one of the Leary tribe) falls 'with a shoe-maker's knife sticking under his arm-pit'. In 'The Rodd Street Revolution', in *Green Ginger*, Morrison refers to 'the mysterious laws which make all jobbing shoemakers swarthy and ill-shaved and politically rebellious' (p.157); the most famous radical shoemaker was the Chartist Thomas Cooper (1805–92), author of *The Purgatory of Suicides: A Prison-Rhyme*. Alternatively, some element of the principal modern meaning of 'snob' may be involved, given a positive turn to imply flamboyance.

p.29 knocked out of knowledge: battered unconscious.

p.29 quart pot: i.e. a pewter mug. Morrison observed: 'At a beer-house in such a locality (such a house as Mother Gapp's in my book) beer is only served in pewter pots . . . A customer specifically demanding beer in a glass is met with flat denial, though beer can be sold more profitably by the glass than by measure; and the reason is that brawlers, women especially, are apt to break a glass at the rim, and, taking the bottom in the palm of the hand, stab at faces with the jagged points' ('What is a Realist?' pp.333–4).

p.29 Cocko Harnwell: contraction of 'cock o' the walk' (crack man on the street) or an allusion to cock-fighting, meaning a spirited fighter. In noting 'cock' as 'a familiar term of appreciation among the vulgar', *OED* highlights the nuance 'swaggering'.

p.30 cleanliness was resented in the Jago: middle-class perception of the urban poor was structured by an early awareness of the need for improved sanitation in those slum areas that fuelled the cross-class threat from cholera and typhoid. Cleanliness being 'next to godliness' (Father Sturt appears 'whole and unsoiled'), a discourse of class difference structured the poor as by nature ungodly and dirty – the 'Great Unwashed' versus 'washed and well-dressed people' (Chap. 2). Physiognomical text-books such as George Simms' codified and reinforced the point: 'Where there exists a high organization, the individual – be he man or animal – is endowed with a greater or less elevation of nature, and in virtue of this he recoils from the useless contact with inorganic matter, or organic matter of a very low type. This feeling springs from the natural law which attracts like to like. On the other hand, where the organization of the individual is of a low type, as evinced by coarse hair, skin, &c., there is no great revulsion against close association with dirt, because there is a large proportion of the grosser materials in the composition of his frame, in comparison with the amount of soul he is able to boast of' (*Physiognomy Illustrated; or, Nature's Revelations of Character* (London: L. N. Fowler, 1891 10th edition), p.225). Simms clinched his point with opposed illustrations of 'Cleanness Large – The Duchess of Kent, the mother of Her Majesty, Queen Victoria, the Noble Queen' and 'Cleanness Small – Nathaniel Bentley, the dirtiest man in England'. In *The Road to Wigan Pier* George Orwell recorded having to overcome precisely this inculcated sense of class difference.

p.30 assumption of superiority: like 'narking', a grievous fault in the culture of the urban poor and working class.

p.30 Ginger Stagg: by occupation Ginger Stagg is a lob-crawler (*see below*), but 'Stag' – in addition to generating the pun 'at bay' – has some provenance in slang as meaning a person who provides false alibis for payment.

p.30 Pud Palmer: 'Palmer' carries the meaning of a petty criminal adept at sleight of hand (palming coins, cards or dice).

p.31 driving in bungs: breaking into unopened casks of beer or spirits by staving in the wood or cork used to stopper the 'bung-hole'.

p.31 Sally Green ... dangled a long bunch of clotted hair: cf. Jay: 'In this street are two great rival families, two different schools of philosophy, two claimants to the homage and honour of the rest ... Women even take part, biting at each other's faces, and tearing at each other's hair' (p.106).

p.32 lodging-house poker: with the implication of its being larger and heavier than the domestic version; iron rather than brass may be implied.

p.32 Pigeony Poll: *OED*, while not recording 'pigeony', notes use of 'pigeon' into the seventeenth century to mean 'a young woman, a girl; a sweetheart'. More common meanings of 'pigeon', still widely current in the nineteenth century, and not without some relevance to the presentation of Poll, were 'coward; simpleton, dupe'.

p.32 cadged and wrote begging screeves: to cadge is to beg (more literally than in the familar modern use of the word). Systematic ('professional') writing of begging letters addressed to people known to have come into wealth was an attested occupation of the semi-criminal.

See Mayhew, *London Labour* I, 313: '"He writes a good hand," exclaimed one as the screever wrote the petition."

p.35 truck: the wheelwright George Sturt described a 'truck': 'A little light hand-cart it was – a panelled box (made for strength) with T handle ... Its main use was for the morning papers. Two boys took it to the station, threw into it the parcel of newspapers, then brought it at a run to the shop ... You could hear divers trucks rattling about the ancient street' (p.97).

p.35 Fag Dawson: 'fag' was thieves' slang for pickpocket.

p.37 Aaron Weech: despite the name 'Aaron', Morrison and Jay insisted that Weech was not Jewish (or, rather, that his original was not). The textual Weech has, however, been widely read as an anti-Semitic portrait in the same vein as Dickens's Fagin. If Weech is not Jewish, Morrison's fences usually were. Cohen plainly is, and Morrison's portrait of Issy Marks ('Snorkey Timms, His Marks' in *Green Ginger*) is hardly ambiguous. Weech's first name seems a pointed allusion to the first Jewish priest, the brother of Moses, significantly associated with making the golden calf while Moses was receiving the Ten Commandments.

p.37 no Sabbath-breaker: the Act of Uniformity (1551) first placed Sunday observance on the statute book and was followed through the centuries by a number of Sunday Observance, or Lord's Day Acts. An Act of 1871 had in fact considerably reduced the restrictions of the Lord's Days Acts on Sunday trading. Sabbatarianism, however, as it derived from the Ten Commandments, remained a strong tendency among the respectable.

p.38 given anything kindly and ungrudgingly: an episode strongly echoing Oliver Twist's introduction to his 'benefactor' and 'patron' Fagin. *See* R. A. Colby, 'Oliver's Progeny – Some Unfortunate Foundlings', *Dickens Quarterly*, 4, ii (1987), 109–121.

p.39 tapping of the forefinger beside the nose: gestural code for knowingness, but in particular a characteristic of Fagin: see Cruikshank's illustration to *Oliver Twist*, 'The Jew and Morris both begin to understand Each Other'.

p.40 clean the knives: to avoid corrosion, steel knives of the period required vigorous scouring; this was often done by a 'knife-boy', either manually on a 'knife-board' or using a 'knife-machine'.

p.40 broad pennies: while eighteenth-century pennies had been larger, 'broad' may refer to the comfortably large dimensions, in Dicky's eyes, of the Victorian penny as opposed to the ha'penny and farthing. Alternatively, 'a broad' formerly meant an unclipped coin (usually gold), and so a figurative sense of 'sound' or 'whole' may be in play.

p.44 American make: automated mass production and design innovations that reduced the number of working parts made mid-nineteenth-century United States the world's leading clock-making nation. The 'American clock' was consequently a byword for utter cheapness.

p.44 corpse: *Notes and Queries* (1884) reported that 'to corpse' was 'one of many customary and coarse ways of menacing the infliction of death. It is horribly familiar in London' (*OED*).

p.45 In the swe-e-et by an' by: popular hymn by Sanford Fillmore Bennett (1836–98), included in Moody and Sankey's hymn-book and frequently printed separately for display purposes.

p.45 grocers' almanacks: pictorial calendars distributed as advertising; here serving as cheap substitutes for pictures. Compare the heroine's home in *Liza of Lambeth* (Chap. 8): 'there were two almanacks several years old, one with a coloured portrait of the Marquess of Lorne, very handsome and elegantly dressed, the object of Mrs Kemp's adoration since her husband's demise; the other a Jubilee portrait of the Queen, somewhat losing in dignity by a moustache which Liza in an irreverent moment had smeared on with charcoal.'

p.45 Sunday School Anniversary bills: later termed 'Sunday-school festival bills'.

p.46 Roper's tools ... were the most valuable things in the place: with Bethnal Green, Shoreditch was a wood-working and furniture-making area. As a cabinet-maker (and thus highly skilled) Roper would be responsible for supplying his own tools; in stealing them, Old Fisher steals Roper's means of living. In *To London Town* Butson's tools are in pawn 'and a man felt discouraged from looking for a job when his tools were "put away", and he had no money to redeem them' (p.173). In 'The Nicobar Bullion Case' a man working as a ship's steward keeps by him the tools of his original trade of boiler-maker because 'that sort of man doesn't like parting with his tools' (*Chronicles of Martin Hewitt*, p.62).

p.47 Elementary Education Act ... Board School: the 1870 Education Act established board schools: there was one in Nichol Street, and Morrison places one in Honey Lane (Mead Street). Elected school boards had powers to build and maintain schools out of the rates. Support by parliamentary grant was also available to board schools and existing schools in particularly poor areas. In 'From Thirteen to Seventeen' Besant noted discontent that the London rate for board schools had risen to ninepence in the pound, unenthusiastically observing: 'The children leave the Board Schools, for the most part, at the age of thirteen, when they have passed the standard which exempts them from further attendance; or if they are half-timers, they remain until they are fourteen' (p.29). Elsewhere, while doubting the practical value of what was learned in board schools, he acknowledged their 'civilizing influence' in abolishing 'much of the old savagery' (*East London*, p.127).

p.47 tickets were to be had: philanthropists have often distributed dedicated vouchers rather than coin to ensure that welfare is applied to ends defined by the giver rather than the recipient. However, once vouchers were exchanged for goods, the underworld offered a 'regular tariff in gin for charity-given shirts and boots and groceries' (Morrison, 'A Blot on St Basil', in *Divers Vanities*, p.196). Jay opposed the manipulative use of tickets: 'I was not a ticket-machine' (p.28).

p.48 parson: active and resolute: as the *Blackwood's* reviewer noted (*see* 'Morrison and his Critics'), a description which suggests F. D. Maurice's 'Muscular Christianity' movement.

p.49 have the police at instant call: 'There was, for some time, a rooted suspicion that I might be in some way connected with the police': Jay, p.35.

p.49 amazed by sudden address in his own name: 'I soon learned [their right names], somewhat to their surprise': Jay, p.37.

p.50 loaves and sixpences: quibble on the 'loaves and fishes' of the feeding of the five thousand (Matthew, 14.17); widely used as a metaphor for the 'perks' of religious observance.

p.50 since the parish came into being: 1867.

p.53 straps: i.e. leather straps for sharpening razors.

p.54 shining, round metal boxes, notably decorated with coloured pictures: probably examples of popular German export tin-plate and clockwork manufacture of the period.

p.56 Gently Does the Trick: probably the tune of a parlour song of the period.

p.59 offering a quart pot: 'One of my new Club members rushed half-tipsy out of a public-house, and, to the evident enjoyment of his companions at the bar window, insulted me by offering me a pot of beer. I took the proffered pewter-pot, and, flinging the contents in his face, told him to recollect whom he was addressing; a rebuke, I am bound to say, he took in good part, and one apparently much appreciated by his friends': Jay, pp.35–6.

p.60 take away his character: a key point of tension when Jay accuses Tommy Irishman of stealing the Club's bagatelle balls: '"Do you," he cried, "take away my character?" "I do not," I calmly retorted, "you possess no character to take away"': Jay, p.41.

p.62 High Mob: with deficiencies in policing and social adminis-tration, the East End has a long history of criminal gangs or mobs, including the Kray brothers in the postwar period, in which the gang (paradoxically, from a middle-class perspective) is a partly benign presence, 'deeply reverenced' by the community, 'stared at' and 'envied'.

p.62 flourishing practitioners: *Cornhill Magazine* (Nov. 1862): 'Every professional thief is considered as belonging to the branch of thieving in which he excels the most, and he is named after it.'

p.62 the mag: a halfpenny, in the context of 'mag flying' or illegal pitch-and-toss rackets (*see* 'pitch-and-toss' below).

p.62 the mace: swindling, robbery by fraud. Snorkey Timms, one of Morrison's dramatized guides to the London underworld, renders 'macing the digs' as 'takin' lodgin's on the strength of 'is luggage an' slidin' off with anything 'e might find. So that a bag stuffed with bricks was just wha. 'e'd ave, natural enough.' ('His Tale of Bricks', in *Divers Vanities*, p.188.)

p.62 the broads: playing cards, for such scams as 'Find the Lady' and 'Crown and Anchor'.

p.62 welshers: swindlers who act as bookmakers but abscond with the money laid as bets.

p.62 snidesmen: counterfeiters or passers of counterfeit coin ('snide-pitchers').

p.62 exchange and house of call: dealing room or 'stock exchange'; 'house where journeymen of a particular trade assemble, where carriers call for commissions, or where various persons in request may be heard of' (*OED*). The terms are used in part ironically, but in noting the 'vast systematic organized depredation' of shipping and the docks, Besant observed: 'To make robbery successful, there must be accomplices, receiving-houses, fences, a way to dispose of the goods ... All the public-houses were secret markets attended by grocers and other tradesmen where the booty was sold by auction, and, to escape detection, fictitious bills and accounts were given and received' ('A Riverside Parish', p.115). This is the world of Morrison's *The Hole in the Wall*.

p.62 ice-cream coat: fur coat, cf. Jay, p.119: '"Half your luck!" called out a talkative youngster to a horrified lady-visitor from the West End in a new fur coat. "After you with the ice-cream coat! I suppose you did a click yesterday." It was in no sense meant as impertinence, but only as a cheerful and hearty greeting.'

p.62 brimmy: presumably a contraction of 'brimmingly', with a figurative sense of 'complete' or 'excellent'.

p.63 the only way out: weighted phrase both in colloquial expression and in Social Problem discourse (repeated on the novel's last page). Jacob Riis wrote of the Bowery in *How the Other Half Lives* (1890): 'The one way out [that the sanitarian of the last generation] saw – rapid transit to the suburbs – has brought no relief. We know now that there is no way out.' William Booth gave the phrase a more optimistic (though to such as Jay and Morrison, foolishly blithe) colouring in the title of his *In Darkest England and the Way Out* (1890). That there are only two 'ways out' of the East End – boxing or crime – remains a common sentiment in the area.

p.63 and that cut short at a third of the usual span of days: i.e. the faction fight has only lasted a third of the normal period, and so the High Mobsmen are not yet back in circulation.

p.64 the dispensary was no charitable institution: charity-supported 'dispensaries' did exist, supplying medicine and advice free of charge.

p.64   hospital letters: documents enabling the bearer to seek treatment in a charitable hospital, cf. 'Maternity Society letter' (Chap. 27), entitling prospective mother to assistance in childbirth.

p.64   who subscribed: i.e. contributed to the charity that ran the hospital concerned.

p.64   Turkey rhubarb and sulphuric acid ... their opposite effects: Turkey (alternatively 'Russian') rhubarb was a medicinal rootstock originally imported from China and Tibet through Turkey or Russia; its effects were initially purgative but subsequently astringent. Sulphur and its compounds were used as laxatives.

p.64   two or three other drugs in hand: cf. George Sturt: 'You took risks, for it cost too much to go to a doctor. You took powders too! ... There were convenient doses to be got at a grocer's – senna, rhubarb, camomile, Stedman's powders, and a loathsome brown powder we called "Grandmother's powder" which we hated – fortunately, for it contained some form of mercury' (p.134).

p.65   Ross on nerve and brain troubles: James Ross (1837–92), physician working in Newchurch, Rossendale and subsequently at Manchester Infirmary; appointed Professor of Medicine at Owens College, Manchester in 1887; author of Treatise on Diseases of the Nervous System (1881).

p.65   fluid bought at a chandler's shop and called milk: chandlers (sellers of hardware and domestic goods) often also sold food (cf. Nan May's shop in To London Town); adulteration of milk in London was an issue from the eighteenth century through to the twentieth. See A. Hardy, 'Diagnosis, Death and Diet: The Case of London, 1750–1909', Journal of Interdisciplinary History, 18, iii (1988), 387–401.

p.66   little 'ymn: Weech's smattering of religious knowledge derives from the culture of Sunday school. His 'little hymn' alludes to one of the innumerable collections of hymns for 'little children / folk / ones,' of which Isaac Watt's (1674–1748), Ann Taylor's (1782–1866) and Mrs Cecil Alexander's (1818–95) were some of the best known. The phrase 'Little Hymn-Book' frequently occurs in the titles of such collections.

p.66   it's wuss to break the fust commandment: the first commandment is in fact 'Thou shalt have no other gods before me'; beyond the obvious irony, Weech presumably means the ninth: 'Thou shalt not bear false witness against thy neighbour': Exodus 20.3,16.

p.68 stall-farming: sub-letting sub-divided properties (akin to stalls in a stable) on a nightly basis.

p.68 pitch-and-toss: gambling game endemic in the slums of Europe and the USA, hard to police because requiring no special equipment. Three coins are tossed in the air from the finger-ends; bets are made on the balance of heads and tails resulting. *OED* cites the *Standard* (1892): 'There were usually three or four in a gang, one acting as the "magflyer", the "mag" being the coin, another as the caller of the odds or amounts, a third as treasurer.' 'Tossing rings' attracted hundreds of gamblers, dealt in large sums of money and into the twentieth century their control was violently disputed: *see*, for example, J. P. Bean, *The Sheffied Gang Wars* (Sheffield: D & D Publications, 1981). Besant notes Sunday as the great gambling day in the East End; Jay specifically records that in Orange Court (Jago Court) 'every Sunday crowds of men and boys assembled to play pitch-and-toss' (p.61).

p.69 Him as done the sparks in from Regent Street for nine centuries o' quids: the one who fenced the diamonds from the Regent Street robbery for £900. Regent Street was famous for both jewellery shops and its 'smash-and-grab' robberies.

p.69 five stretch: five-year term of imprisonment.

p.70 sash-line ... sash: cord which controls the movement of a vertically sliding wooden window.

p.70 measles or whooping cough: common and potentially fatal childhood diseases. Measles could cause brain damage, while complications of whooping cough included damage to the nervous system, haemorrhage and pneumonia.

p.72 rough application of the main hits and guards: Morrison himself is reported to have boxed and his status as an aficionado of the ring and its technicalities is apparent in this description, as also in his short story 'Three Rounds' in *Mean Streets* and the prize-fight in *Cunning Murrell*. In his *Daily News* interview Morrison spoke of conversations with inhabitants of the Old Nichol: 'we used to talk of all kinds of things, especially boxing. The Nichol has sent out some of our best boxers.' In 1896 Clarence Rook, author of *The Hooligan*

Nights and the publisher Grant Richards were also visitors to prize-fights (Green, p.xviii). *See* S. Shipley, 'Tom Causer of Bermondsey – A Boxer Hero of the 1890s', *History Workshop – A Journal of Socialist and Feminist Historians*, no. 15 (1983), 28–59. However, with its 'holds' (including 'chancery', a wrestling head-hold) this is no purist's boxing match.

p.77 Six bloomin' long months in a prison: a song of the prostitute and her male accomplice: possibly from the music-hall; more probably a street-song actually collected in the Old Nichol: cf. Jay, p.116: 'The very sin which is most common in the streets of London is practised here more for the pure sake of robbery and theft than for anything else, and even children see no harm in the universal practice of the wretched street-walker who with her confederate persuades

> A man to come down our alley
> And then take his money away.

In the expression 'the Jago chant', 'chant' signifies not just song but, in thieves' slang, a name, address or designating mark.

p.78 'wide as Broad Street': extremely knowing and crafty: Jay drew attention to the expression (p.37).

p.79 Mansion House Fund: charitable fund initiated by the Lord Mayor of London (officially residing at the Mansion House), normally in response to a hard winter, an epidemic or adverse trade. In context Morrison is almost certainly alluding to a fund for the unemployed opened in the 1880s – and with the same jaundiced view of it as Besant: a 'mighty migration' of 'hungry applicants arrived by every train'; 'they gave up work in order to be eligible'; 'when the day of distribution arrived they fought for admission, they threatened to brain the distributors, they took tickets which entitled them to food and sold them at the public house; in the end that act of charity developed and strengthened the pauper spirit in hundreds of thousands' (*East London*, p.343).

p.79 Merely-Soft: utterly silly and sentimental. In his *Daily News* interview Morrison declared 'the false sentiment of the day is the curse of the country'.

p.79 Fluffy Pike: 'Fluffy' was slang for drunk. *OED* quotes a report of a man being charged with being 'fluffy and disorderly'.

p.80 jumped, swung on horizontal bars, boxed: the Muscular

Christianity movement and public school ethos of *mens sana in corpore sano* (a healthy mind in a healthy body) validated sport, including boxing, in the East End. The aim was to channel savage street violence into 'duello'. '[They] get rid of the devil in the gymnasium with the boxing-gloves and with single stick; they contract habits of order and discipline; they become infected with some of the upper-class ideals, especially as regards honor and honesty, purity and temperance' (Besant, *East London*, p.172).

p.80 **certain new millionaire:** Jay reports courting 'a wealthy City magnate'; a donation of £1,000 through the trustees of a philanthropist Jay referred to as 'Betty Dash' largely enabled his church-building project (pp.47; 56).

p.80 **sudden quacksalver, a Panjandrum of philanthropy, a mummer of the market-place, who undertook, for a fixed sum, to abolish poverty and sin together:** Morrison endorsed Jay's fears that William Booth's Salvation Army would monopolize charitable donation and damage parish-based social work. Booth complained of a 'whole vocabulary of vituperation' used against him. 'Sudden quacksalver' implies an upstart salesman of patent medicines. 'Panjandrum' was a mock-title invented by Samuel Foote (1720–77) in a passage of nonsense designed to test the memory of the actor Charles Macklin (*c.*1699–1797); Morrison might well have encountered its use in Henry Kingsley's novel *Ravenshoe* (1862). The 'Grand Panjandrum' of G. E. Farrow, whose children's books included *The Wallypug of Why* (1895), *The Little Panjandrum's Dodo* (1898) and *The New Panjandrum* (1902), is normally addressed as 'Your Supreme Importance'. Jay's parish was near Salvation Army headquarters at 188 Whitechapel Road: a contemporary print shows the name of the 'Rev. W. Booth' strikingly prominent on boards and placards (*see* McCarthy, p.88). 'Mummer of the marketplace' refers to Booth's appearances at public meetings and use of modern advertising methods. The 'fixed sum' that Booth initially sought for his work was £100,000.

p.80 **new gaudery:** the Salvation Army's military-style ranks, its uniforms, standards, bands and processions.

p.80 **club at which boxing was allowed, and dominoes – flat ungodliness:** Jay reports a Baptist preacher's objections to boxing and the circulation of fears among his parishioners that boxing resulted in damnation: 'so disturbed were the minds of some of my people, that I announced a sermon on the subject, "May a Christian box?"' (p.88).

Others were wary of dominoes: 'I recollect being surprised at the horror with which a few regarded dominoes – "devil's dice", as they called them – whilst all united in looking on cards as innocuous – a fact, no doubt, owing to the amount of gambling with dominoes in most public-houses' (p.34).

p.81   Father Sturt! – the name itself was sheer papistry: the Oxford Movement had resulted in a largely accepted High Church presence in the Anglican Church, though middle-class suspicion of both Catholicism and Anglo-Catholicism was common enough. In the East End, St. George's-in-the-East had been an influential centre of ritualism: *see* J. S. Reed, 'Ritualism Rampant in East London – Anglo-Catholicism and the Urban Poor,' *Victorian Studies*, 31, iii (1988), 375–403. Besant noted some features of Jay's services that could have fuelled charges of 'papistry', including incense and processions involving 'banners and crosses'. Morrison, however, makes clear that Sturt's title of 'Father' principally stems from the Jagos themselves, a stock strongly indicated as Irish by such names as Leary, Flynn, Rafferty and Regan. Jay indicated that an 'Irish element' was 'not wanting' in his parish and specifically mentioned parishioners nicknamed 'Tommy Irishman' and 'Wild Irishman' (pp.37; 105). 'Father' also functions as a kind of nickname in the world of aliases into which Henry Sturt enters.

p.81   Jago death-rate ruled full four times that of all London: Boulton confirmed this figure in writing about the novel for the *British Review*; Smith notes: 'In 1889 the death rate was 40 per 1000, nearly double that of Bethnal Green as a whole, and four times that of the rest of London' (p.41).

p.82   six moon: i.e. period of six months imprisonment.

p.82   blister: medical treatment for serous inflammation; figuratively, an unpleasant but salutary experience – such as Josh's prison sentence.

p.84   futility of attempting compulsion in the Jago: school boards had powers, at first discretionary, subsequently mandatory, to enforce school-attendance. Jay wrote that in Shoreditch 'compulsion is a dead letter' (p.133), but it was one of the new School Board Attendance Officers, John Reeves, working the area between 1872 and 1907, who left an account of the Old Nichol in *Recollections of a School Attendance Officer* (1913).

p.84   fat's a-running: metaphor presumably deriving from roasting meat over a fire. As it draws near being cooked, the fat runs and there is the chance of catching some of the 'drips'.

p.84 great goods depot of a railway company: the Great Eastern Goods Station was situated to the south of the junction of Bethnal Green Road and Shoreditch High Street and its goods depot a little way down the line.

p.85 tobacco factories hard by: Jay refers to theft of tobacco from carts in Shoreditch (p.100).

p.87 carman: van driver. Vans often carried a boy to load and unload goods and to ride at the back to protect the load from pilfering. Hence the expression 'It fell off the back of a van'.

p.87 defamed each other's eyes and mother: euphemism for 'Damn your eyes, you bastard.'

p.87 slate pencil: schoolchildren wrote on wood-framed slates which could be wiped clean for reuse; the 'pencil' was a short rod of slate, sometimes in a paper wrapper, capable of being ground to a point. It produced a grey line on the writing-slate. *See* George Sturt, pp.94–5.

p.87 co-operation: significant political concept of the day. However, Morrison gave anarchism short shrift, was sceptical towards socialism and deploys the term 'co-operation' in the ironic context of a criminal activity (one which survived into 1980s London as 'steaming').

p.88 ball's stopped rollin': presumably an expression from bagatelle, meaning that the opportunity to achieve a large score has now passed.

p.89 Nobber Sugg: 'Nobber' was slang for someone who collected money, though the implication here is probably of a fighter with a predilection for 'nobbing' or beating about the head.

p.90 a clean room, with pictures on the wall, where there were often flowers: Father Sturt's stable-church embodies Jay's priorities: 'The church I had in my mind's eye ... was to be a home as well as a temple ... warm, attractive, hung with pictures and decorated with colours' (p.24).

p.92 good notice ... though most of the amounts would be reduced: Morrison's account differs from *Life in Darkest London* where Jay emphasizes that the site only came into his possession once the tenants had been evicted (pp.60–61).

p.93   **unfailing sanctuary, a city of refuge ever ready, ever secure . . . a godsend:** 'These facilities for escape were doubtless the reason why thieves so often chose this place as a temporary receptacle for what they had taken' (Jay, p.62). The ironic liturgical discourse has a general rather than particular reference.

p.93   **fire-grate adroitly let drop:** 'Two policemen tried one Sunday to go down the narrow entrance to the court, the first, on emerging, at the inner end, was levelled to the ground, though not seriously hurt, by a grate thrown by some one on him out of one of the empty rooms above' (Jay, p.62). In his *Daily News* interview Morrison said that the original of Josh Perrott told him this story and 'C.R.' insisted that Morrison had himself told the story to Jay. However, Jay's book was completed by the end of 1890, so not dependent on Morrison. Perhaps Josh's original told the same story, independently, to both Jay and Morrison.

p.94   **princely wages:** Jay comments on the calls on his income and the difficulties of fund-raising throughout *Life in Darkest London*.

p.94   **instead of being distributed among themselves . . . nothing but an immediate consideration carried weight in the Jago:** 'When I first mentioned building a church, the people suggested instead that any money collected might be far better employed in providing them with food and clothes. I agreed, of course, partly with what they said, but deplored the trait of character which all, like so many wild beasts, exhibited, of clutching at any present advantage, utterly regardless of others, or of the future' (Jay, p.46).

p.95   **tumbrils:** two-wheeled covered cart for carrying tools.

p.96   **not done without payments from the vicar's pocket:** 'One man demanded compensation on the ground that, in a moment of abstraction, he had placed an old mattress on the top of a cage containing a canary, and sitting down had crushed it flat. Another was so persistent in protesting his inability to provide a home for his family, that I felt almost forced to hire a room elsewhere for him, paying, however, only one week's rental' (Jay, p.62).

p.97   **their prosperous season:** much casual work was seasonal; girls who made matches in winter might work in jam factories in the summer. Market-porters would be busiest in late summer and autumn. Winter generally produced less work and more social distress.

p.97 out-and-out downy benjamins: totally 'sharp' coats ('benjies' deriving from Benjamin and his coat of many colours: Genesis, 37.3). As applied to a person, 'downy' meant wideawake or knowing.

p.97 bang-up kicksies, cut saucy, with artful buttons and a double fakement: splendid trousers (cf. 'kecks'), stylishly tailored with decoratively placed buttons and double trimming.

p.97 daisies: boots (Cockney rhyming slang, via 'daisy-roots' – from the idea of their being 'hard to pull up').

p.97 fishmonger's frails: woven rush-baskets. Morrison's Essex conjuror (in *Cunning Murrell*) is distinguished by his umbrella and 'frail basket'; East Anglian ports supplied fish to London.

p.97 weaving of rush-bags ... profit ... the business: despite irony about the scale of return on Mrs Bates' 'business', the idea of 'profit' is relevant since in many of the home-working trades (including garment-making), the worker had to take into account the cost of those materials that they had themselves to buy and supply.

p.98 wide sashes of the old 'weavers' windows': 'The Jago actually contained within its borders a large silk manufactory': Traill, *The New Fiction and Other Essays on Literary Subjects* (London: Hurst and Blackett, 1897), p.26. 'There are silk-weavers in Spitalfields and Bethnal Green. An attempt has been made to revive the trade; meantime, many of the old houses remain with their wide windows on the first floor' (Besant, *East London*, pp.202–3).

p.98 rooms which the wreckers – no jack-a-dandies neither – flatly refused to enter: 'Jack-a-dandies' implies weak, flashily dressed effeminate men. Jay: 'The workmen absolutely refused to enter this room at first, because it was so indescribably filthy. ... The workmen at last only consented to enter it on the promise of a liberal allowance of beer to each' (p.115).

p.99 Mr Grinder: a quibble on 'organ-grinder' (in the context of his 'Italian warehouse') may be involved, but principally an allusion to the trade of oil-and-colourman. Pigment, or 'colour', had to be 'ground' and mixed with oil to make paint. Robert Tressell was to use the name 'Grinder' for an exploiting employer (kin to 'Sweater'), but Morrison's character is an earstwhile errand boy and 'no bad fellow'.

p.100 collect a little dirt, and rub it down the front of his apron: the new apprentice dirtying himself to create the appearance of an old hand is part of the mythology of work. In *To London Town* Johnny May, as new engineering apprentice, wants to get his gleaming coffee-can smoky. In Walter Greenwood's *Love on the Dole* the new apprentice dirties his face, is sent for the 'long stand' (the 'round square' in Johnny's case) and, like Johnny, encounters sordid and humiliating initiation rites.

p.102 brass roastin'-jacks ... smoke-jacks: appliances that kept meat in motion while roasting; machines for turning roasting-spits by making use of the current of hot air in the chimney.

p.104 'Scatter seeds o' kindness' you know, as the – the Psalm says: a typical misattribution on Weech's part.

p.109 crest: tuft on a donkey's head.

p.110 touched for: stole successfully, in the context of picking pockets or petty theft (cf. 'His Tale of Bricks,' p.179); cf. 'he touched me for a fiver.'

p.116 moleskin waistcoat, with pearlies down the front and the artful dodge over the pockets: waistcoat of cotton fustian (a material shaved before dyeing); traditional cockney's mother-of-pearl buttons. The 'artful dodge' suggests a button-down flap to deflect pickpockets.

p.116 She's a fighter ... Rorty SAIRER: 'Rorty' is slang for fine, splendid, jolly. The internal rhymes suggest a music-hall song that encouraged audience participation.

p.116 trap: possibly echoing the planned entrapment of the Turks (and, in the event, Barabas himself) in Marlowe's *Jew of Malta*; both episodes are legible as modelling the damned entering Hell's mouth. Mother Gapp's cellar into which 'the aliens' fall is a 'pit of writhing forms', while the name 'Gapp' itself suggests a gaping mouth or chasm. (Morrison makes some allusion to Renaissance drama in his journalism.)

p.119 leaving shop: unlicensed pawnbroker's.

p.121 dose of the 'cat': cat-o'-nine-tails: abolished in the services in 1881, but still part of the system of judicial corporal punishment. 'The cat ... which is strictly reserved for the very worst cases of all – and then only for men of the strongest physique – is a punishment which leaves its marks in some cases both on body and on mind. It is the one thing the callous, depraved, dehumanized convict stands in fear of': H. B. N., *Penal Servitude* (London: Heinemann, 1903), p. 136.

p.121 bow: ring on a pocket watchcase, to which the chain or ribbon is attached.

p.122 mere Waterbury on a steel guard: cheap stem-wound American watch with a base metal chain. Waterbury watches used a stamped-out mechanism without jewels and were very cheap to buy.

p.122 red clock and slang: gold watch and chain.

p.123 Mogul: Emperor of Delhi; figuratively, a tycoon – usually in 'legitimate' business.

p.123 screwed a chat, nor claimed a peter: to screw a chat was to make a quiet entry into a house; peter-claiming was 'laying hands nonchalantly on unconsidered parcels and bags at railway stations', sometimes involving a swap ('A Conversion', p.258). *See* 'His Tale of Bricks' for a disquisition on the technicalities of the crime (p.180) and the confusions of three peter-claimers accidentally stealing each others' identical brick-filled bags.

p.124 let a great deal of blood – no doubt with benefit: ironic reference to cupping and blood-letting as a medical procedure.

p.124 prince of fences, Ikey Solomons: the historical model for Dickens's Fagin in *Oliver Twist*.

p.124 'front': one who distracts a victim's attention, allowing an accomplice to pick the victim's pocket more easily (cf. 'front man').

p.124 never bought anything himself: *see* the activities of Captain Kemp in *The Hole in the Wall* for a detailed elaboration of this method of the professional fence.

p.128 Snuffy: nickname for someone who takes snuff; also slang for drunken or tipsy.

p.129 penny cast: by analogy with a thrown object, the distance of journey by tram allowable for a penny.

p.129 prosecutor: in the sense of one agreeing to press charges.

p.129 commission agent: someone with authority to act in business for another party (though here used as a loosely defined occupation to conceal the Mobsman's true activities).

p.130 the Old Bailey ... Holloway: the Old Bailey, or Central Criminal Court, adjoined Newgate prison where prisoners due to make a court appearance would be brought from such holding prisons as Holloway. A 'respectable' prisoner recorded being held in Holloway in 1898: 'I ... was put into what is called a furnished cell – that is to say, a cell containing a table and some chairs, with a drugget on the floor, so that it looks something like a private room. ... as long as I was in Holloway I was not altogether a close prisoner. I wore my own clothes, and I had my meals brought in from a restaurant. I also had newspapers and books to read, and I was allowed to write letters and receive visits' (H. B. N., p.14).

p.130 lob-crawler: a robber of 'the till: not narrowly ... the individual till, but broad-mindedly ... the till as a general institution, to be approached in unattended shops by stealthy grovelling on the belly' ('A Conversion', p.257).

p.130 laggin' dues: penal servitude; confinement and specified hard labour.

p.130 Newgate ... before a double iron railing: this scene bears close comparison with Frank Holl's painting 'Newgate – Committed for Trial' (1878) – so much so that the painting comes close to constituting a found illustration to the novel. Along with Luke Fildes and Hubert von Herkomer, Holl was a notable social realist painter whose work appeared in the *Graphic* during the 1870s. While not depicting a 'screaming hubbub' (though a baby may be crying), Holl does show a woman with two bewildered children looking at her husband through the wire-netted 'double iron railing'. The husband lounges against the bars on his side. Holl's prisoner is a young clerk rather than a Josh Perrott, but his manner suggests that he too has 'little to say'. As in Morrison's scene, the prisoner is among other prisoners while his wife must communicate with him in the presence of other visitors (and a prison-officer). While the scene has a generic status, Morrison might well have seen Holl's painting, or a reproduction of it. (http://www.rhbnc.ac.uk/ART/art4.html; Royal Holloway Art Collection.)

p.131 Recorder: city or borough magistrate with criminal and civil jurisdiction.

p.131 **Parkhurst ... easier conditions:** 'First offenders condemned to penal servitude, after a short time in a local gaol, are, as a rule, sent to Lewes prison to serve their separate confinement, and are afterwards removed either to Portland or to Parkhurst, the only two convict prisons where first offenders are sent': H. B. N., pp.26–7. Josh serves what would normally have been nine months of separate (or effectively solitary) confinement (23 hours a day alone in a cell, of which 8 were spent in work) at Chelmsford Prison, and is then transferred to Portland. H. B. N. was in poor health and was duly sent to Parkhurst, 'a special place of confinement for invalid or weak-minded prisoners who are brought there from all the other convict prisons as soon as their condition is considered serious' (p.148).

p.133 **howling sea of human wreckage:** significant metaphor in Social Problem discourse: *see* folding frontispiece to William Booth's *In Darkest England and the Way Out* and its image of drowning people pulled to safety by Salvation Army officers out of a sea labelled 'Starvation', 'Unemployed', 'Drunkenness', etc. (also reproduced in McCarthy, pp.96–7).

p.133 **'in the country':** euphemism for imprisonment, playing on upper-class idea of possessing town and country houses.

p.133 **ticket-of-leave:** colloquial name for an 'order of licence' giving a convict liberty before expiry of sentence, the remission involved being dependent on good conduct. The ticket could be remitted on petition to the Home Secretary.

p.134 **making shirts:** Mayhew isolated shirt-finishing as one of the most exploitative kinds of home-working. *See also* Morrison's 'Whitechapel.'

p.134 **twopence farthing ... Support Home Industries:** Jay mentions a rate of tuppence farthing a gross, judging the task two hours' work (p.22), seven gross representing a fourteen hour day (besides time for collection and delivery). Conditions at Bryant and May's factory had included harsh fines and poor ventilation (understood to foster phosphorus-induced skin and bone cancers); these considerations prompted Annie Besant's article 'White Slavery in London' and the Matchgirls' Strike of 1888. The ironic force of 'public-spirited' evokes the contrast between such matters and the public image of 'England's Glory' match-boxes decorated jingoistically with union jacks, an imperial dreadnought in full steam and the motto 'Support Home

Industries.' (It is with the bitter remark 'support 'ome industries' that Josh stamps on Em's match-boxes.) 'C.R.' reported that Morrison tried 'in his own person what it feels like to earn a living by making match-boxes'. Sweden was the principal overseas competition in the manufacture of matches. For a photograph of match-box homeworkers, *see* McCarthy, p.65; *see also* Mrs Layton's memories in Margaret Llewelyn-Davies, ed., *Life As We Have Known It* (London: Hogarth Press, 1931).

p.135 **half-quarter hundredweight of coals:** i.e. one stone or fourteen pounds (slightly more than six kilograms).

p.136 **police-court birch:** corporal punishment; flogging with a birch rod. Magistrates could order up to twenty-five strokes for those under sixteen years of age; not more than twelve strokes for those under fourteen.

p.137 **reformatory ... 'schooling':** young offenders were often sent to standard prisons; in 1903, H. B. N. commented, 'only ten years ago over two hundred children under twelve years of age, and over three thousand aged between twelve and sixteen, were annually committed to prison' (p.251). Alternatively, for committing crimes otherwise punishable by penal servitude, detention in a Reformatory School could be ordered for not less than two years and not more than five. The Prisons Committee of 1894 recommended great extension of provision for young offenders and the establishment of Borstal followed.

p.137 **outdoor parish relief ... guardians:** provision for the sick and destitute through the parish, or a Union of parishes, took the form either of the workhouse or 'outdoor relief' given in the homes of the able-bodied. Boards of Guardians, administering such provision, were introduced by the Poor Law Amendment Act of 1834.

p.138 **solemn and most circumstantial Lie:** *As You Like It*, V iv.66–100. In Touchstone's seven-point scale of quarrelling, the charge of 'Lie Circumstantial' is the most extreme short of the 'Lie Direct': 'I durst go no further than the Lie Circumstantial, nor he durst not give me the Lie Direct. And so we measured swords and parted' (ll.82–5).

p.139 **unregarded turnip:** episode echoing Jay, p.113.

p.140 **right of rats to multiply their thousands:** as spoken by a surgeon, these words may be designed to refute the liberal East-End doctor in Margaret Harkness's novel *Captain Lobe*: Ledger (p.80) notes that Harkness's surgeon criticizes 'eugenic theorists who explain degeneration through theories of heredity'; 'They talk such rubbish. They cannot, or will not, see that while the environment of these people remains what it is, they will indulge in the only two enjoyments they can command.'

p.143 County Council: in 1889 London County Council took over responsibility for this area from the Metropolitan Board of Works; the 'Boundary Street Scheme' had the distinction of being the first major project in slum-clearance undertaken by the Council.

p.143 crude yellow brick of the barrack dwellings: in *East London*, Besant criticized the barrack-like nature of the new buildings and the tenants' lack of control over their new homes. Charles Booth observed that the rents were too high and the conditions of occupancy restrictive: 'the result is that the new buildings are occupied by a different class, largely Jews' (cit. Smith, p.44); in his *Daily News* interview Morrison observed of the Old Nichol that 'no jew would be tolerated there for a moment'. *See* 'Morrison and his Critics' for Jack London's comments.

p.143 earned his marks: good conduct system. 'Having earned the maximum number of marks for good conduct without forfeiting any, I was discharged': H. B. N., p.48. Josh earns enough to serve less than four years.

p.144 safe from ... the reformatory now, being well over the age: i.e. over sixteen.

p.145 sevenpence is half a gallon: i.e. the price of four pints of beer.

p.145 'out' ... 'fall': go out thieving; get caught or arrested, cf. 'Bob the Bender fell in Broad Street.'

p.145 'Spect 'im up tonight: i.e. Josh will arrive from Portland on the 'up' train.

p.146 Jago hair was commonly cut in another place: i.e. prison: 'Before, however, being taken to my cell in the hospital [at Wormwood Scrubs], I was measured and weighed, and had all my hair clipped off': H.B.N., p.25.

p.146 Band-of-Hope air: influential total-abstinence association. 'The drunkenness was appalling. ... Reeling men and women singing one minute, fighting and cursing the next were everywhere. ... The

Blue Ribbon Army and the Salvation Army together with the Bands of Hope, and Adult Temperance Societies, did a grand work in their campaign against intemperance in and around Bethnal Green, but the improved social conditions including education, better facilities for recreation and enjoyment have played a large part': Le May, p. 33.

p.147 Fair's fair, as the apostle David says in the Proverbs: Weech's most egregious and complex Biblical confusion: the saying is not Biblical; the Book of Proverbs is associated with Solomon, David's son; David was not an apostle.

p.147 Wot a blessed release!: in his anxiety Weech misapplies a cliché used of death as a release from illness; with inadvertent humour he pursues the idea of release into a misquotation that confuses the 'happy condition' of freedom in the Lord with freedom from the 'lor' (law, police).

p.147 'friendly lead': 'Among the poorer classes in London, an entertainment given by friends, for the benefit of a person in distress, etc.' (*OED*).

p.147 relish: savoury variation on a staple diet. Besant wrote of a factory girl: 'She made her breakfast on tea, bread and margarine, and a "relish". The relish included many possibilities. It depended mainly on the day of the week. It is obvious that what one can afford on a Monday is unattainable on a Friday. On Monday it might be a herring or a haddock, an egg or a rasher of bacon. On Friday and Saturday it would be a sprig of water-cress or a pickle' (*East London*, p.137).

p.148 prison gratuity: in the case of a man serving three years, 'a few shillings' (H. B. N., p.263).

p.148 run the gauntlet of Prisoners' Aid Societies: part of the running joke about Josh's aversion to work; such societies met men leaving prison and aimed to guide them into work. Alfred Alsop's *Down in the Slums* suggests that they were easily evaded.

p.148 Em ... drank her allowance of gin: the early introduction of children to spirits was a strong theme in fictional and documentary accounts of the slums, accentuated by the participation of the Temperance Movement in social work. In Phil May's 'In an East End Gin Shop' a mother stands calmly holding a tankard while her ragged liitle girl drinks from it (*see* Besant, *East London*, p.125).

p.152   step-dance: 'Dance intended for the display of special steps by an individual performer' (*OED*).

p.152   gallows-flap: possibly a specific dance, or a black-humoured pantomime of the movements of a man being hanged: cf. Cruikshank's illustration 'Master Bates Explains a Professional Technicality' in *Oliver Twist.*

p.155   St Leonard's, hard by: St Leonard, Shoreditch, was the parish adjoining Holy Trinity to its north and west, its church standing beyond Shoreditch High Street, on the eastern side of Kingsland Road, at the junction with Hackney Road. Keating prints 'close by' rather than the first edition's 'hard by'; the latter term may risk suggesting the church was nearer to Weech's establishment in Meakin Street than would have been the case.

p.156   striking-box: 'The metal box on a door-jamb which receives the end of the bolt of the lock when the door is locked' (*OED*).

p.156   loo table: Keating prints the simpler 'low table'. but the first edition reading is quite coherent: 'loo table' was a general trade term for a kind of round table (originally associated with the popular card game 'loo'). Josh later recalls it specifically as a 'round table'.

p.156   coloured wall-texts: popular Victorian decoration: sentimental or Biblical quotation, printed or embroidered and usually framed. Implied as the source of some of Weech's fractured pious sentiments.

p.158   bull's-eye: police-issue lantern with hemispherical lens giving a powerful beam.

p.161   Heap on a shutter: 'If you dropped dead "in a fit" you would be "brought home on a shutter", as there was no ambulance, but every shop had shutters' (George Sturt, p.133).

p.163   Lion and Unicorn: royal coat of arms.

p.163   take his gruel: gruel was standard prison fare; synecdoche for judicial punishment.

p.164   bunch of flowers: originally carried to ward off typhus (prison fever).

p.165   trap: a cage with a contrivance for releasing the birds quickly.

p.165   They wouldn't have given any more in Club Row: if they had

been sold live in the fancy bird market in Club Row, the pigeons would
have fetched no more money than they did dead at the poulterer's.

p.165   four-legged linnet ... two-headed sheep: freak shows, animal
and human, authentic and fake, were common features of Victorian
fairgrounds. On Fair Day at Farnham 'there was a rich selection of fat
ladies, bearded ladies, abortions of all sorts' (George Sturt, p.108).

p.166   soft mortarboard: Black Cap, traditionally donned by judges
in pronouncing the death sentence.

p.166   Clerk of Arraigns: Court officer recording judicial decisions.

p.167   fourpenny-doss-houses: some dosshouses, or common lodging houses, charged less than fourpence a night, though tuppence or
less might only bring the chance of sleeping across a rope slung across
the room. For a print, *see* McCarthy, p.33.

p.167   the gipsies that used to live at the Mount years ago: Morrison
reported that well into the eighteenth century a fort called 'The Mount'
stood in the area of the Whitechapel Road ('down near the London
Hospital, and opposite the Pavilion Theatre'). The site had subsequently
been built over with a terrace of shops that maintained the name. *See*
his article 'Whitechapel.'

**p.174   I am the resurrection and the life ... Man that is born of
woman ... In the midst of life ...:**   Book of Common Prayer.
Morrison's ellipsis functions to highlight the words that follow in the
Order for the Burial of the Dead: 'We are in death'.

p.170   doubly sealed of the outcasts: 'Outcast' was a key word in
Social Problem discourse, notably deployed in Andrew Mearns' *Bitter
Cry of Outcast London* (1883).

p.171   How good for them all to go off easily together: suicide (e.g.
Neddy Wright) and domicide were themes of turn-of-the-century
depictions of poverty: cf. Thomas Hardy, *Jude the Obscure*; London,
The People of the Abyss and Tressell, *The Ragged Trousered
Philanthropists*.

p.172   leather-aproned: emblem of the shoemaker (here, Bobby
Roper).

GLOSSARY

———

Below are listed some less familiar words and meanings not treated in the Notes.

AMAIN, *with full force; violently*
AREA, *yard; open place; basement stairwell*
ASSORTMENT, *unsorting*

BARNEY, *argument, fight, commotion*
BEDESMAN, *proxy paid or endowed to pray for others*
BEER-ENGINES, *pumps drawing beer from cask to bar*
BILLYCOCK, *round, low-crowned felt hat*
BOB, *one shilling (twelve pence)*
BREAK, *collection; whip-round*
BRICKBAT, *broken brick (used as missile)*
BUST; BUSTER, *burglary; burglar*

CASE-KNIFE, *sheath-knife*
CHIVE, *stab*
CLAIM, *steal, 'lift'*
CLICKER, *thief*
COMPASSED, *brought about*
COP, *steal*
COPPER, *laundry boiler made of iron or copper*
CORNEOUS, *horny*
CRANK, *(of machinery) weak, shaky*
CRANKY, *shaky, crazy*
CROAK, *die*
CROOK, ON THE, *dishonestly; criminally*
CUT HIS LUCKY, *escaped; went when the going was good*

DAVY, *affidavit, legal deposition*
DIPPER, *pickpocket*

FAINT, *(of glue) feeble, lacking in strength*
FARTHING, *quarter of an old penny*

FASTNESS, *secure place; place of safety*
FEE-FAW-FUM, *nonsense fit only to terrify a child*
FENCE, *receiver of stolen goods*
FLAMING, *gaudy, 'loud'*
FLIMPED, *robbed, usually by a team of thieves*
FULLIED, *committed for trial at a higher court*

GILT, *money*
GONOPH, *petty thief*
GOSSIP, *old woman*

HALF-A-CROWN, *two shillings and sixpence*
HANDERS, *caning on the hands*
HARDBAKE, *slab (almond) toffee*
HOOK, *thief; steal (cf. 'Hookey Street')*

IKEY, *Jewish*

JAMES, *jemmy, burglar's crowbar*

LAG; LAGGING, *imprison, sentence to penal servitude; period of penal servitude*
LATHERS, *beats; thrashes*

MAZZARD, *head*
MECHANIC, *workman; skilled labourer*
MILCH-COW, *source of profit; person from whom money is easily taken*
MILLING, *boxing*
MINIM, *sixtieth part of a fluid drachm*

NEDDY, *life-preserver; stick, or bludgeon loaded with lead*

OOF, *money ('ooftish': see Liza of Lambeth, ch. 3)*
'OOKS, *see 'hook'*
OPPOSITES, *opponents*

POGUE-HUNTER, *pickpocket dealing in purses*
PROP, *piece of jewellery with pin*

QUARTERN LOAVES, *four-pound loaves*
QUODDIN', *serving a prison sentence*

RED, *gold*
ROTTED, *chaffed, bantered, teased*

RUM, *odd, queer*
RUSTY, *(of clothes) showing age or use; shabby, worn, faded*

SHALLOW, *costermonger's cart*
SMUG, *arrest*
SNUGGERY, *snug place or room; otherwise, small bar in a pub*
SOVEREIGN, *gold coin worth one pound (twenty shillings)*
SPECIE, *coin, as opposed to (traceable) paper money*
SPECIFICS, *medicines or remedies*
SPLIT, *detective; informer*
SQUEEGED, *squeezed, compressed*
STIR, *prison*

THICK, *united, solid ('thick as thieves'; 'thick as glue')*
TOFF, *gentleman*
TOG(S), *clothing, clothes*
TOKE, *bread*
TOY AND TACKLE, *watch and chain*
TURNIN' OVER, *search on suspicion; fleece, rob*
TURN-UP, *fight, commotion*
TWIRLS, *skeleton keys*

UXTER, *money*

WATCH-GUARD, *chain, cord or ribbon securing a watch to clothing*
WELL-PLUCKED, *full of pluck*
WIDE, *knowing, street-wise; able to fence with the law*
WORKED OFF, *disposed of and got done with*
WRITHEN, *subjected to writhing; contorted*

YANNUPS, *money*
YULLER, *'yellow metal'; gold*

MORRISON AND HIS CRITICS

A *Child of the Jago* was published in the shockwave created by *Tales of Mean Streets* and the promotion of the novel took advantage of that response. Moreover, reviewers tended to approach *A Child of the Jago* as a product of underlying processes and techniques gaining ground on various fronts – the methods of the realist. In 1899 Morrison himself blurred matters in another way by reclassifying *Tales of Mean Streets*, *A Child of the Jago* and the more mellow and diverse *To London Town* as a trilogy. There was no formal necessity for this retrospective trilogization, but the earlier books having been criticized for excesses in treatment and selectivity of focus, it was a reframing that invited reassessment of the balance of subject matter and tone over three, rather than just one or two books. Reviewers of *To London Town* responded positively to the gesture. This anthology consequently collects responses to *A Child of the Jago*, some comments on *Tales of Mean Streets* that initiated continuing controversy and a snippet or two on *To London Town*. Any narrative of the reception of *A Child of the Jago* would be incomplete without them. The anthology, however, begins with a letter throwing new light on Morrison's first published writing.

(a) An unpublished letter by Arthur Morrison:

Morrison reflects on his earliest ventures in writing:
Salcombe House
Loughton
Essex

August 19th 1907

Dear Sir,
My first published manuscript was the first manuscript I wrote for publication – in other words my first effort was accepted. It was nothing very ambitious, though I was very young at the time, for it was twenty-six or perhaps twenty-seven years ago. The thing

was verse – people used to begin with verse in those days – and I earnestly intended it to be comic. It appeared in a cycling magazine well known at the time, called, I think, *Cycling*. It was in the time of the tall bicycle and some genius had invented a machine of that sort which would double up and go into a carpet bag. My verse described certain tragic misunderstandings on the part of somebody who [heard] overheard a conversation about a carpet bag wherein were stowed a 'head', a 'neck', a 'backbone', different [parts] pieces of a 'felloe' and similar parts of a bicycle. I had no idea of taking to literature as a vocation at that time, [but I] – I was a boy – but afterwards contributed very extensively to the cycling press of the eighties; which consisted, as a fact, of some half a dozen flourishing periodicals. My first attempt on the more regular press was a sketch printed in the *Globe*. I forget its subject and its date, except that it must have been about 1885 [or 1886]

Yours faithfully,

Arthur Morrison.

Walter J. Roberts Esq.

(Reproduced courtesy of The Bancroft Library, University of California, Berkeley.)

(b) Some responses to Morrison's early writing:

The National Observer *recommends Morrison's detective stories* Martin Hewitt: Investigator:

The stories are without exception so exciting that we defy the reader to begin any one without finishing it at a sitting. There is no 'meandering', and there is a very unusual amount of briskness, vigour and ingenuity. The book is well bound, printed and illustrated. We recommend it to bored persons suffering the martyrdom of a family party, to harassed persons encompassed about with bills, and to cheerful people weary of neurotic problems – feeling sure that they will thank us. (*National Observer* (*c.*1894); extract as printed in first edition of *Chronicles of Martin Hewitt* (1895).)

The Bookman *dwells on the absence of the 'moral showman' in the 'strong' but 'ungenial' stories of 'Tales of Mean Streets':*

The East End and its dwellers have never before been painted from the same standpoint, nor in so vigorous and independent a

fashion. That it gives the inevitable picture which sojourners in
the neighbourhood must carry away, we certainly do not assert
... Mr Morrison's intention has been to tell just what he has seen,
idealising nothing and keeping back little. He has carried it out
with a frankness which no doubt some readers will term brutal,
and which certainly wants some courage to face. They are pictures
of misery, cruelty, sordidness, he gives us for the most part,
pictures rather than descriptions; the moral showman never
appears at all to pull a long face, or shake his head, or say 'How
pitiful!' or 'How wrong!' The reader is left to make his own
reflections, and they will not be comfortable ones ... Mr Morrison
has plainly a bias; and who has not? With the right or wrong of
that bias literary criticism has nothing to do provided he gives it
logical and forcible expression. ... It is fair to say there is
something wanting in his picture – something pertaining to
rational happiness and unselfish endeavour, which experience has
led one to expect in streets however mean. ... The book is far
from heartless; indeed, possibly it is just because the observer's
feelings were not of that easy kind that can be relieved by mere
words of pity that his stories are so grim and so ungenial. ('Tales
of Mean Streets', *Bookman* (London), 7 (Jan. 1895), 120–121.)

The Spectator *famously joins battle over the representativeness of
Morrison's short stories; if the East End really is this land of Yahoos,
society deserves to be 'smashed to atoms':*

These tales paint with a marvellous literary skill and force the life
which the author by implication alleges to be the normal life of
the London poor. Were this the East-End, the whole of the East-
End, and were the East-End nothing but this, then indeed are we
of all men most miserable. If the squalor, cruelty, the drunkenness,
the deadly and grinding monotony, the total lack of all that is
wholesome and loveable in human nature, here so vividly depicted,
were really typical of the poorer streets of London, we should
have to admit that we are face to face with a moral situation as
awful and as terrifying as any that the world has ever encountered.
If ... the social and political forces now at work were giving us
such people as their normal product, one must feel that our society
is rotten to the core, and that the sooner it is smashed to atoms
the better. But we do not believe that the life here set forth is
typical ... We do not say that Mr Morrison has not drawn from
the life. He may have done so and yet not painted the typical East-

Ender. What we assert is that he has taken the worst characters in Mr Booth's Class A – the class of the semi-criminals and the morally and physically degraded – and has set them up, or appeared to set them up, as if they were truly representative of East London. But Class A, as Mr Booth showed us, is some only 9 per cent. of the East End . . .

If we read a vivid account of the cruel and savage husband in Mayfair we recognise easily enough that he is not a type of the West-End husband. We know, however, so little of East-End life at first-hand that we are apt to treat everything depicted with an East-End atmosphere as typical. It is the mistake of the traveller also who goes to the East and happens, as he well may, on some occasional piece of humanity or cruelty, as the case may be. Down it goes in his note-book as an instance of normal Arab goodness or wickedness, and unless he is able to live down this impression he is apt to think of 'all Eastern peoples' as tinged with the particular vice or virtue which he came across in so sensational a way . . .

God knows there is much there to be morally and physically mended . . . By all means let us abate the evils of London life, but do not let us delude ourselves into imagining that half London is inhabited by a race of Yahoos. ('Tales of Mean Streets', *Spectator*, 74, 9 March 1895, 329.)

Arthur Morrison responds to the Spectator:

SIR, – Your reviewer treats my 'Tales of Mean Streets' with a kindness which I acknowledge with gratitude, – a kindness which I might venture to call extreme were I in any way entitled to qualify his judgement in a matter of purely literary criticism. But I hope he will allow me to suggest that a very natural personal antipathy to squalor and some of its accompaniments has led him to some misconception of my view of life in East London, – life which, if I may say so, I *do* happen to know at first hand, and without the help of a note-book. I do not present Billy Chope as a type of all dwellers in the East End; an effort to typify the people of a city on one character would be foolish indeed. Chope is a blackguard in a book of all sorts, among whom the blackguards are in what is, I hope, a just minority. There are fourteen members in the collection, of which the story of Lizerunt is only one. . . . I am loth to be considered to have generalised half London as a race of Yahoos, – as loth as to be thought to suppose the world (which I did not attempt to cram into my book) a place without light and sunshine. ('"Tales of Mean Streets": To the Editor of the "Spectator"', *Spectator*, 74, 16 Mar. 1895, 360.)

'Chelifer' (Robert Hughes) turns to Arthur Morrison's 'Tales of Mean Streets' as a touchstone against which to measure Stephen Crane's depiction of American slum life:

Probably the strongest piece of slum writing we have is 'Maggie', by Mr Stephen Crane, which was published some years ago with a pen-name for the writer and no name at all for the publishers. But merit will out, and the unclaimed foundling attracted no little attention, though by no means as much as it deserves. The keenness of the wit, the minuteness of the observation, and the bitterness of the cynicism resemble Morrison's work. ('The Justification of Slum Stories', *Godey's Magazine*, 131 (October 1895), 431. For a similar strategy *see* Frank Norris (author of *The Octopus*), 'Stephen Crane's Stories of Life in the Slums: *Maggie* and *George's Mother*', *The Wave*, 15 (4 July 1896), 13.)

(c) Promoting A Child of the Jago:

On first publication of *A Child of the Jago* in book form, Morrison was presented on the title-page as 'Author of *Tales of Mean Streets*'. The volume also included a selection of extracts from reviews of those tales. Common enough practices, these touches served to extend sales of the stories and promote *A Child of the Jago*. However, the existence of only a few of these particular reviews – which demonstrate the consciousness of Morrison's writing within which first readings of *A Child of the Jago* occurred – has been recorded by scholarship. Moreover, as epitext, they constitute what Roland Barthes called a 'reading protocol'. Edited to omit most reference to the detail of the stories, they offered broad statements about the character and virtues of Morrison's writing which readers might apply to *A Child of the Jago*. In the absence of an introduction, the extracts guided the response of the novel's original readers.

The reviews were pointedly selected and not edited with great candour (ellipses seldom being signalled). A review seen as hostile (such as the *Spectator*'s or the *Bookman*'s) was not even mentioned. Alienating comments in otherwise favourable reviews were silently excised and only the most flattering of reservations survived. With this caveat, I have reproduced the extracts (introductory summaries and bibliographical references apart) as they were presented in *A Child of the Jago* in 1896, though in the case of the first review – to show the scale of editing – I have presented a full text, bracketing the excisions and emphasizing the portion that was used.

'Extraordinary detail' and 'true humanity' without, like George Gissing, 'missing the fun': the Athenaeum *finds 'Tales of Mean Streets' 'absolutely convincing':*

[Mr Arthur Morrison's *Tales of Mean Streets* are] **told with consummate art and extraordinary detail. Not less remarkable is the restraint which the author puts upon himself, with the result that the reader is often startled apparently without cause, the effect is produced so simply.** [It is for that reason absolutely convincing. Some of the tales, indeed, are less convincing than others. The author occasionally swerves from that austere reserve which is the guardian of his devotion to truth, and takes full advantage of a farcical situation. Thus you feel that 'The Red Cow Group' and 'That Brute Simmons' do not live in the same street with 'Lizerunt' and 'A Poor Stick'. But they relieve the prevailing sombreness a little, and for a moment we forget the squalid misery and grimy horror. To understand the author's standpoint you must read the finely written introduction. Unlike the author of 'The Netherworld', he does not miss the fun, but finds it lamentably deficient. Consequently you suspect that the pity or repugnance he feels has so modified his impression of what he describes, that occasionally he almost seems to darken the shadows merely to emphasize their darkness. 'Love-making in this street,' he says, 'is a dreary thing when one thinks of love-making in other places.' No doubt; but why compare? Comparisons must surely to some extent falsify our estimate of the value of the street to its inhabitants. And yet, as we have said, these tales are] **instinct with truth, and presented with an art as delicate as it is strenuous and unerring.** [No thought of poetic justice is ever allowed to lead the author astray. He tells a plain, unvarnished tale, and the very truth of it makes for beauty.] **He gets so near to life, and so convincingly, that the artist himself is never in view; and his art, by its very fineness, effaces itself. Thus the humour is never forced, the pathos never worked up to. You come on them with a feeling of surprise, because they seem to be there of themselves,** [and you acquit the author any intention in the matter. True, the humour is grim, the pathos bleak, the irony cruel. The narrative breaks off suddenly, but you have been told enough. Grimness, squalor, misery meet you on every page; but] **in what you feel is the true humanity of the book lies its justification, the permanence of its interest, and its indubitable triumph.** ('Tales of Mean Streets', *Athenaeum*, 3500 (24 Nov. 1894), 712–13.)

'*Appalling', with 'a thrilling sense of reality*':
A great book. The author's method is amazingly effective, and produces a thrilling sense of reality. The writer lays upon us a masterhand. The book is simply appalling and irresistible in its interest. It is humorous also; without humour it would not make the mark it is certain to make. (*World*, c.1894/5; extract as printed in the first edition of *A Child of the Jago*.)

The National Observer *finds 'pitiful tragedy undressed' in a work combining the exquisiteness of a Tennyson lyric with 'murderous fact*':
The art of it leaves as little to be desired as the art of Tennyson's most exquisite lyric. For the rest, it is humorous, tearful, horrible, murderous fact. Was there ever quite so much pitiful tragedy undressed in a few pages of plain prose, as that which charges every word of [Morrison's story] 'Behind the Shade'? The gaunt, grisly truth is here and nothing more. But how much! (*National Observer*, c.1894/5; extract as printed in the first edition of *A Child of the Jago*.)

Among so many false claims to being 'New', the Pall Mall Gazette *finds Morrison genuinely new*:
Unquestionably an achievement of art: something more than remarkable. The tune is new in a sense in which the new woman and the new drama, and the new hedonism, and the other clamant bores of the period are not new. To those who care for all humanity and to the true hedonist, it should be something like a godsend. (*Pall Mall Gazette*, c.1894/5; extract as printed in the first edition of *A Child of the Jago*.)

The Morning Post *turns to photography for its laudatory metaphors*:
It is doubtful whether anything more realistic (in the best sense of the term) has been written in our tongue than these sketches of East-end life. Pathos, weird as the scenes that inspire it, yet very

real, is also a marked feature of these powerful pictures taken from the lower social depths. (*Morning Post, c.*1894/5; extract as printed in the first edition of *A Child of the Jago*.)

A bluff, cigar-smoking welcome from the Daily Chronicle:
Well done, uncommonly well done, strong and impressive. (*Daily Chronicle, c.*1894/5; extract as printed in the first edition of *A Child of the Jago*.)

Implying a Ruskinian distinction between books of the moment and books for all time, the Sun *presents Morrison's writing as a direct intervention in social policy:*
Very nearly, if indeed not quite a great book. The book is a genuine success. It is a human document, an eloquent sermon, a plea for the poor, a condemnation of the parsimonious. It ought to be read throughout the length and breadth of London this winter, and it ought to do solid good in its generation, which is more than you can say of most books. (*Daily Chronicle, c.*1894/5; extract as printed in the first edition of *A Child of the Jago*.)

The Critic *looks forward to what will be 'A Child of the Jago':*
A novelist of unusual power has come to the front during the present week ... A quite remarkable literary facility ... Mr Morrison's will be a name to conjure with in another season. (*Critic* (New York), *c.*1894/5; extract as printed in the first edition of *A Child of the Jago*.)

The Saturday Review:
There is perception, imaginative insight, the power of faithful presentation. (*Saturday Review, c.*1894/5; extract as printed in the first edition of *A Child of the Jago*.)

The Irish Daily Independent *looks to Balzac:*
Full of power – and restrained power. An exceedingly strong book; and having written such a first book, Mr Morrison ought to go far. He is occasionally as impressive as Balzac. (*Irish Daily Independent, c.*1894/5; extract as printed in the first edition of *A Child of the Jago*.)

Freeman's Journal *looks to Hogarth*:
> A powerful volume. Painted with the brush of a Hogarth. (*Freeman's Journal*, c.1894/5; extract as printed in the first edition of A Child of the Jago.)

Evelyn Waugh's father, Arthur (who in 1894 published an impassioned defence of 'reticence in literature' in the Yellow Book*), finds latitude enough to approve of Arthur Morrison*:
> Most suggestive and stimulating. Mr Morrison ought to be of the widely read in 1895. (*Weekly Sun*, c.1894/5; extract as printed in the first edition of A Child of the Jago.)

The Review of Reviews:
> In Mr Morrison a new and promising observer and writer has appeared. (*Review of Reviews*, c.1894/5; extract as printed in the first edition of A Child of the Jago.)

The Realm:
> Vivid, engrossing. His work is literature and literature of a high order ... A triumph of effect. (*Realm*, c.1894/5; extract as printed in the first edition of A Child of the Jago. This review also commented that 'such a volume does more to make the West End realise the misery and degradation of the East End than a score of mass meetings in Hyde Park, a wilderness of turgid oratory, a month of sermons' (*see* Krzak.)

The Pall Mall Budget *discovers 'a new sensation'*:
> An experience which comes seldom to those of necessity immersed in the ephemeral literature of their own time – a new sensation. An artist of distinction. (*Pall Mall Budget*, c.1894/5; extract as printed in the first edition of A Child of the Jago.)

The Queen *detects life-sketching*:
> Admirable ... All are drawn with the same firm and dexterous pencil. (*Queen*, c.1894/5; extract as printed in the first edition of A Child of the Jago.)

The Aberdeen Free Press *recognizes an 'extraordinary mind'*:
> The sketches are reflections of an extraordinary mind. Unmistakable genius, delicate and consummate skill. It will bear reading

again and again. Its literary workmanship is of the highest order. (*Aberdeen Free Press*, c.1894/5; extract as printed in the first edition of *A Child of the Jago*.)

(d) A Child of the Jago *and the 'trilogy'*:

H. G. Wells identifies conflicts in Morrison's presentation of nature and nurture:

The son of the alcoholic proletarian, the apparently exhausted topic of Dr Barnardo, has suddenly replaced the woman with the past in the current novel ... Next year the artful publisher will be asking his young authors for books about poor boys born in sin and vermin and displaying with infinite pathos the stunted rudiments of a soul ... It is indisputable that the rediscovery of Oliver Twist is upon us ....

'A Child of the Jago' is indeed indisputably one of the most interesting novels this year has produced. We have admired Mr Morrison already for his 'Lizer'unt'; we have disliked him for his despicable detective stories; and we will frankly confess we did not think Mr Morrison capable of anything nearly so good as this admirably conceived and excellently written story ... It is beyond doubt that Mr Morrison must be full of East End material, and never once through this book does he drop into the pitfall of reporting. 'A Child of the Jago' is one of those rare and satisfactory novels in which almost every sentence has its share in the entire design.

The design, it must be confessed, is a little narrow. It is as if Mr Morrison had determined to write of the Jago and nothing but the Jago. It is the Jago without relativity. The reader will remember the spacious effect at the end of Mr Conrad's 'Outcast of the Islands' when Almayer shook his fist at the night and silence outside his sorrows. Mr Morrison never gets that spacious effect, although he carries his readers through scenes that would light into grandeur at a glance, at the mere turn of a phrase. The trial scene of Josh Perrott for the murder of Weech, and the execution scene that follows, show this peculiar want of breadth in its most typical manner ... The execution is got off in three pages with a flavour of having been written in a hurry, is, indeed a mere sketch of one of the characters for the fuller picture there should have been. It seems all the slighter, because it comes immediately after an elaborately written murder, action as finely executed as one could well imagine, and just before the equally stirring concluding chapter, the killing of Dick Perrott in a street faction fight. Moreover, by this brevity the latter chapter is brought too close to the murder chapter. Instead of crest and trough, a rise and cadence of emotion, we end in a confusion, like water breaking on a rocky beach. Had the father and son been presented in antagonism with some clearly indicated creative and destroying force, with Destiny, with Society or with human Stupidity, the book might have concluded with that perfect unity of effect it needs and does not possess . . .

The origin of the Jago, the place of the Jago in the general scheme of things, the trend of change in it, its probable destiny – such matters are not in his mind. [Quotes the discussion between Father Sturt and the surgeon.] Thus speaks Mr Morrison. It is practical on the face of it, and quite what would occur to a man looking so nearly at Whitechapel that the wider world where the races fight together was hidden. But the fact is that neither ignorance, wrong moral suggestions, nor parasites are inherited; the baby that survives in the Jago must needs have a good physique, the Jago people are racially indistinguishable from the people who send their children to Oxford, and the rate of increase of the Jago population is entirely irrelevant to the problem. The Jago is not a 'black inheritance', it is a black contagion – which alters the whole problem. And Mr Morrison knocks his surgeon's case entirely to pieces by his own story; for he shows, firstly, in Mrs Perrott that to come into the Jago is to assimilate oneself to the Jago; and, secondly, in Kiddo Cook, that a vigorous, useful citizen may come out of it. ('A Slum Novel', *Saturday Review*, 82, 28 November 1896, 573.)

The Athenaeum *is glad to find no 'immorality' in 'A Child of the Jago'
– but finds too many fights, exaggeration and uncertain purpose:*

Realism is so often an excuse for immorality in what is called art, that one can gladly praise Mr Arthur Morrison for a realism which deals frankly with dirt, brutality, and crime. . . . [Quotes the fight between Norah Walsh and Sally Green to show the 'zest of the narrator'.] The human frame can bear a great deal; but if this description is taken literally it is pretty clear that Sally must have been killed on the spot. At another place it is said that a constable was laid low by a fire-grate adroitly let drop from an upper window. 'Laid low' may, of course, mean killed; but if so, the author for once fails to choose the plainest word; if it does not, the exaggeration is palpable. Many pages are devoted to elaborate accounts of free fights, and one chapter describing a single combat furnishes the most disgusting passages in all the book. What is the object of it all? Those who have to pass their time in police courts or in the Central Criminal Court know very well that villainy such as Mr Morrison depicts, and worse, exists in London ... Mr Morrison has nothing new to tell. He is sarcastic about the philanthropists, who surely do not deserve his sarcasm. If his aim is to beguile novel-readers into taking an interest in the slums, it is not to be commended ... Better directed efforts are not wanting and those who are in earnest must deplore the methods of the novelist who dwells upon revolting details of blood and blows. (*'A Child of the Jago', Athenaeum*, 3607, 12 Dec. 1896, 832–3.)

With an opportunity to weigh Morrison against Stephen Crane, Wells' verdict goes to Morrison the 'heavyweight':
The literature of the slum multiplies apace, and just as the mud of the Port of London has proved amenable to Mr Whistler, so the mud of the New York estuary has furnished material for artistic treatment to Mr Crane. Mr Crane, in 'Maggie', shows himself the New York equivalent of Mr Morrison, with perhaps a finer sense of form and beauty and a slenderer physique. He is the light weight of the two. He is far more alert for what the industrious playwright calls the effective 'line', and every chapter cocks its tail with a point to it. He sketches, for instance, the career of Maggie's brother James, and tells of his lusts and brutality. 'Nevertheless,' ends the chapter, he had on a certain starlit evening said wonderingly and quite reverently, 'Dah moon looks like h—l, don't it?' And with that the chapter, rather self-consciously, pauses for your admiration. Of Mr Morrison's 'Dick Perrott' it is not recorded that he ever saw the beauty of moonlight or the stars. But one may doubt, even after the chromatic tumult of 'The Red Badge of Courage', whether Mr Crane is anywhere equal to Mr Morrison's fight between Perrott and Leary. To read that and to turn to Mr Crane's fight between Maggie's brother and her seducer is to turn from power to hysterics. The former is too strong and quiet to quote – it must be read: but of the latter: 'The arms of the combatants whirled in the air like flails. The faces of the men, at first flushed to flame-coloured anger, now began to fade to the

pallor of warriors in the blood and heat of a battle . . . The quiet stranger had sprawled very pyrotechnically out on the sidewalk.'

Which is very fine, no doubt, but much more suggestive of a palette dipped in vodki than of two men fighting. Yet, on the other hand, the emotional power of that concluding chapter of 'Maggie' seems a little out of Mr Morrison's reach – the old woman, drink sodden and obese, stricken with the news of her daughter's death and recalling her one vivid moment of maternal pride.

'Jimmy, boy, go get yer sister! Go get yer sister an' we'll put dah boots on her feet!' ('Another View of "Maggie"', *Saturday Review*, 82 (19 Dec. 1896), 655.)

Morrison entertains Josh Perrott at Loughton, disputes with H. G. Wells on eugenic theory, and explains why he 'killed Dicky Perrott':
'Sometimes I had the people themselves down here to my house in Loughton. One of my chief characters, a fellow as hard as nails, who could stand a punch in the face without flinching, and whom it was said only steel or lead could affect, came several times, and told me gruesome stories and how the thieves made a sanctuary of Orange-court; the inner hell of this awful place . . .'

'Yes, you are right,' went on my host, 'heredity and environment are their greatest enemies. One of the critics in his notice of my book said that 'neither ignorance, wrong moral suggestion, or parasites were hereditary', but he is wrong. Just look at this book of Charles Booth's, 'Pictures of Pauperism', and see the influence of heredity. Look at these long lists of families going back to the third and fourth generation, and all criminals or lunatics. Now and again turns up a respectable artisan, but he is a freak, a 'sport', to use the biological term, and he is so rare and startling an exception that he only goes to prove the point . . .'

'How can a half-starved girl of sixteen bear healthy children?' exclaimed Mr Morrison. 'One of the critics says that my Jago people are racially indistinguishable from the people who send their children to Oxford, but you never see a tall man amongst them, all the criminal classes are stunted. They have a certain strength, they can fight for a short time, but they have no staying-power. Take them a five-mile walk and you'll soon find that out. Therefore they have no quality that goes to make a good work-man. It is monstrous that the weak should be destroyed by the strong, but still more so that the strong should be destroyed by the weak ... For my own part, I believe, as Father Jay does, in penal settlements; it would be far cheaper than our present prison system. Why not confine them as lunatics are confined? Let the weed die out, and then proceed to raise the raisable. That is why I killed Dicky Perrott. He could not escape from his environment, and had he lived, would have become perforce, as bad as his surroundings. ('The Children of the Jago: Slum-Life at Close Quarters: A Talk with Mr Arthur Morrison', *Daily News*, 12 Dec. 1896, p.6.)

'C.R.', repudiating a charge of plagiarism, adduces information about the novel's sources and composition:

A writer in the *St. James's Gazette* claims to have discovered the secret of Mr Arthur Morrison's realism ... 'In a sense,' says the reviewer, 'the book has been written before' ... Now five years ago the Rev. Osborne Jay published a little book ... dealing with the same district. ... For example, Mr Jay states in a passage of about thirty lines that faction fights are common in Old Nichol. Mr Morrison gives two chapters of vivid description of a definite faction fight. Mr Jay makes the plain statement that 'women even take part, biting at each other's faces and tearing out each other's hair', while Mr Morrison 'expands' this piece of information into the character of Sally Green, 'the female champion of the old Jago'. Such parallels as these, the writer urges, 'suffice to show how realistic fiction may be written'. Now it will occur to the least reflecting that Mr Morrison must be a much cleverer man than he is, to evolve a realistic story, full of the minutest details of slum-life, from the few bald facts that the *St. James's* reviewer discovers to be common to *Life in Darkest London* and *A Child of the Jago*. Moreover, my own knowledge of Mr Morrison convinced me that this was not the method on which he worked. And in answer to my request he was good enough to relate to me the genesis of his book, and to explain the origin of those points of resemblance which certainly exist between his work and that of Mr Jay.

It was shortly after the publication of *Tales of Mean Streets* that Mr Morrison made the acquaintance of Mr Jay and his parish. Mr Jay, struck by the grim truth of Mr Morrison's work, wrote him a letter of appreciation, which brought the author on a visit of inspection to Old Nichol. Already Mr Morrison had the idea of Dicky Perrott in his mind [I have seen it, among scores of other jotted notions, in one of his old note-books] and was hesitating

whether to place him in Poplar, in Bethnal Green, or elsewhere
... Hither, then, Mr Morrison came day after day for more than
eighteen months, learning every inch of the half-dozen streets –
now improved off the face of the earth – which makes up the
Jago, haunting the public-houses, sitting with the people in their
homes, and even trying in his own person what it feels like to earn
a living by making match-boxes ...

Now, given two men who spend eighteen months or so studying
the lives of its inhabitants, and comparing notes of their discover-
ies and impressions, is it unlikely that when the one sets down the
facts and the other weaves the facts into fiction a similarity should
here and there appear? ('The Methods of Mr Morrison', *Academy*,
1284, 12 Dec. 1896, 531.)

The Bookman *protests against 'orgies of physical violence'*:
This new book of his has pages which it is almost impossible to
read. We do not combat his general attitude at all ... We do not
accuse him of exaggeration, and as to his excesses of realism we
can at least understand the temptation. But to understand does
not take away the right of protest; and we do protest against the
useless riot of brutality, the orgies of physical violence which we
are made witnesses of if we read the book through. Zola has never
outdone some of the pages here in their horrible defiance of any
sensitive feelings we may have. But we declare our right to have
these feelings respected, if not pampered, and our opinion that an
unblinking perusal of these tales of brutal fights would show much
more morbid effeminacy than any shrinking from them would do.
They are no necessary part of Mr Morrison's strenuous and
courageous purpose. ('*A Child of the Jago*', *Bookman* (London),
11 (Dec. 1896), 90–91.)

Blackwood's *reviewer muses on the uses of fiction: recreation or
missionary's medium?*
When [fiction] is not absorbed in the odious question of sex, it is
so overstrained in the pursuit of the unusual, so determined at any
hazard to humanity and with every possible breach of its prevailing laws to get something new ... that its inventions are sometimes monstrous, and its call upon our attention rather an offence
to us than an advantage ...

There is nothing attractive at all in the world which he opens to
our gaze. It is a world without hope or desire or any fair or

pleasant thing, knowing nothing but the foullest sediment of existence, unable to conceive of anything better – brutal, filthy, miserable, yet in a measure content ... It is strange to think upon what rule it is that pictures like these please the imagination, and are received by so many in the character of an entertainment, a portion of the relaxation of life. It may well be that we should see how another part of the world lives ... But ... what are they for? To make us all a kind of missionaries, impelled by disgust and horror, if by no better motive? ... Are we then to take these doubtful tales for amusement? France has accepted a similar kind of amusement from M. Zola; but only when highly spiced with vice and the peculiar kind of garbage upon which the French novel-reader has chosen to feed. Seldom, however, does the historian of the Jago bring in this element to make his horrors palatable. He shows us all the uncleanness of the streets excepting that. So far as we can recollect, the appalling sketch called 'Lizerunt in the Mean Streets', in which the brutality becomes tragic and so justifies itself, is the only one in which the great pollution of all is so much as referred to ...

Fiction is scarcely the medium for a lesson taught in such miserable detail, and in colours so dark and terrible ... Perhaps he thinks it is the best way to seize the attention of the frivolous public; but we think he is mistaken ... On the contrary, the gentlest of readers prefers to be seen with Nordau, or Kidd, or Pearson, quite superior kinds of literature, upon her table. ('A Raid Among Books', *Blackwood's Magazine*, 160:974 (Dec. 1896), 838–44.)

George Gissing is annoyed – and then courted – by Father Jay; he records in his diary spending Christmas Day reading 'A Child of the Jago':

[8 Sept. 1893:] Reading *The Times* at news-room, yesterday, came across a review of a book called 'The Social Problem', by one Revd Osborne Jay, of Shoreditch. In a passage quoted from him I recognized whole sentences taken bodily from 'The Nether World'. Wrote letter to *The Times*.

[9 Sept.:] ... My letter in *The Times*, headed, unfortunately, 'Borrowed Feathers' ...

[11 Sept.:] ... To-day the Revd O. J. writes in *The Times* that I am hard upon him, that he of course meant to quote me, that by some mistake he did not see the proofs of his book, etc. The lamest excuse ...

[13 Sept.:] ... One W. C. Hunt writes to *The Times* to say that the Revd O. Jay entrusted to him the correction of his proofs and *he* is responsible for the omission of inverted commas and of 'some names'. Referring to this the *Westminster Gazette* heads its par[agraph] 'A Printer's Marvellous Confession'. Indeed, it is remarkable enough ...

[21 Dec. 1894:] ... Astonished by letter from Revd Osborne Jay, of Holy Trinity, Shoreditch (the man whose plagiarism I had to write to *The Times* about, last year) inviting me to visit him. Replied genially, of course, and promised to go some day.

[31 Mar. 1895] ... Afternoon to Shoreditch, where I stayed till 6 o'clock with Father Jay, as he is called. Think I see my way to a big book.

[5 July:] ... Invitation from Osborne Jay to the laying of the foundation stone of his new church; can't go ...

[25 Dec. 1896:] Read *A Child of the Jago*. Poor stuff. (Pierre Coustillas, ed., *London and the Life of Literature in Late Victorian England: The Diary of George Gissing* (Hassocks: Harvester, 1978), pp.314–430.)

H. D. Traill launches his influential attack on 'A Child of the Jago', detecting not the 'mud pies' of realism, but 'a fairyland of horror', another 'Voyage to the Houyhnhnms':

It need not surprise us to find our attention solicited by a New Realism, of which the two most obvious things to be said are that it is unreal with the falsity of the half truth, and as old as the habit of exaggeration ...

Mr Arthur Morrison, author of *Tales of Mean Streets* and *A Child of the Jago*, undoubtedly carries heavier guns than Mr Crane. To begin with, he can tell a story ... Many of his characters are vividly and vigorously drawn ... Mr Morrison ... perceives ... that the life of the criminal in his constant struggle with the law, and in perpetual danger from its officers, possesses at least the element of 'sport', and presents features of variety and interest which that of the mere sot and tavern-brawler [in Crane's *Maggie*] cannot possibly offer ... In a word, the English writer differs from the American by all the difference which divides the trained craftsman from the crude amateur, and he deserves to that extent more serious and detailed criticism.

What, however, has most astonished one of Mr Morrison's critics fresh from a perusal of A Child of the Jago, is the impression of extraordinary unreality which, taken as a whole, it leaves behind it. ... He comes out from the Jago with the feelings, not as he had expected, of a man who has just paid a visit to the actual district under the protection of the police, but of one who has just awakened from the dream of a prolonged sojourn in some fairyland of horror ...

No wonder that those who know the East End of London have protested against this picture. The houses in that area of 'two hundred and fifty yards square' have been cleared of its former occupants and their dens, and the original of the Jago has, it is admitted, ceased to exist. But I will make bold to say that as described by Mr Morrison it never did exist. Mr Morrison has simply taken all the types of London misery, foulness and rascality, and 'dumped them down' on the area aforesaid ... It is certainly not realism. It is the idealising method, and its result is as essentially ideal as the Venus of Milo. That it is the idealisation of ugliness, instead of beauty, is a mere detail ... Unless words are to part with all their distinctions of meaning, it can no more be a realistic history of any community of human beings that ever existed on the earth, than is the Voyage to the Houyhnhnms ... The total effect of the story is unreal and phantasmagoric ... ('The New Realism', Fortnightly Review, 67, ns61 (1897), 63–73.)

Dicky Perrott lives; Harold Boulton asserts the accuracy of 'A Child of the Jago':
Incredible as it may appear, the Alsatia known in these pages as the Jago did exist up to three or four years ago, with all its reeking filth and horror, its absolute lawlessness, its frequent murders, its untainted heathendom, and its death-rate four times that of the rest of London. Perrott, the fighting man, the burglar, the murderer, was but one of many such, and the statement that eighty per cent. of the male population in one street were ticket-of-leave men only leads to the conclusion that the remaining twenty per cent. had served their time or not yet been caught. The blood-feuds and faction fights between the Ranns and the Learys, well as they are depicted, as matter of fact fall somewhat short of the hideous reality. In the great historic final fight, renewed at certain hours every day and lasting the best part of a week, one of the most striking incidents has escaped Mr Morrison's researches.

There had been for some days a *crescendo* of weapons as well as a *crescendo* of fury: fists had been discarded for sticks with nails in them, these for pieces of iron, and the climax was evidently at hand when one evening the Dove-Laners, as the author calls them, appeared before a certain house in the hostile quarter and, executing a savage war-dance, proceeded to sharpen knives upon the pavement in front of their foes, as an earnest of what might be expected on the morrow. It so happened that a youth, very much like the Dicky Perrott of the tale, who had at last suc-ceeded in obtaining an honest situation, much to the derision of his friends, was a witness of this war-dance. The old Jago blood within him was too much for this recruit to the ranks of respectability; next day he sallied forth to battle in the ranks of the Jagos, only to fall horribly wounded by a butcher's cleaver, and to be borne off to hospital, where his depositions were taken. Contrary to expectation, after several months he recovered; but of course his situation is gone for ever, and he is to be seen to-day meditating among the ruins of the Jago and waiting for a job to turn up. Whether it is likely to be an honest one after such a failure, who can say?

Here, until quite lately, existed a state of things that no novelist could exaggerate, no reporter over-paint . . .

Mr Morrison's book has appeared just as the old order of things has vanished, and it is therefore timely. It should remain a *locus classicus* for a certain type of nineteenth century barbarism flourishing undisturbed for a while in the midst of our over-civilisation. ('A Novel of the Lowest Life', *British Review*, 9 Jan. 1897, 349.)

The Nation *measures the affective force of 'A Child of the Jago' against Dickens:*

The story of the Jago is a terrible one, very modern in the manner of its telling, but dating back to Charles Dickens in matter, incident, and character. We seem to be reading about the 'Artful Dodger' and 'Poor Jo', 'Tom All-Alones', 'Bill Sykes', 'Nancy' and 'Pecksniff' converted into a fence slightly more degraded, but no more hypocritical and hateful. They are all done in a new way – a harder, more physical, brutal way. We have a stronger realization of their pitiable plight, but are more reconciled to it – it is so hopeless, so inevitable. Our horror is more vivid, our compassion feebler. Undoubtedly a great impetus to philanthropy was given by Dickens's slum stories. He controlled tears and laughter; he made emotional people feel that something must be done, and he forced sentimental people to go and do something at once. It is hardly probable that any burst of sympathetic activity can follow the reading of tales written by the more actual moderns. Literary worth does not spur the general reader to action, and perhaps, with such tales as the 'Child of the Jago', it is the force of the literary presentation which convinces those who can appreciate it of an impotence in action – a conviction to which that sort is ever predisposed. ('*Sir George Tressady* and Other Fiction', *Nation* (New York), 64:1648 (28 Jan. 1897), 70–71.)

Mr Woodland Erlebach, a former manager of the Nichol Street Board School, writes to lend support to Traill's objections:

From a thirty years' acquaintance with the district [Mr Morrison's Jago] I boldly say that the district, though bad enough, was not even thirty years ago so hopelessly bad and vile as this book paints it. (Letter presented by Traill, along with the names of other 'experts' demanded by Morrison, in publishing his revised critique in book form: *The New Fiction and Other Essays on Literary Subjects* (London: Hurst and Blackett, 1897), pp.25–6.)

Aaron Weech lives; Jay describes and defends Morrison's methods:

SIR, – I have for ten years been an inhabitant [and indeed Vicar] of the district the existence of which Mr H. D. Traill appears to doubt – the district described by Mr Arthur Morrison in his novel *A Child of the Jago*. I have much respect for Mr Traill's abilities as a literary critic, and in that respect would not venture to question his opinions; but as regards simple facts I think I may with honesty claim to be an 'expert' in the matter of the life which Mr Morrison has described. I have one thing to say – a thing I have said publicly before – and that is that Mr Morrison's book exhibits with perfect truth the life of my parish as I have known it day by day for ten years.

Who the 'experts' may be who condemn the book I am at a loss to conceive, and Mr Traill does not mention their names. I can think of nobody more entitled to be styled an 'expert' in this matter than Mr Morrison himself, who, after many years of residence and personal study in other parts of the East-End, spent eighteen months in minute personal investigation of my parish – the 'Jago' – before beginning his book; and apart from myself, I have met nobody well-acquainted with the neighbourhood – and I think I know all such people – who does not agree with me that the book presents the place and the people with a sincerity and truth that is wonderful. So far from Mr Morrison's characters being selected from different districts, I know all the originals among my parishioners, and could point them out. As to Aaron Weech [his name is not Queech, nor is he a Jew as Mr Traill supposes], he is alive now and carrying on in his shop. Mr Traill is surprised that readers are 'invited to believe' that cosh-carrying, as described by Mr Morrison, was a general feature in this unhappy parish. I also most earnestly invite Mr Traill to believe it, sad as the fact is. The Bishop of Stepney's organ, *The East London Church Chronicle*, supports Mr Morrison's facts unreservedly, though I trust my own testimony is sufficient. The professional philanthropists who live in the West and talk of the East may disagree with those on the spot who know, but I am sure Mr Traill will weigh their opinions in a just balance. The place is cleared away certainly – or nearly so. But the people still exist, and it was the people who made the place bad, not the place that degraded the people. The problem still exists.

    I am Sir, your obedient servant.

    A. OSBORNE JAY
    Holy Trinity Vicarage,
    Shoreditch, E.

('The New Realism: To the Editor of the Fortnightly Review', *Fortnightly Review*, 67, ns 61 (February 1897), 324.)

Sally Green lives; Morrison contests Traill's label of 'realist' and assumptions about 'process':

To begin with, then, I have never called myself a 'realist', and I have never put forth any of my work as 'realism'. I decline the labels of the schoolmen and the sophisters: being a simple writer of tales, who takes whatever means lie to his hand to present life as he sees it; who 'insists' on no 'process'; and who refuses to be bound by any formula or prescription prepared by the cataloguers and pigeon-holers of literature. This, I am aware, may be an announcement of limited interest: but I think I am justified in making it by reason of the perplexing movements of Mr H. D. Traill in the course of an article on what he calls 'The New Realism' ... The procedure, briefly, is this. The critic begins by calling me, quite gratuitously and of his own motion, a 'realist';

he announces, again quite gratuitously, that realists [and I presumably among them] 'insist' on a certain 'process' in the production of fiction; he proceeds himself to 'insist' on a particular 'process', which he presents ready mixed and of his own discovery; then he produces from his imagination, inspired by the completest ignorance of the life of which I have written, a theory that I have not worked by his process. He compares this theory with his label *Realist*, and decides that there is a disagreement somewhere. And in this way, amiably trotting after his own tail, he arrives at the conclusion that I am a very insincere sort of person, writing the thing which is not in base competition with other realists . . .

Mr H. D. Traill, however, has adventured farther than any other critic in this direction. The Jago, as I have described it, he 'makes bold to say' never existed. Truly, he makes very bold: even so did Dickens's 'amazing alderman' make bold to say that Jacob's Island never existed. In a like degree would he make bold were he to deny the existence of Franz Josef Land. For the only perceptible warrant for his denial is that he has never seen the Jago . . . He cites my description of the 'cosh' and its use – to stun or disable a drunken man decoyed into the Jago for purposes of robbery. He complains that he is invited to believe that 'coshing' was a regular industry of the Jago, practised throughout the whole district, at all times, and by every one who had the means of practising it with success. My actual words were that 'cosh-carrying was near to being the major industry of the Jago', and certainly he is invited to believe this. I know it, Mr Jay knows it, his lay-helper, his curate and his mission-woman know it. Mr Harold Boulton knows it. Mr Traill knows nothing of the Jago at all: therefore he refuses to believe it. That is all . . .

He will not believe in Sally Green, her trick of gnawing the nape, and the incident of the broken bottle assault . . . Sally Green is alive at this moment, and, as I write, it is scarce twenty-four hours since I had sight of a cheek, eye, and temple swollen to the size of a turnip by the application of her boot. Her actual name is not Sally Green – as matter of fact, she chances to bear the surname of one of the most inoffensive literary men alive; but her manner of fighting was such as I have described. She is growing older now, and is losing some of her quickness; consequently she fights rather less, and rarely attempts the difficult tactic that won her supremacy in earlier years. But her temper has not improved, and she is surprisingly ready with a heavy boot. If Mr Traill is willing to risk the boot, it will give me much pleasure to present him to Sally Green in person . . .

A definite accusation is that I have taken bad types from divers districts, and concentrated them in my picture of the Jago. But again Mr Traill mistakes. The original of my Jago was a place to which those types gravitated as by natural law from other parts . . . Not I, but their own propensity, brought these people together.

Mr Traill has discovered that in Josh Perrott's fight with Billy Leary 'every punch, with its effect on the punched part, is faithfully delineated in black and blue, picked out with crimson'. Surprised to learn this, I turned to the book, and succeeded in counting the mere mention [no more] of as many as a dozen blows. Has Mr Traill any conception of how many blows are delivered in, say, a quarter of an hour of a well-stricken fight? Has he ever seen such a fight? . . .

Why does he call my Weech a 'revival' of Fagin? True, he styles him 'Queech', and a Jew – which he isn't; but even that brings him little nearer. Aaron Weech is alive now, and in his shop [though it is not a coffee-shop], and there are hundreds of other men of his class. His likeness to Fagin is as the likeness of Cacus to Jack Sheppard: his trade is the same, and that is all . . .

One thing I regret, and that is that when Mr Traill speaks of Dicky Perrott's story being buried in a mass of squalid irrelevancies, he does not point to some, at least, of the irrelevancies to which he refers; because the information might have been of use to me. There is nothing I am more anxious to exclude from work of mine than irrelevancy. But when I am attempting to depict the squalid surroundings of a boy in a thieves' neighbourhood, and their effect on his character, I am disposed to consider these surroundings no irrelevancies at all, but strict essentials of the picture . . . ('What is a Realist?' *New Review*, 16, 94 (March 1897), 326–336; *see* note on 'Preface'.)

The Critic *sounds the aesthetic note of the 1890s, finding Baudelaire without the beauty and Dickens without the poetry: a novel that leaves 'only a shudder behind':*

Many years ago, a French poet distinguished himself by a volume in which the worship of evil, the adoration of ugliness, was the dominant chord . . . In Baudelaire – in the 'Fleurs du Mal' – it allied itself with beautiful form, and had so far a reason for its existence; an exquisite vase held the fetid unguent, a rare and lovely rhythm threw a panoply of grace over the monstrous limbs...

But what can one say of ugliness unredeemed by beauty of form or grace of utterance – ugliness of toads and adders and creeping things, that freezes and thrills like the Medusa of Leonardo and leaves only a shudder behind? We have tried in vain to read Mr Morrison's book; we must frankly avow ourselves defeated. As a 'tract for the times', supplementing the revelations of Mr Jacob Riis and the philanthropic economists who are investigating East New York and East London, the book is undoubtedly powerful and may serve a good purpose; the very disgust with which we lay it down shows its power... The same talent, remarkable enough, which he displays in painting these brutal Salvador Rosa landscapes, might, if softened a little, have served his purpose infinitely better, and created or evoked the sympathy which he longs for the reader to feel. No one can read nearly 400 pages of unrelieved wretchedness, pessimism and ugliness without an effort too heroic to be expected in these days. The wonderful genius of Victor Hugo triumped over us in 'Les Misérables'; but Victor Hugos are scarce. The 'children of the Jago' [the Five Points of London] are miserable enough in their gaunt poverty, but to make them interesting, a certain transfiguring touch must poetize their habitations, their lives and loves, as Dickens has made them beautiful in little Nell and other immortal figures. If we can neither smile nor weep, we are apt to fall into the rigidity of indifference. ('A Child of the Jago', Critic (New York), 30, ns 27 (24 April 1897), 287–8.)

The Academy *weighs up Morrison's career, suggesting that he should restore the priority of 'human nature' over 'environment':*

Mr Morrison appears to have arrived at a very interesting and critical stage of his career, for no one can say whether promise is going to ripen into performance or not. He is of the French school; Daudet might have taught him his method, and Zola selected his subjects. In his *Jago* he trusted little or nothing to imagination, but a great deal to his notebook... [But] human nature does not alter so much with conditions as he seems to think... Mr Albert Chevalier made his early success by recognising this fact; the coster of his songs is recognisably alive and human. The coster of Mr Morrison does not seem to be a man, but only a stuffed figure carrying a blotch of horrible characteristics ... Moreover, his success has been achieved in pictures of the brutal. There are times when he seems to reflect that, after all, passion and hatred and love and tears and sorrow and forgiveness, if he could but see them, play the same part in the slum that they do in Piccadilly; but so far this discernment has resulted in no more than the reproduction of some of the worst faults of Charles Dickens, catch-penny pathos, and weak sentimentality where he intended real feeling. Mr Morrison never will do first-rate work till he shuts up his Dickens, a writer who had no command of the harsh, bitter cynicism in which Mr Morrison excels, and whose sunny love of what was bright and cheerful is inimitable.

To pronounce any final judgment upon Mr Morrison's writing would be absurd. The truth is, he has not yet found himself; he has not searched his mind so thoroughly as to be able to say how much of it is second-hand Kipling, second-hand Daudet, Dickens and Zola, and what remnant is pure Morrison ... The imitation that is freely pardoned at the beginning of a career is not to be so easily forgiven in more ambitious tasks. So, also, the lack of sympathy – we do not mean pity or compassion so much as the power to enter into and share another's views and thoughts and passions – may be passed by once, but without it there can be no really great imaginative writing. ('Mr Arthur Morrison', *Academy*, 4 December 1897, 493.)

The Daily Telegraph *concedes a 'new Mr Arthur Morrison' in his 1899 novel 'To London Town':*

We have idyllic pictures, woodland scenes full of tenderness and grace ... This is the new Mr Arthur Morrison gracious and tender, sympathetic and human. (Extract as printed in Hutchinson's 1909 catalogue.)

With the evidence of 'To London Town', the Bookman *calls a halt to reproaches against Morrison:*

The reproaches sometimes cast at Mr Morrison that his 'Tales of Mean Streets' and his 'Child of the Jago' gave a one-sided and a very miserable account of East London life, must now cease. It was not a wanton delight in gloom that made him write so harshly of existence in the wildernesses of brick and mortar. He writes his report of life in chapters, and not in one alone can he tell the ultimate truth. But here he comes nearer to doing so. There is something idyllic in the story [of *To London Town*], much that is gentle. But it is no symptom of Mr Morrison's having begun to quail before the spectacle of poverty and sin and suffering. Beauty and goodness are seen in their common struggle against sordid ugliness, but beauty and goodness are uppermost. ('In London Town', *Bookman* (Nov. 1899), 58–9.)

Looking back on his trilogy, Morrison focuses on the short-termism and reversal of moral code of the Jagos:

'I believe that if you could erect a machine at a cost of £500 which would supply them with food and clothes and all the necessities of life for ever, and if you went down to them with the £500 and said, 'Here I have £500 to spend on you. Shall I build a machine, which I can do in a month, to keep you in food and clothes for ever after the month is over, or shall I divide the money among you and give you eighteenpence each on the spot' – I believe if you did that a great shout would go up, 'Give us our eighteenpence'. They are utterly unable to see beyond the present; the idea that at the end of the month the machine would supply them with all they wanted would be quite incomprehensible to them . . .

The moral order of things was reversed in the Jago; this boy was brought up to stealing, and stealing became a moral habit to him. He had never known it was wrong, and could not understand being punished for it. He had no chance. So criminals are made and paupers are brought into the world.' ('New Light on London's Poverty: A Chat with Mr Arthur Morrison', *Cassell's Saturday Journal*, 19 September 1900, 24.)

Edward VII, as Prince of Wales, recalls Dicky Perrott at the official opening of the Boundary Street Scheme flats:

Few, indeed, will forget this site who have read Mr Morrison's pathetic tale of 'A Child of the Jago', and all of us are familiar with the labours of that most excellent philanthropist, Mr Jay, in this neighbourhood. (*The Housing Question in London 1855–1900* (1900); cited by P. J. Keating in his 1969 introduction to *A Child of the Jago*.)

Jane Findlater sketches the evolution of slum fiction, according Morrison a high place – though not the last word:

Many authors, many modes of presentation; but, in spite of this, it is easy to arrange our authors into distinct 'schools', each writing from their own standpoint. The slum and the slum-dweller, then, may be, and have been, treated in (at least) five different ways:

1. As a moral lesson.
2. As a social problem.
3. As an object of pity and terror.
4. As a gladiatorial show.
5. As an amusing study.

The first of these divisions belongs now to a bygone age; the second and third merge into each other; the fourth has not very many exponents; the fifth is the latest evolution of the whole movement ... Dickens from the outset is moralizing; and that is what no modern author would dare to do for a moment – because no one would read his books if he did. The awful retribution of sin, the hard way of the transgressor, is not what we wish to hear about in 1900, whatever the public of earlier days liked. It is much more to our taste to read of the triumph of the transgressor and the total defeat of innocency by inexorable fate ...

The whole school of social reformers sprang into being with *Alton Locke*. ... Surely every unwholesome trade has had its novel; every grievance of the toilers its special pleader in fiction. All honour to the reformers, and long may they blossom and bear fruit. What Kingsley began Besant went on into, and a host of smaller writers, well-intentioned but nameless, followed hard upon their masters. ... This interest in social reform books is certainly more healthy than the rush which was made for the two other classes of slum literature which I have mentioned – i.e. (1) the school of pity and terror, and (2) the school of brutality.

The demand for the first of these is, I hope, explained by the fact that the writers of this school have written so admirably.

It was in 1890 that Gissing brought out that extraordinary book *The Nether World* ... Gissing writes the tragedy of Want. It is not written with brutality, and that is why it is so terrible and undeniable ... As we read we know that every word is true – this is hunger, and heaven help the hungry; – this despair indeed – not the glib despair which the novelists deal in by the page, but that mortal disease of the mind which is past all cure. Gissing has no gospel of hope to offer his readers. ... The lower orders are, to his seeing, one huge tragedy. ... Arthur Morrison became the most prominent exponent of the School of Pity. His *Child of the Jago* continued the tradition at its best, and exhibited the 'relentless' modern method very plainly. For here is the story of a boy of originally good, tender instincts, who, like Oliver Twist, is in training for a thief. Does innocence triumph here? Is there a measure of hope and comfort at the close? Impossible. Dicky Perrott – the 'Oliver' of our day – has never a chance from the cradle to the grave ... We all read the books of Arthur Morrison and shuddered over them; some people were apparently reading them without the shudder, for in 1897 appeared yet another recruit to the ranks of slum literature, who, in slang phrase, seemed to be determined to 'go one better' than his predecessors. The brutal school had appeared ... [Somerset Maugham's] *Liza of Lambeth* appeared in 1897. It is a story of brutal frankness and sickening import ... We are spared nothing: the reek of the streets; the effluvia of unwashed humanity: but worse than all these outside things is the hopeless moral atmosphere in which the characters move. ... Nor does the author seem to write in any spirit of pity, or with any love for the creatures he has made. With a stolid indifference he chronicles their hopeless sufferings; without apparent disgust he details the loathsome vices which degrade them; the whole thing is so gratuitous. Why all these horrors? Why all this filth? ... But this is just where these books fail. Life in the slums has its joys quite as surely if not as evidently, as a life in palaces, and it is ridiculous to suppose that it has not.

This was a fact which was working obscurely in the writings of Arthur Morrison. *The Child of the Jago* scarcely admits the joys of slum-life, but it gives a fair idea of its pleasurable, if savage, excitements – the ecstacy of Dicky Perrott's absorption in the prize fight, the lust of battle, the gratulation of successful thieving – all these dubious joys are freely admitted.

But it remained for yet newer recruits to the slum-writers to discover what I venture to say is more nearly the ultimate truth about slum-dwellers, and to describe this. [William Pett Ridge's] *'Mord Emly* and [Clarence Rook's] *The Hooligan Nights* both give voice to this new discovery, and with admirable art, that is quite without exaggeration, show the wild joys and excitements of slum-life ... There comes the truth; every slum-dweller is not entirely depraved, or desperately miserable. ('The Slum Movement in Fiction', *National Review*, 35 (1900), 447–454.)

Robert Blatchford, editor of the socialist 'Clarion', focuses on Morrison's omissions and ultimate literary limitations:

An infinite deal of nothing has been written about *A Child of the Jago*. The book has been foolishly praised, and as foolishly condemned, and both praise and condemnation have been a source of amusement and suprise to the few who possess real knowledge of both literature and the slums. For it is a fact within the memories of a legion of readers that nearly every feature of the 'Jago' life has been painted in literature before; and it is a fact within the knowledge of innumerable citizens of London, Glasgow, Dublin, Liverpool and Manchester, that the life of the 'Jago', and of all other slums of which the 'Jago' is a type, is more horrible, more miserable, more shameful, and more unspeakable than Mr Morrison has painted it. Mr Morrison ... has *not* presented the 'Jago' in all the colours of its wretchedness and shame. On the contrary, he has excercised a stern artistic reticence.

Let anyone who knows the slums consider how the truth is toned down or evaded in *A Child of the Jago*. What are the two commonest adjectives of the low-life Cockney? No publisher dare print them: yet in 'Jago' conversation hardly a sentence is spoken without their use ... Then nothing is said in Mr Morrison's book as to the sanitary arrangements of the 'Jago', nor is there any indication of the great prevalence of sicknesses, which ... flourish in the slums as fungi flourish upon rotten trees ... In the 'Jago' children are prostitutes before they reach their teens; and it is true that bad as are the morals of the East, they are exceeded by the vileness of the West of London.

There is not a newspaper nor a novelist in these islands who dare tell the whole truth and the real truth about Whitechapel, the Strand, and Piccadilly. ('On Realism', in *My Favourite Books* (London: Walter Scott, 1900), pp.222–53.)

Jack London visits the setting of 'A Child of the Jago' and reflects on the 'mean streets' of the East End:

We next visited the municipal dwellings erected by the London County Council on the site of the slums where lived Arthur Morrison's 'Child of the Jago'. While the buildings housed more people than before, it was much healthier. But the dwellings were inhabited by the better-class workmen and artisans. The slum people had simply drifted on to crowd other slums or to form new slums ...

The City of Dreadful Monotony, the East End is often called, especially by well-fed, optimistic sight-seers, who look over the surface of things and are merely shocked by the intolerable sameness and meanness of it all. ... But [it merits] a worse title. It should be called the City of Degradation.

While it is not a city of slums, as some people imagine, it may well be said to be one gigantic slum. From the standpoint of simple decency and clean manhood and womanhood, any mean street, of all its mean streets, is a slum. ... The mean streets merely look mean from the outside, but inside the walls are to be found squalor, misery, and tragedy ... (*The People of the Abyss* (1903; reptd London; Journeyman, 1977), pp.88–9)

A defender of William Booth turns on such clergy as Jay:
How has [General Booth] been received? And what has he done?

He has been received with an almost unbroken chorus of insult and abuse. Clergymen who have never been heard of outside their own little parishes – who have never shown themselves worthy to tie his shoe, and of whom any thousand put together cannot show as the fruit of their labours one tithe of the souls whom he has rescued from darkness to light and from the power of Satan unto God – have written about him in terms of positive fury. To me there is something absolutely shocking in this fact ... Here is a man who to all his *religious work* – of which the results are incontestible, however much its methods may be disliked – has added a *social work* ample and fruitful enough to furnish out the glory of fifty ordinary reformers, and yet every fussy nobody, every commonplace and routine clergyman, thinks himself justified in speaking of him with scornful disapprobation, and looking down upon him from the whole height of his inferiority. (The Ven. Archdeacon Farrar, 'The "Darkest England" Social Scheme', reprinted from *The Review of the Churches*, in Bramwell Booth, ed., *The Salvation Army: Essays and Sketches* (London: Salvation Army, 1906), pp.206–34.)

With an eye on Morrison's 'Lizerunt', Stephen Leacock satirizes writers of social-reform novels, their descents into the abyss – and earnest critical discussion of their 'methods':
We sat on a low stool immediately beside Mrs Ethelinda Afterthought, who presided in her own gracious fashion over the teaurn.

'So you want to know something of my methods of work?' she said, as she poured hot tea over our leg ... 'I always begin,' said Ethelinda Afterthought, 'with a study.'

'A study?' we queried.

'Yes, I mean a study of actual facts. Take, for example, my *Leaves from the Life of a Steam Laundrywoman* – more tea?'

'No, no,' we said.

'Well, to make that book I first worked two years in a laundry.' ...

'Do you always work on that method?' we asked.

'Always,' she answered. 'For *Frederica of the Factory* I spent six months in a knitting mill. For *Marguerite of the Mud Flats* I made special studies for months and months.'

'Of what sort?' we asked.

'Of mud ...'

'And what are you doing next?' we inquired.

'My next book,' said the Lady Novelist, 'is to be a study – tea? – of the pickle industry – perfectly new ground.'

'A fascinating field,' we murmured.

'And quite new. Several of our writers have done the slaughter-house, and in England a good deal has been done in jam. But so far no one has done pickles. i should like, if I could,' added Ethelinda Afterthought, with the graceful modesty that is charac-teristic of her, 'to make it the first of a series of pickle novels, showing, don't you know, the whole pickle district, and perhaps following a family of pickle workers for four or five generations.' ('Ideal Interviews: IV – With Our Typical Novelists', in his *Frenzied Fiction* (London: John Lane, 1919), pp. 127–36.)

In P. G. Wodehouse's hands, the descent into the abyss becomes a comic vehicle:

'Meadowes,' said Archibald, 'are you busy for the moment?'

'No, sir.'

'Then let us speak for a while on the subject of bread. Do you realize, Meadowes, that there are blokes who can't get bread? They want it, their wives want it, their children are all for it, but in spite of this unanimity what is the upshot? No bread. I'll bet you didn't know that, Meadowes.'

'Yes, sir. There is a great deal of poverty in London.'

'Not really?'

'Oh, yes, indeed, sir. You should go down to a place like Bottleton East. That is where you hear the Voice of the People.'

'What people?'

'The masses, sir. The martyred proletariat. If you are interested in the martyred proletariat, I could supply you with some well-written pamphlets.' ('Archibald and the Masses', in *Young Men in Spats* (London: Herbert Jenkins, 1936), pp.232–60.)

V. S. Pritchett rediscovers for his wartime audience Morrison's account of people who have 'kept their heads above water for a spell':

Let us urge the importance of conditions; but let us not allow them to deflate the imagination or argue away the novelist's chief delight and greatest difficulty: the art of constructing and telling a story complete in itself. For unless he learns this art, a novelist sterilises his power of observation, the power to see stereoscopically and perspectively, and to set moving the congestions of fact that clog an impressionable mind. Arthur Morrison had this power. 'Conditions' were in his bones ... Mr Morrison's early novels and sketches are often modest in their art, like the work of someone learning to write, but they have an anthropological drama of their own ... a sharp-eyed and intimate knowledge of how East End society used to behave as a society, of how it used to deploy its cunning and uphold its customs. Injustice is done and the President of the Immortals has already abandoned the hopeless scene to the human instinct of self-preservation when Mr Morrison comes in to record it ... These novels are not pools of self-pity in the Gissing manner; nor are they worked up with that sadistic touch of angry ecstasy which Dickens brought to his pictures of poverty. In Mr Morrison's book slum life is the accepted life, a dirty but not a turgid stream. In their position, you say – as one ought to say of all human beings – these people have lived, they've kept their heads above water for a spell. Man is the animal who adapts himself. ('Books in General', *New Statesman and Nation*, 22 Jan. 1944, 61.)

Alan Sillitoe, author of 'Saturday Night and Sunday Morning', attacks Arthur Morrison's 'zoo' working people:

Robert Tressell's *The Ragged Trousered Philanthropists* was the first good novel of English working-class life. A generation before it, appeared those of Arthur Morrison, who wrote *A Child of the Jago*, and *Tales of Mean Streets*. Morrison's writing, however, was as slick as the Sunday newspapers, and his pompous and passionless style either lulls you to sleep or makes you distrust it. He wrote from too far above his characters: they lived in a zoo, and were to be regarded with fear, hostility, and derision. His working man was the stereotype [add a dose of dirt for realism] that still plagues English fiction. Robert Tressell, on the other hand, put his ordinary people into correct perspective by relating them to society as a whole. (Alan Sillitoe, 'Introduction' to Robert Tressell's *The Ragged Trousered Philanthropists* (1914; restored ed. 1955; reprinted London: Granada, 1965), pp.7–10.)

Benny Green distinguishes Morrison's authenticity from the many other pens writing about the 'mean streets':

Most of what passes as the literature of mean streets has been composed by well-intentioned respectable gentlemen to whose lives a mean street has no more relevance than a mummy to an Egyptologist's . . .

But there does exist an authentic literature of the urban poor, small in extent perhaps, but intense in effect. Arthur Morrison in particular, in *A Child of the Jago*, *Tales of Mean Streets*, and *The Hole in the Wall*, spared his readers so little in his account of how the slum-dweller lived his life and saw the world that there are moments when the brutalized characters in their stunted surroundings become too awful to read about. Indeed Morrison did his job so convincingly that social engineers since have been misled into thinking that because violence and criminality came out of the Jago, then the Jago can produce nothing but violence and crimi nality. The conclusion is comically false, and Morrison went out of his way to say so, insisting that brutality and crime were only two aspects among many of working-class life and by no means the most dominant. Nor were they exclusive to the working class; there is after all some kinship between the man who shoots a few grouse before having his lunch and his contemporary who squashes a few bedbugs before going to sleep. Most of the residents of Morrison's mean streets, housed in pigsties at the very apogee of Empire, aspired to graduate from the bugs to the grouse, figuratively speaking, by lawful means, and often succeeded. Virtue resided cheek by jowl with vice, sapience often shared a bed with doltishness. ('Introduction' to Clarence Rook's 1899 documentary, *The Hooligan Nights* (Oxford: OUP, 1979), p.viii.)

Roger Henkle argues that Morrison, in terms of the politics of class and gender, constructed an East-End illegible and therefore threatening to its middle-class readers:

Morrison underwent an *embourgeoisement* that took him beyond his East End roots. The dialogue that his writings create is with a middle-class reading audience. But he saw himself as an authentic voice of the urban slum experience ... Morrison rejects the sentimental and the melodramatic for a laconic, unmodulated prose that rarely rises to a dramatic climax. He portrays a world of gratuitous violence which offers up no *meaning* to the middle-class reader; it cannot be integrated into the systems of value, psychology, or material relationship of the middle class ... It is no longer a land of shadows cast by the projections of middle-class subjectivity, no longer a terra incognita to be read in line with the dominant class anxieties and desires. It constitutes its own social order ... At the same time that he asserts this, Morrison also insists upon the enclosed, immobilizing fatality of that world, its immersion in violence, its deadened submission to poverty, its constricting social containment ... For all the efforts of social services to confirm the woman as the ethical center of lower-class life, she turns out in many of these stories, to be as uncontrollable as the men, at her worst, or too passive to resist her own victimization, at her best ...

The circumstances of life in the slums affect the possibilities for writing a traditional male text as well ... Morrison's male protagonists are to a man unfulfilled, fated to frustration. Economic and social conditions force this upon them, but the inchoate natures of all the characters indicate that a full, mutually interdependent code of subject construction is absent. A system such as that of the middle class, in which a female ethical subject balances and validates the agency that is granted to the male, is missing in the nether world ... It is only natural, in a way, that Morrison should turn to some form of *Bildungsroman* for his accounts of life in the East End, since the likely course that the slum culture would take would be to imitate the middle class in its effort to establish for itself a masculine-based, if not patriarchal, order. Tellingly enough, the protagonist in each of these novels is a boy, as if to indicate that mature or 'full' subjectivity is never attained in lower urban existence ...

The popularity of the novel was matched only by the critical outrage over its alleged grossness. Yet the violence is so spectacular, and so emblematic of the ferocity that comes out of lives of depravity and idleness, that the pathology becomes *symbolic* ... The spareness of Morrison's prose, its starkness – held in place by a half-Dickensian ironic narrative commentary – constitutes not realism, at least as the English and French middle-class literary culture knew it, but a symbolic text. So disturbing is his version of slum existence, so alien, so intractable is it to middle-class representation and hegemonizing, that he has to be content with the charges that what he describes *isn't there*. ('Morrison, Gissing and the Stark Reality', *Novel*, 25, iii (1992), 302–20.)

John L. Kijinski sees Morrison as Victorian ethnographer:
During the time Morrison was working on *A Child of the Jago*, British interest in systematic methods for describing 'exotic' populations was at an all time high, as evidenced by the appearance of increasingly professional studies in ethnology, folk-lore, and urban sociology. All of these fields shared in common a method which involved exacting observation by an expert who had qualified himself to present new and systematically organized knowledge on the group being observed ... Morrison prepared himself to produce a portrait of a native population in much the same way as an ethnographer of the time would have. Morrison's (and Jay's) hope that the novel would help to bring about public awareness and reform was also in keeping with the general tendency of Victorian ethnography ...

The reader is given the precise boundaries of the region that will stand at centre focus of the book; Morrison even includes a map of this foreign territory, a 'Sketch Plan of the Old Jago'. But more importantly the reader is made to see that the Jago – though in the heart of London – is as foreign to the average Englishman as any region in Africa ...

What seals the case of the Jagos as a dangerous 'other' within the heart of an advanced civilization, is that ritualized violence as a community response to the environment around them has made the Jagos true aliens, even in such matters as physicality and response to pain. Throughout the novel Morrison develops a picture of residents of the Jago as physically degenerate ... The outsider needs the ethnographer to interpret even the bodies of these natives ...

But even more important than the observable physical differences of the Jagos are the communal styles by which they inflict, observe, and endure violence to the body ... One of the most striking passages describes a woman warrior, much admired for her prowess as a street fighter ... What is absent in the Jago response to this violence is a normal fear of bodily pain or of any empathy for the physical suffering of others. Instead, periods of widespread violence are met with enthusiasm; members of the community become delighted observers or participants.

In this, and in many other ways, Morrison equates the residents of the Jago with natives of a 'less advanced' culture ... He shows that the skilful 'colonial' administrator – in this case an admirable Anglican pastor, 'Father' Sturt, who actually lives and works among his poor parishioners – needs to treat the 'natives' as one would treat large children. ('Ethnography in the East End: Native Customs and Colonial Solutions in *A Child of the Jago*', *English Literature in Transition 1880–1920*, 37, iv (1994), 490–501.)

Krishan Kumar, including Morrison in the category 'novelists of the 1880s', highlights class fears of 'contamination':
There is the fear of 'the residuum' and the concern to prevent the contamination of the respectable poor by the idle and profligate poor. In its most general form this goes right back to the Poor Laws of the sixteenth century, and it was spectacularly confirmed in the New Poor Law of 1834. But it has been shown that even in the supposedly more 'technical' and precise form in which it was formulated by Booth in the 1880s, it had been fully anticipated in the 1860s – specifically in the debates surrounding the Second Reform Bill in Parliament, and in such bodies as the National Association for the Promotion of Social Science. Moreover, the generalization of this perception to society as a whole had already taken place. In so far as the novelists of the 1880s harped on the theme of contamination and contagion – and it underlies much of the imagery of their writing – they were harking back to a mode of analysis that was well established long before the '*grand peur*' of their time. It was not some writer of the 1880s but one in the 1850s – George Godwin – who spoke in 1854 of the haunts of the poor [those 'dark and dangerous places', those 'swamps and shadows'] as 'the festers and malignant sores with which the body of society is spotted'. ('Versions of the Pastoral: Poverty and the Poor in English Fiction', *Journal of Historical Sociology*, 8, i (1995), 1–35.)

Sally Ledger traces in slum-fiction the articulations of imperialism, race theory, degeneration fears and gender:

If the writers of imperial adventure stories appeared to be sanguine about the enduring qualities of the British 'race' at a time when British supremacy appeared to be under threat, the same cannot be said of those social explorers who ventured into the depths of London's slumland. Eugenic sub-texts are strongly in evidence in East End slumland novels and documentary essays as well as in the imperialist adventure stories of the *fin-de-siècle* . . . At quite a deep level, the fictional enactment in imperial adventure stories of an assertion of authority over colonial subjects in distant countries would seem to have been, at least in part, an ideological displacement of the social and political chaos which threatened to engulf Britain, not least in the depths of the East End which was frequently figured in discourse as 'Darkest London' . . . A fear for the future of the British 'race' and its empire and, at the same time, a fear of the British working class, which, amongst other places, appeared to be starving just yards away from the seat of government in London, are manifested here. Whilst they starved quietly, no one much minded, but the fear was that with the rise of the new socialist parties at the *fin-de-siècle* Britain's poor might start to protest . . .

Booth's analysis of 'Darkest England' draws sympathetic attention to the plight of London's prostituted women. He makes a direct analogy between the African women of the Equatorial forest whom Stanley claimed were raped and abused by the Arab traders, and the women of London's East End who were driven by economic distress into prostitution . . . Women figure largely in the fears expressed concerning 'race' degeneration in Britain at the *fin-de-siècle*, not least because of their reproductive function. As a theory of heredity, eugenics was profoundly concerned with women's function as mothers and nurturers of the 'race', most particularly at a time when the 'empire' was felt to be vulnerable and requiring the very 'best of British' to sustain it. The degeneration of women was therefore regarded with even more concern than the perceived degeneration of men in the slumlands. ('In Darkest England: The Terror of Degeneration in *Fin-de-Siècle* Britain', *Literature and History*, III, 4, ii (1995), 71–86.)

SUGGESTIONS FOR FURTHER READING

Richard Benvenuto, 'The Criminal and the Community: Defining Tragic Structure in *A Child of the Jago*', *English Literature in Transition (1880–1920)*, 31, ii (1988), 153–61. A demonstration of the opposing value systems of the Jago and of middle-class Victorian culture through the different ways they respectively interpret the life-stories of Josh and Dicky Perrott.

Vincent Brome, *Four Realist Novelists* (London: Longmans, 1965). Useful discussion of Morrison's writing alongside that of Edwin Pugh, Richard Whiteing and William Pett Ridge.

Robert Calder, 'Arthur Morrison: A Commentary with an Annotated Bibliography of Writings about Him', *English Literature in Transition (1880–1920)*, 28, iii (1985), 276–97. An essential survey of responses to Morrison, embracing both early reviews and later critical studies.

Gill Davies, 'Foreign Bodies. Images of the London Working Class at the End of the Nineteenth Century', *Literature and History*, 14, i (Spring 1988). Interpretation of the rhetoric of images in respresentations of the East End, stressing its colouring by fear of difference and moral panics among the middle class.

Pamela Fox, *Class Fictions: Shame and Resistance in the British Working-Class Novel, 1890–1940* (Durham and London, Duke University Press, 1994). An extensive scholarly and polemical study, in touch with the most recent critical and theoretical discussions of working-class writing; devotes a short section to *A Child of the Jago*.

Roger Henkle, 'Morrison, Gissing and the Stark Reality', *Novel*, 25, iii (1992), 302–20. A posthumously edited essay offering stimulating stances on such topics as: women and working-class culture and the symbolic dimension of *A Child of the Jago*. In focusing on the disturbance that the novel offered to middle-class ideology through its depiction of the capacity of the working class to resist acculturation, Henkle offers a more radical view of Morrison than most.

Peter Keating, *The Working Classes in Victorian Fiction* (London, RKP, 1971). A pioneering study discussing Morrison against the backgrounds of mid-century industrial fiction and the wider phenomenon of the 1890s slum novel; see also Keating's 'Biographical Study' prefacing his edition of *A Child of the Jago*.

Peter Keating, ed., *Into Unknown England 1866–1913* (London: RKP, 1976). An invaluable anthology of the writings of nineteenth-century urban social 'explorers'.

John L. Kijinski, 'Ethnography in the East End: Native Customs and Colonial Solutions in *A Child of the Jago*', *English Literature in Transition*, 37, iv (1994), 490–501. An important contextualization of the novel's themes within the discourse of Victorian popular and scientific ethnography.

H. G. Klaus, ed., *The Rise of Socialist Fiction 1880–1914* (London, Harvester, 1987). As one might expect, little on Morrison but valuable engagement with other fictional versions of the working class from the period of *A Child of the Jago* that puts Morrison's novel into political perspective.

Michael Krzak, 'Arthur Morrison's East End of London', in Jean-Paul Hulin and Pierre Coustillas, eds., *Victorian Writers and the City* (Lille: Univ. de Lille III, 1979), 147–82. Scholarly and thoughtful analysis of a range of Morrison's writing directed towards a sociological understanding of the historical urban culture.

Krishan Kumar, 'Versions of the Pastoral: Poverty and the Poor in English Fiction from the 1840s to the 1950s', *Journal of Historical Sociology*, 8, i (1995), 1–37. A useful historical survey of the larger pattern of fiction about the poor and working class in Britain.

Sally Ledger, 'In Darkest England: The Terror of Degeneration in *Fin-de-Siècle* Britain', *Literature and History*, III, 4, ii (Autumn 1995), 71–86. A wide-ranging exploration of the articulation of degeneration fears, particularly in 1890s fiction, to imperialism, class relationship and gender politics.

Daniel Pick, *Faces of Degeneration: A European Disorder* (Cambridge, CUP, 1986). A pioneering study of theories of degeneration in nineteenth and early twentieth-century culture.

Griselda Pollock, '"With my own eyes": Fetishism, the Labouring Body and the Colour of its Sex', *Art History*, 17, iii (1994), 342–82. Fascinating exploration of visual and verbal representations of working class women, showing with striking force the interrelationship of images of race and gender.

F. S. Schwarzbach, 'Terra Incognita – An Image of the City in English Literature, 1820–1855', in Philip Dodd, ed., *The Art of Travel: Essays on Travel-Writing* (London: Cass, 1982), 61–84. Valuable background to the development of Social Problem discourse of the later nineteenth century.

T. Harper Smith, 'Re-Readings 2: The Jago', *East London Papers*, 2. i (1959), 39–47. Marshals materials and sources in local history concerning the Old Nichol not found elsewhere.

TEXT SUMMARY

Chapter 1

Young Dicky Perrott lives in a crime-ridden East End slum with his shiftless and work-shy father Josh, his listless and self-regarding mother Hannah and his beloved baby sister Looey.

Chapter 2

Philanthropists attempt to raise the cultural and spiritual level of the inhabitants of the East End but, misunderstanding the area and blinded by their own idealism, they miss their mark. At one of their ceremonies Dicky steals the guest of honour's gold watch.

Chapter 3

Josh takes the watch and punishes Dicky; confused, Dicky broods on the nature of justice.

Chapters 4 & 5

Dicky avidly participates in one of the regular Jago faction fights between the Ranns and the Learys, this one leading to the death of Fag Dawson; in addition, Hannah Perrott – carrying Looey across the road – is attacked by Sally Green of the Leary clan.

Chapter 6

Dicky is recruited by Aaron Weech, a receiver of stolen goods who draws children into crime through a mixture of food, sympathy, intimidation and blackmail.

Chapter 7

Dicky sets about thieving with a new earnestness, stealing a cheap clock from a family in his building and along the way making an enemy of Bobby Roper, a young hunchback.

Chapters 8 & 9

Others steal tools belonging to Bobby's father and only the intervention of the new vicar, Henry Sturt, puts an end to the ensuing fight and brings about the restoration of the tools.

Chapter 10

Dicky steals a music-box to compensate the Ropers for stealing their clock – and discovers what it means to be chased as a thief. Sturt helps the Ropers move out of the Jago to a better area.

Chapter 11

Old Beveridge advises Dicky that the only ways out of the Jago are gaol, the gallows or success in the High Mob. Josh tries to set up a fight with Billy Leary. Looey falls ill.

Chapter 12

Weech keeps a close eye on Dicky's industry as a thief.

Chapter 13

Josh wins the long-promised fight with Billy and takes the purse: Looey, however, whose health has been in decline since Sally Green's attack, suddenly deteriorates and dies despite Pigeony Poll's care. Dicky is more affected than are his parents.

Chapter 14

Father Sturt has meanwhile won the trust of the Jagos by the force of his personality and proceeds with his plan to replace part of the slum with a new church, club and night-shelter. Sturt teases Josh about his thieving. Josh acquires the Ropers' clock from Weech.

Chapter 15

Dicky goes to school; his feud with Bobby Roper grows and he becomes involved in 'fat's a-runnin'' robberies.

Chapter 16

Under Father Sturt's influence and to their own surprise, Josh Perrott and Kiddo Cook find themselves at church.

Chapter 17

Evictions from the Jago and demolition of buildings pave the way for Father Sturt's church and social complex.

Chapters 18–21

Dicky's education in crime pauses when Father Sturt helps him to a legitimate job in a shop; Dicky loves his new responsibilities and the prospects they open, but Weech engineers his dismissal and Dicky returns to his old ways – even stealing from his recent employer and placing the goods with Weech.

Chapter 22

A party in time of truce between the Jagos and their old enemies the Dove Laners ends in disaster when the floor of Mother Gapp's public house collapses.

Chapter 23

Without knowing the identity of his victim, Josh breaks into a house and steals a watch and chain belonging to the chief of the High Mob.

Chapters 24 & 25

Josh has difficulty disposing of the watch, but Weech recognizes it and betrays him. Josh is arrested and sent to prison for five years.

Chapters 26–28

The adolescent Dicky, his demoralized mother and new sister Em have to survive on ill-paid work at home, whatever Dicky can steal or earn and whatever Father Sturt or Kiddo Cook can contribute. Hannah gives birth to little Josh. Father Sturt and the surgeon discuss the poor and the brutalized in terms of the problem of their reproducing themselves.

Chapter 29

Dicky and his family get by; more of the Jago is demolished and new Council dwellings are erected.

Chapter 30

As the time for Josh's release approaches, Weech becomes apprehensive and ingratiates himself with Dicky.

Chapter 31

Josh arrives home and is greeted first by his family and then by Father Sturt – who now teases Sam Cash about his thieving.

Chapter 32

Bill Rann and Josh plan to break into Weech's house.

Chapter 33

The burglary is committed, but while Bill has only robbery in mind, Josh intends revenge on Weech for betraying both himself and his son. Weech is savagely killed and Josh is pursued and caught.

Chapters 34–36

Josh is tried at the Old Bailey and sentenced to death. The Ropers' clock, around which his family kneel, will announce the moment of his execution.

Chapter 37

Under the influence of Father Sturt, Kiddo Cook prospers through work, marries Pigeony Poll and moves into the new Council dwellings; Dicky, however, has moments of even greater despair. Skirmishing with the Jago's Dove-Lane enemies, Dicky is stabbed – circumstantially, by Bobby Roper – and dies. His last words assert either the bleak fact of there being a way out of the Jago through an early death – or perhaps the intuition Dicky has sometimes nurtured of there being some better way of living which the circumstances of his environment, and Weech as their instrument, have denied him.

ACKNOWLEDGEMENTS

I am grateful to the Bancroft Library, University of California, Berkeley, for permission to print Arthur Morrison's letter to Walter J. Roberts.

Barbara Dennis, Andrew Hassam, Michael Kakooza, William Price, Allen Samuels, Malcolm Smith and Martin Wright all illuminated corners of Victorian culture which were dark to me. Sophie Gilmartin, John Scattergood and George Walter gave generous long-distance assistance with bibliographical puzzles; Jim Walker, while treading a very different path, eased my introduction to Japanese art. For technical facilities I am grateful to the Media Centre, Library and Academic Computing Services at UWL. In acknowledging my debts to others' research I would particularly stress that this edition would not have been possible without the published researches of P. J. Keating and Michael Krzak.

I also owe a considerable debt to some three hundred students at Lampeter who, over the years, have got up early on Friday mornings in January just to talk about Arthur Morrison.

The editor and publishers wish to thank the following for permission to use copyright material:

ELT Press for material from John L Kijinski, 'Ethnography in the East End: Native Customs and Colonial Solutions in a *A Child of the Jago*', ELT, 37:4 (1994);

NOVEL: A Forum on Fiction, for material from Roger Henkle, 'Morrison, Gissing and the Stark Reality', *Novel*, 25, 3 (Spring 1992). Copyright © 1992 NOVEL Corporation;

A. P. Watt Ltd on behalf of The Literary Estate of the author for H. G. Wells, 'Another View of Maggie' and 'A Slum Novel' from *The Saturday Review*.

Every effort has been made to trace all the copyright holders but if any have been inadvertently overlooked the publishers will be pleased to make the necessary arrangement at the first opportunity.

CLASSIC NOVELS
IN EVERYMAN

The Time Machine
H. G. WELLS

One of the books which defined 'science fiction' – a compelling and tragic story of a brilliant and driven scientist
£3.99

Oliver Twist
CHARLES DICKENS

Arguably the best-loved of Dickens's novels. With all the original illustrations
£4.99

Barchester Towers
ANTHONY TROLLOPE

The second of Trollope's Chronicles of Barsetshire, and one of the funniest of all Victorian novels
£4.99

The Heart of Darkness
JOSEPH CONRAD

Conrad's most intense, subtle, compressed, profound and proleptic work
£3.99

Tess of the d'Urbervilles
THOMAS HARDY

The powerful, poetic classic of wronged innocence
£3.99

Wuthering Heights and Poems
EMILY BRONTË

A powerful work of genius – one of the great masterpieces of literature
£3.99

Pride and Prejudice
JANE AUSTEN

Proposals, rejections, infidelities, elopements, happy marriages – Jane Austen's most popular novel
£2.99

North and South
ELIZABETH GASKELL

A novel of hardship, passion and hard-won wisdom amidst the conflicts of the industrial revolution
£4.99

The Newcomes
W. M. THACKERAY

An exposé of Victorian polite society by one of the nineteenth-century's finest novelists
£6.99

Adam Bede
GEORGE ELIOT

A passionate rural drama enacted at the turn of the eighteenth century
£5.99

All books are available from your local bookshop or direct from:
Littlehampton Book Services Cash Sales, 14 Eldon Way, Lineside Estate,
Littlehampton, West Sussex BN17 7HE *(prices are subject to change)*

To order any of the books, please enclose a cheque (in sterling) made payable to
Littlehampton Book Services, or phone your order through with credit card details (Access,
Visa or Mastercard) on 01903 721596 (24 hour answering service) stating card number
and expiry date. *(Please add £1.25 for package and postage to the total of your order.)*

In the USA, for further information and a complete catalogue call 1-800-526-2778

CLASSIC FICTION
IN EVERYMAN

**The Impressions of
Theophrastus Such**
GEORGE ELIOT
*An amusing collection of character
sketches, and the only paperback
edition available*
£5.99

Frankenstein
MARY SHELLEY
*A masterpiece of Gothic terror in
its original 1818 version*
£3.99

East Lynne
MRS HENRY WOOD
*A classic tale of melodrama,
murder and mystery*
£7.99

**Holiday Romance and
Other Writings for Children**
CHARLES DICKENS
*Dickens's works for children,
including 'The Life of Our Lord'
and 'A Child's History of England',
with original illustrations*
£5.99

The Ebb-Tide
R. L. STEVENSON
*A compelling study of ordinary
people in extreme circumstances*
£4.99

The Three Impostors
ARTHUR MACHEN
*The only edition available
of this cult thriller*
£4.99

Mister Johnson
JOYCE CARY
*The only edition available of this
amusing but disturbing twentieth-
century tale*
£5.99

The Jungle Book
RUDYARD KIPLING
*The classic adventures of Mowgli
and his friends*
£3.99

Glenarvon
LADY CAROLINE LAMB
*The only edition available of the
novel which throws light on the
greatest scandal of the early nineteenth century – the infatuation of
Caroline Lamb with Lord Byron*
£6.99

**Twenty Thousand Leagues
Under the Sea**
JULES VERNE
*Scientific fact combines with
fantasy in this prophetic tale
of underwater adventure*
£4.99

SHORT STORY COLLECTIONS
IN EVERYMAN

The Strange Case of Dr Jekyll and Mr Hyde and Other Stories
R. L. STEVENSON
An exciting selection of gripping tales from a master of suspense
£1.99

Nineteenth-Century American Short Stories
edited by Christopher Bigsby
A selection of the works of Henry James, Edith Wharton, Mark Twain and many other great American writers
£6.99

The Best of Saki
edited by MARTIN STEPHEN
Includes Tobermory, Gabriel Ernest, Svedni Vashtar, The Interlopers, Birds on the Western Front
£4.99

Souls Belated and Other Stories
EDITH WHARTON
Brief, neatly crafted tales exploring a range of themes from big taboo subjects to the subtlest little ironies of social life
£6.99

The Night of the Iguana and Other Stories
TENNESSEE WILLIAMS
Twelve remarkable short stories, each a compelling drama in miniature
£4.99

Selected Short Stories and Poems
THOMAS HARDY
Hardy's most memorable stories and poetry in one volume
£4.99

Selected Tales
HENRY JAMES
Stories portraying the tensions between private life and the outside world
£5.99

The Best of Sherlock Homes
ARTHUR CONAN DOYLE
All the favourite adventures in one volume
£4.99

The Secret Self 1: *Short Stories by Women*
edited by Hermione Lee
'A superb collection' The Guardian
£4.99

All books are available from your local bookshop or direct from:
Littlehampton Book Services Cash Sales, 14 Eldon Way, Lineside Estate,
Littlehampton, West Sussex BN17 7HE (*prices are subject to change*)

To order any of the books, please enclose a cheque (in sterling) made payable to
Littlehampton Book Services, or phone your order through with credit card details (Access,
Visa or Mastercard) on 01903 721596 (24 hour answering service) stating card number
and expiry date. (*Please add £1.25 for package and postage to the total of your order.*)

In the USA, for further information and a complete catalogue call 1-800-526-2778